RIDGE OF GOLD

RIDGE OF GOLD

James Ambrose Brown

St. Martin's Press
New York

RIDGE OF GOLD. Copyright © 1983 by James Ambrose Brown. All rights reserved. Printed in the United States of America. No part of this book may be used or reproduced in any manner whatsoever without written permission except in the case of brief quotations embodied in critical articles or reviews. For information, address St. Martin's Press, 175 Fifth Avenue, New York, N.Y. 10010.

Library of Congress Cataloging in Publication Data
Brown, James Ambrose, 1919-
   Ridge of gold.

   1. Johannesburg (South Africa)—History—Fiction.
I. Title.
PR9369.3.B72R5   1986   823   86-13125
ISBN 0-312-68231-X

First published in the Republic of South Africa
by Jonathan Ball Publishers under the title *The White Locusts*.

10 9 8 7 6 5 4 3 2

RIDGE OF GOLD

Chapter 1

It was cold in that bed-sitter in Bethnal Green. Colder than Leonard Penlynne ever remembered London to be. The body that he had built in ten years of hard physical work in the sun shivered with urgent gooseflesh as he waited for Jessie the maid to bring up a second bucket of hot water from the kitchen. The sun of Kimberley had burned his forearms, neck and face in startling contrast to his body, milk white with its coils of black hair now dripping wet. He had kept the beard and mustache he had grown on the diggings so that when he smiled, and he smiled readily because he was that kind of man, even when things looked at their worst, his swarthy face lit up, revealing strong white teeth.

He was never quite sure when it was that he had come to understand that what he had believed to be ugliness was no disadvantage. At school he had been called 'that dark boy ... what is he? An Assyrian ... some kind of Levantine? How did he get a name like Penlynne?'

It was not until he was twenty that he discovered his presence was disturbing to women. Until then he had taken it for revulsion when they looked away from his heavy eyebrows and blue chin. He was taller than most men he met. His most remarkable feature, however, was his black eyes. His mother's, so it was said.

A woman in Kimberley had told him he had the face of a wounded monkey ... a blend of perplexity, anger and hurt. 'It will go away,' she had assured him, 'when you are rich.'

'And when will that be?' He had turned away from her to look out of the window towards the blue-grey heaps of broken ore.

'Why bother with that now?' she had whispered, pulling him towards her. 'You've plenty of time.'

Well, time had run out on him. He was back where he had started in this damnable London he loathed in its coldest, blackest winter in a decade. The vulnerable look was still there. At least it would have been obvious to a woman. But it had not yet turned to a look of defeat. He could still smile, that extraordinary, unexpected, transforming smile that turned women weak, so that when he took their hands in an introduction – and his hands were always well kept, even when he had done heavy physical work – he never failed to be astonished when they broke the contact as if a shock had gone through them.

The darkness of his brow gave him a saturnine look which had deepened these last six months. He had been depressed, longing for Africa and the easy comradeships.

There was a knock on the door and he realised that the zinc bath had grown cold. Reaching for the worn towel, he stood up and shouted: 'Put it down at the door, Jessie.' He heard the clank of the handle and saw the doorhandle turn slightly.

'Will that be all, Mr Penlynne?' He had once touched her hands by mistake when she was passing a dish to him from the kitchen. He was always quick to give a hand and he was liked for that. Her hands were rough and red. Rougher than his own. He felt a pang for her.

She smiled. He had turned away, embarrassed by the contact. There was Dorothy to consider. Dorothy, whose letters came irregularly from Kimberley and were tantalizingly vague and uncommitted.

'Can I make up the fire, Mr Penlynne?'

'Just now,' he replied and listened in the pause that followed to the door opening a fraction.

'I've a dry towel for you.' The hand came in and let it fall. 'And there's letters for you.'

'Where from?' he said, stepping from the bath.

'Kimberley.' He dripped to the door and reached through with a bare arm. She withheld them with a giggle. He had to extend his arm.

'Give them here,' he said, all thought of the girl wiped out by the proximity of what he longed to handle. Lines in Dorothy's hand. He put the envelope to his nostrils to search for the elusive scent. Weeks of travel had eliminated any trace of her. The second letter was in a hand he did not know but when he turned over the envelope he saw the name Porges and Beit, Diamond Merchants, Paris and Kimberley. The letter was six weeks old. Why should Porges and Beit be trying to reach him here? They knew he had thrown in his hand on the diggings and returned to

England almost as penniless as he had left eight years ago.

He postponed the opening of that letter and sat down to read Dorothy's. It was like being back there in the wood and iron bungalow. He could almost see her sitting at the table, a blanket spread over the tablecloth, her head to one side as she scribbled in that impetuous, impatient way of hers.

In the envelope he found a pressed flower. It seemed almost unbearably precious and he put the letter to his lips. He turned to the letter from Porges and Beit, skipping the pleasantries, looking for the meat.

'... and your reputation is high with us. We know and admire your industry and your grasp of management. Opportunity has arisen in the Transvaal Territory and what we are proposing is to send you to the new gold fields in Johannesburg and district to establish our interests there. Josiah Rawlinson is there ahead of us and has substantial holdings and as you have worked for him in the past and know his methods...'

The letter concluded: 'Our partner Julius Wernher has opened an office in London and will be ready to see you at any time to discuss terms of employment which will be suited to your status. He will arrange your passage First Saloon on the earliest available mailship. Time is vital, Leonard. Rawlinson has been shrewd but there is still great opportunity.'

A week later Penlynne saw his bags carried up the gangway to *The American*. He hardly felt the sleet and the penetrating wind that swept the early morning wharves and wrenched the flames of braziers. The ship was warm and bright, crowded and jostling with good-humoured passengers. Or so it seemed to him as he was helped from his topcoat by a steward. Impulsively he gave the man a five pound note. As he did so he was aware that the act was not one of generosity alone. It was a gesture to the future. And worth it to feel the respect it bought.

He went up to the Smokers' Lounge to see who else was going out. Sharp men, shrewd men, faces honed by experience. Fools, too. You could pick them out. He already knew that Africa was not a land that showed mercy to fools. There were faces here he would never see again and faces that already gleamed with the authority of success. His appearance commanded attention and he felt their eyes on him. Swift looks of speculation which measured a man.

This time, by God, there would be no failure. He felt the elation of being the chosen man. It was as if he had been singled out by fate. And yet the horror of failure was still strong enough to bring a tremor to his fingers as he lit a cigarette. He looked across the polished mahogany of the saloon at the image of himself in the mirrored wall. For the first time he saw the man he was determined to become.

Stewart MacDonald dropped his week-old copy of *The Times* over the ship's side and watched it spread its pages on the dark water of the Thames. Hunched in his old woollen topcoat and tartan muffler, bareheaded, sleet sliding down his cheeks, he gave the black city a curt wave of dismissal. He heard the cries of seamen and the splash of heavy hawsers.

'Let go forrard! Let go aft!'

The Castle Line steamer was edging away from the docks of the East India Basin. It was January 3rd, a bitter, windless wintry Monday in the Year of Our Lord 1890 and Victoria Queen of Great Britain, India and Dominions Overseas.

Stray sheets of ice from the frozen upper reaches of the Thames crackled aside from the sharp iron prow. The newspapers said it was the coldest winter in a decade and Stewart did not doubt it. He had been too footsore, cold and hungry to make the most of the winter revelries on every pond in London. He had stood watching skaters, hearing the bands, spending a penny or two on hot potatoes, enjoying the flaring illuminations and the flushed faces of the girls.

He still found it hard to believe that he was qualified to practise medicine as a Bachelor of Arts and Licentiate of the Glasgow College of Surgeons. He squinted at his father's half-hunter watch, still amazed that it had escaped the pawnshop. His mother had been willing to sell it for textbooks in the long grind of study after he left home in Ayrshire. Often it had been touch and go but he had felt it would be dishonouring to his father to part with it.

Steerage to South Africa wouldn't be so bad ... nothing like the immigrant ships to America. This vessel was the pride of the British mercantile marine, there would be regular meals and dry quarters, vermin-free. He thought hungrily of the coming breakfast. The chalked-up blackboard had promised porridge, hash, Irish stew, bread and butter, tea and coffee. More than he had eaten in a week. He leaned against the rail, his blond head wet in the raw air as the steamship eased out into the Thames. In this moment it was as if the great engines were a part of him, beating for him. The lamps on the quay and the wharves glimmered in a grey gloom but he felt only a soaring of spirit. Forests of masts went by. The rigging of a thousand ships was like a dim winter-stricken wood as the towers, domes and buildings of London slipped past in the sleety darkness. Stewart gripped the rail hard. Whatever was coming he would succeed.

At his final examination, the oral, before the gentlemen examiners of the Glasgow Western Infirmary at Gillmore Hill, old Andrew Buchanan had given his usual lecture on the easy times the medical students had nowadays. Stewart had listened to the old butcher with the respect due to him as a man who could take off a leg in three minutes without anaesthetic. From the walls of the draughty old hall photographs and frozen silhouettes of the grim-faced practitioners of the past glared down. 'And where do you propose to practise the art which has so nearly eluded you ... and what branch?' he heard.

'Tropical medicine, sir – Africa.'

'Is there not enough sickness here in Scotland to suit you?'

Until the results were known Stewart had returned briefly to his mother's cottage on the Ferrygate Farm in Airlie, some twenty miles from Glasgow. He was greeted with embarrassing respect by those he had worked with as a lad and with worshipful awe by his mother.

He walked the fields and lanes with Crudelli's *The Nature, Prevention and Treatment of Malarial Infections*, a paper the Italian had given at the International Medical Congress at Copenhagen in 1884. He came to the conclusion that Crudelli, for all his fame, knew no more about malaria than the Italian peasants he studied. Sometimes he walked behind the plough again, for the sheer joy of feeling the heavy clay underfoot after the cobbled streets of Glasgow, revelling in sunlight and fresh air after the fetid alleys where the poor of the city lived worse than cattle. Plodding behind the plough he found himself doubting that malaria was due to an organism which multiplied in the soil and at night gave off its poisons from fields and marshlands. Already he knew that his profession was unscientifically based, that much of its knowledge was no better than an uncomprehending observation of symptoms.

One thing that astonished him was the unexpected loveliness of Mary Irving, who had been hardly more than a child when he'd left for Glasgow. She was the farmer's daughter, now eighteen and with a restlessness on her that had nothing to do with discontent with her lot. The Irvings were prosperous. She had a wild rose bloom to her and as they strolled the hedgerows in the long autumn evenings, they would stop along the way to kiss and embrace. She smelled of milk and honey. She told him he smelled of carbolic.

'I'm promised to Alex MacFarlane,' she said one evening. He was a ship's engineer at Greenock.

'I hear so,' Stewart said.

He guessed she would have broken her promise for him but he neither took advantage of her readiness to find a place among the haycocks or gave her any reason for making her no offers for a future that was still too remote.

'You'll write sometimes,' she said wistfully the evening he told her he would be going over to Edinburgh to do a labourer's job on the great new cantilever bridge Scottish engineers were throwing across the Firth of Forth. It was his passage money he was after.

'It wouldn't be fair to Alex MacFarlane,' he said

She flared up at that, the red blood bright in her cheeks, and gave a toss of the pitchy hair. 'Your sense of fairplay will be the undoing of you, Stewart.' With that she had turned away and gone up the lane to the farmhouse without a backward look. It had the sound of prophecy in his ears. The Irving women were said to be fey, but she turned with a laugh and a wave.

'If you change your mind, drop me a postcard from Timbuctoo.'

There were hips and haws on the wild roses in the lanes and brambles heavy with ripening fruit. As he went home to pack he heard the mournful cry of the lapwing ... peeweet! peeweet! It seemed to Stewart to share the sadness of his mother.

'I'm home, Mother,' he called out. He could smell her pastry. She had prepared a feast for him tonight. He knew how meagre her meals would be for the following days and wished he felt hungry enough to do her justice.

'Sit down, son,' she said, turning her face aside and hurrying to the kitchen range. They ate together, almost in silence.

'I'll write as soon as I can, Mother.' She rose from her place and he wondered if he would ever see this small bright room again with its brass around the mantelpiece and its bits and pieces of china.

'For you, son,' she said. 'Your father set great store on them.' She put down Stevenson's *Travels with a Donkey* and Thomas Carlyle's *Sartor Resartus*. 'And I know he'd want you to have his watch. He'd have been that prood o' ye, Stewart.'

'Thank you, Mother. I shall treasure it.' He put it in his pocket and saw her smile. It was as if her duty to him was now complete.

There were other muffled figures on deck as London fell back. Sailors were shouting as they pulled the lines aboard and made fast. Sleet slanted into Stewart's face, numbing his cheeks and sliding off the soft blond mustache. A man, smaller than he by a head, came out of the gloom and leaned on the rail.

'Good riddance, I say!' The voice had a high, strong lilting Welsh note. 'I'm Owen Davyd ... and you?'

'Stewart MacDonald. Glasgow.'

'I'm Rhonda Valley, Pontypridd. Miner, what else! Going to gold fields in this Transvaal. Bloody wilds of Africa, mun. And you?'

Stewart was cautious about disclosing his profession. There'd be all kinds in steerage. 'Going out to look around ... there's opportunity.'

'What's your trade then?'

'Ploughman ... I've been a riveter's help.'

'Trade union man?'

'No.'

Owen Davyd gave him a quick look. 'You Scotchmen are too independent for the good of the tradesman. Have you never heard of the great Keir Hardy, one of your own? A great man, a noble tongue and fearless of the exploiters. *Das Kapital* – have you read it? No, and you speak like a man with learning. Karl Marx, greatest teacher since Jesus Christ, no offence, Stewart, if you're religious-minded. It's given to few men to overturn the world!'

Greenwich Hospital had slipped by. The low lying shores of Essex on the left and the green slopes of Kent were hidden in the all pervading, eddying gloom of sleet. Many other ships were coming and going, hooting and braying. There was a bitter stink of coal smoke that stimulated Stewart's senses, then the brown sails of low-hulled barges, braziers glowing on deck.

The Welshman took his silence for being offended.

'Trouble with me ... I talk too much. But how can a man be silent? I've seen heads smashed and the brave banners trampled under the hooves. And if a man stands up and speaks, it's jail. No, start again, mun. New land, no class distinction. Jack as good as his master, I say. Gold mining. Clean work. None of your crawling like a blind mole in the bowels of the earth and you don't own a foot of it! Make your money clean and get home, that's what the lads say. Three hundred of us on this ship. Welshmen, Cousin Jacks – tin miners out of work. All good boys. Bloody lords shut them out ... capitalist arrogance!'

It was on Stewart's tongue to say 'Why don't you stay here and put it right if you feel so strongly?' Why was he leaving himself if it came to that? The very question his examiners had asked and then gone on to discuss 'the world out there'. Its appalling ignorance and backwardness in every respect, particularly in medicine.

There was a furious churning of paddles as the tugboat eased alongside and the pilot came aboard. A bell clanged below.

'That'll be breakfast,' said the small dark man eagerly. 'Shall we go down together, Stewart? Have you a place to sleep yet? I've a billet next me. It's worse than the pit down there. Sleeping anywhere. Open Berth Ticket ... any place the Chief Steward can find. Bathroom, passages. Like sardines on the floor of the dining saloon. Everybody cheerful!'

The black pit dust was already engrained in the Welshman's pores and he was hardly more than his mid-twenties. He must have been at it twelve years already, perhaps more. A pit boy at ten was normal. Wise to be getting out before the coal dust got to the lungs, turning them to the black stones Stewart had seen in the laboratory. Dust that turned the fine singing voices to coughings, gaspings, silence.

He was not sure that he wanted to be adopted by this zealot. He saw the signs of a man who would consume himself and quite likely all associated with him but he went to the table with the Welshman and was introduced as 'our new comrade ... he's going to turn the barren sands of Africa to fruitfulness and feed the hungry.'

Stewart was received with back-slapping and cheers. He marvelled at the excitement, the stirring of the blood that turned ordinary men into conquistadores. There was ample food and they ate like men having their fill for the first time. One dark slip of a boy was chaffed for slipping food into his coat pockets. He could hardly speak a word of English. It was a face too soft and sensitive for the rough and tumble below decks.

'Here, what's this?' The seaman in charge of the mess grabbed up the boy and was emptying his pockets. 'Dirty little kike. Ain't you got enough in front of you then?'

'Let the boy alone!' It was Owen Davyd who came between the man in the white messcoat, red-faced and abusive from the galley, and the face like a frightened animal, cringing away. There was a sympathetic hubbub at the table. The boy gave Owen a look of gratitude. Surely he had a father or brother somewhere here or was he going out alone to join a family already on the gold fields?

'What's your name, boyo?' Owen asked, but the lad pushed his way through the men. 'I was down pit at his age,' Owen said. 'One thing I swear to the Almighty, if he exists at all, things will be different for our children.'

Tilbury Fort slid past, then the Nore's jagged teeth and so out into the Channel. Glint of wintry sun on leaden sea. Pilot and stevedores picked up. Hearty British cheers. Tug falling back as *The American*'s engines reached full power. The crew returning the huzzahs! A sense of the rightness of it all. Bright paintwork and gleaming decks. British solidity. British comfort. British thoroughness. British pride of workmanship. And in the steerage as the sea got up, British breakfast in the scuppers, green-faced immigrants groaning and retching.

The Castle steamer ploughed her way past Herne Bay, Margate, Broadstairs, Ramsgate and there, glinting pale, the white cliffs of Dover.

I wonder, thought Stewart, huddled in his overcoat, how many of us down there will ever see that sight again.

Isadore Isaacs had been two days and nights under the tarpaulin of a lifeboat lashed on the deck of the ship. Nothing in his life had prepared him for the Bay of Biscay. The vessel took dark water over her bows, rose shuddering her entire length and plunged again into the rollers. Spray lashed and drummed on his hiding place. He was so numbed that he no longer felt the ache of every bone and muscle. He had fallen on the stock of cheap cigars he had been taking out as trading stock. Those uncrushed were soaked, and by the smell of his pack some of his patent medicines were smashed. Did it matter, he thought. Yes, it mattered and if they did not throw him overboard he would live to be rich. In any case, he must live for Rachel, his sister Rachel's sake. There had been money enough for only one fare to the gold fields. A half fare. Rachel dressed as a boy, a tender-faced youngster, clothes too large, feet in clumsy boots. A girl of thirteen among that pack of men below decks. He had promised her that after a few hours at sea he would emerge and join her. They would hardly be noticed among the hundreds crammed into steerage. She must think him dead already. Rachel so tender and inexperienced in the ways of the goyim even though she had been born in the dark alleys of Whitechapel in a community of immigrant Jews. As he lay shivering in the bottom of the lifeboat it seemed to him quite likely that he would follow his father. This boat would be his grave. In his delirium the rattling of some piece of loose gear was the rattling of the pyx in which six old men had gathered alms for the poor as the funeral procession passed through the alleys.

Isadore tried to raise himself and get out. Time to mingle with the immigrants, find his sister, make a few sales from his stock and hear the reassuring clink of coins. A litany rang in his head. It was the voice of the ancient Israelite with the straggling white beard and tall old beaver hat singing a prayer of countless verses while the earth was shovelled over his father. Now it was mixed in Isadore's head with Cockles Anti-Bilious Pills for Bile and Alcock's Elixir for the Relief of the Hacking Cough of Consumption.

The boy cried out against the battering wind. The hammering and drumming of taut canvas over his head and the scream of the storm in the steel stays carried his voice away. Suddenly the canvas cover was turned back.

'Poor little kike ... bloody near dead.'

Then the voice of his sister crying, 'Issy ... Issy!' The wild flapping of canvas and the continual shriek of the wind became utterly confused. When he regained his senses he saw that he was in a kind of half-dark cavern, hung with hammocks. Lurching, staggering, cursing men were groping around with lanterns or lying retching and groaning. It had the look and sound of Sheol. The Sheol of his Talmudist father. He tried to rise but firm hands pressed him back.

'Rachel!' he cried. As if in a dream he saw the pale young face above him, sharp and dark-eyed, the cropped hair, the ungainly clothing, heard her voice.

Again he struggled to rise, every instinct crying out to protect her. The cockney English he had spoken for years was forgotten in his anguish. The boy who had run barefoot in the gutters, fought for survival with the energy of a sparrow, knew where to beg, steal and how to earn a few coppers holding horses and running errands ... the Whitechapel urchin was gone. In his delirium he was once more in the Pale. Oh, the oppression of those marshy plains where the heart hungered for sight of a mountain.

'Quiet, boy, quiet,' he heard. The voice was Welsh though he could not have identified it. The hands on him were rough but the tone was gentle. 'Bring cocoa from the bloody galley then. He's near perished.'

'My sister,' he was crying in Yiddish. 'Rachel, Rachel!'

Days were to pass before he understood that the pale Welshman with the mane of pitch black hair was not a tormentor. He had made a place for both of them between his pallet and that of the fair-haired man with the soft brogue of ... no, it was a tongue he had never heard before. But there was sympathy in it. The survival instinct warned that there were men among them who would betray them. In particular he feared the face of Jorley, pale youth, redheaded and furtive. He seemed always to be watching, not Isadore but Rachel. There was a kind of sneering loathing in his expression that the youngster had never seen before. Oh, he had had kicks and blows, been cursed for a dirty sheeny. He had soon learned that laughter is survival, that the ordinary man will turn away with a shrug. Jorley was different.

'He's going to split on us,' he whispered to the Welshman.

'Not while I'm here, boyo.'

Strangest of all to the young Jew was the bond of sympathy

11

which seemed to be growing daily between the Welshman and his sister. He saw that Rachel, so timid and tender, listened to the singsong accents as if he were propounding the Law. She still wore the clothes of a boy, and that troubled her. Was it not scriptural that this was sin?

'Soon, soon,' he kept reassuring her. 'In South Africa it will all be different.' He had to be careful of his own movements but so great was the crush at the tub and the table that he passed almost unnoticed.

'Don't your brother wash then?' he heard one morning. It was the gingerhead, one loutish arm pinning Rachel against the bulkhead.

'Hands off me bruvver,' Isadore said.

At that the hand of Jorley hooked out and ripped at Rachel's shirt. Startling white flesh and budding breasts. 'Ere's seven years good luck,' gloated Jorley, his face suffusing with scarlet. Rachel's eyes were enormous, black-ringed pools of terror. Then, as she fumbled to conceal her girlish body, Isadore smashed his fists into the pale gingery flesh. And he was still smashing at Jorley when he was pulled away by Owen Davyd.

'Don't fink I won't get you for that,' Jorley moaned and wiped a bloody nose with his sleeve before he slunk away.

A girl, by the Lord! Among this crowd. The crude talk, the nakedness. Owen's dark face flushed with instinctive feeling to protect. He was not so astounded after all to find that the sensitive lad who had listened so eagerly to his outpourings had been a girl. It made sense of the bond between them. He put his jacket around her and held her trembling body close.

Later he cornered Jorley. 'I'm marking you, boyo. You spread a word of your filthy tongue around and I'll do for you.' Jorley shrank back from the intense Welshman. He had the hands of a clerk, the shrewd half-worldlywise expression of the immature raised in an environment that had made him a cynic before he was twenty.

'I won't say nuffin...'

'Fair's fair. A chance for all, is it!'

Jorley nodded evasively and began to comb the stiff quiff of oily hair.

Chapter 2

Kitty Loftus found the attitude of the other Second Saloon passengers decidedly standoffish. They were models of the upper servant class, decorous, soberly dressed. Portraits once removed of their employers. Shadows cast to one side to allow the real thing to bask in the sun. Kitty could have amused herself by fitting each to his master or mistress if ever the originals had condescended to visit Second Saloon.

She had been a quick-witted judge of the human scene since childhood. She had had to be. She was used to the superior sniff and the phrase 'theatrical personage'. Yet these were the very same people who on their night off crammed the gods of London and provincial theatres and applauded to the chandeliers.

The Babes in the Wood at the Crystal Palace had been dismissed by the newspapers with amused tolerance. Kitty had been cast as A for Archer in the Alphabet Tableau, the very first to appear on stage, her bust laced into a tunic of Lincoln green, very short, to display the full thighs. She had four witty lines to speak and as she delivered them she winked roguishly at the swells in the boxes and the stalls. When she told 'Old Kroojer' out there in the South African Republic what Mr Gladstone would like to see him do with her arrows it brought down the house every night.

When the curtain fell for the last time on the show that night Kitty had been certain that her future in the theatre was assured. There was a toff in a stage box who had fairly stared her out all night. Who knew where a girl might land up if she played her cards right?

Now she was aboard this steamship and she knew that the contract she had signed to appear in a musical show in the brand new Empire Theatre in Johannesburg wasn't worth a farthing. And the Golden Girls Troupe of Entertainers had been picked for talents other than theatrical. But who would believe her if she tried to speak out to a ship's officer? Some of the other girls looked terrified at the very idea of protesting. Others had accepted with an air of worldly wisdom which Kitty could not condemn. Everything was very nice, splendid beyond the imaginings of girls who had lived, at best, two to an attic room 'and eat when you're lucky!'

Kitty Loftus had knocked around with all kinds since she had run away at thirteen from the kitchen drudgery of a fishmonger's house in Brixton. She had no hard feelings about the past. She had long ago accepted the world for what it was, a kind of arena where you could either tickle the lions or lie down and be eaten. The analogy came easily. Kitty had enjoyed many a penny dinner prefaced with piety at the Girls' Refuge in Great Queen Street, Lincoln's Inn Fields. Prayers first, then potatoes and meat with a slice of bread. But only on Fridays. Somehow she had escaped the obvious and supposedly easier way of earning her living.

There was a stubbornness in her and a vague sense that she was capable of becoming something. Just what, she was not sure. With the girls in the match factory where her mother worked she believed in love that at long last triumphed over every adversity. They regaled each other with such stories while they dipped match sticks in phosphorus and set them to dry and packed them in boxes, for sale at a penny a dozen. Kitty's mother had been a dreamy-eyed woman with surprisingly nimble fingers. As a boxer she could pack thirty-six gross of matches a day and she earned fifteen shillings a week until she contracted the 'fossy jaw'. She had wanted nothing more for Kitty than a safe life as a domestic in some Christian home. She had died believing Kitty was employed as such.

Why make her unhappy in her last days, Kitty thought. It was hard enough for her to die in a Shelter for Women, her bones destroyed by long contact with phosphorus. 'It's not for us to complain,' she always said to Kitty. 'It's not our employers' fault that the brimstone is hurtful.'

At the end Kitty had shuddered to see her, teeth fallen out, her thick red hair reduced to grey wisps. 'Glad you're a good girl, Kit,' were about her last words. The girl's tears had fallen thick and fast but when she had dried them she was determined never to accept the hard life as inevitable.

Taking off her make-up that night in the Crystal Palace dressing room for the chorus Kitty was hardly aware of the reek of sweating bodies, powder, greasepaint and cold cream, or the chatter of twenty young women. The man in the box had given her a signal. As she dabbed and wiped away all traces of the Archer her heart was beating fast beneath the cheap dressing gown. She saw with dismay that the face that emerged in the mirror under the flaring gaslight was not beautiful, as she had hoped. He wouldn't want to be seen with her now. It was goodbye to a ride in a hansom cab and a cosy supper, the kind the other girls boasted about. Nothing improper ... just a bit of fun. She combed out the coarse Titian hair that fell to her waist. It was her best feature, they said. The trouble was her nose. It was short, the mouth too wide and too full and where she had her eyes from she had no idea. Deep, dark green. Perhaps her father. She had never known him or even heard him spoken of. She did know that when her mother was discovered to be pregnant she was put out on the pavement of the Methodist home where she had been the 'general'. How she had found time to fall pregnant was a mystery Kitty had never been able to resolve. She thought it must have been in a state of complete exhaustion.

Yet there must have been times of tenderness in her mother's life, when she had listened with fast-beating heart to the tread on the attic stairs. The match factory came later. Until then Kitty's memories were of being dragged round from soup kitchen to prayer meeting, sleeping in coffin-sided beds, a hundred women to a hall under flaring gas jets. Hymns and prayers and then darkness, snuffling and coughing, tears and groans.

Yet from the kerbsides of London she had absorbed something of the vitality and excitement of a great city at its zenith, something that made her long to reach out and embrace it all with her eyes and senses.

The man who waited outside the dressing room after sending in his card was tall and darkly foreign, his cloak turned back to reveal a slash of scarlet, his white shirt gleaming.

'Claude de la Roche,' he said, kissing her fingers. 'Baron Claude de la Roche ... enchanted by your performance and by your beauty ... enslaved as you can see.'

Her first instinct was one of caution but when she saw the words 'theatrical impressario' on his card she put instinct behind her and grabbed her opportunity. Around her the girls were ooh-ing and aahing. 'I'n't 'e 'andsome then ... lovely! A Frenchie...ooh! Pass 'im on ducks if you don't want 'im!'

This was it then, the eagerly awaited unknown. But no cheek, no fast work with the hands if you please, though some girls would have slid into his embrace the moment they entered the well-sprung intimate darkness of the cab.

They clopped away from the theatres, through the land of gentlemen's clubs, past Hyde Park, further than she had ever been before. London glittered, its lamps shining on Portland stone and ornate railings, on the bare trees in hidden gardens entered only by the few. Her heart beat fast. She allowed him to hold her hand in his gloved one while he told her he had plans for her. No truly. She had amazed him with her ... words failed him.

By the time the cab drew up in a cul-de-sac of three-storied houses she had been persuaded that the generous patrons of the arts on the South African gold fields would welcome her.

Kitty's caution fought with her slum-fired ambition. He was nice. Not as forward as she had feared. He'd like her to meet some of the other girls she'd be going out with, dancers, all very talented, all very charming ladies. She drank a glass of sweet sherry, amazed at the ornate decoration of the room, the rich and airless hangings, pieces of statuary that were surprising to say the least. Wherever did they get such ideas! Immodest to her mind, but very artistic. How airless the room was getting. Innumerable gas jets flared, their white lights rising and falling. Rouged faces gathered around her, white shirts and dark heads. Shrill laughter. Whirling ... whirling. A voice saying, 'It must have gone to her head, poor thing. Carry her up to the Red Room.'

Kitty awoke – it was more a sense of returning from a great distance than awakening – to see a stark naked woman lying on a richly made bed, her limbs languorously outspread, her red hair loose on lacy pillows. At the head of the bed, which she could see perfectly well without raising her head, there were carven cupids frolicking around a sprawling Venus. Kitty put up her hand to touch the figure. This was a dream, surely? She saw, to her astonishment, that the woman above copied her gesture. How strange it was that the white limbs of this woman were sprawled on the covers exactly as her own, that she had the same flaming hair and between her thighs a white linen towel stained with blood. Kitty reached up her hand to touch the apparition. It was on the ceiling!

She had never seen her own body full-length, naked, in a mirror. She was unfamiliar with the globular breasts, the tiny waist and the spread of hips. The full, astonishing beauty of her total nudity as another might see it. She lay for a long while examining the woman in the mirror and she seemed to bear no resemblance to Kitty Loftus. She was like a woman in a picture, the voluptuous woman of a canvas richly framed in gold. Something in the fall of the limbs was shocking but strangely pleasing; both erotic and artless. Her senses were aroused in a way she had never experienced before. It was the same awareness that had been stirred by the scarlet and gold of theatres, the blur of white bosoms in the stalls, the hot perfumed air which wafted over the footlights, the glitter of brass and silver in the orchestra pit, the sweating flesh around her in powder-reeking costumes. It had a quality of beguilement that slid through her loins like an uncoiling serpent.

She tried to sit up. She must break the spell, whatever it was. Her clothing had disappeared, the street-stained boots, the bonnet she had made in imitation of a fashionplate passed round the dressing room 'as worn recently by the beautiful Lady Tankerville at the opening of the Bourne-Jones Exhibition at the New Gallery'.

The waist-nipping corset, the knee-length bloomers and the camisole were gone. So were the thigh-high black stockings. No, one remained. It straggled around her knee. Only this was soft as gossamer. Silk, she thought, and I am no longer Kitty Loftus. It was like some trick of illusion in the pantomime in which a palace was suddenly revealed. Would this scene also fade? It had the quality of an erotic fantasy she had until this moment suppressed for fear of its seductive wickedness, for fear she might enjoy the sensations it aroused.

She had not the slightest memory of how she had come to this room or what had happened. She was curiously unafraid as she lay there, vaguely aware that the curtain would rise tonight on Babes in the Wood without Kitty Loftus. A pleasant languor spread through her limbs and as she drifted she was certain she had been drugged.

She had no memory of being brought aboard the ship but when she finally came to her senses it was to feel an unusual vibration and see sunlight reflecting on white paint. Above her head a photograph of a heavily mustached seaman demonstrated the use of the Patent Safety Lifebelt. She looked at this for some time in an effort to square it with her tiny attic room with the geranium in the aperture of grimy window and with the strange dream of a red room.

There was a woman in the cabin. When she saw that Kitty was awake she hurriedly rose and went out. Kitty heard the key turn in the lock. She tried to rise but found the weight of her limbs impossible to move. She woke to see De la Roche sitting looking at her. He was in white from head to foot.

'Well, Kitty,' he smiled, 'you have been sick. But never mind, you're with us and we're on our way. You'll meet some of the other girls later and I hope you'll be friends. It's always more agreeable for everyone if the girls get on well together, not so, Mrs Brisbane?'

There was something of the pantomime dame about Mrs Brisbane that would have tickled Kitty in other circumstances, a certain masculinity of figure beneath the dark blue serge costume. The heavy frogging and high neckline emphasised a short thick neck that confirmed the impression of severity, even cruelty.

'If it's the show you're anxious about, we've let them know you won't be back, that you have another contract. And considerably more lucrative, Kitty. I think I can promise that you'll be a favourite out there. Not with the miners, common fellows. It's the big men who'll be your clients. You're already a favourite with one. No, I won't mention his name. He's particular about that. But he pays well for the unusual.'

'I was to be in a theatre show,' she blurted.

'Oh, you shall be in a show, don't doubt it.'

'I want to go home.'

'Where's that, Kitty?' He laughed and patted her thigh. 'You shall go home. Just as soon as your contract expires.'

Mrs Brisbane moved closer and the girl saw the strength beneath the whiteness of powder and the heavy use of rouge. 'We don't want to use the needle again, Kitty. We like our girls to be part of the family.'

'I'm British ... this is a British boat.'

'That don't make any difference, dear. There's girls going out all the time and nobody takes no notice as long as they behaves. So be a good girl and don't make no trouble. You'll have a good time. They all do when they settles down.'

Kitty Loftus had not grown up in the rough and tumble of lower city life without learning to use her wits. What De la Roche and Mrs Brisbane took for passive acceptance as she lay back with a nod was, in fact, her decision to bend events to her own will. She would make this work for her. She accepted that she had been 'interfered with', that her deflowering had taken place without her consent and in circumstances beyond her imagining. Part of her did not protest. Many a girl she had rubbed shoulders with had lost her virginity in a dirty lane, brutalised by some rough; others had been sold by their mothers at the age of ... God help us, eleven. There was nothing uncommon about the abuse of poor children. In a way she'd been lucky, one might say.

But the part of Kitty Loftus that was inviolate, the part that insisted that she had the right of refusal of her own body, was outraged and furiously angry. Beneath all that desirable softness – was it De la Roche done it? – there was a girl who had long ago determined to crawl out of the muckheap. In the meantime, what a nice little cabin this was. Polished wood and cheerful bright paint. Her own bunk instead of three in a bed!

When she had dressed and gone into the saloon she had found that the girls looked no different from other women. No more brassy than the ladies of the chorus. They greeted her with cheerful, familiar accents. It was the girls who had come aboard at Lisbon who were so different, so foreign. They were a mixed crowd of Dutch, Italian, Portuguese, some of them not more than fifteen and not a word of English among them. They were herded together, holding hands and rolling their eyes. Then they all took to their bunks seasick and Kitty saw little of them.

The English girls of the Golden Girls Troupe met with cheers and whistles whenever they appeared near the steerage crowd of men. But they were not allowed to go 'down there' as Mrs Brisbane balefully warned. Kitty noticed that the maids and valets, the governesses seen at mealtimes, had very quickly sized up the situation. There was an icy reserve.

The stewards were more familiar. A cabin steward gave Kitty the wink. 'I hear you've been joined by a lot of nuns, miss. We takes a lot of them Portogooses out to the gold fields. Must be a lot of poor sinners out there.'

He raised his arm and pinned her against the bunk. 'Wot abaht a little sample to be goin' on wiv?'

Kitty pushed him violently away.

'You're just a bunch of whores,' he spat. 'If I 'ad me way you wouldn't none of you be on a decent British ship.' His red-faced indignation above the starched uniform had become the image of outraged morality.

It made the girl want to laugh in his face. It was so apiece with the rest of the Second Saloon with their noses in the air. What were they anyway but a bunch of obedient sheep and their good clothes the uniforms of their servitude. They called it 'service' and they would do it for the rest of their lives or until they found themselves discarded.

Chapter 3

That first night on board Leonard Penlynne found himself placed at the captain's table. He came late to it, taking longer than usual over his toilet. He wore evening dress well, the gleam of starched linen setting off his swarthiness. For all the suavity of cut the black suit failed to conceal the essential maleness of the man. He was aware that he would sit at this table by grace of Wernher, not by his own efforts. He was also aware that he had the skills required to shine in any company. He would be sitting down with a countess, a bishop in purple, an Indian army colonel and a leading American mining engineer, gentlemen speculators with titles and newspapermen from the financial and popular press.

As he took his place he was conscious, as always, of the initial sense of shock he created, the momentary hiatus in conversation. Men were taking his measure and women were suddenly conscious of their naked shoulders. For this reason he kept a modest exterior though inwardly he was excited.

He was instantly aware of the young woman three places to his left on the other side of the table, her splendid white neck rising out of a decolletage concealed with white flowers. The face was familiar and yet he was uncertain whether he had seen it before. When their eyes met she smiled, uncertainly, he thought, as if she too were groping to set a name and a place.

Now came the civilised clatter of dinner with its large variety of seasonable things in the shape of fish, flesh and fowl. The discreet drawing of corks, flash of silver and gleam of napery. What a beginning!

'Do you know that we are refrigerated!'
'How remarkable!'
'This is a British ship.'

Katherine Rawlinson was already pointed out as 'the Rawlinson girl ... the Kimberley heiress'. From the flushed enthusiasm of the men and the less cordial expressions of the women she knew with a sinking of her spirits that she was already cast as 'belle of the ship'. She had a longing for the informality of her father's house in Kimberley, open to anyone, cool in the bleaching light of midday under the dusty, drooping pepper trees. She would rather have been hearing the singing and crying out of the Griquas and Coloureds in the locations than this polite babble. The deep sound of the ship's engines could have been the rumble of rock crushers in the Great Hole.

Among the ladies, in the place of honour, was Alice, Countess of Stratford, friendly and beautifully composed without the trace of the hauteur of her own chaperon, Lady Violet, insisted on by her father. It seemed to Katherine that she was always at her elbow and her efforts to pair her off with Charles Warewood, the seventh Viscount Warewood, had really been tedious. She had been a guest at Warewood and admired the beauty of Warwickshire in all its glory of greensward, elm and stream but to marry into the world of Charles Warewood seemed a most unlikely event for a girl of her background. He did not agree and had begged her to encourage him to follow her out to South Africa.

'My regiment will probably go out. Things are boiling up there and it's time those Boers had a hiding!' he'd said.

The gallantries of the men aboard were not entirely unpleasing but she resented the attentions of the man mentioned in the passenger list as Baron de la Roche.

'I have an introduction from Baron de Rothschild to your distinguished father,' he enthused in an accent she could not quite square with his title. Katherine had been glad to be rescued by Mr Walter Gardiner. He was the kind of man she was accustomed to in Kimberley, a mining man and he looked it. The light blue eyes were startling in the sunburned face, yet somehow whimsical, and he did not treat her with this deference she found so irritating. His sheer American exuberance and easy laugh were immediately attractive to her and she was thrilled to hear that he was going to work for her father.

Over coffee he drew her aside, smiling and apologising for his cigar. He had to stoop to speak to her and she saw that his hair was already greying at the temples in a face that was a combination of the practical and the dreamer. She had met so many men of this kind, big-handed, hard-drinking, with a fund of stories about Californian and Australian gold rushes. Tin and copper men. The eternal mineral hunters. Footloose men who earned big money and spent it like water.

'I suppose you are pretty well aware of the reason for my going out to your father, Miss Rawlinson,' he drawled. 'Your father is a shrewd man ... none shrewder. He wouldn't be where he is if he weren't. The fact is, the new gold mines in this place they call the Wit Waters Rand are heading for trouble. May not last another year. I'm going out to make a report for your father. But hell, I shouldn't be boring you with this.'

It was her feeling that he knew he had said too much but his frankness had impressed her. 'Please tell me,' she insisted. They sat together and Gardiner looked around the saloon. He had seen it all before. Gentlemen speculators, newspapermen, professional fortune hunters, clerical gentry and down there below decks three hundred Welshmen, Cornishmen, Canadians, Turks, Armenians and Cypriots – all with that look in their eyes.

'Your father wants the truth about his holdings and he wants it fast. If what he fears is true he'll own the biggest collection of useless rock in Africa. It happened before, in the Lowveld, place called Barberton.'

She felt grateful that he had not treated her with condescension, as if she were a child. Only she knew how gauche and uncertain of herself she was behind the assured features. Or how aware she was of something disturbing about men. She felt this rising in her like a panic as Gardiner rose, pressing her hand and excusing himself. And as she watched his departing back, very tall, with an attractive stoop to his shoulders, his head inclined to one side as if he was ever ready to be agreeable, she was conscious that she was thinking more of him than of her father's anxieties.

He had hardly been gone when his place was taken by 'the dark man', as she had dubbed him at table.

'I believe you are Miss Rawlinson,' he said very civilly. 'I hope I didn't stare too rudely at dinner trying to place you. I worked for your father. You may not remember. You were just a child.'

She was groping among the memories of many men who came to the big brick house with the shady verandah. His eyes must be familiar. One did not forget such eyes, surely.

'Penlynne ... Leonard Penlynne.'

'You must forgive me, Mr Penlynne.'

'It was years ago.' He was astonished that Josiah Rawlinson could have produced such a fine looking girl. As if she were made of another clay altogether. He looked away, conscious that he was confusing her. He had been often to the big brick house with the wide stoep, sometimes straight from her father's claims in his greasy corduroys and muddy boots. He had never hit it off with her father whom he regarded as a petty tyrant with a gift for getting the most out of employees for the minimum reward. It galled him that Rawlinson had respected his energy and organising ability and had never paid him his worth. He had shed no tears when the older man, fighting to retain his hold on his claims, went down before the superior money and skilled manoeuverings of Rhodes and Beit. But he had nothing against the girl. Katherine had then been a small girl in that bachelor household (her mother had died years earlier) and then she had been sent away to school in England.

'Are you going back to Kim?' she asked.

'As a matter of fact, no. Are you going there?'

'I'm going to this new ... Langlaagte. Daddy's built a house there at the new mine.'

'Langlaagte. It'll be dreary there for a girl. I wonder how you'll find it after London?'

'They say Johannesburg's pretty awful, too. Mr Gardiner has been telling me the mines won't last. Do you also think my father might have made a mistake by going there?'

Yes, he made a mistake, Penlynne thought. The mistake was in underestimating me. But he only shrugged and smiled. He looked around the saloon. So that was Walter Gardiner. The man had a big reputation in mining circles and if he was Rawlinson's man he would make a formidable opponent. Poor Katherine, he thought, to be in the centre of that maelstrom so young, so lovely and bound to be sought after by men.

'In my day in Society...' Katherine could hear the approach of Lady Violet and excused herself from Penlynne, as the aristocrat with the face of an ageing bird of uncertain plumage advanced with her arm on that of the Bishop. Her voice had the curiously grating quality Penlynne had always associated with British privilege.

'The two characteristics of English society of the past twenty years are blatant vulgarity and slavish adoration of the Golden Calf. Today, any parvenu with the requisite shekels is accepted. Have you seen the passenger list? Very tolerable for these times, although I must say the intrusion of the Semitic element is unfortunate...'

His Grace, Penlynne noted, did not seem to have any prejudice against the race that had produced his Lord and Master. And my father, for that matter, he added with a mental grin, watching Katherine go through the saloon and out on deck in a flash of colour. He hesitated to follow. After all, she was Rawlinson's daughter and it would be somewhat less than honourable to pursue his instincts with the girl when he was going out to challenge her father. Besides, there was Dorothy.

Katherine climbed the steep companionway to the upper deck, grateful for darkness and cold air, the feeling of being unstifled, watched and manoeuvered at every turn. She had not realized what it was to be the daughter of Josiah Rawlinson until she encountered the subtle mixture of deference and contempt on the faces of the society girls she had 'finished' with in Switzerland. She was glad to be going home, aware as she was of her father's need of her. Suppose he were to fail again? Up there on that wild, barren ridge, treeless and rockstrewn. Langlaagte. It had a dreary sound. The Dutch had named it well. Her father had written her enthusiastically about the house he had built there. 'The first stone house ever seen in these parts – and a fine room for my girl.' She was remembering the evening in Kimberley when he had left the house, grey and concerned. It was just after the big amalgamation of the diamond companies into one, De Beers Consolidated. He came in at about ten o'clock and at once began packing a bag. His whole demeanour had changed from the strain of the past weeks. He had the old look of excitement she had almost forgotten.

'I'm taking the morning stage up country.'

'Am I coming with you?'

'Not this time.' He had said it with a kind of grim-faced enthusiasm like a man going out to face something of unknown proportions with only his courage or his desperation to drive him. She knew that Rhodes and Beit and little Barnato had beaten him in Kimberley and that he'd lost his fortune in the process. He'd gambled up there and won where his rivals had been slow to follow. He was a rich man. Very rich. Rich enough to want his daughter to marry into the nobility. But she knew she'd never marry without love.

The door of the saloon opened and slammed and a man appeared at the top of the companionway. 'I took the liberty of bringing your wrap,' said De la Roche, setting the ermine about her shoulder. She was repelled by his familiarity and started away.

'I hope we shall be good friends, Miss Rawlinson,' he said. 'Do you know that I have admired you for a long time. Ever since your presentation. Ah, yes. I was there at the Debutante's Ball. I saw you make your pretty curtsey to Her Majesty. Who is that, I asked. Oh, that is the beautiful Miss Rawlinson from Kimberley, South Africa. What an occasion! So many fine carriages. Dragoons with drawn swords. What a flaring of gas lights, lovely young ladies on the arms of proud papas. Splendid uniforms. Her Majesty took special notice of you...'

It was the girl's impression that he had never been there, that he had picked up the details in the press. There had been a fuss about the blue-white solitaire she had worn. A debutante was not supposed to exhibit other than a flawless throat but she had worn it because her father had sent it for the occasion and she wanted to please him. He was incensed when the press seized on the jewel as 'an ostentatious vulgarity ... a flaunting of wealth unworthy of the occasion.'

'Do you mind if I smoke, Miss Rawlinson?'

She resented his closeness, his easy assumption that she would accept his flatteries. His use of cologne roused all her girlish scorn. In Kimberley she was more used to the odour of whiskey, sweat and tobacco.

De la Roche talked easily of his connections in French society, of his friendship with Deputies and Ministers of the Chamber. He even hinted an acquaintance with the Comte de Paris ... 'the Pretender to the French throne, you know.'

Katherine pulled away but he detained her.

'You're cold, my dear. How thoughtless of me. In four days we will be at Madeira. The climate is far better than the Riviera and more to be depended on than Egypt. The English colony there is most hospitable. Visitors with the proper credentials find there is hardly a day without a picnic or a tennis party ... imagine!

Blue skies only four days from Europe's winter!'

How far he would have gone with his advances she had no idea. Fortunately at that moment a woman appeared. She gave the impression of someone unsuitably dressed for First Saloon. There was a coarseness about her.

'Excuse me,' said De la Roche, moving quickly towards the woman as Katherine made her retreat.

'You are never to come up here,' said De la Roche in an angry voice. 'Never. I want no connection with anything down there.'

The woman's cold, expressionless mask had gone slack. She groped at his sleeve, pulling him into the shadow of the deckhouse. 'It's the girls, the Lisbon lot. Sick ... real sick.'

'Give them spirits. They'll be all right after Madeira.'

He was furious at the intrusion. He had been on the point of inviting Katherine to accompany him on a horseback jaunt to the plantation of a Portuguese friend. A lamed horse might detain them overnight and his solicitude earn him the gratitude of her father. 'Merde!' he exclaimed, treading out his cheroot.

'It's not the seasickness,' the woman urged.

'What then? Hurry up!'

'I don't know. Vomiting and blood. One of them's passing blood and off her head.'

He knew the Mediterranean. Such a complaint was common in hot weather. The heat of the ship, the change of diet. It could be trifling. He saw panic in the woman's eyes and remembered sweltering Naples. Stifling alleys and summer deaths. Posters with the word 'Cholera'. Who knew where these girls had been recruited?

'Have you touched her?' He stepped back from contact with Mrs Brisbane. 'Wash your hands. Take a hot seawater bath.'

'What's to be done?'

'They're in your charge...' He was fighting to keep down his own panic.

'You must see her. The stench is awful. Shall I get the doctor?'

'Are you mad? And have them all quarantined in Madeira?'

He paced with controlled frenzy, while the squarish hands in their black gloves frantically washed each other.

'Get her into a cabin by herself.'

'It can't be done; they're all full.'

How were they to keep it from the ship's officers until they were past Madeira? Once at sea again they'd find some way to keep it under control. If one died out of twenty it would be no great loss. But he had not worked for this to throw it all away.

'Keep the steward out of there. Here, give him this.' He gave her half a sovereign. 'And keep your mouth shut.'

'There's a doctor in steerage ... a young one.'

It seemed to him unlikely but if there was a qualified man among that mob of penniless hopefuls he'd probably do as he was told for a few gold coins.

Some time in the night Stewart awoke as he often did when some man groped his way past the slung hammocks and made his way up the companionway to the deck or came blundering back searching for his billet in the darkness. A hooded figure was passing down the rows of sleepers. In his half-awakened state it seemed to him to have a quality of menace. It was in the attitude of stooping over this figure and that, shaking and questioning. He sat up. The face under the hood was a woman's – powerful, almost brutal with its deathly white powder. He knew instinctively that she was looking for him.

'You're 'im ... the doctor fellow.'

'Aye,' he said cautiously.

'Come with me. Quick!'

'What do you want with me?' He was rising and putting on his coat. What was happening was like an echo of his student days in the Glasgow slums where he was doing practical work and was wakened by some shawled, beckoning figure, urging him to follow. At that time he often slept among the poor in the stink and squalor of the lodging houses, where in a single room as many as twenty people of both sexes and all ages slept promiscuously together in all degrees of nakedness. What he had seen there of damp, dirt, decay, penury, misery, drunkenness and disease was ineradicable. What stirred him now was the resemblance to it in these rows of sleeping men, groaning, retching, crying out in their sleep. Of course there was no degree of comparison in this to equal that squalor. The men bathed daily in tubs of salt water set out on deck and under the hoses of the seamen ... a great lark it was! But in Glasgow he had learned to smell the distinctive effluvia of typhus and he smelled it now on the woman's hands.

When she unlocked the cabin door up on Second Saloon the

reek of it hit him in the face like a clenched fist. The girl was about sixteen and had evidently been in this state for several days. She had the colouring of a Latin, probably Italian or Portuguese, but the olive flesh of her face and neck was coarsely reddened. She was tossing and turning, moaning and babbling. 'Agua ... agua!' He knew the terrible thirst of typhus and as he held the cup to her lips he noted that where the cup pressed against the red flesh it made a white slash that only slowly recovered its redness.

Stewart threw back the covering and recoiled from the foulness. The woman stood, hand over her nostrils, as if afraid to breathe.

'Why didn't you call the ship's doctor?' he accused. 'You've been hiding this. She must have come aboard sick at Lisbon. She'll have to be quarantined at once.'

'Can't you give her something? It'll be worth your while. She'll get over it in a day or two. She's strong. Maria, the doctor's going to give you something.'

'It's typhus, woman! Is she the only one?'

'The only one, I swear.'

'And the others? The English girls?'

'They're all right.'

'You're the what do they call it ... madame.'

'Chaperon,' she said primly.

'Is that it? And the whoremaster? Is he on board?'

'They're dancers, doctor.'

'And the dancemaster's going First Saloon. It's on your head then.'

'Do something...'

'Open the porthole. Give her air.'

He did it himself, gratefully sucking in the cold night wind. The woman was fumbling in her reticule for money, whining. 'It's a better life for them, the likes of this one. And they gets used to it quick enough. She's no better than dirt where she come from. Some of them marries respectable.'

Stewart shook her off and went out to find the ship's doctor. He was lost in the carpeted corridors and bewildered by the lavish appointments, the glitter of silver, brass and polished wood. He grasped a handrail and went up a wide stairway that led to the Palm Court. There was a hum of polite talk. Card tables were busy and a string quartet played an English air, the musicians bowing away among the greenery.

He hesitated to enter. On the other side he saw what he took to be the officers' quarters and the sick bay. He knocked on several doors without an answer but at the end of the passage a door suddenly slammed open and he was confronted by a steward. 'What you fink you're doin' up 'ere? Get back where you belong!'

'The ship's doctor ... where is he?'

'Sick parade's in the morning.' The steward took him by the arm and dragged him away.

'Let me alone, man. There's typhus in Second Saloon.'

The steward fell back with ludicrous haste. 'Number 43 ... at the end. I've just took 'im in a bottle. 'E's in a filthy mood.' He was all conciliation and eager to be gone. News would be over the ship in a flash.

Stewart knocked on Number 43. A bolt was unshot and he saw a scarlet eye glaring at him through the aperture. 'What do you want, fellow?'

When Stewart told him what he had seen the ship's doctor looked at him with a mixture of contempt and drunken incomprehension. 'Are you ... have you the damned audacity to approach me at this hour, in my q...quarters with some cock 'n bull story? Get to hell back where you came from. Report to sick bay in the morning.'

'My name is Dr MacDonald ... doctor. I believe you had better see this girl at once.'

'Doctor? An unlikely doctor if ever I saw one.' He gulped his liquor and pressed a bell. If he was listening to Stewart's attempt to describe what he had seen he showed no sign of it. When a crewman appeared he showed a sudden change of mood. Winking heavily at the man in the blue jersey, he suggested they all go quietly together to the cabin where Stewart imagined he had seen the typhus case. 'We have another doctor aboard, bosun,' he grinned.

Stewart could not find the cabin again. 'It's here somewhere. She's a Portuguese girl.'

'Portuguese girls,' winked the ship's doctor. 'Now we know what the trouble is, eh, bosun.'

'We do that, sir,' winked the seaman and without warning

Stewart found himself pinioned. 'We'll cool 'im off, sir, never fear.'

In what he took to be the ship's brig he lay down on the iron cot. It was futile to rattle at the door and protest. He began to laugh. What a fool he'd been to suppose that the principle of upper class privilege that operated everything would have ceased just because he had put the shores of England a few hundred miles behind him.

Chapter 4

Was she really leaving England? The long drawn-out summer had lingered into a golden autumn and as the days shortened and darkened there had been the excitement of the London season – the debutante's ball, theatre parties and more invitations than she could cope with. Now as she lay in her bunk, watching the play of light on white paint as the ship rocked in the mild swells, she had a sense of home-coming. The bright light was already a foretaste of Africa. But would she ever be the same again? The society columns had called her 'the Diana of the Veldt' because she rode well. Hers was a tall, straight body, the fine limbs not entirely concealed by the disfiguring fashions she found so irksome, the changes of clothes so boringly necessary. Morning, afternoon and evening.

Before she went to sleep last night Lady Violet had come in with a letter and a look of secret knowledge. Katherine guessed that it was from Charles Warewood. She sighed as she turned over and reached it from the dresser. She liked him well enough when it came to riding and he had a boyish gaiety that made one forget his noble background. The shock of blonde hair that fell over the broad forehead ... really he was most unlike her idea of a soldier and a lord of many acres. He had apologised for falling in love with her, punting her down the river that last afternoon at Warewood Hall. Soldiering was the family tradition.

'All I'm really fit for,' he laughed. 'I know Warewood's a tumbledown old place, with twenty empty bedrooms that haven't been slept in for half a century. But if you were here, it'd be so different. I'd chuck the army and go in for farming. We've still plenty of land that's not overgrown. I know a title's not important to a girl like you. You colonials are so ... so free. Is it true your grandfather was one of the settlers sent out to keep the Kaffirs at bay? I know my regiment fought in the Kaffir Wars...'

The story of how her father had been in his cradle when his

father and brothers were up on the roof of the farmstead beating off the Xhosa had fascinated him.

She felt his restless longing for something he could not express and young as she was she sensed that his longing for her was only part of his yearning to break away from the old and familiar.

'I love this place,' he said as he rested on his pole. 'But one has this awful sense of ... of something coming to an end. Do you know what I mean? Perhaps it's just that you're going and I shall probably never see you again.'

He had none of the hauteur she had come to associate with the aristocracy. Tall, he would be heavier. She admired the unforced ease with others that was the legacy of blood. And his good manners and consideration. But could she love him? She guessed that this letter was a plea.

'It is true the Warewood family is penniless today,' Lady Violet had told her. 'But its position in Society ... the real Society ... is unassailable. I would hesitate to turn him down, Katherine. Think of your father!'

As she broke the seal of the letter she could imagine him sitting at the writing table, spluttering ink on green leather and calling for another pen, a whiskey. Pale and biting his lip as he struggled to say what he meant. Dammit, Katherine, you know I can't put words together. If I could you might not have turned me down so fast. I often ride where we rode together. What grand days they were for me...

She felt her eyes mist. There was an openness, an honesty about Charles that she had felt from the first moment at the Military Gymkhana the 14th Hussars had put on at Preston Park the day she had met him. It was all very splendid. Bunting snapping, parasols in the stands. Champagne and strawberries and splendid uniforms which turned tall men into giants, red faced and fiercely mustached under towering shakos. The smell of hot horseflesh mingled with the suffocating odour of chestnut blossom. Glitter of weapons and thunder of hooves. Turf flying. It was a fine day for 'cutting the Turk's head' as they charged at dummies with flashing steel. There was tent-pegging and a tourney. The officers fought the ranks, sword against lance. The musical ride was all jingling equipment and dancing hooves, sunlight glancing off accoutrements and gleaming horseflesh. But it was the charge that brought everyone to their feet. Charles with his squadron galloping up the green slope against the battery.

A week later had come the invitation to spend a week at Warewood. 'My dear Katherine, he is the seventh viscount!' urged Lady Violet when she hesitated. It was the lady's barely concealed triumph that had given Katherine doubt about the wisdom of acceptance.

This was a sweet and considerate letter. Almost halting in its appeal. 'I shall put all this behind me and come out,' he wrote. 'I understand that I shall have to do something worthy of you.'

As she put the letter into a drawer she was thinking that it was nothing Charles had said or done that had made her hold back. She did not know what, if anything, she felt for him. And yet, surely he was the most romantic figure she would ever meet? Then why was it that she had felt something move in her when the American took her hand? A man she had never seen before in her life. A sensation that had been almost frightening ... everything seemed to rush to her head leaving her in a state of confusion. Perhaps she would see him again this morning. Almost she hoped she might not.

She started at Lady Violet's knock on the door of their interleading cabins. She lay back and pretended to be sleeping. The woman had such searching eyes and she was so insistent on having her way. Katherine knew she would almost certainly enquire about the letter. She'd sit down on the bed and tell her it was for her own good. 'Think of it, my dear child. One of the oldest families in England! Surely you don't think Lord Charles is a common fortune hunter!'

It was her maid Mildred who entered. Still pretending sleep she saw the white kid boots, dress of pale rose shantung, blue sash and a wide Italian straw hat with trailing ribbons to match the fringed parasol. It still amazed her that Mildred was so deft, so clever with clothes and with her hair. She had a pleasant deference that was in no way servile. Katherine was getting rather fond of her, much to Lady Violet's concern.

'What on earth have you got there, Mildred?'

'It's your spine protector, Miss Katherine. It's the tropics, miss. Lady Violet says the sun melts the brain out there.'

'I'll never wear that stupid thing.'

'Oh, Miss Katherine. Suppose you was to get sunstroke? I'd never forgive meself.'

'Mildred dear, I was born in the veld, under a canvas.'

'Oh, miss, you're teasing me.'

It seemed impossible to the girl that anyone so beautiful could have been born under any but the most sheltered circumstances. This talk of being carried on the hip of a Griqua girl, whatever that was!

To Mildred her young mistress was like something out of a picture, some nymph, half-naked and wide-eyed in a Burne-Jones canvas. It was in the fall of her hair, the length of white limb as she rose, her tender young breasts moving against the nightdress.

'Have you got a young man, Mildred?'

'Yes, miss, he's a sojer. He's in India but he writes.'

'Mildred?'

'Yes, miss?'

'Do you think the American gentleman ... Mr Gardiner, is handsome?'

The girl giggled. 'Oh yes, miss. He's a fine looking gentleman.'

'It seems strange he's still a bachelor. His hair's greying already. He must be thirty-five at least, maybe older.'

'That's not old, miss. Not in a man, that is.'

'Lord Warewood wants me to marry him.'

'I thought so, miss.'

'He is twenty-two ... and a soldier.'

'Perhaps you still will, miss.'

'No, I don't believe I will.'

Katherine found the deck thronged with pre-breakfast strollers. Binoculars were being focused and passed to the ladies. Bishop Beddington was wearing a sola topi with a neck flap. Panamas and straws were popular and here and there a bare head braved the cloudless blue.

Walter Gardiner came over as soon as he saw her. 'I've got friends here I'd like you to meet. I'm hoping you and, naturally, Lady Violet, will join me.' His skin was as supple as fine leather, his long upper lip cleanshaven, and when he smiled the sun-darkened face creased in a network of deep wrinkles. His eyes were almost unbearably blue and she turned to look at the shore, unaccountably afraid, with a strange disturbance she had never experienced before. He was so powerfully masculine that when she took the glasses from him it was if a shock had passed through the metal into her hand. She saw the white-fronted houses set in a hollow of dark green mountain.

'I'm surprised more English people don't winter here,' he was saying. 'Here come the bum boats, if you'll excuse the word.' He was teasing her, of course. 'They dive for coins. The decks will be a bazaar by breakfast time ... junk, shells, lace and all that. The island's interesting, geologically. Now you as a girl brought up in mining, you probably have a good eye for a formation.' She could feel his eyes on her body.

'I do believe Lady Violet has agreed to ... to go ashore with the Baron.'

'De la Roche.' If he was put out he shrugged it off with a short laugh which could have been his comment on Lady Violet's ingenuousness.

'He's had an introduction from Baron Rothschild.'

'Rothschild? Oh yes, they all claim to have that!'

He turned away, leaving her puzzled and afraid she had offended him, a man her father thought well enough of to send for urgently. A man whose interest in her was becoming obvious. But perhaps it was only because of her father. If only Lady Violet did not meddle so!

'Well, child, it's all arranged. Morning tea at the English Club, an al fresco luncheon on the mountain and this evening a ball at the Portuguese Club. I believe Lady Cavagnari will be there.'

They were joined at breakfast for the first time by the ship's surgeon. Major Fordyce's military past was evident in his bearing and abruptness. Walter Gardiner put him down for a boozer and Bishop Beddington, after one glance at the surgeon's veined cheeks, thought that whatever his record in the Sudan as surgeon on a Nile gunboat, he was altogether the wrong appointment on a passenger ship. A word to the chairman, Mr Donald Currie, might be effective...

The Countess of Stratford was finding difficulty in the peeling of a mango for the first time. Major Fordyce offered surgical assistance.

'My stewardess tells me,' the countess ventured, 'that there is an unfortunate outbreak of typhus aboard.'

'Where did that story come from?' said Fordyce abruptly.

'Then there is no truth...'

'None. This is a British ship.'

'Here, here!' exclaimed De la Roche loudly.

Leonard Penlynne, who had seen typhus in Kimberley more than once, listened without making his interest too obvious. From the surgeon's red-veined face and his hung-over look it seemed possible that the man was indeed hearing of this for the first time.

Major Fordyce laid down his cutlery and beckoned angrily to the steward who had neglected to spike his coffee with whiskey. 'It would be a pity,' he said, 'if such a rumour were to go further ... entirely unfounded.' He said it with conviction. He had absolutely no recollection of the incident the night before but as he fumbled for words it was crossing his mind that there might be substance in what the countess had said. Had someone come to his door, claiming to be a doctor? He had a vague feeling it might have happened.

'Excuse me,' he said, rising. 'This rumour must be scotched at once.'

'On a ship like this?' said De la Roche, his napkin lightly dabbled at mouth and forehead where an unaccountable dew had arisen.

Typhus had carried off Katherine's mother when she was too young to have known her but for years she had walked on Sundays to the grave to put flowers on the stone marked with the words 'camp fever'. She looked to Leonard Penlynne for reassurance and when he rose from the table he put his hands on her shoulders and she took comfort from the strength in them, turning her face up to see the dark eyes smiling with sympathy and understanding. She was aware by now that he was going out to join Alfred Beit but she did not feel any resentment towards him. There were moments, in fact, when he swam into her consciousness and stood there, his smiling mouth concealed by the curl of beard and mustache, his eyes impenetrable and glittering. He was years younger than the American but it was not the difference in age that brought him into her fantasies as she lay in her bunk, the hot wind of the southern seas blowing in at the open porthole. She was sometimes aware that her thighs were wet...

'I think it's most unlikely,' Penlynne was saying and she felt his fingers slide with the soft material of her dress. Almost at once he straightened up and went out. She looked after him, somehow disturbed and in the moment of indecision she heard Walter Gardiner murmuring beside her, 'Perhaps we shall meet on the mountain today...'

She looked up and nodded.

By the time she was ready to go ashore there was a story going around that a young man from steerage was confined in the ship's brig. They said he had been spreading alarm about typhus. There was not a word of truth in it, Lady Violet insisted. 'I have great faith in the spinal pad.'

The chief steward had made up a luncheon basket and its contents were spread on a tablecloth of Madeira lace. Katherine shaded her eyes to look down on the enamelled blue where the grey hull of the ship lay mirrored, its red funnel scattered across the broken surface and its smoke a mere wisp. She was indifferent to the conversation around her, the tinkle of glassware and drawing of corks.

'Provided care has been taken in the choosing of congenial guests,' said Lady Violet, 'a well arranged picnic is one of the pleasantest forms of entertainment. I believe the picnics at Balmoral are delightful.'

'Ah yes, the dear Queen,' said the countess, who was often a guest at Balmoral but never spoke of it as anything exceptional.

'In my view it is the company that counts. Do you agree, Miss Rawlinson?' said De la Roche. If he was anxious he did not show it. The hand that poured the Johannisberger was steady. Once they were at sea again nature would take its course. His investment was too involved to be prejudiced by faint-heartedness at this stage in the venture. His hope of taking Katherine for a walk had been frustrated. She had also rejected his attempts to assist her mount the donkey, seeming to prefer the hand of the cheerful clergyman. De la Roche had gone to some trouble with his appearance – the white cambric shirt with silk cravat worn sailor-style and the Breton straw hat were calculated to stir admiration. His mirror had assured him that he was in every way an object to excite a young girl.

Lady Violet had noted that Katherine was in one of her wilful moods. She sometimes thought she saw signs of the crude Josiah in the girl and a motherless upbringing in the squalor of the Orange River diggings. Josiah Rawlinson had been heard to boast that Katherine had been suckled by a Hottentot, his enormous laugh shaking the glassware at polite tables. Lady Violet had heard that the gentlemen had been vastly amused by his description of the so-called 'Hottentot Venus' whose *labia majora* had been measured by the explorer Burchell ... at a distance. By sextant. Much coarse laughter.

Lady Violet hoped that this story had been put about by his detractors, other members of what she called 'the Midas class'. The Ecksteins, the Beits, the Wernhers. Baron de la Roche? Well, she knew nothing of the Almanac de Gotha with its lists of the accredited nobility of Europe but by his own account the Frenchman was well connected in polite society.

Katherine stirred restlessly as Lady Violet droned on. 'The two characteristics of English society in the past twenty years have been vulgarity and a slavish adoration of the Golden Calf. Ah well ... *fin de siècle*. Where will it all end, my dear Bishop?'

A gentle snore was the clergyman's only comment. Katherine rose abruptly and walked to the edge of the plateau, the soft wind blowing her skirt against her legs in a movement she found sensuous and languorous. The ribbons trailing from the circle of straw shading the firm young face brushed her cheek like the touch of a hand and she shivered unaccountably.

Far down below on the winding path she saw a man coming up at a brisk walk. She saw with a lurch of her heart that it was Walter Gardiner. Mr Gardiner, as she thought of him. In a few moments he turned the last corner, and came up to her, smiling. He was hatless and carried a prospector's tools.

To Lady Violet's astonishment Katherine took the man's arm and together they moved up the slope and out of sight. De la Roche's face was a study in controlled fury. This time his hand shook as he refilled the clergyman's glass before the Johannisberger quite lost its chill.

'Well, I never!' exclaimed the lady. '*Autre temps, autre moeurs.*' The bridge of her nose had never seemed so sharp.

Chapter 5

Stewart had little sleep that night. Towards morning he dropped off but woke when the ship's engines stopped. He was looking through the porthole when he heard a rattling at the door. A steward came in with a breakfast tray. He nodded civilly and went out. Stewart was lifting the cover on the dish when Fordyce entered.

'Good morning, doctor,' he said in conciliatory tones. 'It's been confirmed that you are a licentiate of Glasgow Infirmary and I hope you have not been too uncomfortable. A mistake has been made and you have my apologies. I have seen the Portuguese girl and confirm your diagnosis. The captain wants this kept under control. The less said the better and no panic. Will you give me your assistance?'

Stewart looked down into the azure water. Bum boats were putting out from shore. 'What do you intend doing?' he said.

'Isolate the patient ... make a thorough check through the ship.'

'Will passengers be going ashore?'

'The captain wishes everything to be kept as normal as possible. We can't afford to be quarantined here, or to cause undue alarm to the authorities. By the time we reach St Helena it will be well under control and there is no fear of its spreading to First Saloon.'

They were only at sea an hour when the order was given to clear out the steerage quarters and hose them down. Everyone below was to be assembled on deck with their gear. Stewart pushed among them, looking for Owen and the youngsters. Fordyce had spoken of a military-style medical inspection. 'They're all men, MacDonald. A short-arm inspection will do no harm. Some of them will be concealing all kinds of filth.'

Stewart found Owen in a distracted state. 'What about these children? Where are we to hide them?'

'Who else knows about Rachel, besides Jorley?'

'The boys have been good about it, no trouble. Eh, little sister!' He put his arm about the girl. 'Never fear, lass. We'll manage.'

'The best thing is ... pass them among the men on deck.'

There was a great press of men on the forward deck when Stewart was called to accompany Fordyce and the ship's master. He had persuaded Fordyce to drop his idea of the strip-naked inspection. 'These men won't stand for it, doctor,' he had advised.

'Somebody brought this filth on board, MacDonald. I'd have the hose on the lot of them.' It was his intention to dress them down like a company of idle soldiers but the captain would not hear of it. It must be 'swab down and fumigate'. It outraged his seaman's pride that a brand new vessel could be harbouring this filthy disease. Typhus was for slave and convict ships. Rotting hulks. God Almighty, this was 1890 and if his ship was packed ... well, the company could not allow the immigrant trade to fall into the hands of foreigners. England had a duty to get its good working stock to the colonies. Wasn't that what the bishop preached on Sunday? Unfortunately it was a fact that there was no control on the influx of Cypriots, Jews, Greeks and Turks, their standards notoriously low.

'What about Jews, Turks and the rest of them? Have we many?' He was addressing the chief steward as they went forward in their gleaming whites, red-faced and immaculate. He knew very well what to expect down there but in his anger he was looking for a scapegoat. Hundreds of faces turned up to him as he mounted the forward hatch to address them. Stewart stood behind him, very conscious of his new position, awkward in white ducks loaned by the fourth mate. He was searching among raw young city faces, the bearded ones of older workers, some mocking and some resentful, lifting their eyes to authority. Expecting to be humiliated.

'They stink like cattle,' said Fordyce.

Stewart was still looking for Owen as the captain spoke.

'Now men, if there are any among you concealing sickness step forward at once.' Silence and then a low growl of anger.

Stewart felt Fordyce stiffen beside him. The turkey face went darker. Suddenly there was an agitation in the press of men. Stewart saw Jorley burst out. He stood shaking, pointing in self-righteous agitation. 'It's them, sir, them two sheenies. 'Im an' his sister – stowaways.'

The crowded deck made way for the master. Owen stood with an arm about Isadore and Rachel. 'They're taking up no room, sir,' he suggested. 'And all the men chip in with a bite of grub. No trouble to anyone, sir, eh mates?'

'Master at Arms!'

'Sir.'

'Confine this man in the brig.'

Rachel flung herself into Owen's arms but she was roughly dragged away. Owen shouted, 'Look after her, mates!' Isadore and Rachel were separated, the boy to be confined below, the girl to be under care of a stewardess. Then came the crew with streaming hoses and it was all over.

In the privacy of the captain's cabin drinks were poured.

'Now gentlemen, I want this cleaned up. What's to be done? I'm in your hands.'

Major Fordyce believed in a 'copious use of alcohol and fresh air.' The infection was communicated through the discharges of the patient and the use of infected drinking water. In a clean ship it could be controlled.

'How long will it continue, Major?'

The surgeon looked doubtful. The seaman turned his impatience on the younger man.

'I've seen this in Glasgow. It can rage for weeks in hot weather.'

'God man, this is not a slum! Fatalities?'

'In confined conditions, one in three.'

'I have six hundred on this ship.'

'There is a new theory,' ventured Stewart and saw Fordyce's expression harden. 'The fever is carried by lice. When a patient scratches a bite he rubs the louse into the wound.'

'Are you suggesting self-inoculation by lice?' Fordyce's face reddened and he burst out laughing. 'I've seen many a typhus patient, never one with a bite.'

'There are no lice on this vessel,' said the captain with indignation.

The girl Maria died when they were a day out of Madeira. The small body, sewn in canvas and covered with the flag of Portugal, slid down the plank. A sobbing cry went up from the women who had boarded with her. Their faces, covered with dark veils, were not the faces Stewart would have associated with harlotry. De la Roche offered him a cheroot.

'I believe there's an English girl, a dancer, come down with it?'

'I can't discuss it,' said Stewart, glad for the first time in his medical career that he could assume the professional mask. But the man insisted and for all his casualness there was a note of concern in his voice that made Stewart wary.

'Is the girl delirious?' the man persisted.

'Yes, now and then.'

'Babbling nonsense?'

'You could call it that.' Abruptly he turned away. Leaving steerage to share a cabin with the fourth officer had been more of a wrench than he bargained for.

'I'll carry your gear, Stewart,' Owen had offered.

'Thanks, I'll manage.' He had shaken hands with the small, wiry man with the angry eyes and the pitworn face.

'Get on with you, mun. Keeping the captain waiting for his dinner.' The Welshman turned away and Stewart had a sudden pang of betrayal. That night when he went in to the First Saloon dining room for the first time he was dazed by the bright lights, the glassware and silver, the smell of rich food mingled with perfume and toiletry. A steward pushed in his chair. For a moment there was a lull in the hum of talk. He took his seat, noting with dismay an array of cutlery as formidable as a surgeon's table.

Stewart had come straight from Kitty Loftus. The ravages of the fever had appalled him. He could do nothing more than apply palliatives. Laudanum, twenty drops. Liquid food. Alcohol forced over the blackened tongue. The expected mental derangement was at its height. She had a recurring fantasy of being screwed down in a coffin and had to be held down, shrieking.

The clatter ceased. Stewards paused in mid-scurry. His Grace was appealing to Almighty God to keep a benevolent eye on the steerage. Stewart picked up a menu card a foot long and embellished with the botanical wonders of the Cape of Good Hope. Strange flowers and strange viands. How did one cope with oysters? Would they be served cooked or in their shells? There was a rustle at his side. He rose with the other gentlemen. He had seen the young lady on deck with the tall American who pushed in her chair. He noted her grateful smile and found his heart beating with alarm at having to cope with such a beauty. But she smiled at him easily.

'I'm Katherine Rawlinson. You must be Doctor MacDonald.'

'Aye,' he lapsed in his confusion.

Across the table he heard an imperious voice: 'These days the truly civilised custom of presenting the *carte* in French is in decline.' She seemed to wait for acceptance or challenge.

'Ah, my dear Lady Violet,' murmured His Grace, 'I believe *Potage à la Parmontier* is potato soup nonetheless.'

'Doctor, what is your opinion?' she challenged.

'I have no French, ma'am,' Stewart admitted, aware of every eye on him. 'But if the menu were in Latin I daresay I'd manage.'

'Well done!' whispered the girl at his side.

The conversation turned to weightier things. Had the conversion of the black tribesmen to Christianity had a restraining and civilising effect?

Leonard Penlynne listened to the word play with a certain sardonic amusement. He had never travelled First Saloon before and he had assumed a gravity he did not feel. His fingers fairly itched to tickle the ivories of the piano in the Palm Court, the way he used to in the bachelors' mess in Kimberley. He had chosen his clothes with expensive care.

'Spare nothing, Leonard,' Wernher had said. 'You are our man now.' And he had given him a card to his tailor in Bond Street. For one who had so recently believed himself wiped out it was an exhilarating experience and he was savouring it.

Wernher had cautioned him to keep his own counsel. 'No point,' he said in his heavily Germanic way, 'in telling the enemy in advance. You will find yourself on board with the American, Walter Gardiner. He is going out for Rawlinson so the less you tell him the better.'

It amused Penlynne to see that the American appeared to have more interest in the Rawlinson girl than in small talk about mining. If Katherine was her father's child she would know how to take care of herself without the attentions of the haggard aristocrat who was her chaperon. When the talk about South Africa and its problems got too much for him to resist putting in his oar Penlynne would retire to his cabin and amuse himself with Rider Haggard's entertaining *King Solomon's Mines*. The man knew his South Africa.

He was about to rise when Walter Gardiner begged Katherine's permission to tell a story he had from a friend in London.

'It's about your father ... do you mind, Miss Rawlinson?'

'I'd rather not hear any more stories about my father,' she said and Penlynne suspected that there were tears not far behind the girl's bright eyes. He had seen through the American's technique of mocking and teasing, provoking her spirit then soothing her with small attentions. He saw that she was already in a confused state of mind.

Penlynne spoke louder than his normal voice at table. It rumbled out of him with a clarity and authority that he had not intended. Every eye turned on him. They saw the dark, strangely ugly face, his black eyes not exactly mocking but somehow compelling. He looked almost rabbinical at that moment. A veritable Saul, thought Bishop Bedford, not without admiration. Who in hell is this, was Gardiner's reaction.

'I believe there are many stories told about Mr Rawlinson,' Penlynne was saying. 'But then, that is the fate of everyone who is anyone in the gold fields. Some of them are even true. Mr Rawlinson has not escaped his share of calumnies.'

'No intention to dishonour the man,' cried Gardiner. 'Far from it. It seems,' he continued, assuming command of the table once more, 'that a batch of raw natives arrived from the reserves, all mission boys, Bishop. They worked like heroes in Mr Rawlinson's mine and when he sent down to inspect them they were singing hymns with touching fervour. Mr Rawlinson was deeply moved by the apparent benefits of a mission education but as he turned to go, believing his labour problems solved by such spiritual fellows, a raw Kaffir, a pagan, pointed to the belt of the loudest hymn-singer. In it were two diamonds. One five carats, one of ten!'

Penlynne saw it was time to go. There wasn't a single mine owner in Kimberley who had not bought and sold diamonds illegally and Rawlinson, for all his indignation about IDB, was as big a rogue as any of them, Barnato included. On the one side they flogged the blacks for theft and on the other they bought stones wherever they were offered.

'What use has the savage for diamonds?' said Lady Violet vehemently.

'Apocryphal, of course,' murmured His Grace.

'I have no doubt that the Almighty granted our nation victory over the Zulus and other savage tribes for His own inscrutable purposes...'

'In any case you need the labour,' smiled Gardiner.

'We are not Boers, Mr Gardiner. We are anxious to create a just society.'

'Do they not keep slaves?' questioned the countess.

'Not since the British freed them,' said the bishop.

'They licked you at ... Majuba, did they not?' Gardiner pursued relentlessly.

'Majuba will not be forgotten,' said Major Fordyce.

There was a general round of hear-hears.

Majuba? Where was that? Stewart listened to the voice of the ruling class. The years of study and his rural background had left him ill-equipped. He was appalled to see how little he knew of political opinions and the currents shaping Imperial strategy, affecting the lives of millions. This bitter talk about blacks and Boers was having its effect on Katherine Rawlinson. Abruptly she left the table.

'Katherine is very young, a mere child,' said Lady Violet, rising to follow.

'I admire independence,' said Gardiner, watching the girl go. The conversation resumed at a more subdued level.

Suddenly the clatter of dishes and cutlery faded. The musicians faltered in mid-bow. At some tables people half-rose from their seats. There was a perceptible gasp. An apparition had appeared among them.

Fogs and mists surrounded Kitty Loftus. Phantoms reached out their wraith shapes with mocking cries. When she reached out to strike at them they receded, leaving her once more in the funnel of darkness. Voices were blurred, seeming to speak no language she had ever heard. A succession of dreams and delusions passed through her mind. There was the recurring horror of being screwed down in the coffin with her mother, shrieking, pounding at the lid. But now there was music ... distantly drawing her. Golden threads of violins and silvery trumpets that brought a smile to the ravaged face. Where did it come from? She must hear it, get close to that delightful sound. Waltzing ... always waltzing. Who is this who dances with her? The smiling, knowing face. Is he the secret one? The one who knows? Take him away! Away! Now she is walking. No, floating along a passage towards brilliant lights over soft carpeting and among strange shapes that glitter hurtfully. Going up a stair. It is the music that is carrying her forward without effort to itself. She is reaching out towards it, to grasp it and possess it.

'Mon Dieu!' cried De la Roche, sinking back in his chair. Stewart leaped from his place and grappled with his patient. She fled from him out into the passage. The saloon door slammed and she was out in the wind and the hot, moist darkness.

De la Roche reached for his wine glass and knocked it over in a puddle of crimson. Was that Kitty Loftus? Was that typhus? The blotched face ... the shaven skull ... the body in the bedraggled nightgown. Till now it had been no more than a word pasted up in public places. He had suffered the inconvenience of being fumigated at the Marseilles railway station where travellers were obliged to wait for fifteen minutes in a closed room while smoking retorts poured out fumes of carbolic acid. But this! Was this the delicious creature who had swayed beside him in the hansom, the lovely body he had coveted when from the cover of the two-way mirror he had watched...

It was a dirty business and he would finish with it as quickly as he was able.

The grey speck that was St Helena rose out of the ocean. A single cloud rested on its bleak profile. At breakfast Stewart listened to talk of the Emperor Napoleon and his empty grave on the island. 'The British know how to salt them away,' said Gardiner. 'Who have you got over there now?'

He lost no opportunity to take a rise out of Her Brittanic Majesty's subjects and to stress the benefits of rebellion. It was Major Fordyce who took him up this time.

'I don't think we have to discuss it, Mr Gardiner. I don't think it's a subject for the ladies.'

'Some Zulu chief, I hear. I thought you had them under control?'

'There has to be order.'

Stewart noticed that a change had come over the surgeon's face. The man was fighting to control his feelings, to prevent himself spilling out some deep-seated emotion. Until this mo-

47

ment he had thought of Fordyce as a typical military surgeon, an antiquated mixture of Crimean War manuals and prejudice. From what he had seen of his work he would hardly have qualified today as a country vet. It was only his service bluff that had carried him through the typhus affair. What was it about the mention of the Zulu captive that had so disturbed him?

Later on he heard the engines stop and there was a knock at his door. It was Fordyce. 'We're going ashore, you and I. We're picking up this fellow Binyani ... Dinizulu, the king, he's staying here until he co-operates. We have to check on his health. It'd never do if it was said that we misuse our political prisoners.'

'You mean ... the king of the Zulus is on St Helena?'

'It was good enough for Napoleon. I wouldn't get worked up about it if I were you, MacDonald. They're savages. All blacks are savages. You should have seen the prisoners of the Mahdi in the Sudan. Verminous, starving, crammed into tiny cells. At the mercy of guards for water, sleeping with the dead. And they were the lucky ones. The others had their heads on sticks. As for their treatment of our women...'

Stewart noticed that sweat had broken out on his face.

'The Zulus – these heroic warriors Mr Rider Haggard is so sentimental about – slitting the bellies of the wounded to let their spirits free. I expect this fellow Binyani will have put on twenty pounds and will have only one regret – going back to his grass hut.'

Stewart began to pack his instruments. Fordyce was the kind who could stand by and see a soldier take a hundred lashes and sit down to a hearty dinner. The surgeon was splashing spirits into a glass.

'Are you going to take a position on the gold mines, doctor?'

'I haven't made any decision, sir.'

'There's a wide field open, very wide.' His whole tone had changed. 'I believe there are only two doctors in Kimberley. Big fees and a good club. I may start a sanatorium in the Karoo. The sea's not for me, MacDonald.'

Leonard Penlynne watched the return to the ship of the small boat with the two doctors. They had been joined by a solitary black figure. He was dressed in ill-fitting European clothes and was barefoot. His shaven head was crowned by a curious black ring that gave his impassive features an air of authority. On the ship's decks the chatter had died away. The only sound was the splash of oars. Hundreds of white faces looked down on the Zulu as he came aboard, his carved stick raised in salute to the uniforms on the bridge.

Penlynne was strangely moved. The gesture by the dignified figure in the military cast-offs moved him in a way he could not explain. He did not feel a conqueror. As manager of more than one diamond mine he had turned men like this away in droves. Barefoot and wearing an old greatcoat or red tunic they would stand and give him the salute once reserved for their great. Nkos. Lord. It had always disturbed him that so often he had to turn away men who had walked to the diggings from hundreds of miles away. Their way of life had been destroyed. They would stand on the edge of the Big Hole and look down with blank faces to where their brothers shouted and laboured among the din of thudding engines.

Some time in the night Stewart was wakened by a cabin steward.

'It's the doctor, sir, he's took real bad.' The man was clearly alarmed but appeared reluctant to say what he had seen though it was Stewart's impression that it was nothing altogether new.

'It's the 'orrors, sir,' the steward confided as he led the way to Fordyce's cabin. ''E sez them Zulus are after 'im.' He threw open the cabin door and Stewart saw a sight so grotesque that he hardly believed his eyes. The surgeon was cowering in the extreme corner of his bunk and when Stewart went towards him Fordyce shrieked in terror. Bedding was thrown about. There was every sign of a ferocious struggle. Yet there had obviously been no one there but the surgeon himself. An empty service revolver lay on the carpet and from the open porthole it seemed that he had been firing it through the aperture.

''Olding them off, sir,' said the steward hoarsely. 'Them Zulus. The major, 'e was with Lord Chelmsford's column in Zululand an' what 'e saw there ... well, sir, it takes him like this.'

Fordyce grasped at Stewart. 'Oh, thank God you've come. We tried to hold out. They got into the hospital with the assegais, butchered the wounded.'

Stewart administered a strong sedative and handed the weapon to the steward. 'Get it out of sight and say nothing of this.' He waited while the sedative took effect, looking down at the distorted face until it had slackened into deep sleep. For the first time he wondered what kind of country he was going to, how he would cope living among a people whose customs and language were so utterly unknown. How many immigrants flooding out to the gold fields had any idea of what British soldiers and settlers had gone through? They saw only the chance for themselves. The rest was already history. This man whom he had despised for his weakness had gone through something in the thickly wooded ravines of Zululand where the impis came on like furies, regardless of the rifles. No one who had not heard the drumming of shields, the deep baying of tens of thousands of voices, could have any idea what the pacification of such a people meant...

Chapter 6

From the deck of the docked *American* it was possible to see the breakwater convicts labouring. In the heavy heat of midday the sound of hammers breaking rock came up to the deck, muffled and delayed. To the watchers it was like watching a pageant instead of the reality of hundreds of men – white, black and brown – labouring side by side, ankles in chains.

Most of the immigrants had already gone ashore. Others were sitting on their gear thumbing phrasebooks 'of the Kaffir tongue' which pamphleteers had assured them would be of advantage when they 'got their boys together'. Written by a pioneer digger of the De Kaap gold rush of some years earlier, the pamphlets informed that 'donkeys or others beasts not being available to carry mining gear, the Kaffirs will be found willing for a small wage and a ration of meal'.

Stewart stood at the rail next to Owen. The Welshman had been freed from the brig and Stewart had been able to tell him that 'the children', as Owen called them, had been allowed to land.

'A Mr Penlynne has paid their passages and put down landing money. The boy will make his way inland to Kimberley, he says.'

'And Rachel?' Owen turned anxious eyes on Stewart.

'She's been taken care of in a Jewish orphanage.'

'Who is this Mr Penlynne then?'

'I don't know anything about him. He's going out to the new gold fields on the Rand.'

'I'd like to thank him. It was a Christian act.'

'And you, Owen? What about you?'

The Welshman waved his arm at the breakwater. 'Is there no getting away from it then? What have they done? Little enough you can be sure. Got drunk, spoke insolent to the magistrate. I never thought, Stewart mun, to find it here. In all this extravagant beauty. And down there the same old cruelty. The whip and the chain. It makes a man despair.'

For some moments they looked on in silence. Then Owen turned to Stewart and wrung his hand. There were tears in his eyes. 'I thank you for your good words on my behalf, otherwise I'd be in irons myself. Look after yourself, Stewart. God willing we'll meet again up there in Transvaal. You'll do it, boyo ... whatever!'

Doves brooded and quarrelled around Stewart's feet. In the drowsy heat of the Cape Town Gardens he nodded, listening for the crunch of gravel under the feet of the ship's surgeon. He had said nothing to the man about the incident in the cabin and Fordyce had no recollection of it. He had been easier to get on with and there might be something in the man's proposition.

'What are your plans?' he had asked the night before the ship docked.

'I'll look around.' Stewart's reply had been deliberately vague. Now, as he waited for Fordyce to turn up, he watched the grotesque crawl of a chameleon along a branch, forked feet reaching out to grasp and secure each move, the frilly dragon head intent on its prey. As he saw the surgeon approach a waitress came to the table. She had the high cheekbones of the East mixed with the blood of the Hottentot. European pigeons strutted pompously about, hardly moving aside as a Malay in a conical coolie's hat, out of some paddy field he could have been, offered him peanuts in twists of newspaper.

'Feed the pigeons, master!'

Fordyce cursed him away in a word of Urdu as he sat down heavily.

'Well, Stewart,' he came straight to the point, 'why not join me in this sanatorium idea of mine? The Karoo air is very beneficial to consumptives. Together you and I could do well. There'd be patients from all over Europe. The work would not be exacting, nature would take its course.'

'I've no money to set up.'

'No matter, I'll find backing for it. Cape Town's full of retired Indian Army surgeons looking for an investment. The Somerset Hospital here was built by one of them.'

'I'm not sure I want to live in a desert.'

'We'd get on well, don't you think?'

Stewart sensed the surgeon's grudging respect for his ability. The man would make use of him if he could. He had no reason to be blunt with him but he felt no particular call to give his life to the wealthy of Europe. His instinct had always drawn him to what his Welsh friend called 'the wretched of the earth'.

'Do you know how many tuberculotics there were in England in this last year? More than a hundred thousand. Of course, we'd get the cream. Society and the nobility. I suggest you take something temporary in Cape Town while I go up and have a look around.'

Seeing that Stewart was reluctant to commit himself, Fordyce rose and put on his sola topi, the green lining giving his red-fleshed face a tinge of decay. 'The offer's open ... I've a business appointment in Adderley Street.'

Stewart sat on alone, watching the white cataract of cloud that poured endlessly over the Table Mountain but never reached the slopes of Oranjezicht, the pleasant suburb between mountain and city. He knew he could be quickly established here. A Glasgow-trained doctor would be welcomed. Why go further? Women with parasols drifted by on the arms of red-jacketed officers and naval men in their blue jackets. He heard the jingle of spurs and the crunch of well-booted feet. The slurring drag of skirts was faintly disturbing to the senses. A military band was trying out some brassy notes. All around him he heard the high-pitched voices of the dark people and everywhere he felt this sense of innocence and lack of sophistication. Was it something to do with the brightness of the light, the soft air? In the distance he could hear the rattle and clatter of horsetrams. A shadow fell and he heard a voice he knew. Doves fluttered away from skirts.

'Miss Loftus,' he said, rising, unaccountably embarrassed.

'Doctor MacDonald, sitting here alone with a Gladstone bag.'

'I was just going,' he said, aware of the dazzling copper of new hair, the low decolletage showing her fine shoulders. Hard to remember her as the shaven girl who had wept at the sight of herself in the mirror she had demanded as soon as recovery began. Or the bitter tears.

'Can I sit down? I want to tell you 'ow grateful I am ... for what you done. I'm free of that one, the Baron. No more a baron than I'm a duchess. Broke me contract – what he sez is a contract. I'm joining a real theatrical company. Mr Theodore Gaunt ... thespian. He knows a professional when he sees one. I'm going to speak proper. Learn Shakespeare an' all. Mr Gaunt's taking the company on tour, Kimberley, then this new Johannesburg. I'm to get twenty pounds a week.'

She had swayed gracefully into a seat, her parasol furling in a swirl of green. 'A cool drink would be nice –'

'Of course, with pleasure.' He had the price of a week's lodgings in his pocket.

'You was so good to me,' she said impulsively.

'Look after yourself, Kitty.'

A man and a woman approached. He was tall, with a kind of exaggerated hauteur. He wore a tall hat, a high collar with a flowing cravat and an opulent tie-pin of paste. He gave Stewart the impression of a faded aristocrat of the '70's. The actor, of course. And the stout lady, perspiring in tight corsetry? No doubt this was Miss Ethel Cholmondeley, 'the famous thespian, tragedian and rival of Duse', as the *Cape Times* paragraphist had described her. About them both Stewart fancied he saw an air of desperation only faintly under control. Their clothes, though superficially elegant, had the marks of hard wear. Particularly their shoes. If Kitty were to have twenty pounds a week, he thought, what would be left for these to live on?

'My dear young lady,' said Gaunt, bowing and taking Kitty's hands without appearing to notice Stewart. 'All is arranged. We have a patron! Mr Barnato himself. We are to play a drama ... The Broken Crock ... from my own modest pen.'

Miss Ethel, Stewart noticed, seemed to be having increasing difficulty with her tight lacing as she saw for the first time 'the noted acquisition to the company'.

'The heat is insupportable. I feel quite faint.' She rolled her eyes piteously.

'Do sit down, my dear,' said Gaunt without a glance at her and took a chair with a kind of tattered regality. 'I believe Beerbohm, Tree and Irving are to follow us into the new Globe Theatre. It will be our privilege to bring Art to the dark hinterland which has so far ...' with magnificent scorn, 'seen nothing but travelling mountebanks ... Wild West shows and nigger minstrels.'

Stewart rose and walked quietly away, leaving Kitty listening with rapt attention to the actor-manager and Miss Ethel panting, 'I believe she is much too young to undertake the role of the ingenue...' The thought crossed Stewart's mind as he made his way to his lodgings that Mr Gaunt's patronage might have already extended itself to Kitty's new wardrobe.

His room looked down on the small town's mixture of East and West, a meeting place of cultures, church spires and minarets, rickshas and locomotives. He could see fishing boats drawn up in Granger Bay and beyond the breakwater was the familiar forest of windjammer masts and the smoke of steamer funnels. From the corner of Lion and Pepper streets he could see the old slave quarters. Most of all it was the sounds that intrigued him. A shouting, singing, humming diversity of peoples. Here was Africa, Europe, Asia. The singing cry of the muezzin came up to him from the Long Street mosque. He waved from the window as a ricksha of sailors went rollicking by. Brown girls with rings in their ears leaned out, beckoning.

He sat down at the open sash and began to write home, a mixture of elation and apprehension in his heart. Over that great mountain barrier of tableland a deep billow of white cloud was rolling, falling, dissolving, never reaching the red roofs below.

'My dear Mother,' he began. 'I have landed in Africa.'

Leonard Penlynne hoped this first evening of his return to Kimberley would be one to remember. He believed it would be. The gifts he had brought Dorothy and her mother had been unwrapped and exclaimed over. The négligé from London brought a blush to Dorothy's cheek and a look that hovered somewhere between consent and shame. He had not been able to touch more than her hand. For two hours he had burned for the opportunity to take her out onto the stoep and in the dark shadow of the water tank grasp her warm buttocks with his hands and touch her more intimately than he had ever done. He felt so ardent that he was sure he could set her on fire with his eyes alone but she sat there, feet together.

God, what fantasies he had had of her. Did she have such fantasies of him? Mrs Orwell's company did not conduce to flights of passionate imagination. But what did she think in the warmth of her bed, the night insects drowsily chirping. Even on the doorstep Dorothy had been restrained and he saw appeal in her eyes rather than ardour. Perhaps it meant 'be patient'.

Outside in the hot dark there was the familiar throb of the Kimberley night. Pumps pumping and drums drumming. And his blood pounding in his ears. How much longer would the old woman keep up her cross-examination? She had plainly forgotten how swarthy he was, he saw that at once in her start. His gifts had not mollified her. Those to Dorothy were altogether too intimate, too suggestive of experience and impatience. What did it matter? He would be taking Dorothy away from her soon enough.

'I shall take good care of your daughter, Mrs Orwell.'

'From what I hear of Johannesburg it is no place for a young woman of refinement.'

'Oh, mother ... please!'

'And when will you be taking my little girl from me?'

'When I have my affairs in hand – with your permission.'

'If I have seemed somewhat reluctant and ungracious, Mr Penlynne, it is simply that I have been disappointed in the institution of marriage. My husband was not a successful man. He had great qualities but no grasp of finance, unlike Mr Rhodes. He finished in a rather inferior position, hence ... our present circumstances. Not what we are accustomed to, Mr Penlynne.'

'I am very sorry to hear of your misfortune.' He was trying to trace the curve of Dorothy's thigh against the softness of the material.

'Do tell me ... is Penlynne a Cornish name?'

He was instantly aware that she was probing his origins for an explanation of his 'Babylonian look' as he sometimes called it himself in moments of self-doubt when he looked at himself in the mirror and wondered how it was that whatever he wore he looked unlike an English gentleman.

'Cornish? No.' He smiled the smile that was hidden in the bearded lips. 'My father's name was Penzlovsky.'

He saw appeal in Dorothy's eyes but he was enjoying himself now.

'Then how, may one ask ...' faltered Mrs Orwell who had gone rigid.

'My mother was a Cornish girl. My father changed his name when they married.'

'A Jew,' said Mrs Orwell faintly.

'By deed poll. It's quite legal.'

'These days one never knows,' said Mrs Orwell. 'And your faith ... today?'

'I have none, frankly. Dorothy may be what she pleases. I do not believe in prescribing faith to others.'

At last Mrs Orwell had permitted them a chance to be alone and at once he took the jeweller's box from his pocket and gave it into her hands. 'It's not much, only two carats. I shall do better, much better for you.'

He put it on her finger and she gave him her lips. Very sweet and soft. Very brief. He was trembling but she did not understand. All he could do was draw her two hands into his own and kiss the palms. He understood that this was the nearest thing to a physical approach he could make at this stage of their relationship, but God, the nearness of her, the swelling of her breasts, the stray tendrils of hair that had fallen over her small ears. Had she any idea of the effect on him? He could hear Mrs Orwell rattling about suggestively in the passage.

'Dorothy ... it's late.'

'Tomorrow,' he said ardently and sought to clasp her.

'Yes, tomorrow.' Her face was bright.

He walked the streets of Kimberley half the night, too worked up to sleep, looking out for familiar places. It was here, in this very tin shanty, that he had been Rawlinson's manager. It had taken him a long time to see through the man's avuncular heartiness, his apparent generosities that were totally fraudulent, his ability to make promises without substance. But now he was Beit's man. Generous Beit, who knew how to use an ambitious man to their mutual advantage.

A woman came up to him in the dark. He could not make out whether she was white or coloured but she was evidently trailing from one bar to another. He caught the reek of her perspiration mingled with jasmine. She had the swelling buttocks he had fantasized over in the Orwell parlour and by the light of the match she struck when she asked for a cigarette he saw the dead white of powder and the bluish red lips of a painted Griqua. When she touched him between the thighs he started back like a stung horse.

'Here,' he said gruffly, 'and on your way.' He thrust half a sovereign into her hand. This was one way out he did not propose to take.

Nothing must distract him from his work as he took over Beit's interests in Johannesburg. Dorothy would follow as soon as he had his grasp on conditions there. The urges of the flesh must wait.

Chapter 7

Josiah Rawlinson's face showed no signs of tender thoughts. Early in life it had set in a defiant immobility. Yet the mouth concealed by the drooping, greying mustache could curve into an unexpected, even charming smile and the ice-blue eyes with which he froze his rivals could positively twinkle when he told stories of the old days.

Ferreira's Camp – that first untidy sprawl of canvas which arose before the White Waters Ridge was proclaimed as a gold field and its streets surveyed – knew him for a rare good man at a banquet. If he was in the humour. Some said Rawlinson was a fair man. Some said he was 'a fair bastard!'

At fifty-one he had something of an imperial girth, the better for displaying watchchains and the silver chronometer that had been his immigrant father's in the 1840's. He wore it as an act of filial piety, he let it be known. Others said he was too mean to buy a modern piece. In his youth he had broken in horses and his hands were still clumsily large and drew attention to the single blue-white diamond on the thumb of his left hand. 'The carbuncle', he had called it. These days his suits were ordered from Savile Row and even in the dust and mire of the new town his English topboots were kept spotless by an attendant black boy.

He was over six feet tall and when he walked among men of any rank or condition they made way. He had a leonine presence. He was used to command, even in his young days when it was only Griqua shepherds or his schoolmates who obeyed for fear of his fists. He was noted for his obstinacy and courage. These qualities, combined with an unexpected gentleness, had made him a successful breeder of Basuto ponies. He used to boast, 'My ponies can carry a man and his gear sixty miles a day!' He loved horses for their beauty and strength. 'I honour the horse,' was one of his sayings. 'He is noble and dependable. I can't say that for many men.'

The habit of command had ultimately made him less approachable but in his earlier days he had the ability to unbend, especially to the digger, the tradesman, the shopkeeper and clerk. He'd clap a hand on a man's shoulder. 'How goes it? How are you making out? How's the claim? Getting good values?'

To his equals he was implacable. Some said it was more than that ... pure hatred of anyone who might rival him. These days he never put his hand in his pocket without a growl, never gave a man a note to his banker – 'Let my friend have a hundred.' He gave nothing for nothing, except advice, and that only when it suited his interests.

Rawlinson still rode well but he was most often seen in a Scotch cart drawn by two white geldings and in the company of his surveyor or one of his managers. He invariably carried a heavy bag on his journeys along the Reef. He had long ago learned that the sight of a gold coin on the table was worth more than any amount in promissory notes to Boer farmers who seldom saw cash and were mostly illiterate.

One of his favourite stories was how had clinched a land deal with a farmer's wife, winning her over in the kitchen with his ready use of Dutch and the chink of coin while Cecil Rhodes was stammering away in the *voorkamer* in his squeaky English...

January 24. It would rain again today. He could smell the pungent, dust-laden dryness. Cumulus clouds were billowing up into the hard porcelain blue, climbing and piling, wreathing and devouring each other in the fury of their energy. When they broke they would lash the red earth, flooding the diggings, swamping out the tent town that still existed on the fringes of the wood, iron and mud-brick buildings beginning to take the shape of streets. He did not fear the hailstones. His corrugated iron roof could cope with that. Hail and violent rain were better than drought. Last year the veld grazing was burnt out for hundreds of miles around. Oxwaggon transport carrying heavy machinery for his mines was held up for weeks.

A man had to learn patience. In Africa there was a time for violent action and a time to gather one's strength for the next advance. Patience was waiting a year for steam boilers and pumps from Europe, goods that came at the pace of oxen a thousand miles from the Cape, by three-month trek through the sweltering plains of Mozambique where malaria, tsetse fly, flooded rivers and corrupt Portuguese officials held back the goods for bribes and delayed transport drivers who went down with fever and dysentery.

Still and all, in the four years he had been on the Transvaal highveld he had made good use of his time, fraternising with the officials of the Republic and yarning with old Kruger on the stoep of his bungalow in Pretoria. He had much in common with the shrewd, dour peasant. The native wars for one. They could cap each other's stories. Rawlinson had fought with the Boers against the Basuto; at twenty-two he had led a storming party against the mountain fortress of Thaba Bosigo. They'd have driven Moshesh out of his lair if all his men had not been killed around him. Somehow his bulk had been immune to bullets. He'd known it was not his day to die.

'Ja, a man knows that,' Kruger acknowledged.

More than once Rawlinson had warned Kruger of the danger of letting the stream of foreign fortune hunters get out of control. 'The Jews, the French, they'll eat you up like locusts, Mr President.'

Kruger shook his massive head. 'The gold won't last. We'll make the best of their experience. The land will be ours again. God gave it to my people and we have faith in Him. In ten years it will be farmland again and their Sodom forgotten!'

Rawlinson nodded sagely but he knew it would be different. What he wanted was to secure his own interests and devil take the rest of them.

The first crash of the breaking storm shook his office. He saw lightning strike the stony ridge of Braamfontein farm. Someone was running across the *plein* from the postal shanty. Thick raindrops spattered the dry red dust. Was this the telegram he was waiting for, news that his Katherine was safe? He had been in a state of anxiety for days since the rumour of typhus on *The American* had reached him. It was all for her, what he was doing here. This and the mansion he was buying in Park Lane, London, to entertain his friends in finance, politics and the aristocracy. When he'd made his killing here he'd live in Europe, sail a steam yacht and entertain princes. It would be a coming 'home' his father would never have dreamed of, that young Richard who'd waded ashore at Delagoa Bay with his bride Martha in his arms and looked with awe and hope at the unbroken bush of the Eastern Cape.

A knighthood? A peerage? Nothing was impossible. The thing was to have a goal and make for it with every fibre of your being. Luck? No luck about it. You saw a finger and you grabbed for the whole hand. And you picked the right man. Christiaan Smit. How many men in this town would have seen good in a Boer lad and given him a chance in an office? A narrow-faced boy with his downy beard and mustache. Smart as a whip. Used to come here with telegrams from the post office. One day he'd stood there in his stained moleskins, his blue eyes very alert in the sun-tanned wedge of face.

'I can help, Mynheer Rawlinson.'

'How's that?' He had pushed over the tobacco pouch.

'No, Mynheer, I don't smoke.'

A Boer that didn't smoke!

By the time the lad had been six months in his office he had devoured every book in the place. Law seemed to fascinate him. 'If Mynheer Rawlinson will send me to Holland Mynheer will not regret it.'

From anyone else in his employ Rawlinson would have taken it for damned impudence. But already this Christiaan had helped him in clinching one of the best deals of his life simply by understanding the mentality of his people. A man could be Boer-born and not know Boers but this lad, he had insight. It was on the farm Eersteplaas. There was gold there ... oh yes, he knew that from personal samplings made without the permission of the owner, old Coet Esterhuysen. When it came to bargaining he took Christiaan along. He thought it would soften the old Boer to see a fine upstanding young Boer on his staff. But it hadn't. Something was wrong. The old man was willing to sell but there was no way to get his signature onto the papers. The old woman sat in her place, weeping.

'But Mynheer, this is our place. How can we part with everything?'

'That is the law, dear lady. Come now, it's a fair price.'

For answer she had flung her apron over her head. 'But everything,' she wailed, casting a piteous glance around her possessions.

'*Voetstoets* – land, house, everything.'

Rawlinson made three separate visits to the land. It was twenty miles from Johannesburg over poor tracks and his temper was rising. 'Now, my boy,' he said to Christiaan one morning, 'I have tried everything with that *ou vrou*; drunk fifty cups of her vile coffee. Counted out the money in front of them. What the devil more do they want?' Obviously they were holding out for something costly.

The trap was spanking along in fine style and it was one of those highveld mornings when it was almost impossible not to burst into song. Christiaan got down to open the farm gate.

'If Mynheer will allow me to speak to Tante,' he said. He went inside and Rawlinson waited, chafing and cursing the horses for stamping at flies. This place was another Rawlinson Star. The values were outstanding. He waited thirty minutes and could stand it no longer. When he got to the house he saw the old woman on the stoep with a pot of geraniums in her hand. Her simple, broad face was alight with pleasure. Had Christiaan committed him then?

'Tante Miems was afraid that *voetstoets* meant she would have to give you her pot of geraniums ... ja, that's all, Mynheer,' said Christiaan with a faint smile.

'There's no other obstacle?'

'None.' *Alle magtig*, what people! He knew he would have lost the deal for sure, him a hard-bargaining, short-tempered man and the old woman as obstinate. He gave Christiaan no reward. The lad had only done what was expected of him. But after that he watched him more closely and saw that he had a way of persuading people. Part charm, part sincerity and part a natural authority.

'I'll pay your law studies in Holland,' he grudged at last when he had closely observed Christiaan for sobriety and thrift. 'You'll pay me back, with interest, and you'll serve me two years without pay.'

The grey-blue eyes of the fair young man crinkled into a smile. He nodded. That was three years back and the boy was passing all his examinations, with flying colours. He was a voracious student and kept in touch with his patron with regular letters. He never asked for money.

A clerk was handing him a telegram. He tore it open and stamped his foot with delight. Kathy was safe in Cape Town! He turned to his clerk. 'Have a fill of my tobacco pouch.' Kathy safe! A man should be generous on such a day. Declare a holiday! But she was still a thousand miles away. The railway only ran as far as Kimberley. After that came three weeks' coaching, drifts swollen by rain, the Vaal River uncrossable for days on end. Coaches overturned. Drivers who were no better than ruffians. No, better she come north with Walter Gardiner. He'd arrange a coach to meet them and Lady Violet – for safety's sake.

He went home to find his evening suit laid out for him. His mouth tightened. He believed Mrs Ferguson did this to remind him he was wifeless. He had never looked at her in that way, not in three years and he supposed he never would. There had been no romance in his life since Sheila. Lovely Sheila, at eighteen the most courted young woman in Kimberley. They were married by magistrate at Barkly. Dead eleven months later. Unbelievable! At first he had looked at his infant daughter with horror. Sheila dead! Why, every man in Kimberley was in love with her. The child had her eyes and as she grew up he seemed to see his wife again ... uncanny!

He'd be a liar if he said there were no women in his life. Camp women, some from Barberton and the De Kaap gold fields, trying their luck again here. Tough baggages they were, but women for all that. And some of them were not all that bad, poor bawds. He'd had dealings with one of them that day in his office. Red Jenny they called her.

'I'm doing business this morning,' she announced. She tossed a pile of share script over his desk. He looked at her in her morning finery, the great feathered hat, lace at her throat (they said that was a sure sign of the pox), the dress of some expensive material. Raw nugget on a gold pin. They told some stories of her goings on.

'Well, Josh, what's it worth?'

'You can burn it. Who paid you with that?'

'Come on, Josh. I'm a lady, y'know.'

'They were worth eight hundred last week.'

'And now?'

'Not worth the paper.'

'Are you playing me fair, Josh?'

'Next time get it in cash.'

She had plenty put by from the lowveld days when she was

more to look at. She'd have her own hotel in another year with the whole world making for Johannesburg and the Main Reef giving up to twelve ounces to the ton. Town had been a madhouse today. These monthly affairs when the Mining Chamber celebrated the new record output of gold were too noisy and too long. The Stock Exchange would be got up like a hothouse with plants and electric lights. This rabble community never lost a chance for a booze-up. Every building in town was covered with flags and bunting. Eckstein's Corner looked like a coon carnival. God alone knew who paid for the champagne and whiskey. Last time Rawlinson's clerks had been fit for nothing next day. Gratifying though it was that so much of the record total had come from Rawlinson's Star, he kept his clerks' noses at their ledgers all day Saturday to teach them the benefit of sobriety in business.

He seldom drank. A man didn't need drink to feel exhilarated in this town. The very dust in the nostrils seemed to stimulate. He was to be main speaker tonight and he would reminisce of the old days of fever, rock falls and typhus, men smothered in the collapse of claims in the Big Hole as it went crazily downward in the blue ground, each claim a menace to the next. Well, Rhodes and Barnato had fixed that. It was all theirs now. No more disputes and fist fights over where a good stone came from. No more small syndicates competing to buy a few feet of the richest ground on earth. Rhodes and his friend Beit, the quiet one, they had it all and ruined him into the bargain. He'd been there first – first to see the wealth for picking up, first to bargain with the Korana *kaptein* Jan Bloem, a yellow man with Hottentot blood who claimed all the land along the Vaal River. Empty land, barren and waterless. Even the river was dry most of the year. It was a wilderness of black stones and thorn trees and Jan Bloem was glad enough to sell a few miles of it for a flock of sheep and a case of Cape smoke. Yes, he'd been beaten in Kimberley where his dear one lay in her grave. But by God, he was ahead of them again.

At dinner tonight he would warn that Rhodes and Beit had killed the individualist, the one-man capitalist. And that grey shadow behind them all – Wernher in his London web.

He knew the potency of ridicule. 'Once upon a time, gentlemen, there were three wise men. They bought their monkey suits in Savile Row, their tie-pins in Kimberley, and they all wore silk hats. The first washed his mustache in French champagne, the second bathed in Vichy water. And the third, gentlemen, he never bathed at all but he used plenty of Eau de Cologne. Gentlemen, there are those among us today who are out to destroy all that we have achieved, to wipe out the small man. Wernher and Beit are out to repeat their grab for Kimberley...'

He finished dressing and drank a rare whiskey-soda. He was getting soft, he knew; running to gut. His features showed signs of battle. An ugly old devil, that's what he'd be in ten years. With a sour face. Did anybody care a damn when he was ruined? When his own shareholders sold him out? Today they tipped hats to him but if the combine got the upper hand here they'd do the same again. Jackals snatching the scraps from the lion's jaws, and they'd lick his bones if they had half a chance.

The dark frock coat sat well on his heavy bulk, emphasising his girth and authority. He'd remind them tonight who they were dealing with. I'm African-born, gentlemen. I speak two kaffir tongues and Dutch. Who are these Jews, these Germans to play their dirty games with me?

A black girl was lighting the lamps, the soft light glowing on the rounded, dark brown flesh. She was curtseying in their way, palms together, withdrawing backwards. A comely people. The lamplight revealed the costly drapes and a marble fireplace, the rich, subdued fire of Turkish rugs. No electric light in this house. It was more important at the mine. And he had a fondness for this kind of light. It was full of memory.

As a youngster the horse trade brought him often to farms. While his Malay driver outspanned the four horses he'd share a pipe with his host. They'd drink *witblits* and shake heads over the treachery of whites who sold guns to the Basuto. Often the talk turned to diamonds. Why had the Lord in His wisdom ordained that the ostrich should have diamonds in its droppings. *Nee, wragtig*! The ways of the Almighty were wonderful!

'Has Oom himself seen any of such stones?' he would query as casually as he was able.

'Nee, a man can't spend his days following an ostrich.'

Then the heavy meal and the even heavier '*Kom laat ons Boeke vat!*' The Bible opened and the patriarch, candle at elbow, tracing the words with his finger, his beard overflowing the pages, his heavy Dutch face solemn as he offered up thanks for his four walls, his reed-thatch roof and his dung-smeared floor.

Diamonds in ostriches! As he knelt, Josiah Rawlinson would be scouring his mind for dry places where there were stony drifts. River-washed pebbles uncovered by drought. There were stories of farm children playing with the pretty pebbles. A diamond in a boy's bag of marbles. Worth six thousand when it was cut. Old fools like this hadn't the wit or energy to look for the fortune lying in the sand.

A-men! And thank you for greasy mutton and bitter coffee. Thank you, Lord, for the pest that killed the oxen and blew up the bellies of the horses. And thank you, *Here*, that the Bushmen and Hottentots are shot out.

He was wrenched back to the present by a group of drunken blacks going past ... Shangaans from Portuguese East. Good miners when they were sober, men who were eight hundred miles from their steamy villages. They'd walked it by game trails from the feverish valleys of the Limpopo up here to the Rand, six thousand feet high and its winds like a whetted knife. Cold, bitter cold in those tin shanties he'd erected and every day reports of deaths. Pneumonia, coughing blood. No stamina.

He rang a bell. 'I want the trap here at seven. With the hood up.'

'Yes, master.' Solomon was a good boy. Zulus made the best house workers. Queer thing ... queer the way they'd been tamed and turned into kitchen boys. Solomon could turn out a roast beef and Yorkshire pud with any white woman and do it for thirty bob a month and his keep – sugar, mealie meal and offal. Rhodes said the Zulus had to be taught the dignity of labour and the benefits of wages. But they wouldn't take underground work. They feared the Serpent Lord of the Underworld.

The singers passed out of earshot and the steady thumping roar of the stamp batteries rose again. Double shifts at the mill. Yes, he was pushing his workmen hard but white men were making double what they earned in Europe. So far no squealing trade unionists. That would come, just as it had in Kimberley. The same breed of men who were rioting and burning at home.

On his last trip to London he'd seen them in Trafalgar Square with their banners, passing insolent resolutions, shouting for a reduction of the 12-hour day without reduction of pay. From his club in St James Street it had been a sobering thing to see the way the mob had pressed along that stately street, smashing windows and hurling missiles at people in carriages. Even, by God, dragging women from them to steal their jewels. In South Audley Street they'd smashed every window and plundered every shop. The *Times* called it 'an infamous rapine which will not easily be forgotten'.

He looked impatiently at his watch. An hour to kill. Ordinarily he'd have been at his desk. He twiddled the diamond pin between his thick fingers. Its facets gleamed in the lamplight. Was it twenty odd years ago already? He remembered it for a bitter July day with thin, wintry sunlight and a keen wind from the south. It came from Antarctica, they said. And it killed the lambs.

That day he'd driven some twenty miles off his usual route. The Malay was muttering. He thought his master was sick in the head when he saw him on his knees, picking up stones in the dry drifts.

'All right, Abdullah,' Rawlinson said as he mounted the vehicle. 'Whip them up. Back to the farm. Van Tonder's farm, man. Where we slept last night.'

He could see the Malay thought he fancied the young woman, but it was the mirror in the bedroom he was after. To rub the pebbles against the glass and see if any glowed. That was the test! But before that there would be hours of talk ... prayers again before he was alone. He must keep calm and behave as if nothing interested him but sheep. And keep his eyes off Van Tonder's daughter. She knew just how to kneel to put ideas into a man's head.

As he said goodnight at last Marie carried the candlestick before him. In the passage she brushed against him and he felt the soft bulk of her thigh. At the door she rolled her eyes and simpered. 'Thanks,' he said, taking the candle, ignoring her unspoken entreaty. But he pressed her hand and that was a mistake...

When the beds had stopped creaking and Van Tonder had begun to snore he blew out the candle and began to test the pebbles. One by one he rubbed them on the glass. No soft glow of fire, nothing but river stones. As he stood there in despair he heard a shuffle of bare feet at the door, the snip of the latch as it rose. Someone rushed into his arms. Someone as plump as a chicken, her flesh yielding beneath the nightgown, her hair down her back and her parted lips seeking his.

'Marie ... what the devil!'

Shivering, shaking, her teeth chattering, she drew him down on the sheepskins, muttering her passion in Dutch and broken English. '*Ag my liefde ... my duifie* ... my love, my dove.' Her hot hands groped for his parts. Josiah flared. Their teeth met in a clash, their noses collided. They slipped and slid and grappled and rolled. His pebbles spilled over the floor of polished dung, oxblood and beeswax. The smell of her was pure animal and he almost shot his bolt before he entered her. She took him frantically, moaning and biting his lips. Then they lay panting. Moonlight quartering the small window fell on her breasts as she drew his head down and nursed him.

'Now we is marry ... *my haartjie* ... my darling!' When he tried to break away she held him with the weight of her massive arms. My God, he thought, what have I done? A girl of fifteen, maybe younger. They developed fast, the farm Dutch. Just like the Kaffirs. How was he to escape? Would she never go back to her own place? What if the *ou vrou* came searching? Or the old man with his *voorlaaier*?

As soon as she had gone he shook up the Malay. The driver thrashed the floor in fright. 'Don't make a sound. Span in the horses. Now!'

So long ago it was. He looked at his watch and found himself laughing. What a way to lose his virginity. He'd never gone back that way. Why think of it now? Suppose that Marie had borne him a child, a brother to Kathy? And Katherine at eighteen? Was she as hot-blooded as Marie? It didn't bear thinking about. And yet some man would have her before long. Marie. Today she'd be a huge *vrou* with a rear on her like a hippo.

It was some weeks before he found his first diamond. It was in the corner of his saddlebag and he almost threw it away in disgust. The hotel where he tested it was no more than a line of rooms with hitching posts outside. When the stone grated on the glass he turned out the lamp and began to rub softly, in a circular motion. Suddenly there was a streak of light. He cried out in elation. He danced and sang. He threw himself on the floor and rolled about. A loud knocking brought him to his senses. He opened the door an inch to see the innkeeper, hear the lisping accents of Lithuania.

'Are you sick? You are sweating.'

'It was the supper. I'm not used to rich food.'

The Jew grinned amiably. 'Ja, ve keep goot tafel.'

A night that changed his life. *His life*. The life of the whole land. Nothing could be the same again. This grey-green desolation was rich beyond imagination. He had wild thoughts of building cities, of being president of a republic whose wealth was diamonds.

I gave them first their diamonds, their Kimberley. And now I've given them this Jo'burg. They mocked me when I bought up the farms. Rawlinson's cabbage patches! They'd stopped mocking soon enough.

The soft voice of the Zulu roused him. He must have drowsed. The tall silk hat was offered with reverence. The hat of a chief.

'Thank you, Solomon.'

'*Nkos!*'

'There will be hell to pay tonight, Solomon.'

'*Yebo, nkos.*'

The crowd between the chains was shouting the odds of shares when he drove up and dismounted. 'What price Rawlinson's Star tonight?' The hubbub ceased in order to hear his reply. He had a sense of being baited.

'Our assets stand tonight at eighteen millions,' he shouted. 'And you have all benefited.' He was pushing into the hall when he was jostled by a man. A face he couldn't identify whispered, 'There's word from the scouts ... values down at the Phoenix.' The mine adjoining the Star. Part of the same reef.

'What's that?' exclaimed Rawlinson but he was carried in by the press behind. Pernicious scouts! He was well versed in their dirty business. Pumping his employees for titbits of information that could be useful on the exchange. The Phoenix was one of his minor holdings. When the reef was first broken there they'd got out incredible values. At thirty feet it was still ten ounces to the ton. He'd been waiting for this change of values. The rock had begun to come up blue and obdurate. It was beginning to refuse the amalgam treatment that released the gold. His chemists were struggling to refine sulphides in which iron, copper, lead and zinc were mixed with gold.

Rawlinson had known for some time that it was going sour. That was when he had hired Walter Gardiner. He had to know the worst. And if it turned out to be pyrites he wanted to know before it leaked out. It could be that Johannesburg was going to be another ghost town. If that was the way it was going he'd have to unload his shares while there was still optimism.

It was then that he saw Leonard Penlynne. He had heard the man was in town but until now he had not encountered him. Penlynne was sitting upright in his chair, the evening suit not ill-fitting but somehow unsuited to the man. It was the massive head of hair accentuated by the black, curling beard and of course, his eyes. Eyes that made him so ... had always made him so ... what was it then? Somehow one seemed to see a naked sword in his hand. He could stare you down. Young ... still damned young but more mature, you could see that. Every antipathy he had ever felt towards him in Kimberley and the Vaal River diggings came surging back. Always independent. Always capable. At this moment he seemed to Rawlinson to be watching this scene of Johannesburg indulgence and self-congratulation with a kind of tolerant ... yes, it was insolence. As if he had no respect whatever for those who had made it. No point in avoiding him though. Better to give him the old employee guff. The ungrudging charm. Heavy hand on the shoulder. There was no woman with him, if that meant anything. Abstemious as ever, too, by the look of the untouched glass.

'Evening, Penlynne,' he said grudgingly, conscious of his own bullheaded, grizzled appearance as he towered over the Englishman. 'What brings you up here? I heard you'd thrown in your hand and bought a mansion in England.'

'Not on what you paid me, Josh.'

'Well, let bygones be bygones. Are you looking for something? I could use you.'

'I have an offer.'

'Who made it?'

'You'll hear soon enough.' It was said pleasantly but he felt a sudden claustrophobia. They were closing in on him. He must strike out. He could read men's faces and Penlynne's had the stamp of a man who knew how to overlay with a quicksilvery charm an impatience to win. Oh, they'd been smart picking him.

He passed through the tiled court into the arched hall. Hubbub ... musicians ... potted palms ... women, some of them seen with their clothes on for the first time. Barnato's so-called actress wife. Bit of the tar-brush there. Who else? Eckstein, Taylor – all of them young. Also Beit's men. Like Penlynne. Who else would he be working for? Why else would he be here? Beit again!

A woman, heavily scented and rustling in some shimmering material, brushed against him. "Ullo, darling!" He pushed on to the top table and sat down, sweating heavily. Fans hardly churned the smoke. Flies sluggish in the heat. Flypapers on the chandeliers black with them. Like dead niggers. The usual extravagance. Orchids. Baskets of Cape grapes. English apples and pears. Pheasant. Tinned oysters. Black Sea caviare. Smoked Scotch salmon. Fortnum and Mason must be making a fortune out of the colonies.

He put two fingers inside his collar and forced a stud. It gave and he could breathe. Now it was comic verse read out by Barnato. Squinting little mountebank. Drunken shrieks from scarlet-faced trollops with bird of paradise feathers in their bird's nest hair. He could see that this was going to turn into one of those banquets that finished around three a.m. with the diners lying among broken crockery, playing spooks with the tablecloths and you'd find some whore with her drawers down in the Gents'. "Scuse me, dear. Taking a sweet pea. Don't tread on me orchid.'

There'd be leapfrog and horseback fighting with wagers for high stakes. Of course the official guests from the Government would all be in their beds long before that stage. But they knew all about it and it got back to Kruger and that was bad for the industry. Next time he went over to Pretoria he'd get a lecture from the old man.

Now it was toasts and he could see that the old Barberton crowd, Taylor and company, were going to drink-up and smash glasses. 'I give you His Excellency the President!' No heel taps. Smash! 'Her Majesty, our beloved sovereign Victoria!' Cheers and crashes. Corks popping. Veuve Cliquot bubbling and foaming. Waiters crunching on broken glass.

'And now, gentlemen ... I ask you to stand and light the torch of liberty.' Knife handles were lit and held up like torches, burning with a bright blue flame. 'To our own Digger's Republic. And down with Tyranny!'

Cheers and smashes. The Dutch officials offended.

Rawlinson rose, pounding the table for silence. He could feel the hostility and before he had spoken a dozen words someone shouted, 'Pyrites! What about pyrites?'

Rawlinson smiled tolerantly. 'We must not think, gentlemen, because some of us lost our fortunes due to pyrites in the Lowveld that the Rand reefs will be a repetition of that disaster. No, here on the Rand our mines have proved payable from the outcrop down. We're at a hundred feet at the Star and still in the banket – no problems.'

He saw something being passed from hand to hand up the table.

'Will the honourable gentleman be kind enough to identify the sample.'

'Certainly, where did you bring it from? A souvenir of the Lowveld. A good enough paperweight, my friend.' He took the hard blue fragment of quartz into his hand and saw the yellow glint, the brassy yellow glint, the brassy yellow of the fatal quartzite.

'Any fool knows this is pyrites.'

'It's from the Phoenix.'

'And that's a thumping lie. I've had no such indications.'

'It came up in the hoist from sampling. Five o'clock shift. From the Y-Slope on the south-east drive.'

'I don't know what you game is, sir. Will you stand up and tell us? And who you're working for.'

'My game is fair play.'

'I don't know your face. You're no employee of mine. I suggest, gentlemen, that this is a barefaced attempt to cause alarm at a moment when we are celebrating a record fifteen thousand ounces a month.'

His eyes came to rest on Leonard Penlynne and he smiled. 'And I suggest, gentlemen, that there are elements among us who are out to create panic for their own ends. Some of us have been here since '85. Some of us had faith when others talked of cabbage patches...' That earned a laugh. 'Now the mice have arrived at the feast, too late for the best cheese. So they must use other methods, methods to depress the market and buy in a climate of panic. Gentlemen ... I reject this foolery with the scorn it deserves. I ask you to rise and I give you a toast to the future – the golden Rand!'

He sat down in a hubbub of stamping feet, huzzahs and whistles. He received some congratulations and he got some looks of an enigmatic kind. A pursing of the mouth from Penlynne. The whimsical, knowing look that had always put his back up. Then he had only to dismiss him. Now he would have to be crushed. The thought that he might have to go through the humiliation of Kimberley again. Its richest man, its representative in the Cape Assembly wiped out. Destroyed because he resisted the take-over. Then that ghastly night when he had had to go knocking on Beit's door.

'What can I do for you, Josh?' Smiling, humble, self-effacing little Beit, working in shirtsleeves in his wood and iron office, swivelling round from the heaps of correspondence he handled himself.

'I'm pulling out of Kimberley.'

'Sorry to hear that ... it's true then?'

As if the man didn't know that the Cape of Good Hope Bank had foreclosed on him. 'All I'm asking. Enough to get me a start in the Transvaal. You'll get it back with interest.'

Beit smiling, his face inscrutable. The face of a man who played the money game for its own sake, for truly there was nothing evident in his way of life of greed or women or possessions. A man without vices ... almost. Was his adulation of Rhodes not a vice? An obsession. Unnatural.

Alfred Beit had lifted his pen, dipped and scribbled, sanded the cheque and blown it clear. 'Will twenty thousand see you through, Josh?' It was said as mildly as if the man was giving away nothing. A tip. Maybe it was this that had stung him so. He remembered sweat and an almost overpowering desire to turn on his heel. He had taken it, hating the man for his charity.

'It's only a loan,' he heard himself saying.

'As you please, Josh,' the accent softly Hebraic. 'It is between us ... it goes no further.'

And now Penlynne was on the Rand. He'd come back in the same boat as Kathy and got up here while Walter Gardiner was still squiring the girl about the Cape. He must telegraph the man tomorrow, urging him to make haste and bring her with him.

She'd be safe enough with that old gargoyle alongside her. He longed to search her face for the love and admiration she'd given him as a child. What picnics they had had together, driving twenty miles from the dry, choking atmosphere of the diggings. Down to the yellow-brown Vaal. Willows and islands of reeds. Weaver birds chattering. The sandbanks from last year's summer floods imprinted with her small footprints. Obstinate even then; self-possessed for one so young. He had never wanted a son. Some deep anger in him could not endure the thought of a rival. But Katherine, child of his love, it was all for her.

Josiah Rawlinson pushed his way out of the Exchange Hall and through the crowd between the chains. He noted grimly that the price of Phoenix was being shouted down fifteen shillings. Let it fall, he thought, signalling for the pony trap. I'll buy them back in the morning.

Chapter 8

Where the top of the pass pierced the Hottentots Holland range the traveller heading north from Cape Town could look back on the old town of Stellenbosch. At the place where the Red Star coach line used to stop to change mule teams the locomotives now took on water. Passengers got down to stretch their legs and breathe cool air after the long confinement. It was the last chance to look back on the sheltered Cape valleys of vineyards and white walls before the twisting passes between the great crags opened the route to the hinterland.

Walter Gardiner took Katherine to see the view. The valley was golden with late afternoon light, the mountains a shadowed mystery of blue. A wind fragrant with *fynbos* gusted and buffeted. He steadied the girl and she pulled off the stifling bonnet to let her hair blow free.

'Times back there in Cape Town,' he said, 'I could have sworn I was living a century back, in Boston. Some nights with the darkies singing you could have been in Atlanta in the sixties.'

She felt his arm tighten and for a moment rested her head against his shoulder. They made their way back to the train to find Lady Violet waiting. 'Katherine, we're boarding now, if you please.'

She did not approve of Walter Gardiner accompanying them and she was making quite certain the American knew it. But Katherine had insisted and Gardiner had said, agreeably enough, that he'd take the next train if she wished but they'd meet all kinds and he might be useful. 'This is not England, ma'am,' he drawled.

'We are not helpless,' said Lady Violet vigorously.

'A third hand at whist will make it more interesting,' he said in that whimsical way she found so irritating, no doubt because she saw that the girl found it so attractive.

'I do not want you walking alone with Mr Gardiner, Katherine. It is simply not done.' She did not want to play the ogre but she saw no other way to control the girl and she was very soon glad of the man's company. The country beyond the range was quite appalling and he amused them very much with talk of South America and India. Indeed, the man was quite fascinating and all the less to be trusted for that. She did not doubt that his attentions to her were to win her favour.

The train stopped at haphazard hamlets where shirt-sleeved storekeepers came out to stare and the coloured people hawked cooldrinks and oranges.

'It's quite unimaginably dreary,' said the Englishwoman.

'You'll come to love it,' said Katherine.

'Never!'

The girl knew that beyond the railway's end they would come on waggons groaning with crated goods and mining machinery, timber and corrugated iron and prefabricated shanties. From horizon to horizon the waggons would be spread out, each making its own track, scores of them, hundreds. As if it were a great migration of people seeking a new life, crawling towards it at the pace of the oxen. Two days later, when they came on the first sight of it, the American watched it with excitement.

'It's California all over,' he marvelled.

'The dryness ... the dust ... one can hardly breathe.'

At the railhead they found a coach waiting. Rawlinson had hired it for their exclusive use. Lady Violet looked at the vehicle with dismay, hardly crediting that the American could be enthusiastic about a vehicle open to the elements, springless, with only leather flaps to keep out the dust.

'This is a real American coach, Katherine,' she heard him enthusing. 'She's an Abbott-Downing of Concord. I never thought to see one again.'

Only an iron sense of duty compelled Lady Violet to go on. If she turned back now this headstrong girl would be an easy prey. She had noted his goings-on in Cape Town, the flutter among the bored wives of the officials. She was certain he had had assignations with more than one. She had seen his face when he returned from outings to far-away beaches and refused his invitations to take Katherine on picnics. What a preposterous liberty! She was not too foolish to see the signs on the faces of a man and a girl who planned a secret meeting. When she tackled Katherine the girl coloured and seemed to become wary, unlike her usual open manner.

'Has Mr Gardiner been anything other than a gentleman? In view of my being your chaperon and this man going out to your father as ... an employee, I have to insist on knowing.'

The upset happened on their return to the hotel in Cape Town after an evening in a fashionable salon in Strand Street. Katherine had broken free of Gardiner's arms in the middle of a waltz and gone out into the courtyard. He had followed.

'You have no right to ask if I am in love with him,' the girl protested.

'I am not speaking of love. Katherine, my dear child, I am an old woman and I am not without experience, believe me. I was not always as you see me now. And I am fond of you. I see something in you of what I was. Perhaps the daughter I never had. But that is no matter. It does matter to me that you should not be treated lightly by a man who is ... for all his attractiveness, which I grant you, a cad.'

'You may not speak of him that way,' Katherine said in a low voice. The dark brown eyes which gave her so singular an appearance, challenged the older woman. She looked splendid in her indignation and confusion. Really she had come on remarkably in so short a time.

'He has made approaches then.'

'I am old enough to know my own mind.'

'That may be ... but my child, you are not old enough to know your own passions. I wish you could see me as a friend, Katherine.'

'I hate to be spied on.' The girl trembled with anger.

'In Society, my child...'

'Trust me ... please.'

'It is not you I mistrust.'

'Mr Gardiner has done nothing you could take exception to.'

'He's very free with his attentions to others. I expect you've seen that.'

'One expects it. He's a man.'

It had been their intention to linger on into the golden Cape autumn when the vineyards shed their leaves and the sun had lost its mid-summer fierceness. There was much to do. Gallops, picnics, a theatre company on a visit, concerts and lectures by the

Royal Society of South Africa. They had been invited to old Dutch homesteads, some of them two centuries old and very agreeable. She had found the Dutch of the Cape quite aristocratic, in a rural sort of way. The older woman was actually relieved when Rawlinson's telegram arrived. Mr Gardiner was urgently required and would he be so kind as to assist Lady Violet and his daughter '... parts of the journey still primitive.'

Indeed they were! Particularly when they had to overnight at dubious 'accommodation houses'. Compared with the lowest English country inns these were deplorable, almost Irish in their squalor! 'One dines,' Lady Violet confided to her journal, 'with a company as crude as the food, a motley of adventurers, financial opportunists, engineers, surveyors and the like, some of them with their wives. Appalling creatures. Parvenues and upstarts. What bad luck we missed the train that carried Lord Randolph Churchill and that lady writer of *The Times*, Diana Chudleigh.'

However much her cold eyes disapproved something within her was beginning to respond. If Africa were to be civilised ... who better than the English to do it?

Gardiner bought the news sheets at small towns and looked for news of the Rand. He found nothing but local news or the reprintings of items from British newspapers. Doings of the Royal Family and troubles in the Balkans seemed absurdly remote in arid little *dorps* where dust devils swirled between flat-topped hovels. What did amaze him was the surge of alien humanity moving north. He was old enough and had seen enough to take a philosophic, even pitying view. He had seen it all before. In jungle and tundra. The hopeful, heated faces were the same. So was this sense of urgency to be there before the next man.

'Look at them,' he said to Katherine. 'Not one in ten is going to finish up any better off than before. But who could make them believe it...'

Hundreds were on foot, humping their gear, shooting for the pot, begging lifts on the groaning freight waggons. Sometimes when their coach stopped to change mules some man would put his grinning, bearded face over the door and cheerily ask for a 'coupla bob' to see him on to the next *dorp*.

'How do they manage?' Katherine asked.

'They'll stop over and work at their trade for a few weeks.

Make a small stake and then go on. A hell of a lot will never get there.' It was hundreds of miles to the eldorado. Some would give up and turn aside to make the best of it in some village along the road. Some would fall prey to rotgut grogshops set up at every likely stopping place – a river drift, a place where two sheep tracks intersected.

She would have her hand in her purse for every man.

'It's not your problem,' Gardiner assured her. She was thinking of her father. It must have been like this for him as a young man.

'Your father!' Gardiner exclaimed. 'He was one of the few that made it.'

Wherever the waggon trains passed in convoys of up to a hundred at a time the veld was denuded and the game shot out. 'Used to be here by the thousand,' the coachdriver told them. 'Now a man got to ride ten miles to get a shot.'

Day after day the empty landscape unwound. They were stifled and choked by dust. At times they looked at each other as if they were seeing strangers. At overnight halts there was little water to spare for bathing. They would dismount with their clothing so full of dust that they could beat it off in clouds.

'One simply had no concept,' murmured Lady Violet. Her features had grown more angular, yet her expression had softened. She was several times violently ill from the motion of the coach. 'Mal de mer ... please ask him to stop.' When she returned, very pale, she always said, 'Forgive me, most unpleasant for you.'

The smell of vomit and eau de cologne lingered.

Gardiner noticed that Katherine always tried to make the woman comfortable and Lady Violet was grateful. 'Thank you, child. So silly of me,' as the girl bathed her face with a cloth and urged her to take a sip of spirits.

Interminable though the journey seemed they were making some forty miles a day under the easiest conditions, using the same route over which the oxwaggon transport would take eight months to reach their destination. The immensity, the harshness, the unyielding and unchanging severity of the landscape made conversation pointless. Besides, they had said all there was to say. To read was impossible. It was hard to remember that there was any other landscape or that they had ever known greenness and air that did not burn the nostrils.

It was the bleached bones by the wayside of this endless trail that most appalled Katherine. She knew she was looking at something she would never forget. Across the waterless stretches and where the shallow pans had dried to leave the brittle hoar of salt or cracked mud lay the skulls and the empty ribcages of draught animals, some brittle and decomposed by twenty years of sun, others still newly whitening.

More than once at a halt Gardiner found her standing looking at the evidence of those who had passed this way.

'I had no idea it was like this,' she murmured.

He put his arm about her. 'Tender hearted, aren't you?' His arm tightened and she made no move to break the contact. He was not sure of her feelings about him or indeed about his own. Under such conditions it was crazy to think about romance but the girl's nearness and the way she occasionally looked at him worked on him. Whenever he handed her down from the coach or helped her mount he felt he'd go crazy. Then he would ride up top with the driver and try not to think about other women … faces, bodies …. hands that had caressed. Women he had deserted … women who had loved him. It was time he married, settled. No, that was unthinkable. The easy unfettered life was too good to throw away. And yet … to possess a woman who was untouched, who would love and admire him and be the mother of his children …. He indulged in fantasies of a great sprawling house on a ridge with a view that went on for miles. He could hear the click of ivory balls in a gunroom hung with trophies. Masculine voices of approval and respect. Their appraisal of the young woman, the beautiful heiress who would preside at his table. Josiah Rawlinson set great store on his daughter and the man who married her would be well set up. The old man was already preparing his withdrawal to a mansion in London. He hankered to be an art collector and by God he certainly had the money to indulge any fancy. He'd want a good man on the Rand. It could work out. He must play the gentleman and not force the girl in any way. There were nights when he found it hard to keep his resolve. The old woman would fall asleep almost at once. One night he heard the door of the shared room open and saw Katherine come out to breathe cool air in the darkness in her night clothes, her hair down her back, her body ripe beneath the slight fabric. It was a torment for him to be aware of her proximity, to know that he had only to seize her in his arms for her to yield. He felt it dishonouring to her, her unawareness of his gaze, and he did not repeat his watching of her through the cracks of the reed door. When he heard her return to her bed he had to get out of the room and walk for an hour under the stars .... Only another five or six days to Kimberley, five more to Potchefstroom. Then a mere eighty miles to the Rand. He must hold on to himself.

One night he went further than usual from the inn, making towards a distant campfire. As he drew closer he heard fiddle and concertina and saw men and women dancing and drinking between the waggons. The music stopped as he came into the firelight.

'Mind if I join the fun?' he said, offering his flask to a black-bearded young man who let go a girl to swig at the flask. The fiddle began to scrape and Gardiner saw the look in the girl's eyes. He grabbed her by the waist and felt her body move with his and her grip on his fingers tighten to his challenge. 'Don't mind 'im,' she said. 'The bottle'll do 'im alright.' The clapping and the stomping made him reckless. He danced her into the darkness. Just as she slid into his embrace and he felt her mouth wet on his own and he was groping to lift her skirts, he was seized from behind and flung to the ground. The black-bearded fellow was grappling for his throat, pinning him down with his booted legs. Gardiner flung himself sideways and his assailant toppled. They both rose. 'Git yer 'ands off my girl, mister,' he heard and there was a flash of steel as the man began to close in, arms spread in the stance of the skilled knife-fighter. Gardiner stepped back and measured the odds. His fists against the blade of a man crazy with jealous rage. It was not the first time he had been in a situation like this and he felt his blood mounting with a wild enjoyment that he recognised as being a necessary releasing of his own frustrations. To smash the bearded face in front of him, to see blood smear the grinning teeth. He feinted with his right and the knifeblade ripped cloth at his side.

'Ernie ... Ernie, let 'im alone,' the girl was shrieking. The music had stopped. There was a tense silence. He lashed out and felt his knuckles on bone. The grin bloodied. Gardiner sprang in and seized the knifehand at the wrist. They struggled chest to chest. A boot shot out and Gardiner was on his back, his face in the gravel. The man came at him with a crouching leap. Gardiner rolled and in a moment had him pinned, face down ... the knife fell. Slowly Gardiner ground his face into the dirt. The wild, delicious feeling of triumph subsided. He rose and dusted himself off. He felt the girl come close behind him, her arms around his waist.

'Get to hell out of it,' he said, suddenly ashamed. It was as if he had done something dishonouring to Katherine. He had never felt anything like it before. They all turned on him at that, jeering him away from the waggons. My God, he thought, I'm softening. Was this the Walter Gardiner who had broken his hands before now in brawls and had a scar from a broken bottle among the fine hair of his scalp? The Gardiner who never left his adversary until he had taught him to eat dust and choke in his blood? All for an eighteen year old chit of a girl who'd never had a man's mouth on hers in her life.

He walked back to the inn and splashed water on his bruised face, wincing at the pain of his hands. I'm too old for this, he was telling himself when he heard the door moving. In the candle he saw the girl from the waggons. Instinctively he put finger to lips and smiled.

'I was worried for you,' she whispered. 'E's a devil with the knife.' She was fingering the slash in his sleeve. 'I'm not 'is girl,' she said with a toss of the head. She was turning back his sleeve and baring his arm ... suddenly seizing it and kissing the graze left by the blade. He saw the faint smear of blood on her mouth and suddenly he was on fire. They were down on the dirty sheepskins and his clothing was open before he realised it, his hands groping for breasts and between her thighs. God dammit, he was starving.

'What's your name, 'andsome?' she asked him as they lay in the aftercalm, her fingers in the coils on his chests. 'I'm Sophie.'

'You're a lovely girl, Sophie.' He blew smoke at the ceiling.

'You won't tell me then!'

'Where are you folks making for?' he countered. They were a party of two or three families who had joined resources and were making for the diggings in Kimberley, unaware that the day of the little man was over.

'Better to try your luck on the Rand,' he said, aware of his affinity for unsettled folk like them.

'Maybe we'll meet up there,' she said a little wistfully.

'I'd like that, Sophie,' he said and he meant it but he knew it would never happen. It was cold as he walked her back to the waggons.

'So long, Sophie,' he said, relinquishing her clasp.

He had some difficulty next morning in explaining the marks on his face. He saw that the coach-driver understood well enough and he warned him with a look not to open his mouth. The surly Australian turned away with a grin. 'Got 'er niles inta ya,' he said with a look at Katherine which the girl did not see.

At midday, when the coach was struggling through dried-up drift sand, the wheels went down to the axles. The driver climbed down, cursing, to flog the mules but the more he cursed the more helplessly they struggled. Gardiner got out. There was nothing unusual in a red-faced mule handler flogging his lathered animals and this man was no different. As he flogged he cursed. 'Git up ... you rat-tailed craphouse!' He beat the lead mule about the head with the butt of his whip as it struggled to get footing.

Suddenly Katherine was at Gardiner's side. He felt her grasp his arm. 'Walter ...' It was the first time she had used his name and he felt a thrill. 'Don't let him do that ... stop him. I can't bear it.' He attempted to lead her away but she broke free and wrestled the whip from the driver's hand. With a stroke she cut him across the face, then raised her arm to strike him again, her face white. The man gaped, then grabbed the whip. He could have felled her but instead he grinned and wiped the livid weal with the back of his hand. He did it with an angry calculation as if measuring the odds ... the big American with his arm about the girl. Then he turned away.

'My dear child!' Lady Violet was aghast.

'I can't bear cruelty,' Katherine said.

'I'll get the mule on its feet,' Gardiner assured her. By God, what a girl, he thought.

The incident reminded Lady Violet of the morning of the otter hunt at Warewood Hall. What a pity Katherine had been more concerned for the otter than for Charles Warewood. The meet was at Warewood Bridge. Punctually at seven o'clock the master was on the bridge and the hounds were thrown off. She sighed at the memory of that glorious morning. The foliage sparkled with undisturbed dewdrops and the early morning sun had turned the old mansion to rose red. 'Is it not glorious?' she cried to Katherine, pointing out the towers, gables, turrets and twisted chimneys. Katherine had been unresponsive, even sulky.

Colonel Walker, the squire of Weston Hall, kept her at his side as he followed his hounds down the river. 'I don't expect you've seen anything like this in Africa,' he laughed. 'By his prints this one's a large dog otter, a very devil with the salmon.'

When the pack finally cornered him up Swindon Beck he put up a most determined fight, doubling and redoubling. Charles Warewood showed her where he was finally at bay. The young lord did not notice the girl's dismay but Lady Violet, clumping behind in stout shoes, saw that she was quite pale.

'I hope he gets away,' Katherine cried.

'They'll finish him now,' said Warewood in high enthusiasm.

'Alright then, Charlie,' said Colonel Walker. 'As Miss Rawlinson's your guest you can have the honour.'

Warewood stepped into the shallows and clubbed the otter. Then, lifting it, he offered it with a grin to Katherine. 'Make you a nice muff.' His open young face shone with excitement.

Katherine had rejected it, blazing up. 'How can you call that hunting? Why, an otter's practically tame. There's no danger in it for you ... or the dogs. I think it's awful.'

She turned about and made for Warewood House, leaving Lady Violet to make apologies for the girl's inexperience of such things and her colonial ignorance.

Katherine's behaviour now was another demonstration of her headstrong nature but the older woman suspected that it was occasioned this time by the close proximity of the American. She was confused and angry with herself. Her emotions had been worked on too long for safety. Would this interminable journey never end? She felt herself to be a stranger and outsider, with Katherine and Gardiner in some secret alliance. Her features grew ever sharper. The journey had aged and exhausted her. Almost as soon as they halted at night she would collapse onto her bed. She would fall asleep and wake to hear laughter, voices on the stoep ... and then silence. She would start up, resolved to go to them but fall back on the hard pallet, incapable of motion.

Sometimes she woke when Katherine crept silently into the room.

'Are you alright, Katherine?' she would gasp.

'Of course, Lady Violet. Whatever are you worrying about?'

It was this change in the girl that made her anxious. Something had happened since the incident of the fallen mule and the older woman dreaded to think what it might be. When she saw the girl slip out of her clothes and put on her night things she caught glimpses of such rosy loveliness, such an unspoiled beauty that her heart fairly ached for the child's future. One thing ... she needed a strong man and there was no doubt that Walter Gardiner was that.

Chapter 9

To Dorothy Penlynne – yes, she was Penlynne now – fingering the gold band around her finger through the gloved hand resting on her husband's arm, it was a journey not merely away from her childhood in Kimberley with all its attendant joys and miseries but a journey towards a union with this man beside her of a kind nothing in her life had prepared her for.

In her courtship she had been aware that she was arousing forces within him that she could only handle by being the jolly sporty girl, the tennis girl and the picnic favourite. She was not afraid but she was wary of the sensations that went through her when she thought of him, particularly at night in the hot feather bed that was soon soaked with her perspiration. She had enjoyed the delicious languors of walking with him, of watching his face as she read him poetry, of feeling the strength of him, as it were, exuding from the hairs of his head and the crisp curling locks of his beard. He was nothing like the man she had imagined herself loving and yet his looks fascinated her. His attraction for her lay, had she but known it, in a kind of force ... a suppression of force. He seemed to excel at everything physical.

Now, as the jolting coach threw her body against his side, she was somehow glad that he had not been able to hire a coach for them alone. She wanted him. She knew that ... but in what way she could not imagine. It was a kind of frightened yearning. The excitement he created in her she expressed in a nervous stream of ideas about the future, her face shining. But when she saw the dark unfathomable look in his eyes and felt his hunger she shrank away. Tonight or tomorrow night he will pierce my body with pain and blood .... She chattered on, everything in her recoiling from the thought.

There were stolen moments when he could turn to her and his lips sought hers, red and full and his mouth moistly sweet, when his hand stole beneath the travelling blanket and caressed the soft inwardness of her thighs and she felt his bone-hard leg pressing against her own. She was caught then between dismay and a thrilling of the flesh. Emotions followed one another so headlong that she could hardly endure them and would withdraw from contact while he went up top to ride with the outside passengers.

That first night on the road they had been separated by circumstances. The lodging house where they were to rest and take fresh horses on the next day separated men and women, each in rough quarters. He swore angrily but she was relieved.

This feeling she had for him. Of course it was love. What else? And his for her? What of the force that compelled him towards her? How was she to deal with something she sensed was infinitely more powerful than anything she had imagined ... not just love letters, ardent looks and pressure of the fingers – delightful these had been – but something that would fling her on her back and thrust and thrust...

On the second day she had a violent headache and backache and that night she began to menstruate. She was so pale and in such pain that he was alarmed. He did not show dismay, more a kind of perplexity, she thought. What were his expectations of her body? Soon she would have to grit her teeth and find out. Love was kindness and pleasure in each other's company. Surely?

Leonard Penlynne had taken the best suite available in the Grand in Rissik Street. French doors opened onto a first floor balcony, facing agreeably north towards the red ridge of Doornfontein. He could afford it. Alfred Beit had been generous about salary and had promised to help build Dorothy a house suited to their position. No doubt Kimberley was still talking of the somewhat unseemly haste in which the marriage had been arranged. Dorothy herself, he knew, would have liked a renewal of courtship, a time to find each other again, but he had insisted she must go with him to Johannesburg.

'I want you at my side from the start,' he said.

Dorothy had always loathed the atmosphere of mining camp poverty, the depressed huddling of shanties and tents. They reminded her of that part of her childhood when her father's profession as land surveyor had kept them too often on the move to have anything better. 'I want a huge house with tall windows ... and a tower where I can climb high enough to see the mountains.'

'You shall have it, I promise. A house where you can let your hair down just for me.' She had laughed delightedly at the remark but when he tried to draw her onto his knee she had stiffened away from further contact. It hurt and puzzled him but he felt confident that when she was away from her mother's home she would be different. She would no longer primly adjust her skirt and rising, wih a quick kiss on his cheek, go to the piano. She adored to be swung from the swing in the pepper tree. It was both a delight and a torment to him in those brief days before the wedding. It would all change once she was really alone with him....

So he had imagined but they had been a week in Johannesburg and she had proved a reluctant bride. It dismayed him that anyone so feminine and so bursting with vitality and high spirits could turn into another woman when faced with the marriage bed. What have I done wrong, he wondered. He was reluctant to force himself on her, hoping only that he would kindle the ardour he suspected lay beneath the withdrawn exterior.

He had wanted to show her off at the banquet tonight and was dismayed when she had refused, pleading a violent headache. He was sympathetic. In any case he had been more anxious to see Rawlinson's reaction to the sample of pyritic quartz than anything else. He had to admit that the old pirate had handled the challenge with style but there was no doubt that he had understood that the battle lines were drawn. He left the Exchange Hall in a mood of elation.

'Feeling better?' he asked as he entered the bedroom. She put aside her book. She was wearing a nightdress of some soft material that clung to her body. The bedding had slid to the floor as the night was hot. She looked more desirable than he could bear as she leaned down to draw the sheet about her.

'Don't do that,' he smiled encouragingly, drawing it away from her grasp.

'How was it, the banquet?' she asked.
'I'd have enjoyed it more had you been there.'
'Next time. Was Barney there?'
'Yes.'

'Who else?'

'Rawlinson ... the whole crowd.'

'Has the daughter arrived yet?'

'Not that I know of.'

'She was a wild little thing.'

He saw with rising impatience that she was going to keep up the flow of petty talk that might deflect his intention.

'Was there any trouble?' An edge in her voice.

'What kind of trouble?' He was naked under his silk gown.

'High jinks ... the kind of childishness that seems to amuse some grown-up men.' She turned her head on the pillow towards the drapes. 'Tell me what Rawlinson said.'

'Damn Rawlinson ... where is it?'

'What?'

'That thing of yours, the pessary. Didn't Jameson fit you?'

'I hate it. It hurts. It's so humiliating. You men have no idea what it's like to be examined. To be probed and have things pushed into one. He told me I need a small operation. But I don't want it here, in this awful town.'

'I know about the operation, Dotty. You shall have it as soon as I can get you over to London. But it's nothing serious he told me. It shouldn't prevent us. In any case you need time to settle down before we think of a family. Till then, my dearest, love is not just having children.'

'I'm not very good to you in the way you want, Pen,' she said timidly, 'but I do love you so.' She turned her face into the pillow and he saw her shoulders shake. At once he felt remorse. Was he pressing her too hard, expecting too much, too soon?

'Listen,' he said, 'tomorrow we'll go out to Eckstein's plantation ... see how the pines are coming on.'

'Oh, I'd like that, Penny. The Rand's so barren and bleak. Just to smell pines will be heaven. Pen, are you going somewhere?' He was pulling on his trousers.

'I'm going to get some work done. Finish a report for Beit. A block of claims he ought to buy at once. Go to sleep. See you at breakfast.'

'Must you?' But she seemed relieved.

There was work enough on his desk to keep him till dawn if he chose. He could work off his frustration. The devil was that he desired her so much. He took up the report by his metallurgist

John Watson and began to read confirmation of what he had suspected after the first visit to the amalgamation sheds. He had watched the sludge of powdered ore pass over tables coated with mercury, Watson explaining at his elbow.

'Suddenly we're into this refractory ore. It means that the amalgam which absorbed the gold ... well, it's no longer doing its job. It's being eaten up by sulphides of other minerals. It was easy in the oxidised banket near the surface –'

'What are you recovering, John?'

'Less than forty per cent. Oh, the gold's in the amalgam alright but we can't get it back by the old method. In money terms what we're recovering now is hardly enough to pay for the mercury we're using.'

Now he was looking at Watson's latest figures. Today's tests showed that just under sixty per cent of the gold had been dumped with the tailings. That means, he thought grimly, there's more value in the tailings than on the tables. It couldn't go on. Hundreds of thousands of pounds worth of machinery were on indent. Huge new sheds were under erection for up to fifty stamps under one roof. At this rate they would be erected in time to be useless. And who was to pay for their delivery six thousand miles from the place of manufacture? No wonder Beit wanted him here in a hurry. Pyrites! There had to be a way of licking the problem.

He turned out the gas jets, locked the office door and went out into the night. Silence and stars. He looked at his watch. Two thirty a.m. The roar of the batteries sounded like distant surf. Pounding out fortunes, but for how long?

He passed black men crouching in doorways, hands held out to braziers of glowing wood. Barefoot, they wore the ragged castoffs of white men which seemed to rob them of their native dignity. Primitives here to hack wealth from the shafts and tunnels of their masters. Undoubtedly his countrymen were right when they saw it as the right of the civilised to conquer and rule. He paused at the chains outside the Stock Exchange. Even if you didn't have a farthing in cash you bought and sold on this market. He had never been a gambler. Always the man to work like a slave for someone else. Beit trusted him. Loyalty could be a damnable fault. Some day he might have to compromise, look out for Number One. And if ever there was a town where a man could get rich easily it was this Johannesburg.

He had walked as far as a part of town he had never seen before. He was among the canvas booths and tin shanties of Ferreira's Camp. Stench of ordure and rotting. Sudden whiffs of oriental cooking mingled with the raw fumes of liquor brewing. He was revolted by the squalor, the filth underfoot. Not that it was anything new. The ten years he had spent on the river diggings and in Kimberley had inured him to hardship. Even as a manager he had taken his coat off and toiled in the muck with the next man, accepting the challenge and the adventure of it, the rough comradeship of men his own age in a situation where social rank and education meant nothing.

Now he was nearly thirty. A married man. This was no place to stand thinking of the past but its spell compelled him to walk on, his heart filling with the desire to achieve. Scaffolding and sundried bricks and half-built walls proclaimed terraces of new houses; spec builders were making money. Barnato was into property, already owning large sections of land for future suburbs. Still dirt cheap. Up here was the *kloof* where Barnato's water company had shrewdly dammed off the Klip River. Now he controlled the town's water supply and all they got was a trickle of red water for an hour a day. Higher up on the ridge he made out the gables and turrets of Barnato's new house, now nearing completion. Coach-houses and quarters for European servants. Every stick and stone brought out from Europe. And yet Barnato's background was not all that different from his own. Give me a year, he thought.

Was that the cry of a dog? No, hyena. They sometimes came in this close at night to devour the dead horseflesh and stinking ox carcases along the coach road from Potchefstroom. The train would stop that, if it ever got here with Kruger's delaying tactics. The old man was postponing the evil day which could not be held off forever. The hyena giggled again. Then a shot and silence.

He stepped aside as a pony trap approached. It went by with a woman inside it. She'd been out at Rawlinson's, no doubt. It had never been his style, not since he met Dotty, so impetuous, so eager to please him in everything else. She'd learned French for his sake and read the novels he chose for her. Why was the act of married love so repugnant to her? Could he blame her mother for that or was it something about himself that distressed her? In their courtship he had written her passionate letters but was always disappointed by the coolness of her replies. He did not want to be called 'Dear Old Comrade and Pal'. He had wanted the excitement of premarital fencing and, yes, the underlying tension between a man and a woman restrained by social convention but burning none the less and hardly able to wait for the wedding night...

He had rushed Dorothy into it and it had been disastrous. He would be gentle with her, bide his time and everything would come right. He would rather not send her to Europe for the small operation. Perhaps with some persuasion she would allow Starr Jameson to do it. He must not press her...

Earlier that night Josiah Rawlinson was standing in his shirtsleeves paging through the photograph album when he heard the expected knock on his bedroom door. He looked at the mantelpiece clock as a matter of habit. Invariably punctual, his housekeeper entered, the invaluable Muriel Ferguson, soberly dressed with a glint of gold at the throat of the high bodice, her skirts trailing the oregon floorboards. Thirty-five-ish, he imagined. Soldier's widow. A decent creature, no beauty and maybe it was just as well. What he'd call a lumpish figure but an agreeable face. Lost her husband at Majuba, one of the redcoated lads who'd tried conclusions with the Boers up there on the crest of the hill the Zulus called 'the hill of doves'. When the sun rose the Boers had their sights on the *rooibaadjies*. Their morale was low after the disaster to British arms at Isandhlwana when the impis got in among them with the stabbing spear. Many had deserted. A man like Andrew Ferguson in uniform for the Queen's shilling might well have been one of the deserters. If he was he'd like as not have finished up in the lowveld riding supplies between Delagoa Bay and the De Kaap gold fields. And no doubt long dead of the fever. At any rate Muriel Ferguson had never had a scratch of the pen from him since.

She often found Rawlinson looking at photographs in the album. He was not as hard a man as they made out. He closed it in some embarrassment. He had been looking at the photos of those months ... the too brief months with his Sheila. He saw a girl in a high-buttoned dress of some white floral stuff, holding an open book in her hand and gazing into some unknown that only she appeared to see. The soft brown of the photo had not aged. Sixteen then, blue ribbons in her long fair hair. Here was one of the bridegroom, Captain Rawlinson of the Kimberley Volunteer Cavalry, hands clasping the hilt of his sword. There was no photo record of Katherine at her mother's breast but he remembered her infant mouth tugging at the dark teats of the Griqua, spilling milk, tiny hands grasping, sucking so vigorously, as if she would draw the very life and strength out of the surrogate mother. And he had laughed, 'Take all you can get, my girl! Grab it with both hands!'

'I'm looking at pictures of my girl, Mrs Ferguson.'

'I see that, sir, and you longing to see her.' She walked to the window and pulled the heavy drapes together, lowering the wick of the lamp with a deft touch. He liked the thrift of it.

'You had none of your own, I suppose.'

'It wasna the Lord's will, sir.'

'You miss your kirk, Mrs Ferguson?'

'Aye, I do that, in this godless place.'

'I had a man in my office today, a Father Murphy, hoping to start a refuge for orphans.'

'A Roman,' she said, perceptibly shocked.

'I gave him fifty.'

'You're aye generous, sir.'

He saw that to her Presbyterian soul it had been misplaced generosity. 'I'll do the same for your kirk when I'm called on,' he smiled and saw her face soften.

'Will that be all tonight, sir?'

He waited until she reached the door. 'I've a late caller. I'll let him in by the side door,' he said, watching her face for the slight stiffening of disapproval. He wondered if she counted the visits. A man was by no means dead at fifty-one even if the doctors said he was. He had bought a box of medical books for the mine hospital, second-hand, property of a doctor who was more interested in ivory hunting than the hippocratic arts and had got himself tossed by a rhino. Dipping into it with a layman's curiosity he had turned to 'obesity' – to which he showed a tendency these days – and found a remark which made him re-read the passage.

'... the male climacteric, while not so definite as the female, is marked by obesity and a general lowering of the activity of the catabolic glands...' What glands? 'There is a tendency to atrophy of the testes...'

Well, the lass who was dropped off by the closed carriage doing its nightly rounds was the best cure for that. A bagful of French tricks was the right stuff for the old catabolic. Not that he felt much like it tonight, with Penlynne here. That sample of blue-grey quartz with its rash of yellow pyrites was enough to put a man off his stroke.

Why should he fear Penlynne? The man had a record of failure so far. It was irrational. Yet sometimes the irrational, the sensation in the gut, was the true indicator. Penlynne was a man to look out for. And with Beit appointing him to be his man on the Rand it could mean that the real battle for control was about to start. Not that he didn't have a head start but now the dirty work would begin. The jostling of interests, the looking for the chinks in the other man's armour and the smashing of him before he got too powerful. They'd done it to him in the past. Well, they'd find out he was too big to be broken again.

Dorothy Penlynne walked in the plantation of young pines. The hot scent rose all around her. The pines were hardly more than head high but already they had changed the aspect of the veld. Mr Eckstein called this the Sachsenwald. Trust a German to plant pines! Sentiment mixed with shrewd business. Mining timber and Christmas garlands. So Pen said.

The young woman carried a leatherbound edition of Wordsworth. Byron was too clever for her taste. She liked to dream over misty landscapes and unfathomable lakes she had never seen. Pen had promised her travel abroad. Dear, hardworking Pen with his merry eyes and love of gaiety. It had been so agreeable during their courtship. A kind of delightful game in which she had discovered the pleasure of having power over this ardent young man she could draw to her feet, sighing and laying his dark head on her lap to be petted. She called this vaguely stirring pastime 'spooning' and it could have lasted forever as far as she was concerned. It gave her a sense of worth that was a new experience.

In Kimberley he had visited her in the wood and iron house which was within earshot of the coloured location. She had hated that. She still flushed at the memory of his first call. Mother had so obviously been imbibing. Her face was hectic and her hair ends kept escaping from their pins and the moment she had seen Pen's toney clothes and heard his accent she had begun to talk of her father's people who were 'so well-connected' in the Eastern Cape. 'We have considerable land there, Mr Penlynne ... and property. Here, as you see, Mr Orwell was not a practical man though he has employment of some responsibility with De Beers – Mr Rhodes and Mr Barnato, you know.'

It had been awful but Pen had been a lamb. Never seemed to notice her state. Later he joked, 'My dearest, I was too far gone on you to even notice what she looked like or hear a word she said.' It wasn't true. He was too sharp for that but it was dear of him to pretend. And of course Pen knew the exact details of her father's new job as a diamond search officer. It was a disgusting thing to ask a decent man to do but someone had to. There was so much stealing from the sorting tables. The natives swallowed them and the search officer had to ... every time she smelled Jeyes fluid or castor oil she felt quite faint.

Father may have been a failure in the world where wealth came easily to some. Not ruthless enough. Dead now, poor dear. She never walked in the veld but she remembered how he'd shown her the marvel of plants that lived without water. Insects, birds and trees. She remembered long rambles over the harsh land and everywhere the miracle of life.

'...Marvellously adapted, you see ... much better than we have. They belong here, you see. The conditions of Africa have made them what they are.'

Dorothy walked on through the young pines, quite heady with the scent of them, her parasol furled. She had never blamed her father for his failure, seeing him as a figure to be pitied. There had been an evening on the stoep with Pen when her mother had been sober. She was at her worst then, quietly bitter and caustic.

'You'll hardly believe it, Mr Penlynne, but I have a claim to be the discoverer of the first diamonds here. Oh yes, that surprised you. We were picnicking. Where the Big Hole is now there was a small *koppie* and I prodded up this huge stone with my parasol. My husband recognised it at once. Twenty carats, would you believe!'

As she walked Dorothy prodded the ground with a kind of aimless desperation. Memories were too disturbing. One should never give rein to them. Father had taken up claims but none of them were worth much and then the bottom had fallen out of diamonds on world markets. She remembered him saying, 'Every shop girl in London's wearing them!'

What a wretched little house it had been and how she longed to escape from it and the mood of despair and gloom that had settled over Kimberley with the mines half-closed and thousands out of work.

Tall grasses bowed with heavy seed-heads parted before her skirts. Heat and an odour of dry earth assailed her senses. A widow bird lifted from among the grasses, its long black tail fluttering like a widow's crepe. The Zulus called it 'iSakabuli'. Father called it the 'Kaffir finch' and told her that before their defeat the warriors used to wear its plumes.

Things like that came back unbidden. She could think of her father only with affection. The memory of her mother was painful. 'There are things about marriage that are frankly ... distasteful to decent women. You must learn to put up with them, however. That is a wife's duty, however repugnant.'

After an occasion when she had found Penlynne kissing Dorothy with more ardour than prudence, her mother had told the girl, 'Men are like dogs – worse than dogs.'

The image which that remark provoked had revolted Dorothy. But Pen was different from other men, wasn't he? The picture postcards he showed her of London art galleries he had visited showed the naked bodies of women. 'Statuary is so innocent,' he pointed out. 'Classic nakedness is quite sterile, don't you think? It's the marble, of course. You'd never think they were modelled on flesh and blood, would you?'

'It's art, isn't it, Pen?' Groping for the meaning.

'Yes. It has nothing to do with the crudity of life. It's for the higher emotions.'

When he spoke of art and music and the theatre she felt safer with him. He was so ardent in everything and he promised her a European trip when he'd made his fortune. It was his Europeanness that fascinated her most, his quick wit and urbanity. So different from the men he was manager over. And yet he was not too fastidious to 'muck in with them'. He was brave too and he hated braggarts and bullies. Above all, he despised meanness.

'Do you know, Dot...' This was when he was still working for

Josiah Rawlinson, managing one of his companies. 'The man does his own shopping ... doesn't trust anyone else to go to the fruit market. Only he knows how to bargain with the coolies. Then he comes to the diggings and watches every stone, having saved himself a shilling on greens. Who could work for a man like that?'

Before their marriage in the Anglican church in Kimberley they had gone together to the manse to learn more of the duties and vows of the married state. She had prayed quite fervently to understand all that was implied but it was mostly about a woman's duty to her husband and the meaning of marriage being 'fruitfulness'.

Pen had put his arm about her afterwards and laughed. 'He made it seem like you're to be a brood mare, old girl. I think rather we ought to see old Starr Jameson; he's a rattling good medic. I think he could, you know, assist. I don't think we want a family right off, do you? Not till we're getting somewhere. He's so sympathetic and you know him well enough not to be, well, embarrassed.'

He took her ardently into his arms. 'He'll fit you.'

'How do you mean ... fit?'

'It'll come better from him, don't you think?'

'You mean he'll talk about having babies?'

'About not having babies, that's the point.'

She had gone to Dr Jameson almost totally ignorant, aware that however unpleasant it would be it had to be faced as part of her duty. Not that she did not feel an excitement that was almost an exaltation. Kind of sacrificial. The 'altar of Hymen' had been a recurrent phrase in her head. When he used the word 'amenorrhea' it was meaningless to her. She saw the vivid little face of the doctor grow more concerned, or was it merely curious when she admitted to having an absence of menstruation.

'Never?'

'Never,' she admitted. 'Once or twice, a little ... perhaps.'

Her mother had said, 'Count yourself lucky.' Some girls had it at fourteen, some even younger and they all hated it. Some had headaches and backaches and had to stay in bed.

She had an immediate fear of abnormality, of being imperfect as a woman. Jameson looked into her eyes, pulling down the lids for signs of bloodlessness. In her case it was more likely due to psychic origins than anaemia. Marriage would no doubt effect a cure. Penlynne was a good man. He'd give her the security she had lacked.

'Will you please remove your skirt and loosen your other clothing. Nurse will help you.'

She lay on her side on the blanketed table and he approached her from behind. 'This is the ring pessary. I'm going to fit you. I shan't hurt.' In his gloved hand he was holding the vulcanite ring between thumb and forefinger, his index finger extending the rubber membrane. She felt the thrust of the device, upwards and backwards, the probing finger pushing. The thing twisting and settling. A choking nausea rose in her throat and she retched. 'There,' he was saying, 'you won't find it difficult with the applicator. Once in six weeks is enough but you must douche the vagina daily.'

Were these the marital duties her mother had found so distasteful? He spoke of them as if they were nothing. Afterwards when she had dressed he asked her to sit down for a moment. 'Mrs Penlynne,' he began, 'I believe a small operation will be necessary before you can become a mother. Nothing seriously amiss. We won't worry about it for the present, but should you decide you wish to start a family come and see me again. Otherwise nothing to bother you. Perfectly normal.'

But could she be perfectly normal if she was in need of 'a slight adjustment', as he had put it. To be married, was it was always to be like this? This feeling of an ultimate privacy torn away. She got up, eyes downcast, feeling she could never greet him in the street again.

She was broken out of her reverie by the sound of her horse whinnying. What could be wrong? She retraced her steps to where she had tethered him to a tree. He was throwing back his head and rolling his eyes.

'Steady, boy. What is it?'

Something rose out of the long grass. She saw naked black flesh. She was knocked heavily to the ground. She caught her breath at the stench of the heavy body. She tried to cry out but her throat constricted in terror.

It was just after dusk. The highveld sun had gone down into the haze of dust in a blaze of orange. Darkness swiftly followed. The coach Rawlinson had hired to bring Katherine and Walter Gardiner to Johannesburg splashed through the shallow drift at Fordsburg and began to climb the last hill to the town. Ahead they could see gaslight streets and the great blocks of darkness where nothing was yet built. They were to put up at an hotel that night and meet Katherine's father and go out to Langlaagte in the morning. The prospect of hot baths and comfort seemed unbelievable.

Gardiner had got up on the box to see the new gold town emerge from among the fires and lights of the hovels and shanties on its outskirts. There, in the middle of nowhere, he saw a square mile of ... not civilisation. It was too raw, too sudden for that. It was a kind of scarecrow copy of a European metropolis. He had seen gold towns in America but none had prepared him for stone and brick buildings of quality and architectural grace. Money was being spent here. They meant it to last, this little enclave of Europe imposing itself on African nakedness. Corinthian columns and Gothic turrets, quarried stone and plateglass cheek by jowl with corrugated iron.

The driver pulled up. 'Look's like a mob's out.'

'Can you go around, reach the hotel another way?'

The coach pushed slowly through the crowd but eventually could go no further. The crowd was excited and Gardiner knew that look. He got down from the box and pulled down the side flaps of the coach. Both women were looking apprehensive.

'What is it?' Katherine asked.

'I don't know but it looks unhealthy.'

The coach rocked as men climbed on it. They paid no attention to those inside. All their attention was focused on something up ahead.

'Aye, they've got him. There he goes ... up wi' him! Kick, you bastard!' Then came the roar of approval and the coach rocked as the mob pushed forward to see every detail of the spectacle. Bottles were lifted to faces inflamed with angry enthusiasm.

'Don't look,' said Gardiner and put himself between the girl and the thing he could see suspended by the neck from the scaffold planking of a two-storey building. 'Scum of Europe,' she heard him swear as he put his arms around her.

'What is it?' she repeated.

'A lynching.' He was to find out much later that Katherine had never heard of such a thing and at the hotel where Rawlinson was waiting for them he was greeted with the words '...an ugly business ... not our way. I'm sorry you had to arrive tonight. A poor welcome, Lady Violet. It's a rough town and there's no control.'

He took Gardiner aside a few paces into the carpeted hall with its rich panelling aglow in the soft light of electricity. 'Wife of a colleague ... ugly business. It's been a madhouse for two days but they caught him tonight.'

'And the woman?'

'She'll mend, I'm told.'

'Who was he, the black?'

'There are sixty thousand of them on the Reef, Shangaans mostly ... Mozambiquers ... Portuguese Kaffirs. This one was a Basuto. Good mine boys when they're sober. It's the drink makes them mad. Poison, most of it.' Then affably, 'How was the trip? Thanks for looking after my girl.'

'It was a pleasure.'

The noise brought Stephen Yeatsman to the window of the hotel room he was sharing with two others, both of them artists employed by the *Illustrated London News*. It was the best accommodation they could get but they were all in high spirits. Stephen had assignments from the *Manchester Guardian* and was to write a 'Letter from Johannesburg' for *The Liberal Weekly*. He had been sitting shirt-sleeved by the open window, scribbling his impressions after twelve hours in this town. 'It almost vibrates with energy,' he had noted, and gone on to describe some of its curiosities.

'The Johannesburg Exchange and Chambers Company building is worth riding ten miles to see with its arched windows and decorative plasterwork, surrounded at all hours by brokers, touts and buyers shouting and waving script. I must confess the names mean nothing to me – The Royal, The Wolshingham, The Nabob ... King Solomon and The Teutonia. No doubt they say much about the genesis of population and its aspirations to wealth. In a city bar I watched a curious game played between gentlemen in elegant suits and polished shoes, rolled brim bowlers and much ornamentation in the way of gold tie-pins and cuff links. It was called 'tempting the fly', itself a commentary on this endless scourge in a town where hundreds of oxen are 'outspanned'. Each player had a lump of sugar in front of him on the bar counter and on each lump was a Kruger sovereign. Above them in the smoky atmosphere flies buzzed by the thousand. Suddenly a fly swooped and landed on a piece of sugar. Gold coins clinked into the waistcoat pocket of the winner and there were cries of "Champagne all round!"'

Perhaps he had better not miss what was going on. He put notebook and pencils into his pocket, closed the window to keep further dust from swelling the pages of his writings with red powder and went out. At this end of town it was suddenly and curiously drained of movement. Bars stood open and empty. Bootblacks, beggars and whining hawkers were conspicuous by their absence. Traders had put up their shutters. In the distance he saw the white glare of naphtha lamps and the red of torches.

An hour later he came back to his hotel and sat down in his room. He was not a drinker but what he had seen had so disgusted him that he found himself gulping raw spirits as with trembling fingers he grasped his pen and tried to set down what he had seen. In his shock he could at first think only how untypical of his race it had seemed. Yet there were many voices shouting encouragement in English as well as those in Turkish, Armenian, Greek and God alone knows what languages.

What was it that came over men in a place like this where a woman could not walk in the streets without being accosted in six languages and propositioned by barefoot blacks in stinking blankets. Something raw and ugly. Greed and lust out of control. So different from the order of England, the birthright of respect for right and decency.

He wrote for hours and, after sleeping fully clothed on top of his bed, went out at first light to see the sequel...

No one claimed the body. Cut down it lay in the street. It was the object of abuse. Drunks urinated on it. By midnight the dogs were tearing away. Thrown onto a cart next morning it was trundled out of town to the area allocated to Kaffir dead. It was close by the cesspools where the Fingoes emptied the nightsoil carts. A row of holes was already dug in the dark red clay. Corpses were picked up every morning and the graves were unmarked. Police records stated: 'Unknown Kaffir, male.'

Stephen Yeatsman stood by to see the grave filled in by shovelling, dusty blacks. Their fluttering rags seemed to him to give them the aspect of serfs in some mediaeval tapestry. The diggers grinned when he pointed and questioned.

'Bad man ... skellum, baas.'

He had come here after last night's affair to observe the last of it and make his report on what he had been told was the first lynching on the Rand. A man in priest's clothing was pausing at each grave, saying a few words and making the motions of a cross in the air. The priest stopped. 'Father Murphy, St Mary's. I just commend their poor souls to their Maker.'

Yeatsman was strangely moved by the graveyard with its backdrop of an unfinished town. It did not seem to him other than splendid that his countrymen were shaping this territory to suit their own purposes. What shocked him in last night's affair was that there were so many foreigners involved. He saw only one hope for this stewpot of races – British rule. At Oxford he had heard John Ruskin's passionate oration on the duty of the Anglo-Saxon race to impose its still undegenerate culture on the world. He had come out to this country under the inspiration of Ruskin's appeal to British youth. 'England must found colonies as far and as fast as she is able ... advance the power of our land ... make all the world a source of light.'

Cheering undergraduates. Flushed faces of the best and noblest of England's youth. How they had responded! Now he had to square his idealism with last night's disgusting episode.

He looked up to see a black man salute him. He saw the meagre and faded orange blanket. He was standing by the grave of the Basuto. On his bare arm Yeatsman saw the brass disc that proclaimed his number 4454 Star GM. A countryman of the dead man. Brother?

He felt in his pocket for a coin that would in some way distance him from the episode but found to his surprise that he could not do it.

Stephen Yeatsman would probably never learn a word of the black man's language. He knew that. If he had he would have understood that as the man turned away from him he said: 'The white locusts have eaten up the land.'

Chapter 10

If Rawlinson was put out by Walter Gardiner's apparent indifference to his house at this first serious talk between the magnate and the engineer he was too shrewd to show it. He guessed it was the American's way of establishing his authority as his own man. He grudgingly conceded that this was a good thing. Up to a point. He was a fine looking man, this Gardiner. He conceded that too. There was just a hint that his hardness was past its peak and that the face, reamed by sun and weather, would ultimately set in self-indulgent folds. Rawlinson saw him right off as a high-living man. But his reputation in hardrock mining was unequalled. It gave him the kind of easy confidence Rawlinson was not accustomed to having around him. He understood well enough now why Lady Violet had not wished him to be along on the trip from the Cape.

The man had shown no sign of going over the score with Katherine. He was too well controlled for that. It was Katherine her father looked at twice, as if to see some subtle change in her. To him she was still a child and it gave him a profound shock to see her admiration for the man. She hung on his every word while he gave that easy, bantering laugh.

'Your daughter's been showing me your country. A finer guide I couldn't have, sir.'

Rawlinson had formed these impressions in the first twenty-four hours since Katherine's homecoming. This was their first meeting to discuss technical problems facing the mines and try as he would the older man could not keep his mind on the main business. He kept measuring the man as a man.

'Well, sir,' said Gardiner, turning from the Gothic window and measuring his employer. He believed he could get on with him if he made certain that Rawlinson did not underestimate his worth. But for Katherine's sake he was prepared to play a waiting game. He had tentatively suggested to Katherine that he might ask her father's permission to court her. She had hesitated.

'He won't like this, Walter. I've been all he's had for years. If he thinks someone else means more to me...' She looked down as if confused. He saw how her face lit up with tenderness when she talked of her father and it gave him a pang, a momentary doubt in himself.

'Don't worry, I won't rush him.'

'In any case I want more time to think about it myself.'

When she appealed to him like that he understood well enough what she meant and he respected her for it. It showed a maturity unusual for her age in a girl who had been indulged since childhood. He could wait. There was an unexpected pleasure in waiting. An anticipatory thrill he had all but forgotten.

'Every stick and stone of this place came out from Europe, Gardiner,' Rawlinson was saying.

'I see that, sir. Very impressive.' He did not say that he had seen as good up jungle rivers in South America in goldrush towns that had been as quickly swallowed by jungle as they had arisen. He was remembering the abandoned cities of India's early cultures, now the abode of monkeys and bats. Man made and man moved on. It had always been his way.

'I'll put it to you straight, Gardiner. The Rand's been built on a bluff so far, stock market *verneukerij*, as the Dutchmen say. Oh, the gold values are there but most of the trash making money here have only one interest and that's rigging the market for quick profits. Shares change hands like bits of paper. Solid values mean next to nothing; dividends are meaningless. Any rumour is good enough to move the market. We have a rotten reputation as an investment centre. London and the Continent — they won't look at us after the Lowveld crash. And now, just when I'm building confidence in good returns for capital investment, there's this.'

The American turned over the piece of blue-grey quartz.

'If you're into pyrites it's finished.'

'I didn't bring you out here to write my epitaph. I want to know how to beat this thing.'

'There's no way I've ever heard of. You know, of course, that some of the best American engineers and geologists have been over this reef before and written it off as a freak, given it five years at the most.'

The older man gave his head a furious shake. 'There are twenty thousand people here already – never mind the blacks – and an enormous investment of capital. If what you say is fact it'll be abandoned in six months. Go back to the Dutchmen and the Kaffirs to fight over. I won't let that happen without a fight.'

'Give me a few weeks and I'll report.'

'One thing about me, Gardiner – I never underestimate human ingenuity. If you can tell me how to beat this thing there's a fortune in it for you ... I'm talking about millions. I hired you because you're the best. I didn't underestimate your value. You're the highest paid man who ever walked this land.'

'I believe I'll earn it, sir,' the American smiled.

'Everything's open to you. Everything's at your disposal. Just ask.'

He did not ask the American to stay as his house guest and as he watched the man mount and ride off he understood well enough that he had good reason for his reluctance to see over much of the man under the same roof as Katherine.

It was strange to have women in the house again. Already he felt a certain friction. Lady Violet had shown hauteur towards his housekeeper. The English woman had run her gloved hand down the bannister and exclaimed in disgust at red dust on her fingertips.

'I'm sorry, ma'am,' Muriel Ferguson had said without humility. 'It's nae possible to keep the dust oot in this town. It's in the bed linen and the food. And the bathwater's red as weel.'

She seemed to have deliberately coarsened her brogue. That amused Rawlinson. One woman, bony and imperious, her profile hawklike and haughty, the commoner with her broad, stolid face, her heavy bosom and a severity of expression no less than the lady's. But already the Scot had tasted the free air of Africa. Widow or not she was in a town where men outnumbered women to the extent that any woman, even over thirty, could pick and choose. Not that the whores didn't marry fast enough. You'd see them in theatre boxes with their husbands – Armenians, Turks and Germans. Rouged and glittering. Cypriots and Greeks married only girls sent out from home. But nobody cared a damn. In ten years today's strumpets would be the new nobility.

For Rawlinson, if it came to a choice between Mrs Ferguson and Lady Violet, it would not be the gentlewoman. How to get rid of her now she had chaperoned Katherine so far? Maybe Muriel Ferguson would have some ideas.

His main concern was Katherine. He cursed the necessity that had brought her out on the same ship as Gardiner and the way they had been forced into each other's company on the long journey from the Cape. Lady Violet had brought up the proposal by Lord Charles, 7th Viscount Warewood.

'She's turned him down, foolish child. For no good reason that I can see.'

He could see that she took it as a personal failure and it pleased him to have the advantage. 'She knows her own mind,' he said dourly.

'I suppose it's the American,' said the lady. 'What impudence. An employee.'

'My dear lady, you would do well to remember your own position.' Then, relenting, his curiosity getting the upper hand, 'This Warewood. What's he do?'

'Do ... Mr Rawlinson!' The idea of Lord Charles doing anything more than ennobling the realm gave Lady Violet a momentary start. 'The nobility are in politics, the House of Lords, the Army.'

Rawlinson checked her with an abrupt, 'This Randolph Churchill, he's a lord. He's writing pieces for *The Times*, blackguarding the Kruger Republic. He was here, asking questions, looking for information on shares. Going up to Matabeleland looking for mining concessions. Ain't that work?'

'Lord Randolph married an American woman.'

'That explains it.' Tongue in cheek.

'She is quite notorious in London.'

'Oh yes ... Randy! Frankly speaking I'd rather my girl married in a practical way.'

'Lord Charles is a soldier!'

'Then he's an idiot, I expect. I never met one who wasn't.'

The tone of the conversation was such that when Lady Violet retired to the well-furnished guest suite she noted in her journal: 'If Mr Rawlinson is ever elevated to the peerage there is no doubt that he will have his escutcheon emblazoned on his coal scuttle. He is the kind of Midas who will have his pheasants shot for him.'

She looked at her travel-weary features in the mirror. A sudden great weariness descended on her spirits. She had imagined that Mr Rawlinson would be a way out of her penurious state but really, the man was the complete Philistine. No doubt he would be gentleman enough to pay her passage back home where she would use such influence as she hoped she might still muster to find a place in a refuge for Unfortunate Gentlewomen. A grace-and-favour residence from Her Majesty was beyond her influence. What a pity she had found neither grace nor favour with this ... this boor.

In his study Rawlinson blew smoke rings into the silver-tipped kudu horn trophy above his desk. He spat in the wastepaper basket and stretched his well-trousered legs. A connection with the nobility would be a useful door-opener in Europe but what the Rawlinson interests demanded was vigorous blood. A grandson who would inherit his own spirit. He was beginning to see the American in a more favourable light.

He had bought Katherine a young spirited stallion as a surprise. He would watch her from the window when she mounted. She looked superb in the London-tailored habit but it shocked him to see that she now rode side-saddle. As a child she had ridden like a boy. Now he saw the womanly fall of her skirt as her leg crooked over the saddle horn and saw with a kind of embarrassment and apprehension the undulating motion of her body. Sometimes she looked up at the window and waved her crop while the black groom checked the animal. He was amazed at the strength in her small, capable hands. When she returned from riding with Walter Gardiner and he saw her slide from the saddle, the man's hands spanning her waist, the smiles that passed between them, he had to turn away. He knew he had lost her even before the man spoke for her – as he would.

He armed himself with arguments. She's too young for you, man. She's still a child. But every time he saw them together, heads close, or walking the garden paths out of earshot, laughing and larking, he had to steel himself. Was it the loss of the child he feared ... or giving her to this man? He could not have said and he refused to face the question square on. I'll wait, he decided. It may all come to nothing. And in the meantime he needed Gardiner.

It was like her father, Katherine thought, to invite the new doctor he had appointed to the mine hospital to have dinner with them. It was the accustomed way in her father's home and part of her accustomed way of life. In Kimberley the door had always been open to anyone. She had found the English so different and she had long ago decided that she would never be able to conform to the ideas Lady Violet continually thrust on her. Her father's new wealth was not easy to accept. She truly felt that the earlier life in more modest surroundings had been easier. She could no longer wander about the house barefoot or with her hair down or burst through doors unannounced. Being a woman was one thing ... she was glad of that with its prospects of happiness and the still vague future of wifehood and motherhood. Being a lady was another. So when her father announced at breakfast that he'd asked the new doctor around to the evening meal she was unexpectedly light-hearted.

'He turned up at my office with a card from my agent in Cape Town ... Scotch. Looks like a good worker. Came out steerage.' That was a commendation.

The truth was that Katherine was confused by events and lonely in the big house. She had no female companionship. All the friends of her girlhood were in Kimberley. There was only the Englishwoman of whom she was heartily sick and the Scotch housekeeper. She could have been friendly with her but Lady Violet saw to it that Mrs Ferguson kept her place.

Town was too dangerous to roam alone. Women were continually molested. Her father, being unmarried, had not had invitations on her behalf to the circles where women were engaged in tea-making and good works. In any case, his wealth and position had to some extent isolated him from the simple things. So she was very often alone.

Why was she so disturbed by the thought of the young Scots doctor sitting at her father's table that night? They had never done more than exchange polite conversation and once, when they had danced aboard ship, he had awkwardly touched the bare flesh of her back with his naked hand and apologised for not being gloved. There was an essential goodness about him that she had never sensed in Walter. She was realizing then, as she thought of it, that she was actually more afraid of her lover than in love with him. Not actual fear, physically, but a strange, inward shrinking from his dominance, his assurance.

How nice it would be if she did not have to make up her mind. Why not just be friends with both of them? Suppose the young doctor were to ask to see more of her? Would she refuse him even at this late stage of her romance with Walter? Perhaps she was simply trying to escape from the whole idea of marriage. Too sudden. Too early.

And yet there was this continual empty ache in her breast, a confusion of mind that often brought tears to her eyes as if she were looking on a beautiful, unknown landscape and going with regret on a journey of no return without having ventured further into it. It was almost as if she were hoping to be saved from Gardiner. If only she had someone to confide in.

'Yes, father,' she heard herself saying. 'I think Dr MacDonald will be just the man for the mine hospital.'

She was missing the company of Mildred, her maid, who was four years older than herself and had left her service in Cape Town. She had asked her father to write and offer Mildred the chance to come north to Johannesburg and she was daily expecting a reply.

Often she found herself looking forward to seeing Walter with a mingling of excitement and dread. His notes, which he sent from places like Springs, thirty miles away, would turn up at intervals. Terse and unromantic. She would lie down on the chaise longue and stare at the ceiling, wondering what it was about the paper in her hand with its few scribbled lines that had such an effect on her.

She was always hoping to see the words: Be with you tomorrow, sweetheart. Yet when she saw them she would find herself full of apprehension. She kept every note as well as the ribbons from bouquets in a heart-shaped violet chocolate box – the most romantic expression of his affection so far. She thought she understood his reticence. It was not yet possible for him to show a more open affection. To her father she still felt the love of her girlhood but it was now tempered by a caution and reserve which prevented her from blurting out her feelings. In any case they were often of so intimate and disturbing a nature that they were impossible to communicate. She knew that he felt hurt by her withdrawal, hurt and puzzled, and he tried to regain his position by gifts and awkward moments when he would try to pull her onto his knee ... 'like I always did when you were a child.'

From her upstairs bedroom she could look out over the young trees and several acres of garden beginning to flourish in the red clay. There were English shrubs and exotics from Natal, pines and plane trees. Privet hedges were taking shape and walks had been laid out shaded by pergolas which would soon be covered with flowering creepers. There was a flourishing kitchen garden tilled by an industrious Tamil from Natal.

The new house was far superior to the house at Langlaagte where he still spent some time to be near the Star.

'You like this house, Kathy?'

She could see that he was groping around the subject of her relationship with Walter. 'Yes, it's beautiful.'

'It'll be yours ...' he left the sentence unfinished but Walter was obviously very much in his thoughts for he began on mine talk. It was the kind of talk she had often listened to in Kimberley, sitting on a box at the open bedroom door while he whetted his razor and shaved. She felt a pang for him, knowing that he was trying to recover something.

'I'm paying recruiters exorbitant sums to sign on these Kaffirs. Miserable fever-ridden specimens from Moçambique, even as far as Nyasa. And they either die on me or the recruiter steals them back and sells them to my competitors. What can you do when four out of ten are dead in a few months? Who's to pay for a hospital – the mine owners? The government's taking it all in taxes. It's their business ... and what with falling values it could all come to nothing, so Gardiner says. His report's bad; it's pyrites from one end of the reef to the other.'

She put her arms around him. 'I'm sorry, father.'

'He's asked for your hand.' This came as a shock to her. She turned away. She could feel her father's eyes on her back but she did not turn to face him.

'Do you care for him, girl?'

'What did you tell him?' she said, the shock of the announcement still uppermost.

'Do you love him?' he persisted. He was standing very close behind her now and she felt his hands on her shoulders. She

111

turned and put her face against his. They were both trembling as he tilted her face up to meet his eyes.

'I see you do,' he said. As he said it it was like a confirmation in her heart. Yes, she would accept this thing and the rest would surely follow.

She was dressing for dinner, missing the jokes she would have been sharing with Mildred, when she heard carriage wheels in the drive and looked down to see Walter throwing the reins to the groom. She saw him look up at the windows and something instinctive made her step back. She listened to his brisk step to the front door and heard the bell echoing through the lower house. Then his voice.

'Tell Miss Katherine Mr Gardiner's here.'

Had her father known he was coming tonight? Was there to be an announcement at dinner and would she find herself engaged to this man who so disturbed her that at times she could think of nothing else?

When she met Walter in the drawing room all the reservations she had felt in the past days vanished. She could hardly meet his eyes. He was in evening dress with a glint of gold on his shirt front and the flash of diamonds in his cuffs. He looked supremely at ease as he leaned against the stone fireplace, drawing on a cigar. He carried her hand to his lips and she heard him murmur, 'You're looking very lovely tonight, Kate. Just as I expected.'

His confident masculinity almost overpowered her. It was all she could do to retain her composure. He drew her against him and she felt his lips, hard and possessive on her own and she was yielding, giving in as she had never done before, her knees weak.

She had put weeks of resistance and indecision behind her. Yes, she loved him and her trembling lips told him the same. They broke apart as her father entered, his expression startled but not dismayed. Downstairs the brass gong began to boom its brazen summons from between the supporting tusks of a wild boar.

'What's holding young Stewart MacDonald?' Rawlinson addressed the table half an hour later. He was put out that the courtesy he had offered his new employee had been taken so lightly. Surely he had not been mistaken in the man? Coming as it did on top of his disturbed state of mind over Katherine and the further report from Gardiner – expected and inevitable – he drank more than was normal for him and by the time Stewart was announced he was flushed and truculent.

Rawlinson's dinners were usually stolidly English, often stolidly Scotch. Tonight Muriel Ferguson had put on a green pea soup, veal cutlets with french beans from the garden, a saddle of stringy mutton with new potatoes and suet pudding – to which Rawlinson was very partial. She hovered around the servery while the Zulu butler, white-gloved, served, sweat glistening on his forehead.

She announced 'Doctor MacDonald' rather abruptly, seeming to take it as an affront to Scotland that a compatriot had missed the first course and the best of the mutton.

'You're late,' said Rawlinson dourly, his napkin tucked into his waistcoat. He was perspiring heavily and his coat had been discarded with the soup.

'I'm sorry, sir. I had an emergency.' MacDonald took his seat opposite Katherine and the American. He was rather white-faced.

'Could it not have waited? Never mind, never mind. Eat your dinner. We'll talk about it later. You must be in good appetite after a fortnight in Mrs Ferreira's boarding house.'

It was not Stewart MacDonald's way to be socially outgoing and he found the dinner difficult. He felt himself to have become the centre of attention and even criticism. His own nervousness seemed to heighten a nervousness already apparent at the table, and besides, he had been shaken by his first inspection of the Rawlinson Star mine hospital. He was afraid that if he were asked his impressions he would blurt out the truth.

In the iron sheds which accommodated the patients he had found surgical cases lying in pus and blood with only an ignorant black in attendance. Equipment of the most elementary kind was not available and men with every kind of tropical disease from beri-beri to hookworm were lying cheek by jowl. While part of him had risen to the challenge he was dismayed to have such responsibility and shamed that he was sitting at this table when the ward he had left was full of stoical, uncomplaining blacks. He had lost his first case on the table only an hour ago.

His hand trembled as he raised the sherry glass. Katherine, with quick sympathy, noted the trouble in the clear grey-blue eyes that could conceal nothing.

'You'll get used to it, MacDonald,' he heard the American saying. 'It's the same wherever you go. Hazards of the mining game.'

'It's all so ... primitive, sir,' said Stewart.

'I've hired you to see to it, MacDonald,' his employer said. 'Your predecessor was more interested in the stock market.'

'I'll do my best.'

'That's fair enough,' said Rawlinson avuncularly. 'I'll give you a ready ear. Are you married yet?'

'No, sir.'

'I'm building married quarters at the Star. Nothing fancy but more than some of them were used to at home.'

As he spoke Stewart noticed that the American's hand came to cover that of the girl at his side and he found himself thinking of Mary Irving. The image of her rose up so suddenly it was as if she had walked into the room. Involuntarily he looked towards the door. Was she thinking of him at that moment?

The Bechstein grand in the drawing room was slightly out of tune. It had suffered the vagaries of heat and sea air and had spent four months in a crate in an oxwaggon. But it looked handsome and when Walter persuaded her Katherine sat down to play.

'Will you turn for me, doctor?' she said. He watched her hands on the keys and her intent expression and when she raised her eyes to indicate a turn she looked so radiantly young and so endowed with every charm that he could not help wondering at her obvious attachment to this man so much older than herself. Often her eyes went from the music sheet to the tall figure leaning against the mantelpiece and when their eyes met she smiled and her fingers stumbled.

'You play very sweetly, Miss Rawlinson,' he assured her.

She smiled up at him and he saw that her mind was far from the music. He knew it was only a courtesy when the American invited him to accompany the couple to the opera at The Globe. He excused himself and took his leave. Already the spectre of the wards was rising as he went down the long carpeted stairway to the door where a servant handed him his hat and helped him into his coat with its shabby collar and cuffs.

The carriage with Katherine and her escort passed him on the road about ten minutes later. They did not appear to notice him as he trudged back to Mrs Ferreira's rooms. Katherine was leaning on the man's shoulder.

That one will lack nothing in her life, he thought. Strange though that her father was willing to give her to so much older a man. Greying already. The rich had their reasons.

Chapter 11

By the time he had been three months at Rawlinson's Star Gold Mining Company Stewart MacDonald had had his fill of shocks. He had soon found out that doctors on other mines gave only a few hours a week to patients in the corrugated iron sheds so euphemistically called hospitals. The white wards were usually in the care of a discharged army medical corporal, more often drunk than sober. Rough surgery and the crude care of fellow blacks was the rule for the half-naked tribesmen. It was the same from one end of the Reef to the other. Doctors from the Continent could hardly talk to their white patients let alone understand an assortment of African languages. Stewart saw and learned more in a few weeks than he had in five years of study.

'It's an eye-opener,' he wrote his mother in Ayrshire. He was at it from first light till the brief African dusk. In the evenings he worked by the harsh flare of naphtha lamps. His aim was to bring some order and system into it, divide medical from surgical cases, keep down sepsis and put a brake on the stream of cases that ended in a barrow wheeled to the mortuary and out to a hasty burial.

He grew careless of his appearance. There was simply no time for clean boots, fresh linen and a shaven face. Easier to let his beard grow. Often he would hardly have fallen into a stupored sleep than he would be wakened by a black orderly and stagger out to face some crisis. He had quickly learned the basic words of his trade in what was called 'kitchen kaffir'. Phrases like 'a boy is dead ... he drilled into a misfire hole' were answered by *'tata lo muntu file lapa lo Dead House!'*

Sometimes in his stumbling weariness he hardly knew what he was about. What was there to keep him here? A two year contract with Rawlinson? He had thought it good money but soon found that there was little left over after he had paid for his new lodgings in the wood and iron house opposite the canteen near

Number One Shaft. Contracts in Johannesburg meant little. Men changed jobs every day in a restless migration that drove mine managers crazy. A few bob a shift extra and they were gone. He could have walked out and started in town as a general practitioner. Rawlinson would have shrugged it off soon enough. The man had no real concern for his workers. Tonnage was all he cared about. Keep the stamps battering away. Keep up the ceaseless flow of shattered rock. The noise was unending. Underground was some mad inferno where sweating, naked blacks, unrecognisable with rock dust, shovelled the rock shattered by the unending explosions. Choking in the fumes and the dust raised by the hand drills they slogged into the rock face with heavy hammers. Around them on every ledge candles gave the caves and tunnels the aspect of some mediaeval hell.

'I imagined they were panning gold in the streams,' he wrote his mother. 'They're a hundred feet down already, chasing after the seam of gold they call "the reef".' He did not tell her how it was with him. He sent her two pounds a week. She wrote back humbly. She could not use such a sum. It was far beyond any expectations. She'd put a pound of it in the post office against his return.

In a recent letter she wrote: 'Mary Irving has broken off with Alex MacFarlane.' The innocent remark was somehow heavy with suggestion. Would Mary know me the way I am now, he wondered. For a moment the racket from the canteen faded. Instead he heard the harsh cawing of rooks in the bare elms and looked back on the tracks he and Mary left in the snow up there in the Top Field ... first time he ever walked her out. She was twelve and he was fourteen, his voice not properly broken. What was it she wanted of him? And he with her? They touched and broke away, rolling in the snow, grappling and mauling. Then suddenly her mouth was on his, open and wet, amazing in its fleshy sweetness and somehow frightening. No, not frightening. More like a foretaste of something yet to be experienced. What a sense of wonder and delight in the words 'I love ye, Stewart'.

Should he write to her? Was that what his mother was hinting? Go home and court her? He searched the words for deeper meaning. The very name conjured up her face. Sixteen years old, her eyes challenging from beneath the thick black tresses. Dark brown, impenetrable eyes. Mary, laughing and always evading, yet being closer than he could stand. Had that been love? If he had taken her in his arms at that moment would she have taken up with a ship's engineer from Greenock with his Third's Ticket? I was only a first-year medical student. You couldn't keep a girl waiting all that time.

Then another letter from his mother. 'Mary Irving was over today. She's asking to be remembered to you.' Almost as if his mother was urging it on him. Could a man ask a girl brought up in the solid comfort of Ferrygate Farm to come out to a place like this? Mind you, he'd seen carts from the brickfields lumbering to the sites of raw new houses and waggonloads of furniture coming up in crates from the coast. There was a school and churches being built but after the snug propriety of Ferrygate and the secure order of life there would she be the kind of girl to accept the confusion and disorder of the Rand?

He would sometimes wake up at night and wonder what it would be like to put out his hand and touch her. In the meantime he could only try to imagine how good it would be to come back to a small house and find that she had heated water for his bath. It would only be a tin bath in the kitchen but there'd be a smiling face to greet him and while she soaped his back he'd tell her how things were going. Not the worst things, the kind of things he couldn't get Rawlinson to listen to. He had begged the owner to come and see for himself. If Mary were here he would be able to talk it through. 'Something has to be done about improving diet ... mealie meal and treacle five days a week and a pound of meat and vegetables on Wednesdays and Saturdays ... is it reasonable to expect men to keep up with the heavy work underground...?'

In his loneliness there were times when he caught himself saying things like this aloud. As if she were in the next room. A girl who had lived the practical life of farming would understand. And these were men, not animals. He imagined her compassion and indignation. But mostly he thought of the cheerful house and the way she'd make things. He'd imagined that work was everything. What a fool he had been to cut himself off from the joys other men of his age shared with their wives. Mary could be here now. Come out, I need you!

What a way to court a girl. There would have to be an exchange of letters and he knew that as soon as he had made up his mind he would write to her warmly, imagining the way she would respond. A little cautious at first. She'd read a lot into very little – just as he would, searching the page for signs of longing and affection. Hungry for an endearment. Yes, that's how it would be. Mary. Dear Mary. Mary, my dear ... I know I've taken a long time to say what has been in my heart these weeks...

He wrote many letters like this in his head, especially at his new quarters where he was getting out the beginnings of a statistical record. The main headings were death from accidents, death from enteric and other fevers, death from pneumonia and other respiratory diseases ... unknown. He knew it would be months before a pattern emerged. In the meantime he'd have to ask Rawlinson for more money and a house in the married quarters. Poor things, they were. No more than a kitchen, a living room and a bedroom. He could furnish it roughly before she came. But oh, she'd have to be brave to face this after Ferrygate where she'd been surrounded by good old solid pieces, things in the family for generations. The wag-at-the-wall clock that wagged its brass pendulum in the hall, the huge family kitchen with its polished and scrubbed oak. She'd be better off with some young man who'd one day take over his father's farm. The laird's son and the many acres of Rocky Hill.

Mary, dear Mary, won't you come out and help me make a home here? The climate is wonderful and I often think of you and wonder if you still have a small place for me in your thoughts.

Martin Griffiths, the mine manager, was angry about the monthly reports he was putting before Rawlinson. When Stewart added death from liquor there was a confrontation. The Welshman was under pressure to get out tonnage and was continually harrassed by his employer.

'I know about it as well as you do, MacDonald. There's no way to stop this traffic so you do your job and I'll do mine. There's nothing I can do to stop the boozer, the 'iSidakewa'. It's the same on every mine. It's the drink they come for.'

He gave Stewart a long challenging stare as if to face him down and then relented. 'You're doing alright ... keep it up. I'm not against you. Things will change. They'll bloody well have to!'

'I'm not trying to interfere, Mr Griffiths. Surely it's best for everyone if we improve conditions?'

'Look, lad, the owners can get all the labour they want. They don't care a tinker's curse. You'll not be the first doctor who gave up. One thing I will say ... the men say you're doing a good job.'

The small word of commendation meant a great deal but nothing changed. Whenever the black workers came up to the surface they made for the shanty grog shops. He often woke up in the morning to find men lying in the street, insensible, sometimes dead. It was then that he would think of moving to town. There were a score of doctors doing very well, taking adverts in the newspapers. Well dressed and driving their own rigs. Surely that's what Mary would expect of him? Not the down-at-heel character he had become. Why not reach for the rewards of good living and community respect? Life had been hard enough so far.

He was seriously thinking of resigning when something happened to change his mind. He was walking between the compound and his quarters when he heard a horse behind him and stepped aside to see Katherine Rawlinson. She reined in and he gave her a hand down from the saddle. He was taken aback by the richness of her clothing and by the well-groomed animal's impatient trampling.

'How are you, Dr MacDonald?' she asked in a friendly way. While they made small talk he had a sudden surge of hope that he might reach her father through her.

'I'm to be engaged,' she said. 'I hope you'll come to my party.'

'Oh aye,' he laughed. He was thinking he'd have to buy a decent suit. A ready-made would cost sixty shillings. 'Miss Rawlinson, you'll forgive me if I ask a favour.'

'If I can ... surely.'

'I've been hoping your father would come to see the needs of the hospital.'

She frowned. 'He's always so busy. I hardly see him.' Then as he so plainly showed his disappointment, she promised to speak to her father that evening. As she rode off he had a feeling of renewed hope. Things would be improved. In the spurt of optimism he went to his table and wrote the long-delayed letter to Ferrygate Farm.

He was in the compound about a week later when he was hailed by a man getting down from a dray loaded with liquor crates. 'Dr MacDonald. How long have you been here? Don't you remember me?' The voice was slightly foreign.

'Oh aye.' He felt a surge of hostility. It was the whoremaster De la Roche. He was well turned out in polished boots, riding breeches and white Indian cotton shirting; his dark skin had darkened further in sun and fresh air. He looked brutally healthy and prosperous.

'I'm in the liquor business, MacDonald.'

'Oh, what became of the other trade?'

De la Roche took it in his stride. 'They're all nicely settled on their backs. Half are married already. How's doctoring? You could make a fortune here in the pox cure business.'

'I'm busy enough with the results of liquor.'

'It's a public service, doctor. The cup that cheers. Would you deny them that? We bring it in by mule caravan from Delagoa Bay. It's a hard game. We lose animals and transport riders. It's tsetse country.'

'I understood you made it here.'

'We doctor it here. It's German potato spirit. Comes out by German East Africa Steamship Company – I've shares in that. Colonial spirit, they call it.'

Stewart turned his back on the man. He was seething with anger.

'I saw a friend, a mutual friend, the other night. You remember Kitty Loftus, the redhead? You look surprised. Everybody turns up here sooner or later.' He laughed. 'She's back in the trade. Don't worry, I mean the stage. I sent my card round; no hard feelings. I'd have taken her to supper but she was getting all the attention she wanted.'

'Good day, baron.'

'I've dropped the title. This is a republic.'

'If you ever had one.'

'Doctor! A word of advice. Grab all you can while it's going. It's not going to last.'

Stewart went into his shanty dispensary. He dashed the sweat from his forehead. Everyone in this town seemed under a curse, a kind of frenzy. Was this what he wanted? Was this what he had asked Mary Irving to share with him? Yet there were people trying to bring in some sense of order and decency. The nuns at St Mary's had opened an orphanage and a school. The rich soil was perfect for vegetable gardens. Roses and shrubs from many lands flourished. The bright sunshine and thin air of the plateau gave a constant sense of exhilaration. One had to remember that only four years ago it was barren rock and treeless ridges.

In April the days were shortening towards his first winter on the Rand. They told him it would be bitterly cold and he dreaded the effect on his charges, especially the ones they called 'tropicals'. There was still no sign of Rawlinson's visit and when he received an invitation to Katherine's engagement party – yes, he remembered the American – he was sure she'd never even spoken to her father.

However, Rawlinson arrived unannounced. He was gruff and abrupt.

'I've come at your request, MacDonald. I hope you're not wasting my time.'

Stewart saw that the man was in no mood for sweet reasonableness. He must tackle him softly. But it went against the grain when he thought of him, up there in his mansion, ready to spend any kind of money on his daughter. And down here, squalor and suffering.

'Let's hear it, MacDonald. I haven't all day.'

'My reports, sir. I believe you've had them for a while.'

'I have many things on my plate, MacDonald.' He began to walk down the bare hall of the Kaffir ward. He stopped at a pallet and turned back a blanket from a man's head. 'Well?'

'It's pneumonia, Mr Rawlinson. A man like this comes from the Zambezi Valley ... tropical. They don't take to change. The heat underground and coming off shift into cold air.'

'What do you suggest?'

'We could make a start with a better diet, protective clothing.'

'It's not for me to clothe them. These fellows sell their blankets for drink. I pay fair wages. I don't ask him to come here. He's his own master. Now look here, lad. I told you when you arrived that you could take on private patients, augment your income. Why don't you? Bring out some nice girl. I'll give you one of the houses I'm building for married quarters. Why don't you take your opportunities?'

'Because,' said Stewart carefully, 'I'm needed here.'

It was only when he had said it aloud that he realised that it was indeed the case. It had been enough for him to see some signs of gratitude from faces which otherwise conveyed nothing to him except the enormous gap between them and himself and his abysmal ignorance of their needs, needs that turned them to the *sangoma* and the bones and herbs the witchdoctors brought in and sometimes seemed to cure where he had failed.

Rawlinson stared hard at him, trying to look him down.

'What's this fellow doing here?' He threw back the blanket to reveal the stump of an amputee. 'A Mozambiquer, eh?' He spoke a few words to the man in his own language and Stewart saw him respond.

'Sir, that boy's going to have to get back to his village.'

'They manage, they manage. This is Africa, MacDonald. They're not like us. Time's nothing to them. They've got brothers all along the way.'

'Surely there's no profit in dead workers, sir?'

'I'll thank you to keep your socialism to yourself, doctor.'

The big man walked heavily the length of the ward. 'It all seems in order to me. Keep up the good work. I hope you'll take time to come to my daughter's engagement party.'

He nodded and left. The impression he had made was both awe inspiring and condescending, yet somehow amiable and conciliatory. A man big enough to pause for a moment from great affairs.

'Well I'm damned,' said Stewart aloud.

Griffiths, who had seen Rawlinson to his Scotch cart and had had a few words with him, came over sympathetically.

'I told you you'd get nowhere. Just do your best, same as the rest of us.'

Leonard Penlynne watched the Kimberley coach pull away from the Zeederberg office in Plein Street. He had an overwhelming sense of desolation, of everything he had hoped for with Dorothy falling to pieces. He understood very well that after an experience like hers a woman of sensitivity could not be expected to brazen it out in such a small community. Every eye was on her. Even in sympathy it had been a torment.

She had submitted to a medical examination, moaning and weeping into her pillow. A strange doctor, a newcomer. He had thought it better to have her looked at by a stranger, rather than someone who knew her socially.

'She's not injured,' he reported to Penlynne. 'But her nervous condition is poor. I'd advise getting her away to Europe for a few months. With her medical history she should be seen by a specialist in women's complaints.'

Penlynne, watching the dust of the departing vehicle, was remembering how they had brought her back to the hotel, her hands covering her face, shuddering away from any contact.

'Don't touch me ... I can't bear to be touched.' She had lain in the veld for hours before rising and making her way back.

'It's me, Pen, your husband, darling girl.'

'Don't put on the light, for pity's sake.'

'They'll hang the brute,' he said harshly.

Dorothy sat up, her eyes staring, then fell back, shuddering.

'I love you, Dotty,' he comforted, stroking her hair. 'I'll always love you. I'll take care of you. I'll build you that house. Far out on the ridge, walls all around and the kind of garden you like, shrubs and roses and surprises, lily ponds and statuary. Italian.'

'I want never to have existed,' she moaned.

'Don't say that, Dotty.'

Her hotel room was filled with flowers. People were sympathetic for a couple of weeks but when she would not see anyone they ceased to enquire. She had no wish to emerge. She ate in her room, refusing to go out. He took a separate room. Well, he had done without a woman in his life for months on end in Kimberley. He'd never been a man for camp females and he would not be starting now.

Where will it all end, he asked himself. Some women were afraid of physical love. He'd been unlucky. In every other way she had been a good wife. A dear, amusing companion, sensitive and imaginative. Full of a restless energy that matched his own. When she came back it would be better. It would be forgotten. He would spare no expense to have her in the best hands. Till then he would work. Nothing else would have any meaning for him. Yet he could not help wondering: would it ever be any different with Dorothy, especially now? He'd be a man without a wife, without sons. What kind of future was that?

Dorothy wrote to him from Kimberley, Barkly East (where she told her mother as little as possible) and Cape Town, where she embarked on the new fast mail steamer, *The Scot*. She wrote from London to tell him Beit's partner Wernher had met her and made discreet arrangements in Harley Street. Wernher wrote to Penlynne sympathetically. 'There's a man in Vienna ... a Dr

Freud. I could make an approach to him.' He was touched. Wernher and Beit were always so sympathetic and decent. They'd offered to pay for everything. Penlynne refused. It hadn't been for want of hard work that he hadn't made his pile alongside Barnato and Rhodes in Kimberley. They and Beit had just been that extra notch sharper. Well, he was learning.

It was over a month before he took up a standing invitation from Barnato to drop in at his box at The Globe. Why not, he thought. He had been through a particularly worrying day. A report from the metallurgist John Watson made clear that the pyrites factor had gained the upper hand. Every one of the group's holdings was on the point of losing money.

Watson wrote: 'I recommend that you bring out a man called MacForrest. He is a Scottish chemist working with the practical application of chemicals to refractory ores. I worked with him in Edinburgh and I believe he is now busy on experimental work with cyanide potassium. He is the kind of man who would respond to a challenge. Unless some simple, cheap solution is found, there is, as you know, every prospect of the mills closing within a few months.'

Sitting shirt-sleeved in his office, alone at ten o'clock, Penlynne poured a whiskey and leaned back. He had not come up here as Beit's trusted man to see every hope dashed to the ground. At the same time he felt absolutely powerless in the situation. The only hope on the horizon was some man he had never heard of tinkering with cyanide – and six thousand miles away. Faint sounds of revelry came from bars along the street, a piano jangling, discordant singing, sounds with which he had long been familiar. At first it had been part of the easy comradeship of young men on the make. Now he associated it with his own failure. He was still an employed man. Highly paid, even well off, but the fruits of his initiative were going to Beit and Wernher. He was left out of the big deals that passed between men of real power. But suppose he went home now and made contact with this Scotch chemist? It would be a stroke that neither Beit nor Wernher would be able to ignore.

He paced excitedly. It must be done without Rawlinson knowing. He'd put it about that he had gone over to support his wife with her medical problem. As his spirits rose he had a sudden craving for excitement, to shake off depression and feel his blood running fast. Yes, he'd drop in at The Globe. He'd surely earned an hour of relaxation.

He was a fastidious man. He kept a fresh collar and tie in his desk and a soft cloth to dust off his boots. He took off the paper cuffs and ran a comb through his thick hair. He touched the ends of his mustache with pomade; the faint scent of apples in the jar reminded him of the English autumn, the loft at home stacked with pippins.

He took a ricksha to the theatre and went into the theatre bar. The price of options was being more heatedly discussed than the play. Gas chandeliers flared on cut glass crystal. The long bar glittered with brass and polished mahogany. The atmosphere was thick with blue smoke. Mirrors reflected the faces of men he knew by sight and repute. Hard, shrewd men with hard, gaudy women flashing their shoulders and showing their legs. The Globe was little better than a knockshop with its supper rooms and cubicles. He felt distaste. The fastidious in him recoiled but something else stirred in him ... he felt a kind of choking excitement. A rouged girl frou-froued up to him and made a mouth. He could smell her scent and feel the movement of her breasts against him. He put a sovereign on the counter and nodded to the barman. 'Drink for the lady.'

In Barnato's box he found an empty French champagne bottle floating in an icebucket of tepid water. What with the heat of the iron roof, the flare of footlights and the heavy carpeting and drapes the place was stifling, but the compelling magic of illumination in darkness, with painted faces and figures making grand gestures against painted scenery, caught at his senses.

The situation in the play was not unlike his own. A cold wife and a man torn between his duty to her and his natural desires. Of course there was no one in his life like the young woman playing the mistress, nor could there be. But sitting there in the stuffy darkness he indulged the fantasy that there might be. The acting ranged from mediocre to downright amateur, yet every scene was applauded to the zenith. He saw women sobbing and men tugging at their starched collars.

When he lifted the opera glasses and focused his attention on Kitty Loftus, playing Helen, what he saw in the intimacy of the close-up made him catch his breath. Panting bosom and arched neck. Glittering green eyes enhanced by heavy use of cosmetics.

He noted the suppleness of her movements, the toss of that startling head and the shape of limbs subtly exaggerated by her clothing. Sometimes it seemed to him that she looked straight into his eyes.

Dorothy's lack of ardour had been a goad to him. At first he had lavished her with gifts and flowers and with affectionate notes. He knew now that the rape had ended all possibility of normal intercourse between them, certainly for a long time. With tenderness and care some women might recover. He doubted Dorothy was one of these. Whatever he did from now on that would go against his conscience and his affection for her he determined he would spare no effort one day to make it up to her somehow.

He got up and left the auditorium before the final curtain. There was a chill wind blowing outside and the dust was flying. Ricksha boys were crouching out of the blast and cab horses stood with their backs to the flying grit. He hesitated a moment about going backstage, then decided against it. He'd send her flowers and his card in the morning.

In the event he did not do so. He could not bring himself to betray his wife. In the cold light of day it seemed a shoddy way to behave. A few nights passed before he returned to the theatre and again he found himself enchanted by Kitty Loftus. Perhaps it was his heated imagination but she seemed to him to send him glances, especially when the curtains parted to the final applause and he clapped enthusiastically. One night he drank more than he intended to ... and that was that. He knew as he walked backstage with the carriage waiting outside that he had embarked on something from which he had now no intention of turning back.

Chapter 12

Less than a week before the formal announcement of Katherine's engagement to Walter Gardiner a tall, fair-haired young man, slightly stooping – as if embarrassed by his height – but bearing the unmistakable stamp of a British officer, approached the entrance of the Grand Hotel. He paused before stepping inside and stood looking around as the Zulu who had followed with his baggage in his ricksha capered and grinned.

So this was Johannesburg. After the melancholy wastes of the Orange Free State it certainly had the look of a metropolis, but God it was a ramshackle hole for all that. Hard to credit that a girl like Katherine could choose to live here. He had telegraphed her from the Cape to say that he would soon be up. He had hardly expected a carriage to meet him but he still had high hopes of impressing her. There was every chance that he would be given an appointment as a military attaché to the High Commissioner in Pretoria. Life could be about to flower for him.

He had brought several cabin trunks of clothing. All the usual, and a pair of excellent guns, not handmade for him – he could not afford that – but the property of his late uncle who had given Katherine such a devil of a time at Warewood with his mania for hunting foxes. The old fellow spent every day of his life beating covers for what he called 'vermin' – but would have died without. Charles' face lit up as he remembered those candlelit dinners at Warewood, the warm light on Katherine's shoulders, the scarlet features of his uncle. 'But dammit, Charles, she's a top-class filly for all her being a colonial.'

Yes, she was a top-class filly alright and this time he would not take no for an answer. He had sent his valet ahead of him with his card to announce his arrival and to enquire when he might call. 'Hope this will not be too great a shock!' he'd scribbled.

He was having a drink in the hotel bar, surveying with good humour the motley crowd (he'd never heard such a babble of talk in his life) when his man returned with a note. It was in the familiar handwriting. The truth was he had kept every line she had ever written to him and the sight of it now made his heart lurch. He put a gold coin on the counter and told his man to 'cut off upstairs and look out something decent ... a suit, not a uniform.' Then he swallowed his drink and tore open the note. He was suddenly enveloped in an awareness of her and despite all he could do his eyes prickled with tears.

'Bad news?' said someone at his elbow.

'I don't expect so,' he grinned.

'My dear Charles: What a marvellous surprise that you should turn up in time...' The noise, the smells, the crude imitation fashionableness of the saloon with its flashing mirrors and carpeting ... suddenly it was all inexpressibly tawdry and not to be borne. She was inviting him to her engagement party. Keeping a place on her card for him. Perhaps the Lancers! Well, the gentlemanly thing would be to send along a gift and wish her the best.

That evening as he was sitting in the bar, trying to avoid the attentions of women and the equally blatant approaches of men with 'financial propositions', he saw an advertisement in *The Oracle*. Men were wanted to join Captain Hardcastle in an adventure that would 'redound to their credit'! Seven shillings a day and all found. Good mounts!

Matabeleland. Where the devil was that? And what the devil did anything matter now anyway?

The night of Katherine Rawlinson's engagement party there was some trouble with the electric light plant at the big house in Doornfontein and at the last moment there had been a panic to light lamps and candles. The flash storm of the afternoon had flooded the engine house and hail had stripped the young trees to shreds and battered shrubs to the ground.

Fortunately the ballroom and hall had been decorated earlier with greenery and tubs of hydrangeas, potted palms, azaleas and a profusion of lilies. But when the fans ceased to churn the air in the ballroom became as humid as a hothouse.

Muriel Ferguson had been steady and managed things without panic. Katherine was firmly under the command of Lady Violet as far as the protocol of the affair was concerned. It was she who had pressed for strict control of the invitation list and had supervised the printing of cards. No one could have guessed, as she stood at the head of the stairs, that she was contemplating the scene of her defeat. Katherine was to marry the American after all. Young Charles Warewood had turned up too late and had gone off to Matabeleland to recoup the fortunes of the Warewoods, or at worst to take back some trophies to the mess of the 14th Lancers.

Lady Violet had told Rawlinson that she would consider it her duty to remain with Katherine until she married. He agreed but did not press her to stay longer. If she was shocked by what amounted to dismissal it was not evident in the straightness of her back, the haughty lift of her chin. For some time now she had given up her secret ambition of becoming Rawlinson's wife. The truth was that in this atmosphere of crudity and push, the mixture of the uncouth with the cultivated, the scrambling after wealth and the vulgarity of its spending, the decayed gentlewoman, obsessed with gentility and the manners of a generation past, was experiencing the revival of an ancient spirit all but obliterated.

She had decided to stay here to see this 'England in Africa' (as she dubbed it) become a possession of Her Majesty. She wanted to organise ladies' committees and patriotic functions. She was on fire to stand on platforms draped with the Union Jack and be chairlady of the League of Loyal Ladies. She thought it an outrage that these Dutch, so crude, so uncultivated, so dishonest, so boorish, should have the benefit of this country. She believed it was the duty of her kind to develop the land not for the upstart entrepreneurs of Europe but as a kind of garden estate with good shooting and plenty of servants for people like Charles Warewood.

After the wedding she could no longer pretend to be a guest in this house. Where then? She gripped the balustrade to control the trembling of her hand, gathered herself and knocked on Katherine's door.

Muriel Ferguson was on her knees with a mouthful of pins, making an adjustment to the length of Katherine's dress.

'We're no' finished yet,' she called out.

The girl's hair was about her shoulders; the flower she was to wear was on the dressing table lying next to the necklace that was a betrothal gift from Walter Gardiner. In the soft light of an oil lamp Katherine's shoulders and arms glowed. Her face was pale and her eyes glittered with a kind of feverishness.

Muriel Ferguson, at her feet, was perspiring heavily. There were dark stains under the armpits of her dress. She fussed about her 'puir motherless bairn', but was plainly approving of the match. She thought Charles Warewood a 'miserable body ... a puir thing'. Similar Scots terms of opprobrium had described his length, breadth and penniless estate. Gardiner was 'a mon indeed!' and she had taken it on herself to counsel him to be 'gentle wi' my lassie'.

'You may leave us now, Mrs Ferguson,' said Lady Violet.

'I'll be leaving the minute the hem's right and no' a minute before.' The housekeeper's face was red with possessiveness and the pleasure of knowing herself indispensable. In any case, she knew very well that Lady Violet's days in this house were numbered.

Mr Rawlinson had made it clear as crystal. He had even called her Muriel (though he apologised right after for the liberty and kept his face and voice cold for some time). The girl was ready for marriage and she needed a man with experience and a firm hand to manage the wilful, stubborn streak of Rawlinson in her. She was nervous tonight ... 'and nae wonder!'

Muriel Ferguson had seen them embracing many a night in the garden down at the end of the walk where the cypresses were planted around a Venetian well-head of white marble. She had seen the girl's face when she came indoors. The pair of them were off horse riding in the veld at every opportunity. And where did he take her those nights when he called for her in a closed cab? She smiled. She had not forgotten the touch of a man's hand. She sometimes felt her blood stir when she and the master were alone in this great empty house. He in the library and she in the kitchen preparing his meal. After all, she was still in her thirties and had once been known for a bonnie lass. She had her kirk but no woman, even a good woman, could sleep with a Bible between her legs.

'There now! You're a picture, lass.' She patted Katherine's cheek. To her surprise Katherine put her arms about her and she could feel the girl's body trembling.

'You're missing your mother on a day like this.'

There was a crunch and clatter of carriage wheels in the drive.

'He's here!' cried Katherine.

'Awa' ye go and receive your guests!'

At that moment the engine in the garden started up and throughout the house the lights came on.

Claude de la Roche had not received an invitation to Katherine's engagement party but he knew the value in Johannesburg of the costly gift. He had handed his offering to Lady Violet, who, although she was doubtful he had been included on her list, introduced him to Rawlinson as 'Baron'.

De la Roche shrugged the title aside. 'No need for such distinctions in Johannesburg society,' he murmured. His gift was placed with the others. Gold and diamond predominated but the Sèvres cupids he presented were unique.

He noted Gardiner's eye on him more than once and when he presented himself to Katherine to dance her card was already filled. 'My felicitations ... lovelier than ever, Miss Rawlinson.'

Katherine received his compliments without remark. No matter, the beauty of the town was here in the startling red hair and pallor of Kitty Loftus, the actress. Dancing in the arms of that fellow Penlynne she looked through him as if he did not exist. Good luck to her! He hoped for Penlynne's sake she could give a better performance in bed than she did in the theatre.

He moved about the reception rooms. He noted Barnato and Sammy Marks, both big in the liquor trade. He nodded to them and to various others of Russian extraction with their overdressed wives. They had got in early and already they were in control of everything that counted. But he was optimistic that he was not too late to make a killing for himself. His connection with the Sociétè Française de Distillerie earned him a nod from Sammy Marks that he took for a compliment.

In the atmosphere of Johannesburg De la Roche had found what he craved. What a man did and how his fortune was made was of no consequence. He caught the eye of the haughty Lady Violet. He knew she was looking down her nose at him. He shrugged. Her kind were irrelevant in a society where only failure to make money was despised. Here was the exhilaration he needed. This is my oyster, he exulted. There was money to be made in anything and everything but liquor had seemed to him to be the easiest, fastest route. His false credentials had easily raised a bank loan and he was importing and distributing 'superior French cognac', bottling it himself with the aid of a few blacks in a tin shanty in Ferreirastown. It sold under two labels.

To the European bars and hotels it was Five Star Liqueur Brandy. To the mine canteens and grog shops along the Reef it went by the name 'Kaffir Brandy'. The white drinkers paid double for the refinement of their palates, but the recipe was basically sulphate of copper, green tea, acetic acid and oil of nerolin, in a base of spirit distilled from Prussian potatoes. The black man's brew was given the approved bite by the addition of cayenne pepper tincture, sulphuric and nitric acid. Both concoctions were coloured by burnt sugar and bottled in the endless collection of empties picked up in canteens and back streets and labelled to suit. The chemicals were supplied by a firm of wholesale chemists and the spirit from the Sociétè Française de Distillerie's plant on the banks of the Crocodile River at the border of Mozambique and the South African Republic.

It was almost too easy, except that recently he had received threatening notes to close down or be closed. It made him very indignant about the protection offered by the police of the Kruger government. They looked after the people who paid best and if it came to a fight he knew he could expect no help. Any night now he was expecting to find his warehouse burnt down.

He was strolling back from the Rawlinson home to his hotel when some instinct turned his feet towards his warehouse. In the doorway he saw a young man crouching, arms about his knees, head on his pack. Another Peruvian, he thought, stirring him with his boot.

'Get up. Out of there.'

'Sir, I want work. I can do anything. I know this trade, sir. I worked for Friedlander and Herzfield. I did everything – runner, tout, lookout.'

It would be useful to have someone work for him who knew the methods of the big man, but why should he believe the fellow? He could have been sent to spy on him.

'Why come to me?'

'They held back my wages, sir.'

Yes, that was plausible. 'You stole from them, I expect.'

'No more than they had of mine.'

'I know you're lying.' He took some coins from his purse and dropped them. 'Look after this place tonight. I'll speak to you in the morning. What's your name?'

'Isaacs, sir.'

'You're London ... you talk like Barnato.'

The boy was grinning. 'Sound of Bow Bells, sir, Cheapside.'

'A Cockney Jew!'

''at's me, sir, a proper Lunnoner.'

Isadore Isaacs cried his thanks after the back of De la Roche. A proper gent, he could see that. Flash 'arry. Reg'lar toff. It was the first Christian act anyone had done towards him in this town. Friedlander had been a proper swine. He'd been with that firm only a few weeks. He was too sharp for them and when they topped his wages – 'your contribution to the synagogue we're collecting to build' – he'd had enough. He was giving no *gelt* of his for any bloody Temple Israel. He'd had enough of that from his father. Wanted him to be a Talmudist, a respected man. England was to have been the land flowing with milk and honey but it turned out that his father's only escape was the prayer house, the *taleth* over his head, swaying and rocking, his heart hungering for the Holy Mount of Zion. His father had dreamed of the time when the poor would be poor no longer but Isadore preferred his English rags and the life of the street to the *kaftan* and the prayer house.

At twelve he knew where he was going. It was the day he came back to the alley where the sun never reached. 'Papa, today I saw one of us, a Jew, riding in a golden coach with six white horses. Lord Mayor of London.'

'We are strangers here,' his father cried. 'And you are not yet *barmitzvah*.' The sin his father cried out against was to reject his Jewishness. He had run barefoot in the filth of the gutters since he was six, talked Cockney with the vigour of a cock sparrow, knew where to beg and where to steal food and how to fight with his fists and his feet. More important, he knew when not to fight, when it was better to soften an enemy with a smile....

It gave him a bitter pleasure to think that he had spent his first weeks in this new country in the trade his father feared more than death. To work in a *korchma*! In a flash his memory was taking him down the stone steps of a cellar in the *podol*. The Russians who lived in the *krashtshatnik* quarter of that stinking town in Galicia, of wretched memory, came of a Saturday night to the drink cellars. You found no Jews down there, only *goyim*. Cab drivers and porters, tradesmen and students. The tavern-keeper would lift his glass to the drinkers, a tiny thimbleful of vodka, and drink '*le chaim* ... to life!'

In his father's eyes to be a publican was to be lost. But how else was a man to make the means to escape from the Pale? Galicia, Volhynia and Pondolia. Oh, the oppression of those marshy plains where the heart hungered for the sight of a hill! And if a man escaped he would be robbed at the frontier posts by officials when he tried to bribe his way to freedom on a borrowed passport. It had made Isadore's heart swell with anger to hear his father speak of it.

It broke his heart to have to leave his sister Rachel in the Jewish orphanage. 'I'll come back for you, Rachel,' he'd said, 'I promise,' and they had clung together, weeping. He had humped his pack to the Rand, sleeping in farm outhouses, selling a few trinkets and the *boererate* prized by the Boers for their herbal properties. Sometimes he got a night's lodging in an outhouse with the Kaffirs. They were as poor as he was but they shared their food, even though he was not a brother. He had been robbed by fellow Jews who made off with his pack. But when he saw Johannesburg he knew that his luck must turn. He'd start anywhere, do anything, and when he had a stake he'd send for his sister.

Nothing had prepared him for the shock of finding himself just one of hundreds of foreign Jews walking the streets, standing at street corners with a tray of rubbish goods ... Kaffir truck. But every time he saw Barnato go by in his coach with outriders in cocked hats and Barney nodding and smiling, his name on every man's lips, it was then he knew he'd make it too.

Jingling north from Khama's country with fifty good men, making for Lobengula's territory. Long hours in the saddle and rough company. It seemed to Charles Warewood to be a good cure for love and, with luck, by the time he returned from this adventure the pain of losing Katherine would have ceased. He rode with a continual ache and numbness of spirit that made him dull company. Everyone in this expedition was riding away from something. There was a seasoning of well-salted Bechuanaland Border Police. Good horsemen, good shots. The rest were adventurers and hard cases. No questions asked. They had been promised cattle farms and gold claims up there in the new lands Rhodes was bargaining for from the Matabele and the Mashona. Perhaps he would stay there himself. It didn't matter. All he wanted was to get Johannesburg behind him.

He had not wanted to be anything more than Trooper Warewood, but Major Hamilton took one look at him and did not even ask the stock questions, 'Can you shoot? Can you ride?' He knew an officer when he saw one.

'What's your regiment, Warewood?' he asked bluntly.

'As of the moment ... none,' Charles said.

'I need a good officer.'

'Being a trooper will suit me, sir.'

'Alright, have it your own way. Seven shillings a day all found. Horse and rifle thrown in. Suit you?'

The place was called Pitsani. They unsaddled and bathed in the Molopo River and watered the horses and oxen pulling the commissariat waggons. So far there had only been two places where it had been possible to get water, both of them foul and trampled by cattle. The horses were heavily laden, each carrying on the saddle an extra pair of horseshoes, cavalry cloak, blanket, hard tack, waterbottle and biltong.

Charles was lathering his face and having a rather painful shave of his tender skin when Major Hamilton came over. 'Get your kit over to HQ, Warewood,' he ordered. 'I want you with me.'

Charles did not argue. Already he knew that he was set apart by the men. A man could not shrug off his station that easily. Not that he took Hamilton for a gentleman. He was about thirty, tall and lean with eyes as black as stones in a skin weathered by years in the saddle. He was a hard-drinking man who lay down in his cups and rose up sober. A colonial by his speech and style.

Charles kept his mouth shut and rode beside Hamilton. It was not his business to ask what the operation was about. He wanted nothing more than an opportunity to forget. She was beyond him now, wife of another. How good it would have been to share his life with her. Well, she had been straight about it from the start. Never given him anything to hope for. Yet surely there had been times when they had found a remarkable harmony...

'Riding away from a woman, Warewood?' Hamilton grinned.

Charles touched his spur to his mount and trotted ahead.

The next waterhole was eighty miles ahead at Silenia. All the small waterholes along the way had dried up. The bush was drab and lifeless, the ground hard as iron. So far all Charles knew, all anyone knew (though the column was rife with rumours), was that the major had secret orders from Rhodes.

Quite soon Hamilton was calling Charles 'Charlie' and inviting him to drinks at sundown. Hamilton never let on what the column was after. He talked about hunting and farming and he seemed to have expectations of a large sum of money. One night when he had drunk more than usual he told Charles he had Rhodes's order to capture Lobengula.

'That's what it's all about, Charlie boy. The old savage is in the way. With him gone Rhodes will get the mining concessions he needs. Oh, we're not going to hurt him, you know. Just take him into protection ... from his own warriors, you know. Some of them are impatient with his rule, not the rightful king.'

Charles knew and respected the name of Rhodes. Was there anyone at home who didn't? He had not understood the reason for the pair of Maxim guns, glinting with brass and steel under canvas on a waggon, but if Mr Rhodes had authorised this march there was no need to doubt.

The further north they rode the harder the drought. To Charles it was unimaginable, a hell after the soft air and green fields of Warewood, blue smoke hanging above the elms and gentle rain. At some waterholes they had to dig several feet and scoop water for the horses with their hats. The lowing and bellowing of thirsty draft oxen and the yelling of the black drivers seemed to be always in his ears. When the quick-burning fires of thorns died down lion came in close and attempted to seize the oxen. Katherine did not become less sharp in his consciousness.

Gradually Hamilton grew more open about his orders. The black king had swopped his country for a thousand Lee Metfords and ten thousand cartridges. When Mr Rhodes sent in his engineers to claim his concession rights the old savage had denied signing anything.

'Sitting up there in his royal hut, swilling champagne with his five hundred wives! What is he anyway and his father before him, that murdering Umsiligaas. He was the one who wiped out every living thing in the Transvaal. It was butchery, Charlie, hut

137

burning and woman stealing. Rhodes will change all that. Make it a white man's country.'

'So we're going in to finish the argument?'

'That's it, Charlie. Finish and *klaar*, as the Dutchmen say.'

Early next morning the column moved out, heading for the Shashi River. From there it was still three hundred miles to Gubulawayo, as Lobengula called his capital. A fortnight's riding at twenty miles a day. Ample time to let his pain subside ... except that somehow it did not diminish. He rode all the time with Katherine's image in his heart. At times she seemed more real to him than she had been in reality.

Hamilton, riding at his side, talked incessantly. 'You'll soon see the Matopo Hills. Boulders as big as houses. The blacks call it sacred ground. That's where they buried Lobengula's father. Fine country, grand country. Pretty as a park. Good hunting, plenty of water. Gold, too!'

Charles cast an appreciative eye on the rich grasslands the column was crossing, the animals quickly getting back into condition, coats lustrous and eyes gleaming. It was enough to gladden a man's heart after the wilderness of Khama's country. It was at sundown that they got their first sight of Tati Trading Store. A few miners' huts, windlasses and a small stamp battery. It was the hour when smoke should have been rising from cooking fires with natives driving cattle back to stone kraals and miners on the stoep of the store drinking sundowners.

Major Hamilton lowered his glasses. 'It looks deserted. Take a section in, Charlie. I don't like the look of it.' In the uncanny silence Charles could hear the stamp and snort of horses suddenly checked, smelling water ahead. He rode forward with a trooper. Dismounting, they hitched their horses. Already they could see the looted store spilling goods onto the stoep. Inside it was a shambles. There were several dead men lying gashed and ghastly behind the counters. Glints of cartridge cases showed they had made a fight of it. Flour bags torn open, dried peas, Kaffir corn, coffee and sugar trampled, bolts of cloth and wire. Scattered beads. Their boots crunched and slid on the debris. There was a sharp, sweet stench. Under the tin roof and in that heat ... probably yesterday. No women, thank God. Silence. Not even the screech of guineafowl coming in to roost. From the stench coming up the mine shaft there were more bodies down there.

Charles noticed that the sun had turned into a blob of blood. This was the first time he had been exposed to death and every nerve was aquiver, his senses incredibly heightened. For a moment the sun perched on a heap of enormous boulders, then melted around it. He could feel sweat run down his legs. Salt stung his eyes. Simultaneously the boulders were turning into immense black eggs that seemed to have fallen from the night.

'We better be reporting back, sir,' the trooper said uneasily.

Hamilton was cool. 'I expect they were sent here to deal with us. There won't be trouble tonight. You can hear 'em ten miles off when they mean business.' He did not uncover the Maxims. In daylight they rode on. Everywhere they saw signs of the Matabele raiders. The villages of the Makalala were circles of white ashes on red soil. Head-high corn was trampled, cattle driven off.

'They regard the Makalala as fair game,' Hamilton grinned. 'The old man's past controlling the young bloods, Charlie. They've got to wet their spears before they can wed, and they're hot blooded. Now you're beginning to understand, eh!'

They saw no sign of warriors all next day. They had evidently withdrawn to the military kraals on Lobengula's side of the border. That night the major got drunk.

'Charlie, boy, my orders are to get to Gabulawayo and grab that old nigger and cut his bloody throat. An' in earnest of my services, Chas, Mr Rhodes undertakes to pay me a hundred and fifty thousand jimmy o' goblins. An' no questions. When it's done no one'll give a damn. Get him out of there, dead or alive. That's what Rhodes said. An' it's in my contract. Raise a force ... 'cetra, 'cetra. I have the great man's sig... signature on it.'

'I don't believe it, Hamilton.'

'Ah, the young idealist ... Queen and Country.'

'You lied to me, Major.'

'It's war, Charlie ... war.'

'You told me we were to remove Lobengula to a place of safety where he could make his decision without danger from the *indunas* against him making the concession. This sounds like murder.'

'Wasn't that murder you saw at Tati, eh?'

Charles had no answer. That night he went down with fever for the first time. He was seized with teeth-chattering rigours that were followed by drenching sweats. His whole body shook. In his delirium he called again and again for Katherine. At dawn the major came to his tent. 'I'm leaving you quinine and a Kaffir boy. Also two horses I can't spare. When you're up to it, ride back. They'll look after you at Shoshung, at Smith's cattle post. Too bad you're going to miss the fun.'

Chapter 13

The house called Bloukoppen had belonged to Karl Marloth. Penlynne thought there was a whiff of Mad Ludwig of Bavaria about its turrets and stained glass. He liked Marloth. The German was a man of immense enthusiasm, as reckless as he was good-humoured. Generous too. Some of his hunches had been inspired. Others were disastrous. It gave Penlynne no pleasure that the company he represented was taking over Bloukoppen in settlement of one of Marloth's mistakes. The big German, red-faced and fleshy, met him at the door.

It was like stepping into an improbable compromise between a Bavarian *Schloss* and an oriental bazaar. Marloth greeted him without resentment. 'It's yours...' If he felt a pang about parting with the house he did not show it.

All Johannesburg had watched Bloukoppen rise from the stony hill. German stonemasons cut the blocks on the site. Every piece of timber and pane of glass were imported.

'I'm on my travels again. A man must keep moving. If I stay too long in one place I do foolish things.'

Marloth took Penlynne to the windows looking north to the mountains. In the hard blue small dark specks were circling.

'Vultures,' said Marloth. It could have been a comment but he said it without being aware of it. It was Penlynne who felt the word.

In the gardens the German was experimenting with asparagus and strawberries and in a glass house he was raising orchids from the forests of Natal. Smiling ruefully, he waved his hand around. 'Enjoy it, my friend.' He took a bottle from his pocket and showed Penlynne a yellow stone with a greyish fibre.

'This is the material of the future. It has remarkable properties. There is a mountain of it in the Zoutpansberg. This is the *linum vivum* the Romans used to wrap the bodies of the emperors before burning them. In this way they saved the sacred ashes. It will have a thousand uses in the coming century.'

Penlynne saw that the man's enthusiasm was less for the strange mineral than for the quest. This was the man who had mapped the course of the Vaal River, drifting down it in a rotten boat with a black servant and an umbrella. He had been the first to foresee a gold town on the Reef with thousands of men employed. It was the vision that counted for him, not the achievement. What he found he shared. When he gambled he lost. He'd turn up again with another fortune. And lose it.

Penlynne went back to Bloukoppen several times before he made up his mind. This was where he would install Kitty Loftus.

Kitty ran from room to room. In each she found something to exclaim over. Carpets, hangings, the electric chandeliers in the reception rooms, the heavy, carved furniture with gnomes, eagles and hobgoblins. Gloomily Bavarian and immense. The bathroom was tiled to the ceiling. The bath itself was of Chinese porcelain and stood in an island of peacock blue mosaic. The library and music room were panelled and ceilings throughout were Italian stucco work. In every room there were fireplaces of pure Carara marble.

'Well, Katushka, what do you think?'

'It's ... wonderful, Penny.'

He was delighted with the slight hesitation. 'Good enough for you?' he asked, smiling.

'It's for us,' she said quickly, falling into a chair of deep green velvet. The red hair and the translucence of her skin took his breath away. He was still not accustomed to the feeling that she was his. He knelt at her feet and removed her shoes. The small, perfectly shaped feet were like something cut in white marble, the tiny blue blood vessels like some marvellous inlay. She was watching him with those astonishing, lustrous green eyes, something enigmatic in her expression, as if she too were catching at something that might not last but was ready with him to make the best of it.

'I'm going to carry you upstairs,' he said.

'Just now,' she laughed. 'First tell me ... is it really yours? You mean you bought it for us?'

'My dear child, I'm not that wealthy yet.'

'Then how?'

'Nothing dishonest. Bloukoppen was security. It's the kind of thing that happens in a town like this. Fools like Marloth lose fortunes in one night. This time I'm the lucky one. Don't worry, I'm not a gambler. It's not going to vanish overnight. I'm far too ambitious for that.'

He watched her moving about the room, touching things almost diffidently, as if afraid they might fall apart. 'The silver in the drawers, the linen too?' she asked.

'Everything.'

'It don't seem possible.'

'It don't, do it!'

Her gaze went past him into the tiled hallway hung with tapestries and up the stairs to the door of the main bedroom. Mistress of Bloukoppen, that's what Penny had called her. She had been in this town one short year and this was her house. She was to live with a man of distinction. Everyone said he was going to be rich and important. And he had chosen her. She wandered through the downstairs rooms, holding his hand like a child, hardly hearing him expounding his vision of what Johannesburg could become. Her interest at this moment was the house. He could go on talking about art galleries and parks ... her plans, indeed her world, stopped here. She could imagine nothing further.

Everything was exactly as the German had left it. In perfect order. Even the servants were hers to order. When she thought of that she had to repress an instinct to burst out laughing. All of them, so solemn and respectful. So much to learn if she was to please Pen. From the first he had been the perfect gentleman, handing her down from the cab and watching her safely into her room at the Two Flags Hotel, a wood and iron building with a row of outside rooms. Then one Sunday he had taken her to the Wanderer's Club to watch him play cricket. She had lunched with his friends and he had introduced her casually. She understood that he had taken her there deliberately, to show them his intention. Perhaps to see their reaction.

She smiled at her recollection of her first entry into the clubhouse on Penlynne's arm, the stunned way the men had looked at her, admiring her openly and quite surprised to find that an actress at close quarters was actually quite modest. They were a jolly bunch those gentlemen in white flannels, club ties round their waists and sporty little caps.

She had understood that she was on the threshold of a totally different world. She had been very precise when choosing her words and had carefully checked her natural exuberance all afternoon. She wanted Penny to be proud of her. She was far less talkative than usual, knowing that after they left there would be much speculation about their relationship. Penlynne had shepherded her about the clubhouse, never leaving her side for a moment, making it quite clear that he wanted her for his own.

When he told her he was married she tried not to show her dismay. She had seen him alone in the theatre box before he sent her flowers and his card. She accepted it as just her luck that he could not be wholly hers.

'Where is she?' she asked.

'Under medical care in Europe.'

'How long will she be gone?'

'Month ... maybe longer. I don't know.'

'I expect you love her very much,' she said, her eyes smarting with indignant tears.

'She can never be all I want, Kitty.'

He looked at her with such hungry longing that she stretched out her hand and ran it gently down the side of his face. Now she was all sympathy for him.

'I know I'm being a fool,' she said, 'and I ought to tell you to go.'

'Don't. Please don't.' He had seized her hand and was covering it with kisses. She had been quite overcome by his ardour. Afterwards, as she lay in his arms, he spoke of his loneliness, the burden of his work and the envy and shrewdness of his competitors. His pleadings that he could not get on without her touched her deeply enough for her to accept that she could not be the first thing in his life. Somehow she did not expect it, not in the beginning at any rate. Bit by bit he told her about Dorothy. She was living with his father and unmarried sisters.

'I seem to fit in here better than I had imagined,' she wrote. She had been advised about the operation but shrank from it. She had developed a taste for expensive things and in his guilt he sent her more than he could really afford.

By the time she felt secure in Penlynne's affections Kitty wanted to hear no more of this Dorothy. All her life she had tackled problems head on, often using difficulties to her advantage by shifting her desires to meet her circumstances. Very early on she had learned to be practical in everything.

'I think we've talked enough about Dorothy,' she told him. 'Not that I'm not sorry for her, going through that. So can we forget about her please?'

It was shortly after this that he called for her one day with the trap and told her he had something to show her. He had a way of being secretive...

Now as she walked from room to room she was asking herself if this meant that his wife had told him she would not be returning. She heard his footsteps behind her and felt his arms go about her waist.

'We're going to give a splendid party,' he said. 'I want to show off my beautiful lady to the whole town.' Surely he would not say this if something had not come up? But she held her peace, her heart beating fast in anticipation. Would he have brought her here to this house if it were otherwise?

'I may have to leave you for a little while.'

He saw that she was bewildered and groping to understand. She broke out of his arms, her face suddenly suffused with dismay. 'But you only just come.'

He knew he would be gone at least three months. There was no other way to convince himself that this Scotch chemist had come up with a possible solution to the pyrites problem. The man had sent Penlynne a copy of his formal application for a patent. 'If it is accepted,' he wrote, 'it is my intention to form a gold extraction company. Capital will be available, I hope.'

Penlynne had telegraphed him immediately. 'Have formed a gold extraction syndicate here. Offer you ample capital for field tests of process and substantial royalties for exclusive rights to recovery process.'

He had MacForrest's reply in his pocket. 'Look forward to negotiating with you in person.'

'We'll have a week or so together before I go.'

'But why must you go? It's 'er!'

'It's business ... and of course I must see her. You wouldn't expect me not to, surely. Come, don't let's spoil our first night here together.' He saw that she was trying to pull herself together.

'I'll just 'ave to get used to it, won't I?'

Her mother used to say: you get nothing for nothing.

Walter Gardiner lay soaking in the tub, a cigar in his mouth and a glass of Scotch whiskey in his hand, the real stuff, malt, peat moss and burn water. This was no Delagoa Bay spirit doctored with creosote, oil of cognac and filtered through oak sawdust for flavour. Everything in this town was a counterfeit and even the damned reef they'd built it on was playing them false. When you got through what they called the banket the gold-bearing conglomerate gave way to blue quartzite. He had been working over the length of the Wit Waters Rand for months now and in that time the values in recovered gold had fallen steadily. They were already throwing away more gold in the tailing from the mines than they were able to refine. Rawlinson's Star was comparatively immune so far. He was still getting out the rich, free-milling ores. But pyrites had shown up recently. It was just a matter of time and he'd be in the same trouble as the rest.

The Dutchmen in Pretoria were right. London, Paris and Berlin were right when they refused to invest. The handsome buildings, every stone of them handcut and waggoned up here to the plateau with their pillared renaissance fronts were as phoney as a dud nickel. Nobody would admit what was coming. They were all in too deep. You could hear the shouting at the stock exchange half a mile away. Nothing was based on true values. Any rumour, even a rumour of a rumour, kept the bubble from bursting.

Barney Barnato had only to drive through town in that crazy six-horse Lord Mayor of London rig of his, with outriders in three-cornered hats, for the market to jump. Well, Barnato was into it deep and he had to keep up the edifice to safeguard his interests in real estate, light and water and city tramways.

'Kathy!' he shouted. 'Freshen my drink, will you.'

They were going to dinner at her father's that night and he expected a repetition of his so far futile efforts to convince his father-in-law that every known method of recovery was useless here. He was thinking of his last confrontation with the old man.

'There's no answer and you know it. Metallurgists all over the world have tried to crack this one. There's no known way through the sulphide zone.'

The ageing man with his drooping mustache, thickened waist and angry blue eyes had pleaded. 'Walter. We have to tell them the values are still there. There's to be no panic. Confidence has to be maintained.'

'Even if it leads to an almighty smash.'

'I'll pick up the pieces if it does.'

Katherine came into the bathroom and bent her head to receive his kiss. 'That's enough,' he said. 'By God, we've got to go out just now.' She turned away and looked at him sprawling in the water. It still seemed unbelievable to her that she was this man's wife, that she lay in his arms every night. It had not been easy at first. All her instincts had been to give herself to him in some kind of overwhelming surge of emotion that would make everything simple. Perhaps he had expected too much of her ... or she of him. The honeymoon had been a time of realisation that he was a man of the world and she was at heart still the girl raised in Kimberley.

That had been some time ago and it was better now ... she was pleasing him. She had quickly realised that he had been with too many other women, too many skilled women, and she had not been for him what he expected.

She loved him with a kind of desperation that sometimes dismayed her. She had had no inkling of the depth of passion he had aroused in her, a passion that was interwoven with a possessiveness and a desire to claim what was her own that she had never known till now.

On that first night in the bungalow below the ridge at the Orange Grove he had treated her with the gentle consideration he might have used to a child. 'Am I hurting you?' he asked. She had not replied, only drawing him into a deeper penetration, giving small cries and gasps. She had been afraid of his nakedness and touch when he had turned out the lamp. Then that moment of blackness, the smell of the expiring wick and suddenly the touch of his naked body against her own.

'My lovely kid. Don't be afraid of me.'

'Teach me ... show me.'

Yes, it was better now because she had learned to accept that he was a deeply restless man and that the energy he gave her was only superficially calming to him. Even on the honeymoon she had found him quickly ... not bored, but somehow prickly and behaving as if he wasn't really there. It was an idyllic place. In the drowsy heat of day the smell of orange blossom was overpowering at times. At night the bushbuck came down from the ridge to nibble the garden. They had only been there a few days when Katherine's pet dog was taken from the stoep by a leopard. They heard the dog howl and ran out too late.

'I'm going after him,' Walter said.

'Not now,' she cried, dismayed by his eagerness.

'Don't you want the cat skin for the library?' he chaffed her as he pulled his legs into his breeches and laced up the leggings.

'I'd hate it. Don't do it, Walter. Please.'

'You're not scared to be alone, are you?' He was sliding a cartridge into the breech of the Mannlicher Special, a wedding gift from her father.

'Of course I'm not scared,' she flared.

'I thought you were so fond of that dog.'

He went out with a hurricane lamp and she heard him stumbling up the *koppie*. She lay in bed, finding herself trembling with resentment. Then she heard only the wind and after a long time a distant shot, quickly followed by another. It was not that he was shooting the beautiful creature, though she hated that in spite of the dog ... it was the way he had left her with such alacrity. She turned her face into the pillow, clenching her teeth, suddenly aware that she knew nothing about this man. In her imagination of life with him it had been a kind of dreamy drifting, as in a boat together going downstream on a summer evening. The reality was this man of strange odours and sudden silences, alternately warm and indifferent.

She lay in the darkness feeling her body never so empty. Some great flying insect was blundering about the rafters, zooming and whirring and knocking. Was it always to be like this? Was marriage this way for everyone? She determined she would not allow him to see how wounded she had been. She would not let her marriage be like this. It only required an act of decision on her part ... and a willingness to relent on his. It would be alright again tomorrow.

That night for the first time in years she dreamed of her mother and that was strange because she had never seen her in the flesh.

Tonight at the dinner table with her father and husband Katherine saw that there was some kind of crisis at hand. Both men were at pains to pretend that there was nothing unusual going on. They talked of the coming prize fight with a purse put up by Barnato. A world title fight, it was being called. A straight up, knock-down bare-fister. Anecdotes flowed and there was a superficial good humour. She was glad to leave them to their port and cigars and almost before she had closed the door she heard her father's voice raised.

'A way must be found...'

'I heard today that Penlynne's onto something...'

'That *muishond.*'

'Do you want to listen, Josh? Alright then. Whatever it is he's playing it pretty close to his chest but the word's out that he's off to Europe.'

'It's that wife of his...'

'It's more than that. Maybe if you made an approach to him before he leaves. You know what it would mean if he comes up with the answer. It could be a case of winner takes all.'

Rawlinson's heavy face darkened. He turned and spat into the empty fireplace. At the mention of Penlynne all his resentment for the Kimberley crowd flared up. They had sent Penlynne up here to undermine him, to seize what he had made for himself. Approach him on bended knees? Never!

'It could be to your advantage to get together with this man. He's smart as a whip. Your two groups, the big ones; no point in trying to buck each other. That's the way to hell, Josh. Talk to him. Make him see that it's for the good of the Rand that you're approaching him. If this chemist...'

'What chemist? Who are you talking about?' It had come into Rawlinson's mind with a jolt that when he was last overseas he had read of a Scotch chemist ... what was the name?... tinkering with the use of gold in photography. He had thought nothing of it, having been preoccupied with his search for the Park Lane house and his plans for a private collection of paintings and sculpture. He'd had Katherine on his mind. Marriage for her. London's financial world had been cool towards him and he'd spent his energies trying to turn the stream of capital towards his interests.

'A man called MacForrest,' Gardiner said.

That was the fellow alright. The piece had been in a technical journal and had hinted at a practical use for the solubility of gold in a solution of cyanide. The thought sobered him. Suppose Penlynne had already moved to secure the process? If it turned out to be workable the man could have the key to the whole reef; every gold mine's output in his pocket.

He could feel his heart pounding as his mind filled with rage and resentment.

'Are you feeling alright, Josh?' questioned Gardiner. He saw that the colour which had flooded the older man's face had receded. He was blotched and sweating. He had never seen Rawlinson take on like this before. The man had always showed himself as a rock, impervious to pain and insult.

'Why not make a deal with him now?' he urged. 'Offer to come in with him. Share all the costs of bringing out MacForrest and setting up a laboratory or whatever it'll need.'

He put a drink into his father-in-law's hand and the older man gulped at the spirits. The hard hand wiped the thin line of his mouth under the brush mustache. What Gardiner said made sense but to go cap in hand to that man – dammit, he could crush the man under his boot like a worm. He was worth over a million sterling. The Star was still milling free ores. It was the least affected of them all. He could afford to hold on long enough to see Beit's interests crumble to nothing and Penlynne to despair. It was a long way from a test tube of cyanide and a speck of gold in a laboratory to a process that could be used on the kind of tonnage of rock the Rand was milling every month. Millions of tons. The strategy was to hold on through the coming collapse and then pick up the bargains. Go it alone. It had always been his way.

'I'll have nothing to do with that man,' he said dourly.

'Let me talk to him, Josh,' the American urged. 'I won't make it look like an approach from you.'

'Keep away from him, do you hear!' Rawlinson went to the window and stood with his hand on the drapes, looking out over the town and the growing dumps that represented his triumph so far. His head was bursting. By God, he would grind that upstart Penlynne into the dust. The crowd of them. Beit and Barnato – especially those two. Beit who had ruined him in Kimberley and paid him off with a beggarly twenty thousand, a sop to his conscience!

He turned to his son-in-law. 'I believed in this and I made it. I was here before any of them and I'll be here when they're bankrupt.'

'Don't count on that, Josh.'

'I've gambled before, Walter. It's meat and drink to me.'

'You're older now.'

'What do you mean?' The voice choleric, the eyes reddened, his whole mien threatening. The American shrugged and poured himself a whiskey.

'You brought me here to advise you. Don't let Penlynne get his hands on this system.'

'What system? There's no system, only a theory. By the time he's brought out MacForrest ... six months ... a year ... it'll be ruination for most of them. I went by the market today. Do you know what I saw? Furniture, pianos, carpets – anything you can think of. Tools, machinery. Stuff that took months to get here and cost a mint. Going for a song. My boy, the losers are getting out.'

As if the thought refreshed him he sat down and cut a cigar. 'I'll be Sir Josh yet. And after that – the House of Lords.'

'And then?' said Gardiner, unable to check a sardonic note.

'Then? You want to know?' The heavy head lifted in a kind of dignity that cancelled the outburst of a moment ago. 'There are people here and in London who see me in another role ... Governor of the British Transvaal.'

'What about the Dutchmen ... Kruger?'

'They've had their day. They were nothing but a bunch of trekboers with an empty treasury until I came here. It's the taxes on my mines that have built their fancy Palace of Justice, the Raadzaal. It's Rawlinson gold that's paying their officials, keeping their Zuid Afrikaansche Republiek alive with its corruption, bribery and jobs for pals.'

He leaned forward eagerly. 'There are more Englishmen ... more British in their Transvaal than Boers. Johannesburg's worth more than all their Boer republics put together. And we have no say in anything. We're here by the grace of that old tyrant who hates the "*Uitlanders*". When I was in London last ... oh yes, I had talks with ... no names ... the Foreign Office. They can see the way the wind must blow.'

'Are you talking about annexation?'

'I'm talking about the vote for every man in the Transvaal. Not the Kaffirs, mind. Every white man. But that's another story.' He gave a toss of the massive head and a snort and waved Gardiner away. 'I don't need anyone's advice. I can see my way clear to the end. I don't want to talk of it any more, not another word, Walter. How's my girl? How's Kathy?'

'She's well, Josh. Very well.'

'Always been strong and healthy. I'll have a healthy grandson soon, I'm glad of that.'

'Granddaughter, maybe,' laughed Walter.

'I'm looking forward to it. How's the house coming on?'

'Not finished yet.'

'Press on with it.'

'Is it wise?'

'Of course it's wise. I'm paying for it. Gift for my daughter. Best house in the Transvaal.'

The American saw it was useless to argue further. The man's mind was closed to anything but his own schemes. He had his hand on the door when Rawlinson said in a powerful voice. 'Stick with me, Walter. I'm still your best friend.'

It had the sound of a warning to Gardiner. He turned the handle of the door. The old man called after him again.

'One more thing ... I've a surprise for you and Kathy. I'm getting married again. A very good woman, my housekeeper. Say nothing to Katherine. I'll tell her myself.'

As he drove back to their temporary house that night, Katherine's head on his shoulder, Walter Gardiner congratulated himself on the way things had gone for him. His contract with Rawlinson was worked out. He was free to go anywhere he pleased and to take Katherine with him. He had thought vaguely of going up to Matabeleland and scouting the prospects there. There was more gold there than Sheba had ever taken out of it. But he couldn't take Katherine there now, not in her condition. Johannesburg was bad enough with its mud and flies in summer, its dust in winter. But it had its conveniences.

The smart thing to do was make an approach to Penlynne in the morning.

Until the meeting Gardiner knew Penlynne only as a passing face. They had occasionally exchanged nods at the club. Penlynne was never inconspicuous. Apart from his dark, genial ugliness there was his undeniable charisma. He was always surrounded, not just by those who hoped to benefit from the scraps that fell from the young lion's mouth, but by people who found him agreeable, generous-minded and quick to do a good turn. If he was making enemies besides Rawlinson it was certainly not yet evident.

They chose to meet after dark in Penlynne's office. 'Not for reasons of subterfuge, Gardiner,' Penlynne had assured him. 'It's simply more convenient.'

'I agree,' said Gardiner, understanding him perfectly.

'Let's have it then,' Penlynne said.

'I've heard you're forming a syndicate to recover gold from pyritous ore. I want to come in with you.'

'You're Rawlinson's man. You came out to advise him.'

'He's not taking my advice.'

'Are you proposing to give it to me? Sell it to me?'

'I'm proposing to do business with you, yes. My contract with my father-in-law has expired. The old man is convinced there is no future in deep level mining here. I'm convinced there is – if the pyritous ore problem is solved. Rawlinson still thinks that the reef is no more than a tilted riverbed, maybe two hundred feet wide. I believe it's more ... much more. Look here!'

He opened his briefcase and spread out calculations and diagrams. Surveyor's drawings showed the extent of the reef and where it had outcropped along a ridge of some forty miles. Penlynne knew all the names by heart. At twelve and a half penny-weights to the ton millions of ounces of gold had already come out at comparatively shallow depths.

'Not a yard of it but is owned by someone,' Penlynne pointed out.

Gardiner's finger jabbed at the chart. 'Look here ... and here! All these areas. It's only a question of drilling to intersect a diagonal at, say, two thousand feet. Deep? Dammit man, the Comstock Lode in Nevada is already down to three thousand. It's technically possible. In my opinion a syndicate should buy all the claims south of the Main Reef. They're for picking up. The South Dip, I call it.'

Penlynne was impressed by the American's grasp of the geology of the Wit Waters Rand and particularly by his theory that the gold had been depositied on the shore of a primeval sea after washing down from mountains ground to powder aeons earlier.

'I am inclined, Penlynne,' Gardiner said, pacing about, 'and

153

there's been enough geological exploration over the past few years to support this – fragmentary, it's true, and maybe visionary – to support the theory that the shores of this sea I'm talking about had a shoreline some one hundred and fifty miles long. Do you realize what I'm projecting?'

It was a concept so staggering in its implications that Penlynne hardly knew how to react. He simply lay back and let the idea pound into him. He tore open his collar. They were both sweating profusely.

'It's ultimately a question of capital,' Penlynne said. 'I believe I can raise it. We've got coal mines twenty miles away. We've got all the labour in Africa. It all hangs on this man MacForrest. If what I see in that laboratory convinces me, I'm your man. Now let's talk figures.'

Gardiner was ready. 'If I'm right, and I know I'm right, there's payable banket in the deep levels to a value of ... this figure's the estimated tonnage of ore available.'

Penlynne looked at the figures incredulously. 'Are you telling me that there are some one hundred and fifty million ounces of gold down there?' He put pencil to paper. 'You realize you're talking about some five hundred million sterling at today's prices!'

'Damn right I am. What's more, your grandchildren and mine will still be taking it out. It's only a question of having the guts to go for it, developing the technology.'

'And beating the pyrites,' said Penlynne wryly.

'I'm convinced it will be licked.'

'So am I, Gardiner. Let's drink to it!'

Penlynne took out bottle and glasses. He poured for them both without splashing a drop. Their eyes met.

'To the MacForrest Process ... and the deep levels!'

Chapter 14

For Stewart MacDonald life had suddenly blossomed. At the Park Halt where he had first caught sight of Mary she was standing somewhat to one side of the other travellers, looking along the length of the platform among the jostle and jabber, the wrangling of ricksha boys. She looked eagerly expectant and at the same time curiously isolated, as if to his eyes there was no one else there. The wild, red-cheeked girl he remembered from Ferrygate had become a heavy, broad-hipped young woman, full breasted. She wore a huge hat, veiled under her chin, and when he bent to kiss her he had felt the fabric come between their lips. He caught the odour of her from the mass of black hair coiled high on her head.

'So you're here at last, Mary. I've a cab waiting.'

As they drove they held hands and spoke hardly at all. She was looking at everything but he could not take his eyes off her. They were married at the Landdrost's office by civil ceremony as the law required.

'You're MacDonald now,' he said as they came out into the sunlight. There was quite a crowd in the street and for a moment Stewart thought they were at the court for some case or other. Then he saw in a kind of bewilderment that there were women in their best clothes and men with carnations in their buttonholes. With his arm around Mary he heard a spatter of laughter and clapping and recognised faces of men he had seen before only in working clothes. There was a brougham festooned with white ribbons and four white horses with lovers' knots in their tails and manes. Even the driver's whip was ribboned.

It was a crowd from the Scots community and almost before he knew what they were about they had been hustled into the brougham in a storm of rice. The driver flicked up his horses and a man he had never seen before stood up in the outrider's place with bagpipes and people were running from the shops to see the bride.

'You never told me,' she laughed.

'I didna know ma'self ... it's the folk at the mine.'

'Good luck, doctor. God bless ye, doctor – and the bonny bride.'

Stewart sat in a glow of pride and happiness, the ugly town transformed for him by this act of spontaneous goodwill. When they got down at the Grand Hotel, pushing through blacks and whites, there were more peltings of rice and flowers.

'Speech ... speech!' In the sudden sympathetic quiet as he looked around at their faces, he felt Mary's hand tight on his arm.

'I hadna expected anything like this...' he began. 'How did you know?'

'Did ye think ye could hide a lassie like that!'

Then the bagpipes began to squeal and bray and they were piped into the hotel to the foot of the staircase and for hours afterwards there was dancing in the street and singing in the bar. Next morning they heard that the horses had bolted with the brougham, terrified by the bagpipes, and the Zarps were called out to settle the matter of exuberant Scots toasting the bride long after hours.

Upstairs in the double room with its fresh oregon ceiling and smell of new paint they lay in each other's arms until the town fell silent, talking about memories that went back to their childhood. How she remembered him bird nesting and stealing her father's strawberries and how he had once saved her from an angry turkey. 'I wrote your name on the wall at school,' he confessed.

'You gave me a proper red face wi' that. And was it you who put a bunch of primroses in my desk?'

He couldn't remember that but she gave him the credit with eager kisses and then, very tenderly, trembling and unhurriedly, they began to find each other. Far off he could hear the mournful howling of pariah dogs scavenging the streets. She shivered in his arms.

'It's nothing to fear. Only the Kaffir dogs.'

'It's a' sae strange, Stewart.' As he felt her lips trembling on his cheek he felt a resurgence of ardour and again he found her body willing while he kept repeating, 'Oh, I love you ... I love you.'

Shaving on that first morning together he watched her from the mirror, lying in the brass bed, her hair down, in a nightdress with pink ribbons. He saw her clothing from the night before lying partly on the floor, partly on the chair, her white boots and stockings off to one side. Her bridal garter (she had surprised him with that touch) was not to be seen. There was something about the intimacy, the privacy unveiled and the trust in him implicit in the scene that moved him so deeply that he had to put down his razor and kneel at her side.

'Oh, my Mary,' he said. 'You don't know what this means to me.' He felt her hand in his hair and when he looked up he saw that her face was flushed with a rosy tenderness.

'What are we doing today?' she asked.

'Today. Well, first I'll be showing you your new home. Don't expect too much. Don't forget I warned you it's rough. I've a pony trap ... hired ... and the boy'll bring it round after breakfast.'

As they clopped through the town she laughed as she noted the greetings he received. 'You're quite the laird!'

'It's no' me they're looking at,' he said with pride.

They had the wedding photograph taken at the Berlin Salon in Pritchard Street and ordered prints for their families. He refused to sit and have her stand at his side as the German expected. It quite disturbed the man's sense of fitness as they stood side by side, holding each other's hands. Herr Winckler lifted a red face from his black cloth. The informality of it!

As Stewart drove Mary to Langlaagte he noted her reaction to the landscape of brick pits and dumps, abandoned shafts and broken machinery. He was grateful that she attempted to conceal the dismay she must have been feeling. 'I know it's strange and ugly, Mary. I'll make it right for you, I promise. You'll soon make friends. There's a Caledonian Society and good company.'

'I didna expect a paradise,' she said, giving his arm a squeeze. When they got to Langlaagte and the row of mine houses on the barren expanse of veld the door was unlocked.

'There's good soil here,' she said. He carried her over the threshold and saw with delight that the little front room had been transformed with jars of flowers. On the table there were gifts, some wrapped in brown paper, others of domestic articles standing just as they were among bottles of preserves.

'Folk here are sae kind,' she said tremulously.

'Aye, there's good and bad, but mostly good.'

It seemed to him in that moment of joy that nothing brutal or ugly could ever have happened here and that he could now work as he had never done before, not with a bitter and rebellious ambition, driven by his loneliness, but with a sense of the rightness of it. It was sentimental to think that he would do it all for Mary. But that was how he felt.

The iron and wood house was hot, hotter than anything she had ever imagined. 'It's February,' Stewart told her. 'The season's are upside down here. It'll begin to get cooler next month.'

Mary had thrown off everything but the sheet. The pillow was soaked with sweat from her mass of thick black hair. Her nightdress was like a wet rag. The sash window of the bedroom was wide open but she still had a feeling of suffocation. The fly-screening covering the glass increased the airlessness but she had to accept it for without screens the house would be filled with flies in the daytime and flying insects at night.

There were two sounds that predominated at Langlaagte. The never-ending thunder of the stamp batteries crushing rock and the shrilling of cicadas in the long grass. The one dull and heavy, like angry surf, the other thin and high-strung and nervous. At night the insects were louder. Sometimes she got up and walked up and down the stoep, the night air chilling through the wet nightclothes. Padding about on her bare feet she looked at the blaze of stars and the twinkle of lights from the mine.

On their excursions together the veld grasses and rocks seemed harsh to her. 'There's nae place ye can sit, Stewart, and there's nae a tree that ye can call a tree.'

'Well, it's Africa,' he said fondly. When he moved a stone to make a picnic fireplace he uncovered a thing with pincers like a crab, its yellow tail curved to strike with the hooked barb. He took out a specimen bottle and quickly secured it.

'Scorpion,' he grinned. 'You'll get used to it, Mary.'

'I'm hoping you're right,' she said doubtfully.

He put his arms about her. 'It's no' Ayrshire, I know, but it'll be a good place yet, you'll see.'

Before she arrived Stewart had put up some trellising on the stoep and planted a rambler rose. He brought a mine boy over to dig the red earth yard and plant maize. One of the first things he taught her was how to strip the silken tassles off and cook the corn in salt water. 'It's surely only fit for beasts,' she had said until the melting butter and the sweetness of the corn made her exclaim, 'It's nae so bad at that, Stewart.'

He saw with relief that she was settling in. It was six miles from Langlaagte to Johannesburg and she perked up at the sight of the shops, household goods, linen drapers and more than one tea shop. The horse tram ran as far as Joubert Park. There was a bandstand there among the young plane trees and a free concert every Sunday afternoon. Of the horse racing in Pritchard Street on Saturdays she didn't approve. It was too wild for her taste, with the balconies crowded and the betting and drinking.

What she found hardest to get used to was the sultriness as the clouds built up to the regular afternoon thunderstorm. The first time she heard hail on the iron roof she was terrified, and then furious to see her flowerbeds battered by chunks of ice. Torrents of red water rushed by the stoep. Then the sound of rushing and battering was over. The ground steamed and the thunder of the mills took over again. As a farm girl she had no objection to having to draw rain water from the tank under the eaves, though she spoke wistfully of those in town who had water on tap. This was healthier, Stewart assured her, though the danger of cholera from the night-soil disposal was ever present. She was accustomed to oil lamps at Ferrygate but had to smile at the idea of furniture made from the wood of packing cases which had brought out mine machinery.

Stewart was impressed and delighted by her ability to make much of a little. She cut prints and engravings from the illustrated magazines and bought cheap calico from an Indian shop in Ferreira's Camp to cover a settee made for her by the mine carpenter. She embroidered cushions. She bought a piano for five pounds in the market square. She could play little more than a few clumsy bars but to her its high polish and gentility were more important. She stood open sheets of music on it, dusting them every day, and was delighted when she managed to buy a plaster cast of Beethoven for a few pence.

'He's lost his nose,' she said, 'but you'd never notice. Things are so cheap,' she marvelled to Stewart. 'You can pick up anything ye fancy ... a sewing machine for seven shillings. Can ye imagine!'

He did not tell her that the low price of domestic goods was an ominous sign of the times. He watched complacently as she crammed the rooms of the small house with chinaware, carpets, a fine canteen of Sheffield cutlery with the silver nameplate of the previous owner still in the wood. He saw that making the kind of house that she fancied a doctor's wife should preside over was important to her.

She was invited to tea by the mine manager's wife and she was delighted when Mrs Griffiths deigned to return the compliment. Her baking was a triumph and she sang in the kitchen, nostalgic border ballads. Often he would leave early in the morning but she would never let him go without a dish of oatmeal. He was doing the work of a trained nursing sister, a dispenser and a surgeon and when he got home at night he was at the beck and call of the families around them. 'Your private patients,' Rawlinson reminded him, 'and no responsibility of the Star.' Stewart could never turn them away. He was unaware that his popularity was growing.

'You've got a way wi' you, Stewart,' Mary assured him. 'One of these days you'll have your own practice.' He did not tell her that he was still drawn to research. Every day he dealt with cases that were beyond his knowledge. Langlaagte swarmed with flies. In the height of summer not a week passed but an infant died of what they called 'the apricot sickness'. The milk sold from door to door by Boer farmers was suspect.

When he rode out to the nearest supplier he found the cattle kraal foul beyond belief. Ragged, dirty natives were milking into calabashes and tins. He blew up in anger, shouting at the uncomprehending blacks. When he described the place to Mary she reminded him that at Ferrygate the dairy was one of the sweetest places on the farm, shining with polished brass and scoured urns, always in a cheerful clutter and cool, with the smell of buttermilk and fresh butter.

She shared his indignation but she had a wonderful ability to keep the heat out of it so that a problem did not look greater than it was but seemed more approachable. 'Dinna take on so, Stewart. Rome wasna built in a day.'

Young as she was she had a way with the older mine women.

Often he would come in to find her pouring tea for some woman whose swollen eyes proclaimed a domestic upheaval. Their eyes would meet over the teapot and he would realize that this was no place for him. It amazed him how different she was from the wild girl of the woods, so full of life and a passion that had still to find direction.

'Am I enough for you, Mary ... no, tell me truly? I have so little time to be with you.'

'I'm not discontented, my love. Dinna fash yoursel'.'

'I don't deserve you,' he'd say happily.

'There's mony a true word,' she'd give him back.

A letter from her mother told her that the ship's engineer Alex MacFarlane had been lost in a typhoon in the China Sea when the vessel foundered.

Stewart found her in tears over it. 'He was a braw lad, a decent man.' It was easy to be sympathetic with her grief. She had known MacFarlane longer than him and he had not objected to her keeping a photograph of MacFarlane in his seaman's cap. A long, melancholy face that had sent him to the mirror to examine himself.

'I should send this back to his mither, puir soul.'

'Keep it,' he said. He understood that her tears were not for the man but for the link with the past that was broken. So many links broken, so many new ones to forge in a land that still, for all its fascination and challenge, dismayed her by its harshness and brutality. It was when they walked in the garden together, arms about each other, that he knew she found a special solace there that even his love could not give her.

One morning he came back to the cottage to pick up some papers. There was a pony trap hitched at the stoep. Rawlinson's driver gave him a salute. It was not uncommon to see the owner driving around his property with that air of concern for his goods that some people disliked. Stewart found him in the kitchen with a cup of tea. He was at his courtly best. No one could level with his workers better when he had to and for all they said of him, and most of it was true, he was not too big to sit in the kitchen.

He had evidently been charming Mary. She was in high spirits. He was demonstrating for her how 'right here at Langlaagte' he had panned the first gold of the reef.

'Yes, my dear, in a helmet. No, not this very one, but identical. There wasn't a pan handy.' It was a famous story, of course, but she was hearing it for the first time and was suitably impressed.

Rawlinson was dressed in a white suit and a blue cravat with a diamond pin; his boots were immaculate. His coarseness had been softened by good living but his eyes were shrewd and alert and there was no sign of diminished force.

'No, doctor,' he twinkled, 'I'm not here to steal your lovely wife. She wouldn't look twice at me. I just dropped by to see how you were settled. There's nothing like marriage. I lost my first wife ... but never mind that. I've been telling Mrs MacDonald that I hear a lot about your devotion here. Don't think that I don't appreciate what you're doing for these poor devils. I've been raising the matter of improvements with my board but they're a stubborn lot to convince. Still, I'm pressing. Today I'm here on a more personal matter. I've been telling your wife that you've got quite a reputation. You see, I hear everything that goes on.'

It was evident to Stewart that he was working towards something he doubted would be accepted.

'It's my daughter. You've met her at my table. Well, she's in her last couple of months and I want her well taken care of. You can name your fee. I'll stint nothing. You must advise me. Is it safe for her to have my grandchild here or do I send her to Europe? I don't trust your colleagues ... pox doctors and adventurers. Will you take her case, doctor?'

He laid a heavy hand on Stewart's arm.

'I'm not a specialist,' Stewart hesitated. He was near enough to this man as it was without the added burden of his daughter's pregnancy and all it implied. 'Gynaecology's not my strong point, sir.'

'Come now, you're too modest. I hear all the mothers are chasing after you.'

Stewart felt the pressure of his insistence and added to that the look on Mary's face which plainly advised acceptance and gratitude. It should have been a moment of relish, this man's coming to him. He heard himself saying with a stubbornness Mary called his 'black look' that he didn't see himself clear to manage it.

'I'm under heavy pressure here, sir. Cases coming in all the time.'

'I know all about that.' Rawlinson's colour was rising as his irritation mounted. 'Get yourself an assistant. Pick him yourself.' He clearly felt he was being blackmailed. He rose. He had a hold of himself again, taking Mary's hand and pinching her cheek. 'You'll make him see reason, my dear.'

He turned as he mounted the trap. 'She'll expect you at her residence, doctor.'

Stewart went back into the house to find Mary's face a study in anger. 'What's got into ye, Stewart? The man's your employer. He's asking you a favour ... and name your own fee. Is it no' an honour to be his family's doctor?'

They had been walking in town not long ago when she had pointed out to him a handsome couple emerging from a shop. He recognised Katherine Gardiner at once and when she nodded to him in passing Mary had been deeply impressed.

'A woman like that for your patient, Stewart. It can mean sae much to us.' He had never imagined Mary wanting more than he was able to give her and it startled him to think that she might have yearnings towards the better side of town. She was cool with him that night.

He lay for a long time staring at the ceiling and it seemed he had only just got off to sleep when he was awakened by the shock of an underground fall. It set off a reverberation that made Mary's ornaments rattle. She stirred and a moment later crept into his arms. She could not get used to rock falls and the sudden knock at the door.

'That was a bad one,' she whispered.

'Aye, heavy.' He comforted her, his senses thrilling to the feel of her body, his nostrils breathing her own special scent, a muskiness that seemed to have its source in the mass of black hair. He was finding her mouth willing when he heard running steps and the door thundered.

'Baas ... *lo smesh lapa panzi.*'

As he pulled on his clothes by candlelight he knew this was going to be a bad one. 'Tell Baas Griffiths I'm coming,' he shouted. As he laced up his boots he could hear Mary rattling in the kitchen. 'I've no time for tea,' he shouted. She was lovely in the glow of the candle in her hand, her breasts full beneath the nightdress, but her eyes were wide with alarm and she was trembling.

It hit him then that this was the real reason for her anxiety for him to take up general practice.

'You'll tak' care, Stewart love.'

'Aye!' He went out into the dark where a mine boy waited with a carbide lamp and by his face he knew that he was about to face something on a scale he had only imagined so far. There was a drive on for tonnage. Early in the week he had spoken to Griffiths about the number of minor injuries coming off shift.

'Production's falling, doctor,' the manager replied. 'We're having to crush more to get out the same values. We're into the hard stuff!'

The rock breakers were driving their teams harder than ever. They worked on contract for big money. The more rock they broke out the higher the pay so they pushed their men. Stewart had been underground several times. It seemed to him to be totally chaotic. The hollowed caverns ran in all directions off the main shaft. Blasting, drilling and rock clearing went on all the time. The whites were experienced in coal and copper. They directed the blacks with kicks, blows and exhortations. Many a man got a fist in his face and went down, then picked up his shovel or jumper and laboured on, knowing that he got good money for this madness. If he had a good *baas* he'd get enough *putu* to fill his belly when he got to the surface. Some whites laboured like fiends, directing the scores of blacks who crouched on their hams, slamming the hand drills into the rock-faces with heavy hammers, and the shovelling away of broken rock. In the clanging, cracking, reverberating caverns men were hardly recognisable for dust as they crawled and crouched among shattered reef and hammered up timbers, coughing in the dust and fumes of explosives.

Stewart had urged Griffiths to do something about the state of hygiene. Men defecated at random, drank fouled water and went on working with septic wounds caused by the handling of quartzite shattered into razor-edged fragments. Rocks crushed bare feet and careless hands. Men with wounds covered with stinking rags had been brought to him only after gangrene had already set in.

Griffiths' reply had been blunt. 'It's my belief it'll all be over in a year. Maybe we'll find gold at depth, I don't know. There's talk of test drilling down to a thousand feet. But if you can't get the ore from the milled rock it's a diminishing asset.' He had waved his arm along the length of the Reef and listed some of the best producers – The Star, Wemmer, City and Suburban, Little Wonder, Roodepoort. They were all doomed.

'Sixty miles of mining and it could all come to nothing,' he shouted above the roar of the open battery where the great iron stamps were shaking the ground.

'You see that dump? There's gold there alright. All we can do is pile it up and hope for a miracle. In the meantime is there any sense in trying to improve conditions for men who come here thinking it's another California? Nuggets as big as your fist? This is for engineers or no one, and even the big men are frightened now.' He shook his head. 'Do your best, lad.'

What Stewart might have answered was drowned by the screaming of a locomotive whistle; it was hauling coal from the Witbank colliery. Rawlinson owned that too, or a substantial part of it. The thing that Stewart marvelled at was that the workers, white and black, accepted the risks. There seemed to be no resentment among them. They were more like soldiers in their attitude of 'it can't happen to me'. One thing he had noted – you never saw a Dutchman underground. The farmers who made a good thing out of selling meat and vegetables took their money and considered them madmen.

These were the things he had mulled over many times but now, as he stumbled over the cocopan rails behind the boss boy, his mind was on what he might find down there. At the open shaft he could make out the glow of light ... yellow of candles and the white glare of carbide but the reek of shattered rock still rose from the hole where a crude iron cage was waiting to take him below.

Griffiths was waiting for him. Together they went down in the hoist, clinging to the cable. Stewart, holding his bag, shouted above the clatter of the descent. 'What happened?'

'The night shift was stoping ... blasting. The whole section came down.'

'How many men in there?'

'God knows. Could be a hundred.' Griffiths was plainly in a state of shock. He had been pulled out of his bed and was none too sober, a waterproof coat thrown over his nightclothes, his feet in rubber boots. At the foot of the shaft he grabbed a carbide lamp from a lashing boy and plunged into the reek, drawing Stewart behind him. The hanging wall gave a sudden crack overhead. Small stuff fell and they ran through it.

'Get timber under here!' Griffiths yelled at a stupefied group crouching in terror of further falls. He struck the hanging with a pinchbar. 'Where's the carpenter ... *upi lo foloman kapenta*?'

Stewart ducked under the loose hanging. It seemed to him that the whole drive might come down any moment behind him. The effect of shattering was appalling. In the lamplight the blue quartz fragments glinted in lethal shards. Now he understood the injuries he had been dealing with. Suddenly he came on a chunk of dark meat with a gleam of bone, a hand sticking abruptly out from a crushing mass, fingers extended. He saw the bright red and his mind told him ... arterial blood. Then a grey ooze of brains mixed with fragments of skull.

'Jesus,' he whimpered. He heard Griffiths hoarse cry as the manager pointed ahead. The main drive had collapsed for twenty yards. Winzes and raises were choked. An iron cocopan had been crushed like a tin can. Stout timbers of pine and blue-gum were shredded as if a hurricane wind had stripped a forest. Water dripped and glistened from ruptured pipes.

They paused in the ominous silence. Griffiths pointed.

'Up there ... there's where they are.' They listened. A groan came out of the veil of dust. They crawled forward. Griffiths held up his light. The man was pinned down by the arm. By his trousers and boots he was a white miner. His dusty face was unrecognisable but the open eyes shone in the flare of carbide. Stewart crept up beside him.

'There's only one way to release him, Griffiths.'

Griffiths nodded. 'We'll get you out, lad,' he said.

'Hold the light closer,' Stewart urged. He clamped the gauze over the grimy and distorted face and let the sweet, heavy liquid drip into the fabric. His senses reeled as fumes rose in the confined space.

'Hold the light steady,' he ordered Griffiths, laying out tourniquet, scalpel, forceps and amputation knife. With his amputation saw he turned to the inert figure. 'I'll have to take the arm...' He was saying it for himself. The man was unconscious.

Chapter 15

Owen Davyd recovered consciousness to find himself in a room with a strange woman bending over him and an excrutiating pain in his shoulder. He tried to get up. 'Where are my mates?' he groaned. In the fever which followed the amputation he had drifted for days in a fantasy that mingled the reality of the rockfall at Rawlinson's Star and the never entirely discarded memory of falling timbers and the fire in the Rhonda Valley pit disaster of his youth.

When the hanging uttered its warning crack he had shouted his Kaffirs away from the workface. His Cornish mate was at the drill, deaf and cursing as the heavy Ingersoll slogged into the rock with brutal percussion. Owen ran in under the hanging where he had been knocking up timbers, to pull his mate clear. At that moment the hanging wall came down. As he lay trapped, still conscious, he could see the broken cavern by the glimmer of hundreds of candles perched on ledges. It was like a page from the Gustav Dore engravings in the family Bible – black fiends in wreathing smoke and dust.

When the fever had passed he knew that the woman was Mary MacDonald, wife of his shipboard friend. They had brought him into their house to recover. He lay in bed from where he could see Mary's vegetable garden through the open door and watch her moving along the rows of beans with a bucket drawn from the rainwater tank. His eyes would dart around the small house, bright with Mary's possessions. It was almost as if he was home again amongst cheerful, familiar things. Bits and pieces, cut paper on kitchen shelves and bright crocks. She even polished the brass of the sink. It brought tears to his eyes. It was like his grandmother's home in the valley. Strange how he measured that time against a happiness that had eluded him ever since. Men had grown bitter in the valley and he had been raised in hard times. The owners had become ever more demanding and unyielding and where his father had gone down the pit cheerfully, drawing good money in his younger days, by the time Owen was old enough to follow wages had fallen and every value had changed.

From small family concerns the mines had become huge agglomerates and the master to whom his father had given a cheerful 'good day' had become an unknown who did not even live in the town.

He had time in the weeks that passed to reflect on many things. But chiefly he had made up his mind the way his life would go from now on. He could dress himself and shave with one hand. He sat in the sunshine getting brown from the waist up. Sensitive about his stump, he joked about it.

Stewart had brought his gear from the single quarters, among other things his battered copies of *The Class Revolution* and Darwin's *The Evolution of Species*. They were like a light in his mind. They made sense where there had been no sense. He had been introduced to these and other works in Cardiff where he was a member of the Workman's Mutual Improvement Society. Those had been thrilling hours. His young mind had been fired as they read and discussed papers they had written on vegetarianism, Darwin and Ruskin. His own paper on Carlysle's *French Revolution* was received with amazement. Andrew Jenkins, a foreman carpenter, had taken him aside afterwards and asked him how he felt about joining a general worker's union.

Now, as he sat under the African sun listening to the roar of the reduction works, hearing the sudden jabber of blacks going by, he wondered why he had hesitated. Had he been afraid to be called a radical, a socialist? Was he only a paper enthusiast for the cause of the workman?

After the fire at the pit he had gone to Cardiff as a trained carpenter and timberman. He got there in time to find eight thousand workers out on strike. He had never imagined a situation where men, fathers of families, could walk the streets, desperate and without a penny.

He found Mary MacDonald sympathetic but uncomprehending.

'...it's because you're a farm girl,' he cried. 'Look, Mary, you've all your life been concerned with the seasons, the natural rhythms. Men are not beasts and beasts are what the capitalists have made of the worker. It's ignorance and oppression and the Church hand-in-glove with the oppressor.'

She was bewildered by the torrent of words.

'Why don't you do something if that's what you think?'

'I'm only a blabbermouth.'

'But you believe in this ... socialism.'

'I've never been a leader, always too ready with words.'

'You could tell them, surely?'

'I'm afraid, Mary, afraid to let loose the anger in me.'

'Don't do it in anger,' she said calmly.

He was grateful for the solid sense of the young woman. How could he tell her what he had seen in those weeks in Cardiff? They'd be meaningless to a girl who had grown up with open skies over her head. Yet he found himself continually returning to the subject.

'It's hard not to be bitter,' he told her. 'Sixty-five men died in that fire, in the Rhonda pit; good men, fathers of children, lads too. No safety precautions, cages too small to take them to surface in time. Men at the workface walking a mile to the shaft from workface. How do you think I felt when an older man gave up his place in the cage for me? Get the next one, he said. And there never was no next one ... and him knowing it.'

'Don't talk of it,' Mary comforted. His thin, hard frame was shaken beyond his control. The anger gushed on. 'After I left the valley I walked to Cardiff looking for work. Anything. It was hell for the working man. Dockers were out on strike, owners called out the soldiers, bloody dragoons on great horses. Drove them up street like cattle ... flat of the blade ... whack-whack! I can still hear it and down under the hooves. All they was doing ... protesting conditions. Employers brought in what they called 'free labour', non-union men, to break the strike. Well, they won and six thousand men were left on the streets without a halfpenny. Rest went back on boss's terms. That's when I started reading Marx and Engels.'

'What will you do?' she asked one morning as they sat together on a bench on the back stoep, she stringing beans, he slicing them clumsily with his one hand. 'Will you go home?'

He had felt that his time in this house was drawing to a close. Not that there was any pressure on him; only that it had to come. Besides, he understood now that for all their good-heartedness

Stewart MacDonald had passed over the borderline that divided the workers from the advantaged. He knew Stewart's beginnings and he admired him for his struggle. But the division was there.

'I'm thinking about it,' he told her.

Six weeks after the accident the mine manager paid his first visit. 'How are you, Owen? I hear you're making progress.'

'I'll manage, Mr Griffiths,' said Owen, fumbling a charge of tobacco into his pipe, tamping it with a blackened forefinger and striking a light.

He guessed what was coming. The Government Mining Inspector had called for an enquiry. He was going to be asked to give evidence. Was this not what he had been waiting for? A chance to speak out?

'There's an opening in the White Time Office, Owen,' Griffiths said. 'Would you be interested?'

'I might at that.'

'There's no workman's compensation, if that's what you're looking for.'

'I'm thinking that I'll have something to say at the enquiry, Mr Griffiths. My mate operating two sloggers, taking another man's job – no fault of his, owner's orders. No time for safety precautions.'

'The job Mr Rawlinson is offering's on the Witbank Colliery.'

'Nicely out of the way then.'

'The money's not fancy, but good enough. I'd take it if I were you. There's not much going for cripples. Better make your mind up quick.'

Griffiths rose and thanked Mary MacDonald for the offer of tea and gave her his wife's greetings and an invitation to supper on Sunday. Fury flared in the Welshman's breast and he fought to control himself and appear indifferent. He heard himself saying with unaccustomed calm. 'As the only survivor it'd be nice and convenient if I disappeared. No enquiry. Matter closed.'

'You can't fight them yourself, Owen,' Mary said.

'I know it. That's why I feel so impotent.'

'Take the offer, Owen. It's not charity.'

'You're right, girl. It's blackmail.'

He had been earning a pound a shift as a shaft timberman and at this moment he had some forty pounds laid by. He had always been a good comrade at the single quarters and at the boarding table he was regarded as a wit. He had not blown his pay on drink and gambling. Some of his friends were even buying shares on the stock exchange. This atmosphere of good money and a chance for a quick win was meat and drink to most of them. It was why they were here in the first place. It was not good ground for trade unionism or craftsmen's guilds and wretched soil for an outcry against the capitalists. There was a mood of recklessness on the workers and if a man dropped out of his job there were ten to take his place. The wastage of human material was sickening but while the fever for gain lasted there could be no effective protest. From one end of the reef to the other it was a whirlpool of workers of all kinds and every trade humping their packs from mine to mine, totally without organisation, without brotherhood.

As he sat in the sun in the MacDonalds' backyard Owen felt with growing conviction that fate had brought him to South Africa. It was an extraordinary realisation, humbling and not a little frightening, to feel one had been chosen. He saw what was needed was a focus of anger and that would hardly come when contract workers were earning a hundred pounds a month and every night in every bar was a roaring carnival. In the meantime, had he any choice other than to grit his teeth and take the job Rawlinson offered?

A few days later Mary found him packing his gear and tools. 'I'm taking the job,' he admitted reluctantly. 'And thank you for all your kindness, I'm not going to forget it. If ever I can do you a good turn...'

They had a bit of a singsong round the piano that night. He felt quite animated and threatened to round up all the Welshmen on the property and sing Land of My Fathers. Stewart threatened to do the same with a hundred Scotsmen, piping and wailing Will ye no' Come Back Again? Then they sat silently and in the distance the mills pounded and pounded. They parted next morning, not without a pang.

Owen Davyd never told them that by the time he went to Griffiths about the promised job it was already taken and the Mines Inspector had signed off the monthly report without demanding an enquiry.

Owen was on his own and he knew what he had to do.

Even on a noisy Saturday night, of all the lodging houses in

171

Claim Street Mrs Ferreira's was the one where almost every door onto the long stoep stood open. Shirt-sleeved men brawled and sang and hurled empties into the road. It was the establishment between two canteens and the one which figured most prominently in the *landdrost*'s court record. Zarps sent there to keep order had their helmets knocked off regularly. Mrs Ferreira collected six pounds a month from each of thirty odd boarders, each of whom was entitled to share a room with three others and the last man in at night slept on the floor where he was lucky if the vermin did not carry him off by morning.

Miems Ferreira was one of those Boer women who had early on decided that the only difference between the *rinderpest* and the *uitlanders* was that one day God would take pity on the four-footed beasts. In the meantime she saw it as her duty to relieve miners, artisans, pen-pushers and shop assistants of their wages. You brought your own blankets and washed in a bucket in the yard. Mealtimes were a brawl down the length of the packing case tables under the all-seeing eye of texts printed in High Dutch. She was tall, angular, gaunt and manless and she ruled with a tongue like a *sjambok* over the scrawny blacks who scrubbed floors and fetched firewood.

She did have her softer moments when she looked at this town and its thousands of newcomers as a wonderful manifestation of the Lord's providence to her. So many golden-fleeced sheep to be sheared. She had banked her week's takings when Owen Davyd clumped onto her stoep with his empty sleeve and his shabby gear and she was feeling benign and motherly. Why this should have been so she could not have explained. Crippled miners were no novelty and poor payers.

'Can you pay a month in advance ... six pounds?' He nodded and when she had seen the colour of his money she showed him where to sling his gear in one of the rooms in a square compound next to the iron lean-to where the kitchen smoked.

Owen Davyd noted two iron cots and a torn grass mat, no window and hardly a hair's breadth between the beds. A guttered candle, dirty blankets and a stink of male sweat completed the furnishings. 'You're lucky,' she told him. 'The man in that bed ... yesterday he died. The lungs. *Skof is op die tafel* at six and the men is hungry. And the Kaffir girl bring your tea in the morning.'

'It's not Buckingham Palace,' he grinned, 'but I'll take it.' He laid out his gear on the empty bed and went out to look for a room in town and a signwriter to paint the door with the words: 'Union Organiser. General Trades and Mining'. It was harder than he had imagined. Every room in every building was taken at high rents and even before completion. He had to be satisfied with a lean-to against a livery stable where a blacksmith clanged and hammered in a stench of burning hooves and horse urine.

As Stewart MacDonald entered the driveway of the Rawlinson mansion he noticed that the young trees had grown tall since he was last there. He caught the heavy scent of roses from well dunged beds and from the side of the house he heard the whirr of a mower and smelt the newly cut grass. In the open coachhouse he saw the gleam of coachwork and harness and heard the cheerful whistling of a young English stableman teaching a native to currycomb a pair of fine coachhorses. Everywhere he saw the appurtenances of established wealth. Rawlinson was admittedly a millionaire. Stewart was conscious of his dusty boots as he jerked the lion-headed bell-pull. The door was opened by an English housemaid who gave him a curtsy and beckoned him in to a lofty hall where the stained glass of the door made jewelled lights on the dazzle of white marble.

'Take the doctor's hat, Ellen,' he heard. He knew Mrs Rawlinson of old but was not prepared for the change in her appearance. It was not so much the clothes as her bearing. Previously she had had the look of a woman who knew her position to a hair in the home of a widower. A pleasant firmness mixed with deference. Now he saw that she had assumed her new position with an added firmness, as if she were ready to challenge anyone who might dispute a housekeeper's right to marry the richest man in the Transvaal. There was authority in the way she held out her hand to him. 'Please come upstairs, doctor. Katherine and her husband live in the north wing. Their house is no' yet ready and the bairn will likely be born here. He's away a lot, her husband, so it's as well she's wi' her father.'

She opened a door off the landing. 'Katherine, he's here ... Dr MacDonald.' A slight softening of her expression as if pleased by their common Scots blood, and him a thorough, conscientious man already with a reputation. 'I'll see you on the way out, doctor,' she said and he took it as imperative and not a social pleasantry. How had Katherine taken the new situation, he wondered.

She was lying on a chaise longue at the window. The shutters were closed and late afternoon sunshine streamed through in golden bars that striped the floor. He was startled by her appearance. Some women bloomed in pregnancy. Katherine's thickened body and the slight oedema of the lower limbs indicated the last two months of pregnancy. Her hair was carefully dressed and her clothing loose. Her face was paler than he remembered, with a tendency to puffiness and her eyes dark-circled. The moment he saw her he could understand her father's anxiety.

Though the possibility of one of the toxaemias of pregnancy seemed unlikely, Katherine's admission of headaches and vomiting might be the first sign of albuminuria. Her blood pressure was higher than he liked but not high enough to be alarming. Was she sleeping well? Was she resting these hot afternoons? Was her appetite good? Vomiting? Well, it sometimes persisted throughout the pregnancy.

'Now if you'll undo your things I'd like to sound your chest.'

She seemed to hesitate. 'Yes ... yes, of course.'

As he held the disc against her chest he saw the heaviness of the full breasts and the wide circle of darkened pigmentation, the prominence of the nipples. He listened for foetal heartbeats. He smiled at the lusty sound and felt her relax.

'Now if you'll just allow me to examine the position, Mrs Gardiner.' He rinsed his hands in the large china basin, pouring cold water from the ornamented jug while she removed her clothing. He probed her with clinical coldness. The uterus had risen through the pelvic brim and was just below the umbilicus. The position of the child was just as it should be.

'My father thinks I should have the baby in Europe.' He guessed she was pressing him for a denial of this. 'I'd rather it were here. I know my husband would want it.'

Now that she had recovered from her uncertainty and rearranged her clothing some of her colour had returned. In spite of the change in her features he was struck by the fine bone structure and her splendid dark eyes. He heard himself asking if Mr Gardiner was well.

'Oh, Walter ... yes. He has to travel a lot on mining affairs. He's not here at the moment.'

He thought he detected a slight tone of distress in her manner when she spoke of Gardiner. He said something about avoiding a sexual relationship during the last six weeks and she appeared not to hear. He turned to say goodbye at the door and saw that she had lain back with an expression of low-spirited weariness strange in a young woman her age and one he remembered for her liveliness on board *The American*.

Muriel Rawlinson intercepted him in the hall. 'You can give me your report, doctor. I'll see it gets to Katherine's father.'

'Thank you, Mrs Rawlinson, but I would like a few words with Mr Gardiner.'

'Do that verra thing doctor ... if ye can find him.'

The flash of stiff-mouthed housekeeper betrayed the servant she had been. Then she corrected herself. 'Very well, doctor. I shall certainly give him your message to see you the minute he returns. In the meantime, I tak' it you'll see Katherine again in a few days. Is she weel?'

'Well enough,' he said formally.

'Ellen, the doctor's hat, if you please.'

As Stewart took his hat from the maid he noticed that the girl had been over it with a hatbrush. He felt himself growing hot and that infuriated him as he pushed his bicycle down the gravelled path and paused at the gate to put on his trouser clips. Then he was flying down the hard red road towards the town, suddenly laughing his head off. There was something about pretentiousness that he found quite ridiculous. As he whizzed past people he knew he guessed they stopped to look back after him. I'll be one of the town characters just now if I dinna watch it, he grinned.

Chapter 16

Dorothy Penlynne went down by train to the docks at Southampton with her husband. They had the compartment to themselves. They were very silent. Everything that had to be said had been spoken and they were both feeling rather forlorn. Looking at the sweet, almost demure face beneath the veil, Penlynne was reminded of the brightness of her hazel eyes when she lit up with excitement, which was often enough. She was still an enthusiast, thank God. Her small feet peeped out beneath the hem of the travelling suit and he remembered his shock, the sheer physical thrill he had first experienced when he saw her naked ankles and the superb swell of calf. Not pretty, no, but a face one remembered for its vitality. Excellent white teeth and yes, a smile that made you overlook the nose that was less than perfect. Looking at her gazing so pensively out of the steamy window he thought: I believe if you asked me now I'd take you out with me and to blazes with Kitty.

Her gaze suddenly challenged him. Too loudly he said, 'I asked Wernher to renew the lease of your apartment, Dotty. If you decide to come out it can simply expire or he can make it available to company people on furlough. Alfred Beit is very run down.'

'I don't think I like the idea of others using it,' she said. She understood well enough that his renewal of the lease had come as an answer to the unspoken thing between them. It illustrated the hesitation on both sides for her to return to South Africa. Renewing the lease meant he was prepared to wait a little longer to have her at his side in Johannesburg. He had been so understanding during his visit, just like the old adoring Penny who could refuse her nothing.

Her gaze returned to the rainy landscape. Penlynne saw her reply as meaning that she was still uncertain about resuming her life with him. As the rows of gloomy warehouses went by, some of them suddenly illuminated with those shafts of pure light she associated with English landscape painting, so that they were momentarily transformed, painting she had been so delighted to share with him, he was thinking that this new Dorothy had so much more to offer than mere sex. Did it really matter so much in the challenges he would have to face out there? He was enchanted by the change in her, the evidence of a growing maturity. What a woman she would be in her thirties! The bright but rather awkward girl he had married had become a woman of fashionable taste, not a taste imposed on her by others but her own. She had opinions on art and politics which had been respectfully listened to in more than one salon.

It had amazed him to hear her outspokenness on the duty of the British nation to civilise and rule in South Africa. At one dinner, attended by Joseph Chamberlain, the Colonial Secretary, the entire table had been hushed to listen to her.

'A very interesting woman, Mrs Penlynne,' Chamberlain observed to him over the port. 'Colonial born, I understand. Perhaps we can keep in touch, Penlynne.'

He had no idea what the man meant but it had come to Penlynne with a shock that he had grossly underrated this woman and he had the first inkling in his life that all things were not accomplished by men.

Her clothes were a pleasure to him. Costly, but a reflection of his improved financial status since becoming Beit's manager in Johannesburg. Wives of wealthy men Penlynne had known in Kimberley had introduced Dorothy to *haute couture* and when he rode with her in Rotten Row heads turned. She showed particular feeling for painting and sculpture and her taste in fine furnishings, fabrics and costly *objets d'art* indicated that she would be the *chatelaine par excellence* in the new home they had spoken of building in Johannesburg ... if all went as he hoped.

Now as the docks approached Penlynne put these musings aside. He hoped to heaven that MacForrest had not missed the connection from Scotland to Southampton. The man was erratic. Dorothy's lowering of her veil and the shadowy blueness of it hazing her cheek reminded him of how she had raised the veil the day he arrived and their lips had met in what was for him as much a question as a greeting, sweet though her lips had been.

She had been medically examined in both London and Paris

and a small operation had been effective in restoring the potency of the fallopian tubes closed by inflammation.

They had managed a weekend in Paris where they were equally delighted by the elegance and refinement of French life into which they were introduced through Penlynne's friendship with Jules Porges, the diamond merchant he had known so well in Kimberley. He saw that this was Dorothy's real element and that she had taken to it as if she had never been raised in a wood and iron shanty in the dust, heat and squalor of the diggings. It was ironic, perhaps, that Kimberley had begun to improve socially just at the time he brought her to Johannesburg ... well, it would work out.

She had been warm and loving to him and put a good face on it when his desire overcame his reluctance to force himself on her. On the ferry back to Folkestone she had put her head close to his. 'Would you be happy if I were to fall pregnant?'

'I'd be delighted, Dotty.'

'I'll cable if I am,' she said.

It was a moment when he might well have urged her to come back with him. But the unspoken had stood between them. For her part she was aware that Penlynne had an eye for women and they responded to his easy charm. Many of his associates here in London had the means to support the fast women seen in the upper echelons of society, at the Savoy, the races, at the very places she most admired for their chic and indeed, she could not but admire them for their insouciance, their insolent indifference to opinion.

Dorothy knew that if she did not return to Johannesburg with him at once it would be a long time before she saw him again, perhaps even a year. She did not like to imagine him acting in the way of his associates. She had tried to reassure herself by assuming that his business affairs would make him too busy to think of such things. When she hazarded the question about his loneliness without her and would it not be better if she accompanied him he had parried it.

And now this matter of the lease...

As the train pulled into the dock siding he leaned across suddenly and put a long flat case into her gloved hands. 'Don't open it now,' he smiled as he kissed her cheek through the veil. And then, as if he had kept it as a final discouragement to her return,

'Think about the new house. Look out for furnishings and fabrics. Don't spare anything. Get a good architect to make some preliminary sketches and send them out. But don't count on it. I may get back to the Transvaal and find it's all over.'

Once he was on the docks he was preoccupied. There were many people he knew and she saw old friends too. But he was on the lookout for the Scotch chemist and in a fever in case the man would miss the boat. In a way it was a relief to Dorothy when Barney Barnato turned up, greeted her and went up the gangway with a flock of pressmen at his heels. She thought he looked older and less than normally buoyant, but as vulgar and common as ever. He would never be one of *'le monde'*, she thought, whereas Penlynne carried his new status as if born to it.

Alexander MacForrest was supervising the loading of crates. Several were marked 'Cyanide/Poison'. The Scotsman was watching complacently as dockers swung the crates into the hold. 'There's enough poison in that to kill the population of London,' he remarked as Penlynne greeted him. He was a cheerful, bony man, red-faced and red-haired, careless in his clothing, his shoes stained by chemicals. Penlynne introduced him to Dorothy as 'the man who's going to save our skins'.

She watched *The Scot* until it was out of sight down the Thames. In the train to London she opened his gift – a case of carefully matched pearls with the note, 'Since diamonds are so cheap and you are ever dear.' She wept a little and as soon as she was in her apartment sat down to write him.

The Scot had been at sea several days before Penlynne discovered that Barnato was aboard. He was keeping to his stateroom. It seemed unlike the man who was noted for his exuberance and conviviality, adept at witty off-the-cuff speeches and who invariably put up prizes for the ship's fancy dress ball. The whisper went around that he was ill. He had been to London to see specialists and he was only returning to South Africa 'on account of the situation'.

There is always 'a situation' out there, thought Penlynne. He sent in a note with a steward. When he saw Barnato he was shocked by the change in his appearance. He was sitting up in bed surrounded by papers. He looked old for a man in his early forties but his greying hair had been carefully quiffed and tinted by his man and he was shaven.

What Penlynne noted at once was his apprehensive look and his gathering up of his papers with trembling hands. 'A minute ... just a minute. Take these, Wilson. A cigar and a drink for Mr Penlynne. Well, Pen, me ole cock sparrow, I've 'ad an exhaustin' time in Lunnon. Seen everyone from the Lord Mayor to the Home Secretary. Did you see Rhodes? Well, he's been there drummin' up support for his Charter Company. He wants Matabele gold to finance this looney idea of his – a railway from Cape to Cairo. Every shopgirl in Lunnon's wearing diamonds ... two a penny. The supply has got to be controlled. All the crowned heads of Europe are fighting for a piece of Africa. No, Pen, things are not what they was. The old days in Kim when I slept under a sheet of corrugated iron and was on me uppers. Where's it all gone to, Pen? The comradeship, the good times!

'Now I'm chairman of De Beers and Christ knows what else. I'm an old man already. Making that first million, that was it, Pen. You'll do it, you'll make it yet. You're ambitious and you've got the right people behind you. If it don't all fall apart.'

He fell back on the pillows and his man put a glass of water to his lips. 'There's nothing in it, Pen. It's the day of the politicians, the big carve up. We show the Dutchmen what their country's worth and they bleed us white with taxes, the bastards. It's bribes and jobs for pals and enemies in high places ... enemies everywhere. I'm weary of it and sick to the 'eart. There's going to be a smash up, Pen. England won't stand for Kruger's nonsense, treating us like dogs. They'll have a war. It'll all be for nothing. The Dutchmen will fight, you know. They already beat us at Majuba and they're getting arms from the Huns.'

His pince-nez fell from the bridge of his nose and he lay exhausted on the pillows. It was hard to remember that this was the swaggering little genius who had pulled off some of the biggest financial coups ever heard of. His weakness was his awe of men with the right pedigree and the right education. They wouldn't let a Jew be a member of the Kimberley Club. They said it was a fact that Rhodes's offer to get him elected to the club had been decisive in their fight against each other for sole possession of the Kimberley mines. Talk about Esau selling his birthright for a mess of potage.

Barnato ranted on for an hour. 'By God, Pen, I've worked harder than ten men and if I've made a fortune it's because I was the best man. Some win, some lose. That's the game and no man can say he came to Barnato to ask a favour and got turned down. If I die tomorrow I know there's enough for my wife and kids. Can a man do more than that? I'm tired, Pen, tired out, and there's nothing but trouble waiting for me out there ... this pyrites business. It's going to be the end of us all.'

Penlynne listened in silence, sometimes responding with a nod, watching with one eye the growing ash on his cigar. It was like some augury. If it fell before Barnato finished talking it would be significant. But in what way? Barnato could see nothing but defeat ahead. Suppose he was right? Suppose MacForrest was an impractical man, incapable of turning theory into practice? He was remembering the scene in the laboratory, the bitter, penetrating stench of potassium cyanide fumes. He believed he had seen the incredible happen there, MacForrest saying, 'After the solution has been decanted from the undissolved residues, we get the gold by precipitating the solution on zinc...'

'Yes, but can it be done in quantity?'

'Why not? It only requires extension of the apparatus.'

It was in his mind to tell Barnato what he had seen, tell him that the man who could change everything was on board. Instead he rose. 'They're missing you on the sports committee, Barney.'

'I've no heart for it, Pen.'

'Come on, man. Put on your clothes. A walk around the deck'll blow the cobwebs away.'

'Tomorrow, mebbe.'

The Barnato of ten years ago would have had his gaze firmly fixed on a way out of the impasse and on the next million. He had never cared a damn about the politics of the Transvaal but he knew to a penny how much it cost to put the right official in his pocket. He knew how to talk the market up and down. The tune Barnato had piped at breakfast had Johannesburg dancing all day. The old Barnato would have known every detail of the deal with MacForrest by now. He'd have been in on it and the wires would be humming. It was pathetic to see this little man who had boasted that the market value of his holdings was ten times greater than their issued capital. 'All bluff, Pen. All done by mirrors. The old sleight of 'and!'

Penlynne's heart was racing. If men of Barnato's calibre had lost confidence it meant their grip on the Rand was slackening. How wrong they were to throw in now. He walked the deck alone. He felt incredibly elated. *The Scot* was three days past Tenerife in mild blue sea with flying fish scudding away from her prow. The mailship from Cape Town was expected to pass about midday. There would be the usual exchange of signals. The coming ship was eight days out from South Africa and she'd carry the latest news.

The passing of two steamboats in that immensity of ocean was always a thrill. It was seen first as a smudge of smoke on the curve of the horizon. Then the white hull would emerge as it were from the other side of the earth. Cheers and scarves waving. Signal flags snapping. Flash of lamps.

Penlynne had been invited onto the bridge. He was sipping a glass of sherry with other favoured passengers when the cry went up. 'There she is!' Signal lamps began to blink. Penlynne went close to hear the yeoman of signals spelling out the message. He could hardly believe the sentence growing on the pad. 'Panic on Rand ... Johannesburg Stock Exchange crash ... gold shares half in value ... trains from city packed.'

Then there came a bellowing of sirens. White plumes of steam stabbed the almost unbearable blue of sea and sky. Black smoke belched as full steam was resumed. Already the ship with the news was dwindling. There was a hubbub about him; he saw dismay on many faces. He left the bridge abruptly. He wanted to be alone, to let no one see the elation he could hardly repress. It was as if the heavens had opened and he had heard a voice cry 'Your time has come! This is the chance you've been waiting for.' He ran down the steps towards his cabin. Before he had reached it he had made up his mind. He would buy, buy, buy. He was in a fever to get to Cape Town and the cable office. The train north would take only two days, fourteen hours. In the meantime he must think calmly, logically. Plan his strategy for the future. And keep his mouth shut. Assume the gloomy look of others caught up in the whirlwind of inflated values, trading in paper.

He rose at a knock at his cabin door. 'Who is it?'

'MacForrest, Mr Penlynne.'

Penlynne saw at once that MacForrest was in a state of alarm. 'They tell me it's panic out there in Johannesburg. Does it look as if we're going to get there too late? I'd have liked the opportunity to test my process.'

'You'll have your chance. I believe in your process. Keep it to yourself and you'll be well repaid. I'll cover all your expenses and we'll set up your test plant if we're the only two men left on the Rand.'

'Aye, but if they leave, what then?'

'They'll be back, never fear.' Penlynne did not add 'And when they do it'll be to find that everything's in my pocket.' Beit had the resources to back him in all he planned and he was confident he would.

For the next few days he walked the decks and sat up late into the night reading the report given him by the American engineer Walter Gardiner after the latter's late night visit to his office shortly before he left for London.

Since then Penlynne had wondered how Gardiner had come by his knowledge of MacForrest and the agreement they had tentatively arranged even before their meeting. Was it something he had said in an unguarded moment? If so, to whom? Someone who knew them both. In a moment of shock he had thought: Kitty? He had instantly rejected it and yet ... he could not always be with her. Secrets were hard to keep in Johannesburg.

They were a day off Cape Town. *The Scot*'s steam yacht hull which had made her the fastest ship afloat was sliding gracefully down the first of the long blue slopes of the Cape 'rollers', as they called the swell where the two oceans met. Penlynne steadied himself at the rail. He was framing the telegraph, for the hundredth time, which he would get off to Gardiner the moment he landed. 'Buy South Dip claims on my authority.' He had no doubt that Alfred Beit would back his judgement and if he didn't it would be a *fait accompli*. Gardiner would strike a hard bargain for his knowledge and skills. But he knew his mining and one must be generous as well as bold.

Chapter 17

There were times when Muriel Rawlinson wondered if her husband's disinclination to hear what she said was due to increasing deafness or to the obstinacy of a fifty-five year old man who had had his own way all his life. He had become surly and uncommunicative in the last few months. The flare up of zest he had enjoyed at the time of their marriage was over. Then he had driven her over her properties far and wide, showing her with pride the extent of his holdings in coal and engineering as well as gold mining.

She was twenty years his junior and a handsome woman. In the years she had kept house for him she had admired his energy, his power to make decisions and his authority. That she might share his bed some day had seemed unlikely. She had been a good servant, dutiful and loyal ... and sometimes disapproving. This business of women who came in closed cabs late at night – she had always showed him a tight face next morning or asked him for a donation to the building fund for the Presbyterian kirk.

One day before he had suggested marriage she had come on her employer sitting heavily in his armchair. She had never seen him in such a mood of despondency. Impulsively she had knelt at his side and taken his hand, his huge work-scarred hand with its crushed fingernail, incongruous against fine linen and the great diamond he wore on his thumb. He had been taken aback and touched. When she rose, flustered by her boldness, he detained her.

'I'm a lonely man, Muriel Ferguson,' he said. 'You lost your husband at Majuba years back, so you know what it is to be lonely.'

'I do, sir.'

'Do you know I've taken a lease on a Park Lane house in London and I'm thinking of retiring there and leaving a manager here. There's an ill wind blowing, Muriel. I don't like it. I've a fancy to collect fine paintings and live in peace. Leave them to their squabbles. How would you fancy such a life, Muriel?'

'I'd be honoured to be your housekeeper, sir.'

'I'm talking about me as Sir Josh and you as Lady Rawlinson.'

She saw the sparkle in the blue eyes, deepset in flesh under the entanglement of greying eyebrows, and felt his strength as he drew her down on his knees. He was chuckling and fondling her, his face reddening.

'I think you could safely assume I've enough for two, and you know my ways. You know I'm a difficult blighter at times but I've got my good points.' He groaned. 'Between the two of us my son-in-law's been a disappointment. Oh, he's a good mining man but I expected more loyalty, fool that I am. You can't buy loyalty, Muriel. I thought the two of us would spend more time together in the evenings, playing chess and a game of billiards. We got on well at first but it hasn't worked out. He thinks he can do better with Penlynne...'

For a moment he flushed dangerously. 'But what the devil!' He pressed her closer, kissing her clumsily. 'What do you say? You and me in a beautiful house in London, my grandson up from school for the holidays, being raised like a gentleman?'

She laughed. 'You'll spoil that bairn, that's for sure.' She rose from his grasp and straightened her skirts. 'I don't know that my husband's dead,' she said primly. 'He went missing, presumed dead.'

'He's officially dead. I looked into that long ago.'

Since Muriel Ferguson's marriage to Rawlinson Katherine and Gardiner had moved into their own house. She knew everything that went on in that house just as she had known the relationship between the two men could not endure long. She thought the American an opportunist and one to watch out for and she knew that Katherine was often alone.

At the time of their marriage Josiah Rawlinson had talked a great deal about going to London. The Park Lane house had been furnished at great expense. It had been featured in the London press as an example of the riches of the Transvaal. Purchases of Old Masters for Rawlinson's art gallery on advice of the director of the National Gallery had created a stir. However, he seemed impossible to budge from Johannesburg. The pyrites problem obsessed him and his distrust of deep level mining had grown more profound. 'Vast cost and no proof of success,' he said repeatedly in the local newspapers. 'Madness to attempt it.'

He was bitter that Penlynne had refused him participation in the Gold Recovery Syndicate. She could see that his exclusion by his young rival and his son-in-law had wounded him deeply. He blamed Gardiner, of course.

'I'd smash him if it wasn't for Kathy's sake,' he often told her and then, somewhat lightened, 'Well, if they pull it off I'll buy into it in London. Either that or I'll challenge the rights of this Alexander MacForrest to patent the process. Any chemist can do it. Penlynne's mad to offer him ten per cent on every ounce of gold recovered. They tell me the process is going to recover eighty percent. Do they want to make this chemist a millionaire in a year? Without a penny of risk to him!'

'Don't distress yourself, Jo. Let them do what they like. You can't stop it and you've enough, surely.'

'Don't tell me my business, woman.'

Stewart MacDonald had examined Rawlinson for his increasing deafness. He put it down to an injury suffered in a blasting explosion some years earlier when Josiah had impulsively gone into a stope to examine a misfire. The charge had exploded. The eardrum had long since healed but now he often heard bells ringing in his skull. He noticed sometimes these days the looks that passed between his directors at the boardroom table when things went past him. He knew that his irascibility had reached a point where some of them would be glad to have him permanently in London as absentee chairman.

Muriel urged him to join the exodus from town. He didn't seem to hear very well but when she asked him for an increase in her housekeeping money he flared up.

'Make do,' he said curtly.

'What's wrang wi' ye, Josiah Rawlinson?' She lapsed into her broadest brogue. 'Ye were a generous man no' sae long ago. Ye've changed then!'

But he was not listening. When they married he had not told her of his secret desire to breed a son of his own. Thinking of it now, he was uncertain whether the idea had formed in his mind as early as that or whether it was later, after Gardiner had spurned his leadership and Katherine had given him no comfort.

'I should have known you were a barren mare,' he blurted out to her one day. She had suffered other insults from him but this was too much. She left the room and he found himself alone in his library for the remainder of the evening. Next day she found an uncut version of a Dickens library volume in the hearth. *Bleak House*. She had to laugh and she almost relented her anger when she saw him wandering about the garden basking in the salutes of the Tamil and his assistant gardeners.

She sat in the sewing room and scrutinised the visiting cards on a silver tray. It never failed to please her that it was now she who received the cards. There were begging letters by the score. She gave these short shrift but one caught her eye. It was from Lady Violet Hurlingham begging to remind Mr Rawlinson of her services to the family and praying assistance 'in these troubled times'. There had been, she wrote, some difficulty about a bank draft from England.

Muriel Rawlinson was about to pitch it into the grate when something stayed her hand. She was thinking how much more galling it would be if Lady Violet were to receive a personal note. She would ask her husband to sign a modest cheque and include it.

She found such small triumphs infinitely satisfying.

The black butler came to her one afternoon, looking uncertain. There was a young AmaBoer in the hall. He would not go away. He was asking for the master. This black from the kraal, ten years ago a wearer of skins, stood before his mistress in starched whites. Already he had assumed the smooth, superior face of the top house servant.

Muriel went into the hall. The Boer was a young man, soft-bearded, standing hat in hand. He did not seem to be overawed by the marble underfoot or the heavy staircase that gave access to the galleries left and right of the stained glass window.

'And what is it you want with Mr Rawlinson?' she asked.

'A few words,' he smiled.

'Does he know you, Mr ...?'

'My name is Christiaan Smit.'

At that moment the door of the library opened and her husband appeared. He looked over his spectacles, his great height hunched from bowing over papers.

'Christiaan!' he exclaimed. 'I got your letter...' Then he went off into a stream of Dutch. 'We are old friends, Muriel,' he said in English to his wife as he closed the library door.

She had looked keenly at the slightly built young man with the cornflower eyes and the soft young goatee. Though he was modestly dressed in city clothes there was a look of the backvelder about him. A certain leanness and the look of far distances in eyes she found peculiarly compelling, even disturbing by their unusual quality of ... what was it? Seeing through you? And yet not seeing you at all.

'Let's have a look at you,' she heard her husband cry. When she brought them coffee the young man rose courteously and called her '*tante*', bowing in the Dutch manner. Her husband's face was flushed and his voice loud.

'This is Christiaan Smit ... Advocate Smit. Yes, a graduate of law school at Utrecht, Holland.' She had seldom seen him so excited. 'An example of the new Boer, Muriel. Look at him! Born in a pondok with a mud floor. I'm right, I always said it. These people have the makings of a great nation. I can also call myself a Boer, an Afrikaner, not so, Christiaan? He's to take up an appointment in the office of the Attorney General in Pretoria.'

When the young man had left she said nothing, waiting for him to speak. She had never seen him in such high good humour. 'People say I'm a hard man. A man who'll never put his hand in his pocket for anyone. Well, then. Six years ago I sent that boy to Holland to finish his education. One of the best decisions of my life!'

'But why ... why this one?'

Rawlinson paused and seemed to look through her. After some time he said quietly. 'A whim. Call it a whim.'

It was on the tip of her tongue to say: you never do anything for no reason but she restrained herself.

'Advocate Smit,' he said again, as if tasting the words. 'That young man will go far. I don't make mistakes in my judgement of men. He'll be a leader, you'll see I'm right. I gave him his chance and he won't forget it.'

'What use can he be to you?'

'A brilliant man in the right place. And that place is Pretoria.'

He chuckled and pulled her onto his knee for the first time in weeks. 'Here, what about a kiss?'

As an orphan Christiaan Smit had trekked with his uncle's family to the lowveld. In winter they pastured the stock there, shot what they needed, dried the meat and trekked back to the farm to raise maize in summer. Four times a year they inspanned the oxen to go to *nachtmaal* in Pretoria with its excitements of dancing and sports. Sometimes his older cousins went off on kommando in the wars against the Kaffirs.

He could have grown up like the others but there was a restlessness on him. It was in the mud and wattle house of the German missionary Hans Erlanger that he first realized he had been born to idleness and ignorance. The sharp-faced German and his skinny wife were translating the New Testament into a Kaffir tongue.

'Why?' Christiaan asked.

'Why, boy? Do you not know that the entrance of truth bringeth light?' He had gone back to the *pondok* where he and his cousins slept on shakedowns on the floor of the same room and their parents had a separate chamber divided only by a curtain of hessian sacking. His uncle could read the Holy Bible only with great labour. His cousins were illiterate. And so, he had suddenly realized, was he.

He went back to Erlanger and blurted out: 'I want to learn.'

By the time the Erlangers died of fever he was fifteen. He had good German, some Hollands and his mind had been fired by the wonders of the Hellenic civilisation. He had taken to Greek in the original with a strange appetite for its beauty and lucidity. Out at elbows he knew himself to be, but his mind was on fire.

The eldest cousin Willem mocked him. 'What's this ... chicken scratches!' But when he tossed the Greek lexicon among the fowls Christiaan, only shoulder high to the brawny youth with his swarthy chin, laid him on his back. With bleeding knuckles he retrieved the precious book.

'Will you look at him,' Willem muttered. 'The little *predikant*. The *meester*. Why don't you go down to the *hokkies* and learn the pigs to read?'

Christiaan only gave him a look from those blue eyes which already had the power to make others lower their gaze. He still respected his uncle's authority and admitted his right to punish his family and servants with the rod. He sjamboked Willem when he lied about lying with the Kaffir maid and it was Christiaan who bathed his cousin's wounds as he lay groaning in the dark under the reed thatch.

'Are you not glad I got a beating?' Willem asked, wincing at the salt Christiaan put on the raw stripes.

'You're my cousin.'

'You're a *sonderling*, a queer one. You're not one of us.'

'What do you mean?'

Willem laughed. 'You'll find out.' Then he had grasped Christiaan's hand. 'Don't tell father I said it.'

By the time he was seventeen he knew in his heart it was time for him to go. His uncle berated him when he came to tell him it was his intention to go to Johannesburg and again when he persisted. He saw the old man was troubled in spirit. One evening, when the Bible reading was over, his uncle detained him.

'Christiaan, it's time for you to hear the truth. Your mother came here to the farm. She was carrying you. She was my older brother's child. He drove her from the farm when he knew her shame. Men had been there, Englishmen, Jews, all kinds. One of them was your father. Ruffians who came looking for diamonds ... there by the Vaal.'

Christiaan ran out into the darkness. At his mother's grave he crouched by the headstone. She had died when he was too young to remember her. Keener than his own misery he felt an overwhelming pity for the girl she had been, no older than he was now.

Someone was calling his name. It was his cousin Anna. 'Chris ... Chris, come home! Chris. Where are you?'

He walked away from her, stumbling and weeping. Pity for himself and hatred for his unknown father. Footsteps and Anna's figure looming out of the darkness. 'Come here, dear Chris. I love you so.'

He clung to her. Anna had always been his favourite. It was Anna who mended his clothes and urged him to eat, putting pap and coffee before him when he was in one of his moods. When he had a few coppers it was for Anna he bought trinkets from the *smous*. He stood trembling in her arms, feeling the strength and goodness of her.

'I hate them. All of them.'

'Come home. Come home with me.'

'I'm leaving. I'll never come back.'

'Come back for me,' she pleaded. 'Give me your promise.'
'One day I'll come back for you,' he said solemnly. They clung together, kissing and sobbing.

Chapter 18

There was enthusiastic applause in the music room. Echoes of *Marche Militaire* lingered around the Steinway grand. While the string quartet – the German consul and his wife, a Hollander official of the Kruger administration and Nellmapius himself – prepared their music officers of the Staats Artillerie in dress uniform and guests in evening dress rose for a moment to take the air on the verandah of Hugo Nellmapius's sumptuous home.

At least thirty had sat down to dinner at the long mahogany table, sparkling with crystal and silver in a room heady with the perfume of women and tropical flowers. Nellmapius was proud of the golden Tokay he served. 'Our own Hungarian wine,' he boasted, 'and what better in which to drink a toast to our new fatherland ... the Republic!'

Chairs had scraped back and glasses were raised. There was a glitter in every eye. The women seemed more animated, more beautiful in the fever of enthusiasm that gave the lightest remark a semblance of wit and brilliance.

After the women had left the table and retired to the drawing room the men's talk turned to the coming campaign against Magato, up there in his mountain redoubt in the Zoutpansberg, refusing to pay taxes, murdering farmers and driving off stock. The boast was, 'We'll bring him back in irons. Hang him on the town gallows!' Upstart Kaffir! The sooner that business was cleaned up the better and the land put out to cultivation and settlement. The older men talked of past campaigns against the tribes. Rawlinson was in good form. He built a breastwork of peaches and grapes on the white tablecloth to demonstrate how the crafty Moshesh had defended the crags of Basutoland.

'I turned around ... there at the top in a storm of bullets, rocks and spears ... and there wasn't a man alive behind me.'

'Ah, but that was many years ago,' someone said.

'A man never forgets a brave enemy,' Rawlinson said. He

turned to Louis Joubert. 'Now Louis, as commandant I expect you to take good care of Christiaan here. Not that he needs a nursemaid but we don't want to lose the next State Attorney. There's a time coming, gentlemen, when the Republic will require shrewdness as much as skill at arms. Brains to match the sharpest in Europe.'

Christiaan, in a dark suit, his eyes on the tablecloth, twirled a glass of untouched port. He had not wanted to become a centre of attention but it seemed unavoidable. Since his success in several cases he had found himself greeted on all sides. This invitation was typical of his acceptance into Pretoria society. He was still astonished at the deference to his opinions by older men. He intended to keep a cool head and cultivate the ability to stand aside from the emotions of the day. He would never allow himself to lose judgement. These men around the table were inflamed with martial ardour. For days past men on shaggy ponies had been coming in. The church square was crammed with waggons. Burghers from all the districts around were forming into groups of twenty-five men under a corporal. The town buzzed with military preparations and cheered whenever the artillery dashed by in a clatter of hooves and gun carriages with brand new German guns.

The Magato campaign would be no more than a *wapenschouw*, a try-out for the gunners. The campaign had been ordered for the autumn, after the worst summer of horse sickness in memory. A sturdy beast, on its feet in the morning would be a carcass by nightfall, its belly blown, choked to death in bloody foam.

Standing with his arm around the waist of his young daughter Irene, the Hungarian with his sad eyes that belied his charm and gaiety among his guests, shook hands with Christiaan as he took his leave. 'A moment,' he said, leading the young man along the verandah. 'You're going to need a good horse. I want you to come out to my farm at Ses Myl Spruit and pick the best you can find.'

Christiaan could see the white blur of Irene hovering in the background against the dark green richness of trees and shrubs. 'Thank you, Oom Hugo,' he declined. 'I planned to get a pair of horses at my uncle's farm at Kameelfontein.'

'Kameelfontein! There isn't a live horse within twenty miles of there. No lad, it's a gift from Mr Rawlinson, a blue roan, well salted, and a Basuto pony to carry your baggage. Don't disappoint him ... and don't say I told you.'

As he strolled back to his lodgings through the fragrant night Christiaan had a mind to refuse the gift. How could he do otherwise when he was already so indebted to Oom Josiah for his education, first in Stellenbosch and then in Holland. Something in him had now rebelled in the taking of gifts. A stubborn unwillingness to be in any man's debt. Too many of his people were being corrupted by *uitlanders* seeking favours and concessions. Some said there wasn't an honest official left in government. They were not building manorial houses on their salaries. His own tastes were simple and he determined they always would be.

These days he often thought of Anna and his boyhood promise to return to her. Nearly seven years ago. If she remembered him it would be as the boy she had comforted that night when he left the farm, wounded to the heart and confused. It had seemed to him then that to find the man who had wronged his mother would be the consuming passion of his life. Ah well, the pain lessened and one forgot. Or did one ever quite lose the deep sense of having been wronged?

From Holland he had written to Anna several times. He had been intensely lonely in the cold attic room in Utrecht, a blanket about his knees, his hands blue and his knuckles chapped. He had written long letters, not love letters, more like letters to a favourite sister, scribbled up there under the eaves, the tiles streaming with rain and so cold in the long winters that he could hardly hold the pen. He had poured out visionary ideas about himself and the future of his land. She wrote back eagerly, letters that delighted him with their evidence of a lively intelligence, a warm spirit and an expanding mind. She had an intense interest in his studies but there was never a hint of the deeper relationship he longed for. Perhaps she wanted no more than a sisterly relationship now she was a grown woman.

Why did he remember her so vividly now? While mixing this evening with the cream of Pretoria society, he had felt a curious sense of betrayal, as if he did not actually belong among this wealth and ostentation – crystal chandeliers, Italian marble and inlaid woods, oriental and Aubusson carpets. In such houses the reins of power were held, the true reins of power which controlled state officials and those in the seats of authority.

He knew himself to be the equal of any man when it came to a matching of minds. Was it power he wanted? Power to change the destiny of his people? What if the coming campaign against the Venda chief proved him to be lacking in courage? A man did not know his worth until he had faced steel.

And then there was Anna...

He had a sudden panicky feeling that he had left it too late, that he had been altogether too cool, too egotistical in his letters. Had he ever shown her by even the smallest word that there were times when he felt an intense physical longing for her? How could he have been so cold, so insensitive? No wonder her letters had become less frequent. He knew, of course, that she had a concern for him that no one else had ever shown. But then she had always been like that. It was her nature. He had hardly realised it but years had passed. There must have been suitors. Was it possible that she had actually married? But of course she would have told him.

Tomorrow he would ask the commandant general if he could leave the kommando for a few days, cutting across country to Kameelfontein and rejoin the force at the Klein Olifants River. It was here that the kommandos from the eastern districts would be joining the main force in the heart of Magato's country. He had a strong desire to see her face again before whatever must happen.

Almost at the door of his room he decided he must accept Rawlinson's gift. He would need good horses. The decision made, he surrendered to the sensation of yearning he had forbidden himself for so long. How would she look? How would she receive him after so long? He felt a sudden inward quaking. It would be a new relationship, or it would be nothing.

In his excitement he could not go to bed. He took up his stick and went out again and walked through the sleeping town. On every side he saw evidence of a vitality he had never believed possible. His people were wakening. He was stopped at a crossing by a locomotive and flat cars going by. They were from Komatipoort on the Portuguese frontier. On each side of the flat cars he saw crates of heavy weapons. Two of them were carrying the barrels of cannon, siege pieces for the forts being constructed on the hills around the capital by French and German engineers.

Now Kruger had his rail link to the sea in Mozambique he could bring in all the guns he could buy. Gold mining taxes paid for the weapons that would point towards Johannesburg. The irony was not lost to the young lawyer. Everyone in Pretoria talked openly of first settling the Kaffir problem and after that the *uitlanders*, before they got too many and too powerful.

Was it as simple as that? Johannesburg was a foreign city but Pretoria was hardly less. Boers themselves were divided between those who realised what they owed to outsiders and those who bitterly resented them. At the age of twenty-five a man should know what he believed. But did he?

Next day Commandant General Louis Joubert made him a present of a new Mauser and a bandolier of cartridges. Christiaan took the fine weapon into his hands with excitement.

'We shall have thousands of these, *ou mannetjie*,' he heard the older man enthuse. 'God bless you and bring you back. We need you.' Joubert embraced him emotionally and said a few words of prayer over him.

The Pretoria contingent entrained with their horses and baggage, saddlebags packed with *beskuit* and dried meat. The artillery were on the same train and the station was crammed with relations and well-wishers. The artillery band played the *Volkslied*. Heads were bared and women sobbed. Flags fluttered as the locomotive shrieked and the coaches moved out with a final discharge of weapons from the open cars.

No one doubted it was the end of Magato. In all they could muster some five hundred men, including a number of English-speakers called up much against their will. Some few of them agreed that they had a duty to the state even if they did not have full burgher's rights. Here was the seed of future trouble, Christiaan thought. They kept to themselves and there were one or two fist fights with Boers when it came to drawing fodder for the horses. He broke up one of these and got black looks from his own corporal.

Next morning he saddled up while the locomotive took on water. He was roughly chaffed about leaving them so soon – there must be a woman in it. He rode away through the black slag heaps of Witbank's collieries. It was a two-day ride to Kameelfontein over low hills that he remembered covered with tall grasses. Now they were burned and seared by continuous drought. Watercourses that had been choked with ferns and wild flowers were now dry. Weaver birds' nests were empty. In a day's riding he saw no wild life. In all that way he never saw another living soul except one native who fled at first but when Christiaan fired a shot in the air came trembling towards him.

He was an Ndebele, survivor of a kraal destroyed by Magato's raiders in search of cattle. All ... all had been speared. The cattle were already dead. Some unknown scourge had decimated both stock and wild life. Christiaan rode on past empty grass huts, withered and fallen in. Stone kraals empty of beasts. His heart contracted when he thought of what lay ahead. He remembered the farm at Kameelfontein for its fields of mealies beneath a small hill, the bend in the river where the willows trailed their fronds in the brown current in the somnolent daze of midday. The house, as he had it in his eye, had its back to a row of bluegums, its stoep obscured by the orchard. From this far off already you could have heard the shouts of umfaans driving cattle. He had to turn in the saddle to check his bearings and he hardly recognised what he saw. Yes, there was the cemetery. He had almost ridden over it.

Christiaan dismounted and saw his mother's name through a haze of tears. The slate headstone with its crude inscription had fallen over. Even before he reached the house he guessed the worst. From this distance it looked the same but he knew he would find it deserted. He pushed open the door. The house was a shell, the dung floor cracked in crazy fragments. The family must have trekked, taking everything. He had imagined himself dismounting, Anna coming out onto the stoep. The shock of joyful recognition. Her face under the *kappie* warm against his cheek, perhaps wet with tears. Yes, certainly they would both weep. Then she would take him inside. She, very simply dressed in sun-faded calico and he in his new riding breeches and dark blue tunic. A little awkward, coming as he had from a sophisticated setting to this primitive shelter against the Africa that was his heritage, that he loved even in its harshness to man and beast.

Where had he to look for her now?

He found out a week later on the slopes of the Blaauwberg. The Pretoria contingent was bivouacked half a mile from the high crags where Magato had withdrawn with his people, warriors, women and children, all of them deep in the mountain caves beneath the breastworks of boulders poised to be rolled down on the attackers.

He was examining the position through his binoculars when he was hailed by a tall, heavily built man with a full black beard and a swarthy face. He was grabbed in a powerful hug.

'Ja, it's me, little cousin. How is it with you? I'm with the Machadadorp kommando. Man, I would never have recognised you.' His eyes were on the new Mauser and the horses.

'How's it with all at home ... with Anna?'

'She's with the father at Dullstroom. He's too old to ride now.'

Christiaan had an intense desire to grab the man by the shoulders and shake information about Anna out of him. How does she look? Has she suitors? How was it I lost touch with her in the past year? Was it my own movements, mail that had not been delivered for one reason or another? Mail carriers who had failed to deliver letters to the nearest store? It was Africa, after all, not snug and orderly Holland.

'Is Anna well?' he heard himself asking.

'Far as I know,' said Willem indifferently. A sudden hostility came into his eyes. 'Our mother's dead.'

'I didn't know. I'm sorry, Willem.' After all she had brought him up and he felt a pang of remorse. 'I expect Anna's married then...'

'She's got suitors. The predikant and others. Seems they all want a woman who can read and write. She teaches school.'

The big dark man turned to heft a bag of meal off the commissariat waggon. Back over his shoulder he threw the challenge. 'You'd better *maak gou* if that's the way the wind's blowing.'

Christiaan held his tongue.

Willem went on mockingly. 'Your cousins are in my kommando. You can join us if you like.'

'I'm with the commandant, but I'll ask him.'

'Don't do us any favours,' Willem said. Then, digging his heels into his shaggy mount, he cantered away. It seemed incredible to Christiaan that this man had remained so uncouth and illiterate. And yet this was one of his own people. He must not despise him. He had slept on the floor of the house with Willem and the rest of that brawling brood of brothers. Only now did he fully understand what separated him and what it was about him that had always made him the butt of their jokes and their crudities.

For the next few days the kommando was content to send out scouting parties. The battery of guns were sited, the ammunition stacked. Stripped to their waists the gunners indulged in horseplay and waited for orders. Commandant General Joubert had brought his wife. A tent was rigged against the waggon and folding chairs set out. Joubert drank coffee in the shade and discussed tactics with his veld cornets. There was psalm singing and prayers every night. Mrs Joubert was a gentle lady, working texts with her needle and approving of her husband's piety.

'The Lord will deliver Magato into our hands,' Joubert said, combing his massive beard with his fingers. He exuded confidence and to all he showed the same stately courtesy and air of magnanimity.

The kommando waited with increasing impatience for a signal to attack up the slope and break into the caves. Volunteers came forward all the time, offering to make single-handed sorties at night with sticks of dynamite. The commandant thanked them. He was waiting for a sign from Jehovah, pondering the pages of the great black Bible forever open, particularly at the campaigns of Joshua.

'Is it not wonderful, neef,' he confided to Christiaan, 'how the Lord gave Joshua the power to stop the sun for two hours so he could defeat the Canaanites before darkness fell? So what have we to fear! For the godless there can be only his wrath.'

Christiaan put down the copy of the tattered Greek Xenophon he always carried. He felt it was time to speak out. 'Oom Louis,' he said firmly, 'the Middelburg contingent lost more horses today. I saw a dozen oxen lying dead in their traces. This place is unhealthy. We should not delay overlong.'

'We have our *boererate*,' said Joubert mildly. It was the same remark he had made in Pretoria when he gave Christiaan his Mauser. 'Mr Rawlinson offered to equip a Red Cross waggon. I told him we have our remedies and we trust in the Lord. Our president blew his thumb off when his elephant *roer*, his great old musket, exploded. The wound healed very well with cobwebs. He told me himself.

'What are you reading, *neef*?' Joubert looked grave on hearing it was the record of a campaign fought by the old Greeks against the Persians. 'Get rid of it,' he advised Christiaan. 'The Lord abhors the works of the heathen.'

'Commandant,' said Christiaan, 'Xenophon writes here "Let us not wait for others to come to us and call on us to do great deeds. Let us instead be first to summon the rest to the path of honour"!'

'The Lord will choose the right path for us,' answered Joubert gravely. 'He is not to be hurried.' He dipped his *beskuit* into his coffee and ate, then poured his coffee into his saucer and drank. A dribble of coffee wet the beard around the redness of his mouth. 'The Lord will deliver Magato into our hands, as he delivered the hosts of Dingaan into the hands of Piet Cilliers at Blood River.'

A day later scouts brought in a black woman they had come upon drawing water. She told them that Magato's women and children were in the caves with the men. Prinsloo, the artillery commander, asked permission to open fire but Joubert demurred. So did his wife.

'Commandant,' said Prinsloo angrily, 'my horses are going down. In a couple of days I won't be able to move my guns. Will the Commandant not come and see for himself?'

Joubert rose, put on his tall black hat, buttoned the clawhammer coat and offered his arm to his wife. At the nearest battery the farrier had secured a sick horse to the wheel of the gun carriage. The horse was in a pitiable state, its eyelids swollen, froth pouring from mouth and nostrils. A funnel was pushed up one nostril and a gallon of linseed oil mixed with gunpowder poured into the struggling beast. Then the lashings were cut and it staggered away.

Christiaan followed it until it fell and lay heaving. Beyond the artillery camp he could see the carcasses of a number of horses, legs stiff and bellies blown. The stench of corruption came sweet on the wind.

After prayers that evening Joubert looked around his officers and waited for their respectful attention. 'I do not want the blood of Magato's children on my head. We will send an emissary demanding his surrender. We will take him to Pretoria and that will be the end of the matter.'

At once there was a clamour of volunteers. Joubert turned to Christiaan. 'I have chosen Advocate Smit. He has eloquence enough.' His mild eyes seemed to reprove and forgive.

'Commandant,' protested Prinsloo, his features dark with

anger. 'My guns are trained on the caves. At least let us soften them up with a few rounds.' He was supported by the veldcornets, impatient to see the effects of the new breech-loaded guns. Joubert refused.

That evening after prayers Christiaan climbed the slopes to the outpost nearest the caves. He took with him an Ndebele servant of the commandant. Willem was in the outpost with men of the Dullstroom contingent.

'Well, if it isn't the advocate,' he shouted. There was a fire going and a smell of scorched meat. A jug of *karee-mampoer* was going the rounds. There was loud laughter and boasts of 'going up there tonight and smoking the Kaffirs out of their holes'. When Christiaan suggested putting the fire out and mounting a guard Willem led the others in mockery. 'Who sent you to spy on us, little cousin?'

Eventually the men lay down to sleep and the fire burned out. Christiaan and the Ndebele lay down some way from the outpost. The Ndebele was afraid. He told how Magato's men attacked at night, putting entire kraals to the assegai, burning huts and driving off stock and women. It was better, the Ndebele said, to have the protection of the AmaBoere. Christiaan pondered the man's sincerity ... but after all, better to be a live dog than a dead lion. The black man pulled his thin blanket around him and spat tobacco juice from the present of Magaliesberg *twak* given him by Joubert for his services as interpreter.

Christiaan fell asleep among the boulders, his head on the crook of his arm, his Mauser between his legs. He woke stiff and cold at the sound of a disturbance of rocks higher up the slope. The Ndebele was also awake. He was shivering like a dog. Christiaan smelled the rank stench of his fear. Could it be some scavenging animal? He strained his eyes into the darkness. Every rock had the shape of a man's head. The aloes stood out stark against the stars like warriors with raised assegais ... you looked and they had moved closer. Christiaan lay flat, his heart pounding against the hard ground, his limbs awkwardly sprawled as he pushed the Mauser forward. The metal was ice cold and he could smell the breech oil. He could hear nothing but the moan of the wind in the short dry grass. This then was what it took to be a man, this strange elation mixed with fear, this sharpening of every sense.

Then abruptly a muffled cry ... a shriek and another, to his right. The Dullstroom kommando. Someone shouted, 'Oh God! Mercy ... no!' At the scream the Ndebele fled downhill. A dark figure rose up in front of Christiaan, raised to strike. Christiaan flung himself forward, dropping the Mauser, and grappled with the man. The naked oiled flesh slipped through his grasp. He heard the rasping breath and felt the hot thrust of metal into his thigh. He groped at his belt for his knife, lunging upwards at the warrior as he fell.

He came round with the sun warming the tops of the rocks. There was a heavy weight across his legs. He rolled the dead man over, fainted, and revived again. His movement had reopened his wound and both his and the black man's blood was slippery on the rocks.

From below in the valley he heard the thudding concussion as Prinsloo's battery began to search for the range. The shrieking projectiles passed low overhead and exploded some hundreds of yards up the slope. Clanging metal pattered around. Then came the next salvo. This time it was striking the base of the cliffs. Trees and bush were tossed up in fountains of red soil. Now they had found the range. The cannonade went on for some thirty minutes. Then suddenly all was still. The loud chirping of insects resumed. The sun appeared through the thinning smoke. A sudden shouting and cheering. He could hear the corporals leading their men up the slope. Several stumbled past without seeing him, their faces intent on the rocks above. He shouted for help but no one heard. His throat burned with thirst. So this is it, he thought. This is how the redcoats suffered at Majuba. All day in the sun, dying unaided among the rocks.

He felt a dull resentment against his cousins, lying in their blood over there. They had failed the kommando. Their contempt for Magato had been the death of them. Boulders were bounding down the slope. He could hear the clash of men joining in combat above him. Had they stormed the caves? He tried to rise. His eyes blurred and he fell back. Dimly he resolved to beware the over-confidence of men like Willem. He must make it a guiding principle never to move until he saw not just the next step but the entire landscape of possibilities. If he survived his wound he would know how to manage his life. He exulted in the thought. It seemed to him to be a revelation. With the revelation came the certainty that he would live. Anna would be his wife and together...

Chapter 19

Isadore Isaacs slipped the gold watch from his fob pocket and checked it with the station clock. The Hollander station master invited the young man into his office and offered him a Ritmeester.

'Ja, Myhneer Isaacs, Miss Isaacs is down as 1st Class passenger from Cape Town. It's a happy day for you. I will have a cab waiting and take care your sister's luggage is delivered to Hartley's.'

Isadore drew on his cigar and stretched his well-tailored legs, examining his boots for dust. His linen was immaculate. While he waited he pared his nails with a penknife, his brown derby cocked at an angle more self-assured than insolent. It irritated the middle-aged Hollander. He knew a Peruvian when he saw one. It reminded him that he lived in an iron bungalow without even the refinement of a mud-brick lining to cool it. His wife complained that it was impossible to housekeep up to Rotterdam standards in this town of red dust. Yet this young Jew with his beard strongly curling and black as jet was half his age and already kept a suite of rooms in Hartley's Hotel. There was more money in liquor than honest work. Being on the wrong side of the law paid handsomely.

Isadore spun a gold coin on the tabletop and sent it circling towards the station master's hand. Plenty more where that came from. Kaffir canteens. There were two kinds of Jew in Johannesburg and the Hollander disliked them both. The Anglo-Jews with their riches and their English manners and the Peruvians with their poverty and stinking rags. They came in by every train, beady-eyed, shuffling with their bundles and packs. Times were when a man could have been in a ghetto what with the embracings and tears. Runny noses and broken boots. Some still wearing the *kapote* down to their ankles. Now and then a sturdy artisan with his tools. Since when did Jews work with their hands!

'Train late again, eh, station master! Mind you, four hours late is good for the Cape-Transvaal express.'

'This is not Holland, Mr Isaacs. We do our best.'

'I'll be over in the Standard Bar.'

'Goot. I send a boy across.'

Isadore crossed the street. He was continually accosted in Yiddish by the type of Jew he was determined to have nothing to do with. Litvaks from the ghettos of Lithuania. He spoke roughly to them in English. Not that he did not understand their despair but a man couldn't have his hand forever in his pocket. A small loan to set them up with Kaffir truck for the native trade, a stake in a Kaffir eating house. It dismayed him to see what he had been so short a time ago. The worst were those who spoke nostalgically of the old ghetto town his father had emigrated from into the Whitechapel ghetto and a grave in a rain-sodden yard with soot-blackened tombstones. He hadn't been too young when they left the Pale for him to forget entirely the dialect. But when he heard it spoken here it made him cringe. There had been too much shame and abasement. Here he spoke only English. The hungry, frightened boy he had been was gone forever. He was broad enough now to shoulder a man out of his way. He ate well and without conscience. What was kosher to him! Christmas, yes. Yom Kippur, no. He had had enough of ritual piety while his father lived. The old man, God rest his bones, had wanted him to study the Torah and become a *rav*.

In his pocketbook he carried the first photograph taken of Rachel in the House of Shelter in Cape Town – a dark girl amongst others in white smocks and clumsy shoes. She wrote to him regularly. 'I am writing this in my favourite place, under the lemon tree, and I am thinking of you, my brother, and blessing you for being good to your little sister...'

Had he been so generous with little gifts and money to the orphanage as she imagined? His memory of her was of a skinny girl of thirteen when they had travelled together in the steamship *The American* in that crowd of immigrants. How he'd come to his present position was another story. When she asked for news of what he was doing he had always been evasive. 'I'm getting rich for us, my sister. You will never want for anything.'

As he entered the Standard Bar there was a perceptible drop in the level of noise. He looked over the drinkers as Sammy Snyders pushed bottle and glass towards him.

'Has Judelsohn been in yet?'

'Not yet, Mr Isaacs, but there's one of his men over there.' Judelsohn never made a business appointment, or a social one, without one of his 'loyal men' at his back. Isadore measured the powerful young Jew who looked back at him with equal contempt.

'Tell Judelsohn I couldn't wait all day,' he said.

'You sure, Mr Isaacs?'

Isadore shouldered his way out. He went back to the station, his mouth dry. People who ignored an invitation to drink with Smooel Judelsohn were known to have been run down by a cab or found with their features damaged, floating face down in a muddy pool in the flooded Brick Field.

The locomotive whistled at Braamfontein Halt. People were surging to the station. He must look his best. A quick shoe-shine and meet her smiling. Confident. His heart was lifting with anticipation. Sweet Rachel, my sister. Always the one who cared for him. So grave, so earnest, with such an ardent heart. Educated. Trained as a typist already.

He caught his breath when he saw her. A little more than medium height, not beautiful, but bright-faced with heavy, dark eyes under a broad forehead. The mouth generous. Yes, it was the mother's face. It quite choked him up. He went towards the figure dressed in brown, the neat white cuffs and collar. Standing there with her basket, she stared at him but did not recognise the broad young man with the glittering watchchain. Then she cried out his name and darted into his arms.

'Rachel ... little sister.'

'Oh Issy ... dear brother!' Her eyes shone with tears. 'I'd never have known you. So tall ... and the beard!'

'The journey up, how was it?' Holding her, he was almost too moved to trust his voice.

'No, I had food ... in the basket. There was nothing kosher at the halts. Let me see you. After so long. Oh dear, you're an important man already. It makes me quite afraid to see you. So handsome and well dressed.'

'I'm getting there,' he laughed. 'Come, there's a cab.'

'My luggage. It's only a box and a blanket.'

'You shall have everything,' he said.

From the cab he noticed her pleasure and uncertainty. He felt he had to boast about his city. 'It's not much after Cape Town but there are some fine buildings already.' At that moment he saw a sturdy young man in a workman's peaked cap and blue blouse run out towards the cab, waving to Rachel. It shocked him to see the familiarity, the way her face lit up. The cab started away.

'Who is that fellow?' he asked.

'Mr Cahan. He helped me on the train. He's from the old country, a carpenter.'

'Johannesburg is full of fellows like that.'

'I told him you might help him find a place.'

'In this town a man must make his own way. You are my sister.'

He saw that he had bewildered her. Leaning forward, he took her hand. 'Wait till you see your room. I had it specially decorated for you ... until we move into the new house.' He smiled. 'You said you wanted to keep house for your brother.'

'Oh, I do,' she said but the cloud on her brow persisted. He was anxious to make amends.

'I have tickets for the opera tomorrow. They say it's an excellent piece – the Barber of Seville. You'll laugh a lot.'

'Do you ever think of the old days in Whitechapel?' she said.

'Never.'

'Not even of father?'

'Of him ... yes.'

It was then that he noticed that hers was not a laughing face. He thought at once: the orphanage, a gloomy hole. Religious too. Gently he took her hands. 'Look here, Rachel. This is a new place. No one here has time for ... *shechita*.'

'Is there no observance ... no *kashruth*?'

'Yes, there is a congregation, more than one. They do nothing but quarrel.' He dismissed them with a shrug. She persisted. 'There is *yiddishkeit* ... surely?'

'Who needs it? This is a new country. Surely it is not so important?'

He saw that to her it was. 'If one dies ... is there a *chevra kadisha*?'

'You did not come here to die, surely?' He laughed. 'Look at this place. There are opportunities for us. No place else in the world gives us such opportunities. The president respects Jews, makes friends of us.'

207

My God, he was thinking, it's the father's blood in her. I managed to kill it and here it is strong as ever.

'I must seem very ungrateful. After all you've done for me.'

'I have done nothing. You are my sister, my family.'

'I will try to please you, Issy.'

'No. You must do as you believe.' Doubtfully he added, 'There are kosher boarding houses. Filled with the roughest kind. A mattress on the floor if you're lucky. You saw the train; they come in by the hundred.'

'Surely you don't despise your own people ... Isadore?' Her sombre eyes on his face, his clothes, his shining footwear.

'In my house you will run it as you wish, Rachel.'

With that she was satisfied.

They had hardly been an hour in the hotel when he received a message that Smooel Judelsohn was waiting. He excused himself to Rachel. In his room he opened the chest of drawers and tucked the Belgian automatic pistol into his trousers.

'I won't be long,' he assured her.

At the street door he dropped half a sovereign into the hands of an Indian vendor sitting like a burst of eastern colour with marigolds stuck in her dark, piled plaits.

'Take your basket upstairs, Room 23, that one with the balcony. Savvy?' If he was buying a wreath for someone it would not be for Isadore Isaacs. His anger was rising. To be summoned! He knew what was coming. Smiles. Compliments. Then the warning. Get out of liquor if you want to stay healthy.

Smooel Judelsohn! You could feel the treachery even before the man spoke. Isadore smilingly declined the cigar, his heart pounding. He sensed at once this was a court as Judelsohn waved introductions – 'Just family ... my sons Simon and Idel.'

Simon nodded coldly. Idel showed his teeth.

This was the apartment above the wholesale liquor depot. From the yard enclosed by corrugated iron sheeting and gates with barbed wire Isadore could hear the rattling of empty bottles being stacked and smell the familiar sour reek of spirits.

Judelsohn smilingly offered a glass of black tea and lemon from the samovar. A woman entered with a tray of glasses. Judelsohn's daughter, surely. But no, it was his wife Rosetta, tall and slender with an hourglass figure. She smiled with the expression of a trapped animal. Her huge eyes eclipsed the arched nose. The mass of black hair was toweringly pinned with flashing combs. Twenty years Judelsohn's junior, the second wife. Maybe the third. Now he saw that Simon and Idel bore no familial resemblance.

'My wife looks forward to meeting with your sister, newly arrived. Not so, my dear?' Judelsohn said, slipping from heavily accented English to Yiddish.

Rosetta handed Isadore a glass of tea. It seemed to him that she was urging, say yes. Agree. Make whatever it is possible. She bent towards him, her eyes enormous, and he was almost overpowered by the scent of jasmine.

In his chair Judelsohn slumped contentedly. Complacently. The sons looked on, Simon indifferent, Idel sullen.

'In a small city like this,' Judelsohn smiled, 'we Jews should have no differences, no secrets from each other. But such people we are ... when have we ever agreed! Today there is bad feeling about the appointment of a *shammas* for the synagogue ... will this one's uncle be *shochet*, to slaughter beasts, or will it be that one's cousin! These things make divisions. It is very sad, sad to one who has given thousands for the building of the new synagogue. Still, they may overrule my wishes. That is the Jewish way.'

Come to the point, thought Isadore. Enough of the softening up.

'Another glass of tea .... May I call you Isadore? I have been impressed, yes, impressed, by your progress here. A pedlar's pack not long ago, today prospering. What a pity you are working against my interests. That is our way, I agree. It is a free land. But together we could both prosper ... greatly. Do you not agree?'

'I am satisfied,' said Isadore. He rose. 'Thank you for the tea.' He looked coolly at his watch and bowed to Rosetta. Judelsohn's sons rose together. Their father had not moved.

'You have not heard me out,' said Judelsohn. 'You will go far if you do not go too fast.' The smile seemed to have become fixed. The face was spreading, exuding oil. His head moved and Rosetta vanished from the room. The sons blocked the doorway. Judelsohn's middle finger began to stroke the arm of the chair. His voice was reasonable.

'You break the law, Isadore. Ah, you say, what is that? Everybody does that, even Judelsohn. But Judelsohn knows the law. Judelsohn has connections. Judelsohn prospers because he knows how these things must be done, to please *all*. Now comes this unbroken pony. Trampling, breaking, pasturing himself in other men's fields. Some would want to break his spirit. Judelsohn is different. I say, put a bridle on him and he'll be worth his oats. Now listen. There is only one liquor king here. There is no room for little princes. Be my friend and I will make you, today, a captain in my family. You will be area boss of the eastern districts, sharing in all profits of the business. That is how well I regard you.'

'And my bottling factory, my Kaffir canteen outlets?'

'All illegal, you know.'

'You would make them legal?'

'There is talk of heavy police raids on illegal premises.' A sorrowful shake of the head.

'There is also talk of prohibition, no more liquor for Kaffirs,' said Isadore, matching the older man's tone.

Judelsohn smiled. 'It is a good reason to make one family now. Fight together.'

Isadore could feel the hardness of the automatic pistol under his waistcoat and its pressure against his thigh. For a moment he thought to use it. No, control. Patience. A few smiles cost nothing. Yet he knew that his refusal was a declaration of war. It was Isadore Isaacs against this man and his family, masters of the central Rand in the wholesale liquor trade, suppliers to every bar and hotel. What hope had he against Judelsohn and the other area kings? Next to gold it was liquor that had made the Rand what it was. Especially the Kaffir trade. He had learned that quickly enough while he worked for De la Roche.

He should give in now, take the share Judelsohn offered. And he might have done it if he had not caught the look that passed between Simon and Idel. The wide-eyed unsmiling stares they turned on him said plainly: our father may be a fool. In the end you will have to settle with us. Isadore knew all there was to know about Judelsohn's influence over magistrates, the police, the public prosecutors. He was even above the power of Government, at least here in Johannesburg. Yet it was the sons' faces Isadore wanted to smash.

'You'll let me have your answer, Isadore,' said Judelsohn.

'I will.'

'Bring your sister to visit. My wife would enjoy her company.'

Isadore left the house. It was sparse and ugly despite the man's wealth, with the smell of kosher cooking in his nostrils. The kitchen door suddenly opened and he saw Rosetta. She looked directly at him. She said nothing. It was a look that lingered and with it the smell of jasmine.

Sometimes the white canvas above his head swung from left to right. At others it seemed to rise up vertically and lurch over. At the end of the tunnel was an aperture of hurtful blue, though at times it was dark and silent. At other times he heard the grumbling of the wheels grinding over rocks. All these things were identified in his mind by pain. Christiaan Smit would not have recognised himself in the tossing scarecrow with sunken eyes and yellow sprouting beard. The small waggon, pulled by two starveling horses, struggled across an infinity of veld.

His attendant was the same Ndebele man who had fled downhill when the attack came. His wound was a suppurating mess. He had no memory now of having refused the opportunity of returning to Pretoria with the victorious commando, insisting that he would be alright. His one coherent thought had been to get to Dullstroom where he would find Anna. She seemed to him to be the haven he must reach, or die.

By the third day he was out of his mind, babbling Greek hexametres from the *Iliad*. In all of this the voice and presence of Anna, sometimes as a child, sometimes as a woman, was the only thing that brought him balm. What mental pictures he had of her were a blend of the fourteen year old she had been when he left home in that night of revelation ... that, and his imaginings of her from her letters. Now she would be a woman in her twenties, subduing a lively intelligence beneath a gentleness of spirit that he imagined could only have grown with the years.

In moments of consciousness he cursed the frightened Ndebele, urging him to make haste because he had a vision of Anna, her hand on the arm of a shadow man, walking and smiling together. Then he would try to rise and drive the waggon himself and the Ndebele had to hold him down until the frenzy passed.

Now he was lying in a cool dark room, shutters closed. Someone was moving. He could hear water being poured and feel the covers removed from his leg. Low voices in consultation.

'Well, we have saved it at any rate, but it was touch and go. He'll always limp.'

Then the murmur of a woman's voice.

'Is that you, Anna?' he cried.

'Oh, good. He's awake,' he heard her exclaim. And then the shadow unreality became the dreamed-of presence as she took his hand and pressed it to her breast.

'Lie quiet. Don't try to move,' she was saying and he could feel tears on his face, trickling freely among the stubble beard. He was not sure whose tears they were, only conscious of the firm cool hand and the softness of her breast. 'Don't leave me,' he said.

'No, I'm here,' she said quietly and he could feel the beat of her heart.

'How long have I been here?'

'A week already.'

'That man I saw you with ... walking together.'

'No, it was the doctor.'

'Oh, thank God,' he said, tears flowing. 'And I am not too late?'

But she had glided from the room, hushing him with her finger to his lips and a touch to his brow. Then he slept heavily, sinking into a deep sleep of peace. In the days that followed his uncle came often to his bedside and mourned his sons. At a stroke his family had been taken from him. First the wife, then the boys. It made no sense to him. 'The will of the Lord ... the will of the Lord!' He muttered this like an incantation that brought him no relief.

Christiaan had feared this man, his anger and his scorn. But now the old fellow clung to him as if he were one of his own. 'You and Anna are all I have now.' Then he would talk about returning to the old place at Kameelfontein when the summer rains began. In his mind it was all the doings of the godless *uitlanders*. When they had been driven from the land the hand of the Lord would be lifted from his people. The locust and the rinderpest and the iron drought. 'I'll ride again,' the old man would cry. 'Against them! The English.'

'I don't doubt that day will come, Oom Hannes,' Christiaan said.

Anna came and went. He would listen for her footsteps in the passage and try to catch the cadences of her voice in the distance. Sometimes he was conscious that she had seen him in his nakedness. She was already in his mind his wife. But what was he in hers? An object of compassion? An outlet of her womanliness? Her cousin?

The Ndebele brought him a fine blackwood stick carved with a serpent around its length. He realized that the limp would remain. Anna returned to her schoolroom duties which took her away for hours by day and at night she sat next to the lamp preparing lessons for the next day. Sometimes she played the organ in the front room. When he recognised snatches of Bach his heart soared. Often they talked quietly about his studies in Holland, sometimes of his benefactor Rawlinson. When he caught her eyes she would look down or turn away. The intimacy he had experienced during his illness seemed to him to have been illusory. He could not understand why things had changed.

One day he could stand it no longer. The schoolroom was a mile away but he walked the distance, glad that it would give him time to compose what he had to say. For a lawyer he felt singularly wordless and dry of mouth. Years later children who witnessed what happened that morning could still laugh. A limping *oom* with a short yellow beard and light blue eyes suddenly burst into the room. It was just a mud-brick structure with a lean-to roof and a single window. They were scratching on their slates when this apparition appeared. Without a word he took *Juffrou* by the hand and turning to the children, he said, 'It's a holiday. You can go home.' He said it with such cool authority that Miss Anna did not protest.

'Now look here,' he said as the last child went out with a giggle and a backward look. 'I can't stand it any longer, Anna. Will you or won't you marry me? I must have your answer because I'm going back to Pretoria, quite likely tomorrow.'

'You are better now,' she said calmly, sorting through some sheets filled with childrens' writings.

'Please put that down and attend to me. As I see it, you have a commitment to your father. I respect that. He may live with us if you wish it so. I have a debt to him.'

She looked up and he saw that she was neither laughing nor crying. The grave blue eyes were level on his.

'I shall be a limping lawyer all my life,' he said. 'Already I owe my life to you. Do you want to kill me now?' She smiled at that. He was catching the fragrance of her. It seemed to rise all about her in a dizzying haze. And yet she was not beautiful. 'Won't you help me?' he begged, seizing her hands and carrying them to his lips. 'I can't go on without you any longer.'

There were children peeping in at the window and a hen walked in through the open door, then ran out scolding.

'I love you so, Anna.' He lifted her face to his.

'I've loved you all my life,' she said.

Instead of kissing her he ran limping into the veld and stood under a thorn tree. He wanted no one to see him weeping. Slowly she went over to him, the hem of her dress dragging in the small plants. And those who watched as children remembered that they stood locked in each others' arms for a long time.

Chapter 20

From the bedroom window of Bloukoppen Leonard Penlynne could see the glint of early morning sun on the test tanks set up half a mile away. From high up here on the ridge the surface of MacForrest's pools of cyanide had the illusory glint of gold.

Penlynne always rose early and these summer mornings it was light at five. Farm waggons were already trundling into town and water carts were laying the dust. It was an early rising town and in his mood of optimism Penlynne could not have lain a minute longer in bed. He was wearing his silk dressing gown, a present from Kitty – black silk with a golden dragon coiled around the loins when it was closed. He had just slipped out from her side ... she was a late awakener. A night girl.

Before he left the house he loved to walk in the early morning garden, plucking at herbs and examining the growth of the young shrubs and trees. Kitty generally joined him on the terrace, drowsily beautiful. These mornings he ate with relish. Porridge, bacon and eggs, toast and preserves, followed by fresh coffee. Kitty seldom ate breakfast but she often drank a glass of champagne.

It seemed to him an astonishing and marvellous thing that he could be eating here with this woman, fresh and glowing from her bath and barely clothed. The marvel was that she matched his excitement in everything. She responded to his exhilaration.

He spent a lot of time during the day with the chemist. He was convinced that the experimental plant would succeed. MacForrest counselled patience as he worked on the erection of the plant and laboratory. It would take two months to show anything. He would not be hustled. And he made no optimistic pronouncements.

Josiah Rawlinson sometimes turned up. He looked dour and sceptical. Talk in the newspapers and around the bars was pessimistic. Penlynne did not mind. The lower the market fell and the more mining companies went bankrupt the more incredible were the possibilities for himself. One simply had to keep one's nerve. These days when he walked into the Rand Club there were always men anxious to sell out. Frantic men made over their holdings to him for the simple undertaking of clearing their debts and the price of their fare to the coast. He was picking up claims on the South Dip for a few pennies a morgen of land. Alfred Beit backed him to the hilt and allowed him full latitude to buy on his own behalf. Penlynne bargained and bought and sometimes took over claims for the price of the government licence.

Sometimes a cold shiver would come over him when he assessed the extent of his holdings, all on paper. And so far worthless. But at other times, especially when he and Kitty were alone together, he felt he could never fail again. Just the same there were moments when MacForrest's methodical methods irked him beyond control.

'If you hustle me, Mr Penlynne, it'll make no difference. You must trust me or try your hand at black magic or alchemy.'

'Don't forget our deal ... no cure, no pay.'

'And don't *you* forget that when it does work the Gold Recovery Syndicate pays me a royalty on every ounce of gold recovered!'

'Well, let's see it then, Mac.'

They could laugh it off over drinks. The deal was signed and irrevocable. Penlynne had closely watched the heavy cost so far in setting up the machinery to bear the concentrates to the tanks. It was into thousands already. He was exhilarated by the danger of it and Kitty was part of the thrill. Each morning as he dressed, putting a rosebud into his buttonhole, he was amazed at his good luck. He had a sparkle of confidence about him that he knew with amusement made some men tap their foreheads and shake their heads.

Let them. Tomorrow they'd be lifting their hats.

A number of mine managers on the east and west Rand sent in concentrates, hopefully for treatment. MacForrest rubbed his hands. 'Never fear, Mr Penlynne, there's fortunes in that muck.' He would wink and go off in a fit of laughter.

The bitter stench of cyanide blowing over the town roused some anger. Once there was a demonstration outside Penlynne's office. 'This poison on the wind,' was the comment of the Rawlinson press.

MacForrest declared he could smell only roses but he hung skull and crossbone notices on his tanks and posted native watchmen with *kierries* to prevent careless use of the fluid. Some brewers of *skokiaan* would try anything to liven up their poisons.

One morning when he had been at his desk for a couple of hours, Penlynne was surprised to hear Josiah Rawlinson announced. The man had lost weight since his marriage to the Scotch housekeeper. They said she had as tight a hand as he on the purse strings. His clothes hung somewhat on his huge frame. There was snow white in the thicket of tobacco-stained mustache.

'Come in, Josiah,' said Penlynne amiably. 'Sit down, please.' He pulled out a chair. 'Good to see you.'

Rawlinson sat down heavily and removed the white helmet. Penlynne could still feel awe in the sheer presence of the man. 'When will we have to call you Sir Josiah?' he chaffed. Rawlinson waved it aside. He began to talk urgently of the coming elections in the Transvaal. They must create a fund to support the Dutch liberals hostile to Kruger's policies.

'Can I count you in for a thousand, Penlynne?'

'Of course.'

They spoke about the rumour that the Government was to raise another commando to begin fresh hostilities against Magato and his people. The effect on labour could be critical. When there were wars like this the natives deserted the mines in thousands....

All the while Penlynne was aware that they were talking around the real reason for Rawlinson's visit. 'Look here, Penlynne,' he said at last. 'I'm not a man to beat about the bush. This gold recovery business ... I'm uncertain of it, but it might just come off. I know MacForrest's got problems with equipment. Leaky plant, can't control the solution.'

'Some people are hoping for the worst,' said Penlynne.

'I've a proposition, take it or leave it. I'm willing to let your man MacForrest do his experiments at the Star. You'd have direct access to the concentrates and I'd bear fifty per cent of the costs.'

He leaned back like a man who could hardly have made a fairer offer. Penlynne knew the advantage of silence at such moments. Rawlinson was obliged to go on.

'The Star is still recovering sixty-two per cent ... without cyanide...'

'Forty-two,' said Penlynne, lifting a blank sheet of paper and studying it as if it held the latest statistics.

'I don't need you,' said Rawlinson, 'but I'm willing to move with the times. What do you say?'

Penlynne looked across his desk and saw a man who was trying to gain control of a situation which had already slipped through his fingers. 'I'll think about it, Josh,' he said.

'You mean you won't,' said Rawlinson. 'Don't say I didn't make you a fair offer.' He got to his feet, rumbling and blowing, and turned to give Penlynne a last piercing glance. It was a look that had hastened many a man to the wrong decision.

That night Penlynne lay back on the pillows, his head on Kitty's breast, the french doors open to the coolness. 'I've been thinking about Rawlinson's offer. Do you know what he's after, Kitty? Nothing less than the presidency. He asked me for a donation to sweeten the Dutch liberals. He needs Johannesburg to give him the presidency. I think he wants to be seen as the saviour of the town. The Dutch liberals will be used to give us the vote. The mining community will out-vote the Krugerites. And we'll have President Rawlinson. To get the miners behind him he needs to stop the exodus and restore confidence. He can't do that on declining values. That's why he needs me and MacForrest. Why else would he make me such an offer? Certainly not out of his esteem for me.'

Kitty lay looking at the ceiling. What she was hearing concerned her only in so far as it affected her relationship with this man. He bored her when he talked business, but like a good wife would she concealed her boredom and tried to channel his thoughts and words towards their life together and her position as his lady. Occasionally she had tried to test him on his feelings for Dorothy. Would she be returning? It didn't seem like it but there was always the possibility. And then what? It was a subject that had to be very carefully handled. Unless he was in a particularly pliant mood he would not discuss it; neither would he hear anything against Dorothy although Kitty knew that for days at a time and sometimes from one letter to the next he hardly gave her a thought.

Now, as he talked his mining politics, she thought how extraordinary it all was ... Kitty Loftus in a richly furnished room listening with half an ear to Penlynne's talk. A confidante in high affairs.

'Rawlinson doesn't want to see Johannesburg go smash and thousands lose everything; or so he says. He gives this as his reason for backing what he calls a wild chance. Decent of him, don't you think?'

Kitty came quickly back to the present. She leaned over him, feeling his eyes devouring her features. She often found him staring at her as if he were seeing her for the first time.

'I sometimes can't believe it,' he said, lifting her breasts with both hands and kissing her throat. She turned on her back and put his hand between her thighs. She wanted him to stop talking business and reassure her that he would always be her protector.

'You told him "nothing doing", I expect.'

'I told him I'd think about it and talk it over with Gardiner.'

It seemed to him that she stiffened at the name and removed his hand. 'They're in the new house.'

'Yes.'

'Is it better than this one?' She knew that he had been there without her. Although she had said nothing at the time she had resented the slight.

'It's more expensive. Gardiner made a killing before the market crashed. In fact, he caught it both ways. He's got fancy tastes. French chef and an English butler. Also a London nanny for the child.'

'Think she's happy?'

'He seems a reasonable fellow. Good sort. I like him.'

'Well I don't!' She sat up and, naked, walked to the open doors where she stood with her hair falling down her back, her body outlined by the glow of stars so that she looked at him like something out of a voluptuary's imagining.

'I don't like the way he looks at a woman.'

'Good heavens, surely he hasn't offended you?'

'Yes, he has. I was coming out of St Mary's...'

'What on earth were you doing there?'

'Don't laugh at me, Pen. I was raised a Catholic.'

219

'So you were repenting, were you...'

It appeared that she had gone into the church to donate some money for Father Murphy's orphans. As she raised her skirt to step into her carriage Gardiner had lifted his hat and offered her his hand. She had been startled.

'I never forget a pretty face,' he had said, smiling.

'I told him I didn't think I'd ever met him.'

She had signalled her Malay driver to drive on but Gardiner had delayed the carriage and told her that he believed he had seen her aboard *The American*. 'Just a glimpse. You seemed to hide away. And now you're here. How is it I've missed you? Where are you living?'

'How dared he!' said Kitty, breathing furiously.

'Maybe he was only being civil,' Penlynne said. 'He knows very well you've been staying here with me. He's certainly seen us together in town and at the theatre.'

'That's it,' she flushed angrily. 'He's ... making out things.'

'You mean insinuating.'

'Insinuating, yes.'

'Insinuating what?'

'Oh, don't be so stupid. I know how he looked at me. I know what he's getting at alright.'

'Well, we don't have to have him in the house,' said Penlynne calmly. He understood the source of her indignation better than she realised and felt a momentary pang of remorse at having put her in a position where men could assume the right to accost her. He could not afford to fall out with Gardiner. They were in partnership. He went to the window.

'Come back to bed, Kitten. I'll never let anyone hurt you.' Her anger passed and he well knew how to take advantage of her heated blood. The day of the deep levels was coming and he and Gardiner would be in it together. Gardiner was one of the few mining engineers in the world who had experience of shaft sinking beyond a thousand feet.

'We've been invited to the christening party,' he said, trying to soothe her, although strictly speaking this was not true. He had been casually invited by Gardiner while they were out on the south ridge where Gardiner was supervising the erection of a test drill.

'Katherine's had a son,' he had cheerfully informed Penlynne.

'Look in on Sunday morning if you like; we're having him sprinkled.'

Had Kitty been invited there would have been a formal invitation card delivered to the door. There was already a social order and ladies did not receive each other except on their 'At Home' days. Kitty did not receive and was not received.

'I don't know,' she said doubtfully.

'Come on, of course we'll go. I'll enjoy showing you off.'

'Alright, but I'll need a new gown.'

'Get it,' he said and he felt her arms about him.

In the next few days she chattered a lot about the right thing to wear and he indulged her, well aware of the slight tremor in her voice which betrayed her apprehension of how she'd be received by Katherine. Let the stupid bitches think what they like, he thought. No one will dare offend her. In any case Katherine did not strike him as the kind of young woman who would have strongly defined social attitudes. Not yet, at any rate.

In the later weeks of Katherine's pregnancy the condition of pre-natal toxaemia which had concerned Stewart had cleared up. The possibility of eclampsia had diminished. Her natural strength had prevailed. The room was airy and quiet in the daylight hours and Stewart encouraged her to walk about or sit in a chair in her dressing gown. He was sometimes met by her father who gave him a genial smile and accompanied him to the door of the bedchamber.

'This child means a great deal to me, Stewart. I'm grateful for everything you're doing for my daughter. You'll see I won't forget it.'

It sometimes happened that Stewart went directly from Katherine's house to Ferreira's Town. Down there in the warrens of sun-dried brick and iron sheeting the mortality of infants and mothers was shocking. Every time he was called there he found himself contrasting it with the comfort and luxury of the woman on the favoured side of town. Children in what had been the earliest mining camp were born on filthy mattresses or on sheets of newspaper in rooms without water or sanitation. He did what he could....

On the day of the christening Rawlinson met him at the door. He was blazing with good humour and his great booming voice filled the hall as, in frockcoat, carnation in buttonhole, a fine diamond in his dark blue silk cravat, he welcomed friends. Katherine was lounging on a velvet chaise longue, her long hair twisted about her neck. The infant was with his English nurse next door. Katherine gave Stewart her hand and smiled radiantly. The shadows under her eyes had faded. Conscious of her beauty as he had always been, it seemed to him now that she had the added aura of a joy he had never seen in her before. It gave him great pleasure too to see how naturally she welcomed Mary. Difficult now to remember the fifteen hours Katherine had been in labour and how he had told her, 'Don't be afraid to cry out. Don't hold your breath. Shout if you want to.'

He had been anxious too at one stage about a too rapid advance of the head, fearing laceration. It never failed to move him that the son of the rich man and the daughter of the labourer were born in the same gush of water and blood, the small red, crumpled faces astonished and outraged at their expulsion.

Katherine's child had been the first he had seen born with the bag of membranes intact over its head. 'It's a caul, doctor,' the nurse cried.

Muriel Rawlinson set great store by the caul. She insisted it must be dried and preserved. It was a sign of good fortune, she said. The boy would be lucky in love, fearless, and would never be drowned at sea.

Rawlinson wrote Stewart a cheque for a hundred guineas.

'With your permission, Mr Rawlinson, can we say that this money is your contribution towards the establishment of an institution for research? I'm grateful for the improvements at the mine hospital but, respectfully, very much more needs doing there.'

Rawlinson's powerful face lost its geniality.

'Can you afford such lavish gestures, doctor?'

'I'm being paid a good fee by Mr Gardiner.'

'You Scots,' Rawlinson growled. 'You're an obstinate race. Give it here.' He took the cheque, looking directly at Stewart. 'I'll make it a thousand. You can call it the Rawlinson bequest.'

The child had been christened Walter Fairbrother Spencer Gardiner. All names from the American's family. Rawlinson commented sourly, 'No wonder my grandson yelled.' It had been done over Katherine's protests and it was Rawlinson's belief that it was the father's way of asserting his break with the child's grandfather. It affected him more than he admitted. Never having had a son he had promised himself that this boy would lack nothing. Despite his displeasure he had continued legal arrangements to set up a trust for the boy.

'He'll be educated at the best English school ... Eton!' he told Katherine as he took the child in his arms, his great sun-reddened face pressing close to the infant. He was thinking of his own schooling in a single room in a heat-seared Karoo landscape, barefoot, learning his letters from a travelling schoolmaster who went from farm to farm, giving instruction and then moving on. They were mostly drinkers and scapegraces, though some were men of good family. He always stressed: 'I had the best education possible at the time.'

There were expensive gifts for young Spencer Gardiner. A sideboard of christening mugs. Toys far beyond his age, all of them given, Penlynne suspected, in a mood that was far more calculating than tender towards the infant. The board of the Rawlinson Star had been particularly lavish and obsequious in the style of its congratulations. It struck Penlynne that these were aimed more at their chairman than the parents.

Penlynne was at his best on an occasion like this, when friends and rivals, even enemies, could take pleasure in the event for its own sake. A male child was a thing to rejoice over. And not just the family. It enriched everyone to see and exclaim over this mewing scrap of human flesh. Who knew what he would become? Sinner or saint. Every possibility was within him.

When the child was brought in Penlynne took him in his arms for a moment. He could not do so without emotion. Dorothy rose unbidden to his mind. Some day ... some day. He looked across the infant's elaborate gown that all but concealed it as a living thing and found himself looking into the eyes of Kitty. The green eyes were wide and he saw that she was very pale. Beyond her he saw the huffed backs and turned shoulders of women dressed for the occasion, rustling and whispering. Some of them he knew by sight from association with their husbands.

In an instinct to protect Kitty, he said impulsively, 'Hold him!' She took the child without hesitation, warmly and firmly, her face alight with pleasure, and he had a momentary feeling that he was looking at a little gutter urchin sitting on the kerbside in London, her feet in the muck of rainwater and garbage, holding the bundle of rags that was her infant brother.

He saw, too, with a lurch of his heart, how the soft red tendrils of hair fell about her cheeks. My God, he thought, like that cartoon by Leonardo, the same roundness of cheek, the same aura of womanliness.

Muriel Rawlinson descended on the scene and brusquely removed the infant. Penlynne put a good face on it for Kitty's sake but inwardly he was angry and though he had meant to convey his best wishes to Rawlinson in person he took her home at once. She was raging. She stood screaming in the hall after flinging off her hat and gloves. 'Whores! Trollips! Half of them didn't have a rag on their backs a couple of years ago. Who are they to treat me like that? I told you I shouldn't never have gone. You done it to give me a showing up.'

'For God's sake, Kitten, why would I do a thing like that?'

He held her trembling, outraged body against him and presently her lips turned up to his. 'Let's go upstairs,' she whispered.

Katherine missed the incident. Shortly afterwards she took the child upstairs. The affair was becoming rowdy; already there were flushed faces and raised voices. It was only later she learned that 'the Loftus creature' had been soundly snubbed by the assembly of wives.

'Was that necessary?' Katherine asked, disturbed.

'A woman like that!' Muriel Rawlinson sometimes thought that Katherine's leanings towards the lower elements of society and her dismay over what she considered injustices were unsuited to her status. She had been pleased to note that Miss Loftus had left in a huff though Mr Penlynne had not been put out.

'Everyone was welcome,' Katherine said. The incident cast a cloud on an event that had already turned painful to her. Walter had been more than necessarily attentive to a woman who was a stranger to her. She had intended to go directly downstairs again but the nurse insisted she return to bed. She lay tensely, almost counting the departing carriages.

When the last guest had gone Katherine listened for Walter to come up to her room. He had drunk more than usual but one could never tell with Walter because he did not show his liquor. You had to know him as well as she did to recognise that taciturnity and an unexpected melancholy were the signs. In these moods he did not like to be touched. It was as if he were bottling up some fury. Suddenly he looked his age. She had learned to say as little as possible and the next morning would find him boyish, and, if not exactly contrite, considerate. Sometimes flowers arrived; at others some trifling gift. He knew that she was not a woman who set great store on expensive expressions of guilt.

When he was being young and amusing there seemed no great age difference between them and he had an ability to reduce any resistance or resentment she might have to nothing with something as simple as an unexpected caress. She thought of these things as she lay in the great bed, looking forward to his coming up and praising her. As he held the child at the christening he had been so careful and solemn, quite unlike himself, as if he were taking the vows of fatherhood more seriously than his attitude to most things. He seldom told her what he was thinking or what he felt but standing at his side she was certain that he was moved by the tiny grasping hands reaching up at his face and his son's sudden wail as the water wet his head.

She knew that he would never let on what he had felt. If she spoke about it he would make some amiable rejoinder. As she lay, undecided whether or not to go downstairs again and see what was detaining him (quite likely he would be in the billiard room; he did a lot of his thinking and planning bent over the green baize, alone with the clicking of balls) there was a knock on the door. She had hoped for Walter's brief rap but this was her maid's.

'I just came to see if you're comfortable, ma'am.'

'You can take Spencer to the nursery, Mildred, and give him to Sister.' She watched the girl lift the infant and saw the look on her face. She was now Katherine's personal maid but she had become more than that in the final months of Katherine's pregnancy. There was no more than a few years between the young women. Katherine's Kimberley upbringing had not put the barrier between her and Mildred that would have been the case in such a household in England.

'Is Mr Walter in the billiard room, Mildred?'

'I'll see, ma'am.'

Mildred dropped a curtsy, a habit she had never quite discarded despite the relationship between them. She knew every tone of Katherine's voice, especially the note of firmness that came with uncertainty ... and when her voice was near breaking. Mildred had found her unusually depressed after the birth, and more than once in tears. 'I don't know why I'm going on like this,' she sobbed. Mildred knelt at her bedside and stroked her hair. 'Oh, ma'am, he's a beautiful child.'

'It's not the baby...'

'Oh, ma'am, Mr Walter doesn't mean to hurt. It's the way he is. He's been on his own so much.'

Katherine clung to her. 'He'll never say he loves me.'

'Oh, there ma'am, he does. I see him look at you and he's so proud.'

'Is he ... is he really?'

It was as if she were always reaching out for something that he was forever withholding. Not that he denied her anything physical, nor any whim or serious wish. It was simply that he had no understanding of her deeper needs. She was still disturbed by the sheer masculinity of the man and by his authority and the deference of all around him. Among the servants only Mildred stood up to him as if she knew it was her place to stand between the man and the girl, to make excuses for her. Mildred sometimes served at table and she was adept at interpreting the glances and the censored remarks that passed between husband and wife. During the difficult weeks of her pregnancy Katherine had borne his casual treatment with dignity. There had been a night when Mildred, disturbed by a sound in the passage, had found Katherine standing at the door of the master's bedroom (they had slept apart for some weeks). She had led Katherine back to her room. No need to tell her that the bedroom was empty. Suddenly her mistress was sobbing in her arms.

'What am I doing wrong? Why is he punishing me like this?'

Mildred held her. They stood breast to breast, warming each other with the intensity of their feelings. 'Forgive me,' Katherine had said, breaking from the other's arms. 'It's selfish of me.'

'Oh, ma'am ... I miss my man too ... him out there in that India and me not seeing him for two years or more and never knowing if he's alive. I'm longing for him to get his discharge and then ... well, ma'am, his idea is to buy a farm here. He's a sergeant and between us we've a bit put by...'

The aftermath of their coming together on this emotional, almost sisterly level had been an undercurrent of sympathy which had grown stronger, though both were careful to conceal their feelings from Muriel Rawlinson and from the other servants.

That Katherine's husband had been so uncaring on the night of Spencer's christening incensed Mildred on Katherine's part. She went first to his bedroom to see if he was there. The billiard room was also deserted. She went into the library. There was a fire burning but no one there. An empty whiskey glass stood on the arm of his chair. In the hearth there was a crumpled sheet of notepaper, as if he had been reading a letter and tossing it page by page into the fire. She looked over her shoulder. It was page three of a letter from a woman upbraiding him for heartlessness. It occurred to her to take it up to Katherine. Instead, she decided to put it away among her own things. One never knew...

Chapter 21

The day before Leonard Penlynne was due to make an official announcement about progress on the MacForrest Process he and the chemist were together in MacForrest's wood and iron laboratory, shirt-sleeved and soaked in sweat. The chemist's face was averted from Penlynne as he swirled a test tube of cloudy fluid up to the light, shook his head and emptied it.

In the bright sunlight outside the donkey engine thudded and the churning paddles of the test vats swirled the grey ooze to a bitter yellow-foamed broth. The grey fluid was flowing over the zinc on precipitation tables and the residue was piped away to where it formed a bog of grey slime.

'What's gone wrong?' Penlynne asked, trying to keep the note of concern out of his voice. 'You assured me that we'd have an extraction of eighty-two percent. For God's sake, Mac, you've come up with nothing better than we had before.'

'You're rushing me. This work can't be rushed. I warned and warned. The ore here is not the same as the samples I worked with in the lab at home. Those were from Australia. I assumed there'd be little difference. There's no chemical reason I can think of that's preventing the gold from precipitating. I'm fair puzzled, Mr Penlynne.'

He stood in the open door, his red hair fuzzed and grizzled. Lit from behind as he was, Penlynne had a momentary impression that this was a jesting clown. It struck him with an icy chill that the man might be a charlatan. But he must not panic. In a more reasonable tone he said: 'London's waiting for my cable to launch African Gold Recovery. I promised them figures by Monday. What's the exact position?'

The chemist sat down in his stained white coat and acid-deteriorated shoes. The eyes behind the lenses of his glasses were enlarged to a look of exaggerated dismay. 'I hadna reckoned with the acidity. I'll have to experiment with caustic alkalies. What we have here is an auric hydrocyanide and it looks as if it's only imperfectly precipitated by the use of zinc. I'll need caustic soda or potash, in quantity. Theoretically at any rate caustic soda could improve the precipitation.'

'Damn theory, man! If this gets to be known we'll be laughed out of business.'

'I'm a scientist, Mr Penlynne, no' a financier and if you're not willing to go on with this I can soon enough go back to Scotland.'

Penlynne put an arm around him. 'You shall have time,' he assured. But he shrank from the matter of going to the press with news of a further delay. His new company was ready to do business as Rand Mining and Investment. It needed an atmosphere of confidence, particularly in its chairman. Over the past months he had steadily consolidated his holdings. His surveyor's charts showed that he (with Alfred Beit as majority shareholder) had the whole of the South Rand in his grasp. The potential deep levels. Treasure trove of tomorrow when MacForrest got his witch's brew in order. He had miles of land under option on the east and west Rand where the depressed communities had all but abandoned hope.

All that was needed was the spark of MacForrest's success to start the explosion of confidence. And now this setback ... with Rawlinson waiting to ridicule his efforts. He could not face the possibility of being wiped out. Maybe he was young enough, active enough to start again but it was the humiliation he feared. His reputation with Beit and Rhodes. His good name in London, Paris and Berlin. To be labelled just another Jo'burg swindler, market manipulator and fast talker ... it was not to be borne. His reputation in London was growing. Dorothy was mixing in the highest circles of financial society.

Only last week her letter had spoken of the kindness of Madame Porges, a dinner with the Rothschilds at the Savoy. He could not bear to be labelled a 'Peruvian' in such circles after emerging from the dust of fifteen years of toil in Africa. At twenty he had slogged in the dry diggings along the Orange River and been the ill-paid manager of other men's claims. To become a man of probity had become as much his ambition as to be wealthy. Until this moment he had felt assured that his courage in buying when others sold out would be respected. Beit assured him that his shrewdness and coolness would make him a legend wherever men talked money. 'And where is that not!' he had said puckishly.

And now ... another failure thanks to the man who had been so cocksure of his formulae. It was all he could do not to take him by the neck and throw him through the door. 'Listen, Mac, we'll buy up every ounce of caustic soda and potash in the Transvaal. This setback is not to get out. We must find a plausible explanation for delay and announce that the system is showing results.'

MacForrest's face turned obstinate. 'I've a good reputation as a chemist and I want to keep it. I don't care for doing things in secret. My report must go out. "Tests so far inconclusive." It's promised as a matter of scientific duty. Chemists everywhere, and metallurgists, are waiting for it. And so is the press.'

Penlynne saw that much of the objection was pure scientific vanity. He knew that if MacForrest insisted on releasing this negative result he, Penlynne, might as well go and blow his brains out. His shirt was sticking to his back in the oven-heat of the shanty. His cigar was dead in his hand. He had a momentary vision of the last time he had seen Barnato. Now it was he who needed a miracle ... the word of optimism he had then denied.

He walked outside. The hard blue of the midsummer sky promised nothing. Dust devils swirled their red columns between the shanties of Ferreira's Town. Down there tradesmen would be shutting doors and windows, cursing the unmetalled roads and the dust churned by hooves and iron tyres. Men like Rawlinson had sowed the seeds of a metropolis here but it was Penlynne's dream to see its ugliness and brutality transformed; to use that part of his genius that inclined to the aesthetic to transform Johannesburg into a city as stately as it was rich.

'Just give me another month, Mac. Delay your report for a month, that's all I'm asking.' The chemist's mouth set more firmly. 'Confidence is everything. Keep trying. It could be a slight miscalculation in your figures...' He couldn't help noticing the red stubble of two day's beard and the pouched eyes of sleeplessness.

'I dinna miscalculate.'

'If you publish this now ... and I respect your scientific disinterest in money ... just consider that you may never get another such opportunity to prove your process.'

The shaft went deep. MacForrest turned an indignant face; then slowly smiled. 'You know just how to capitalise on a man's weakness, don't you, Mr Penlynne?'

'I won't forget this favour, Mac.'

'I don't count on gratitude,' said MacForrest.

'That's what contracts are for,' said Penlynne with a levity he did not feel. He threw his jacket over his arm. He knew that MacForrest's scruples had been won over, however reluctantly. He walked away from the stinking tanks with their death head signs. He noticed that the rose in his lapel was a mass of wilted petals.... Kitty had put it there only an hour before, lifting her lips to his. My God, he thought, I've been close enough to disaster to contemplate a cupful of that brew. Now all his energies must go into raising the needed chemicals. A calming statement to the press here, a reassuring cable to London – these were the first moves.

He whipped up the pony trap towards town. Hats were lifted in his direction. 'See you at the cricket tomorrow,' he gave them back cheerfully. He was remembering an incident in Kimberley. It had happened when the thousands of individual claims in the Big Hole had become a dangerous mess of shafts with every man's claim undermined by the next. He had gone down in the bucket hoist into one of Rawlinson's claims and was some thirty feet below the surface when he had a sudden awareness of disaster. The light above him went dark. The next man's claim was crumbling and falling in on him.

He was dug out by the frantic efforts of his boss boy. The black face and the glare of sunlight. The transition from death to life had only been a matter of seconds. His thought then had been: I've escaped from the grave.

He had the same sensation now. But how long could it last? It certainly would not outlive another failure by MacForrest. He was still at the mercy of the press, particularly the Rawlinson press. He talked it over with Walter Gardiner. Their intimacy had grown of late. They thought alike on many subjects and he respected the American's judgement.

'It was touch and go today, Walter,' he admitted.

'Why don't you make a bid for *The Oracle*? It needs capital. I'll look into it if you like.'

'No, I think I'll do that myself.'

Steven Yeatsman shifted his body in the swivel chair in his office, blew the red dust off his papers and continued to dip pen in inkwell. Shirt-sleeved, his stiff high collar loosened, he worked by the light of a single bulb under an iron roof without a ceiling. The floor was trampled earth. Bookcases were of the same packing cases that had brought out the printing machines. Dust was ruining his books. Through the aperture to the works came the reek of hot oil, steam, printing ink, sweating men and the pungent odour of fresh newsprint. Amazingly stimulating. It was like a mental aphrodisiac every time he entered his office. That, and the clatter of the flatbed rotary press, the walloping sound of the belts licking around and pulleys powered by the steam engine in the yard.

It was still a marvel to him that what he wrote on this paper came off the press in hundreds of copies twice a week. Black and bold and authoritative. *The Oracle* has spoken! It was on hundreds of breakfast tables, in homes, hotels and clubs. When he walked to the Rand Club of a morning or to the Royal Standard Bar where mining's big men gathered for eleven o'clock drinks, he received civil nods and was aware of a murmur: 'That's Yeatsman.' Two sheets folded made eight pages. He wrote it all and often folded copies too. To him it was a marvel of accurate reporting, shrewd comment and bold criticism. He was twenty-four and he was an editor. Twenty pounds a week and freedom to proclaim his beliefs. Within reason...

It was four months since Penlynne had installed him. In that time he had got to know as much about the MacForrest Process as anyone. As he wrote now he was recording the first success, conscious that he was in on history. MacForrest had done it. What was more the cantankerous old devil had done it in a series of public demonstrations. He had used free milling concentrates, tailings and pyritous ores. In every case the fine gold obtained had been beyond the theoretical extraction. This afternoon Yeatsman had watched the assay of 6,210 lb of pyritous ore submitted for test by the Rawlinson Star Company.

'What I saw there,' Yeatsman wrote, 'will be a matter for public celebration, here and abroad. Despite imperfect equipment and the ridicule of sceptics, Mr MacForrest has persisted over six difficult months. The whole Reef has watched his experiments with hope. Today I saw the culmination as a pellet of glowing gold representing a fine gold extract of 90 percent appeared in the crucible.'

He remembered the thunderstruck expression on Rawlinson's face as the assay was announced. The man got up and stalked away from the refinery. Others crowded around the Scot standing modestly in his stained white coat, his hands busy with congratulations, beaming. 'Oh aye, it's all a question of proportions.' He made it sound as if it had been no more than a juggler's trick.

Yeatsman scribbled on. 'Johannesburg is saved. The great tide of depression and lack of confidence will be turned. This we can confidently predict. Mr Leonard Penlynne will proceed at once with the flotation of his African Gold Recovery Syndicate.'

He went through to the works to watch the compositor set it up, waited for a galley proof and took it personally to Penlynne's office. 'If I were you,' said Penlynne genially, 'I should head this...' And he scribbled on the galley: 'Triumph of Modern Chemistry: Turning Point for Rand'.

Then he waved the young man to the table of drinks. 'I might add for your own information,' he said, 'that the first in this office to seek a contract with us was Josiah Rawlinson. I almost believe he'd rather have seen the industry go under.'

Dorothy Penlynne knew that she had made an impulsive decision. She left the specialist's rooms in Harley Street and went directly to Wernher's office. Her intention was to ask him to cable Penlynne that she was taking the first available boat to South Africa. Dr Berthold had made it clear that her condition was improved to the point where she could resume her marital responsibilities. His unstated suggestion of evasion had dismayed her. She had no idea that anyone, even her doctor, could see through the face she showed to society.

The pregnancy she had hoped for had come to nothing but Berthold had assured her that there was no reason why she should not have children – 'But of course, Mrs Penlynne, one must not delay into the thirties.'

Wernher took her to lunch at the Berkley. 'Your husband made ten thousand this morning,' he told her affably. 'Everything is going just as he foresaw. A remarkable man.' Wernher did not give her any impression that Penlynne would benefit from her return, rather the contrary. He hinted that this was not the time to build their great house on the ridge which she had been discussing with her husband by letter for months past. Penlynne's replies had been brief and noncommital, his letters coming at longer and longer intervals.

'He seems to be working eighteen hours a day,' she told Wernher. 'He's president of the Mining Chamber and on so many committees. Frankly, I'm worried that he's doing too much.' She toyed with a crêpe, pushing it to one side untasted, unaware of the clatter and hum of fashion around her, and watching Wernher's face she was suddenly gripped with the idea that he was warning her not to return.

'You know, of course, that he moved out of the house in Leyds Street? Yes, he's been living in Doornfontein in the house built by Karl Marloth.' Wernher's eyes seemed to be wandering over the other diners. 'The company took it over, you know.'

'That huge tasteless place,' she said, somehow ruffled and distressed. He was ordering coffee, nodding as he unwrapped a Valle Valle cigar. 'How on earth is he coping there alone?' she blurted.

'He was left a good staff. Butler, German housekeeper, coachman. Your husband puts up visiting notables, people we send out.'

Dorothy tried to conceal her surprise. She nodded without expression. Penlynne had said nothing to her of this move. All their correspondence passed between her apartment and his business address. Possibly he had wished her not to distress herself thinking of him alone in that house with twelve bedrooms. She was remembering that there was a side to him other than the hardworking manager. There was the ardent Penlynne with his love of fine things, poetry and music, his fascination with the theatre, his enjoyment of life and gaiety. This ball he was giving without her ... what would people think? She wondered how many would remember her as Mrs Penlynne, victim of that shocking incident. The more she considered it the more convinced she became that Wernher, always a man of deep consideration for her feelings, was trying to spare her now. As senior partner in the firm which had brought Penlynne to Johannesburg to manage its interests, he had been rather like a genial German uncle to Dorothy.

It was Wernher who had found her an apartment and paid her

allowance and her dress bills since she had come to England. It was he who had arranged hospitality for her trips to the Continent. Could it be that he had actually in a subtle way controlled her movements? But why?

All that was independent and impulsive in her revolted at the idea ... and now, was he gently attempting to prevent her return? Although she had been extravagant she still had several hundred pounds in hand from the last quarterly allowance. More than enough to pay her fare back to South Africa without Wernher's help. She saw the bearded, considerate face through the fragrant haze of cigar smoke, watching her with shrewd eyes.

He smiled with sudden enthusiasm. 'There is something here you will not want to miss...' His accent slurring her name in that attractive way. 'Her Majesty is to open the Imperial Institute in South Kensington in a few weeks' time. There is to be a Cape court featuring South African diamonds. We do want you to meet Her Majesty. Penlynne is enthusiastic.'

It was as if he were deliberately heading off her unspoken intention. There was a panic in her heart she could not fathom. Through her inner turmoil she could hear Wernher enthusing about the supper party to follow, a box in the Lyceum Theatre, important contacts useful to her husband.

Suppose she were to turn up in Johannesburg instead? Unannounced! It was the kind of impulsive thing that Penlynne had always found so amusing. He adored the impromptu – the luncheon that turned into a party, the day at the races that went on to be an entertaining weekend. She would travel under her maiden name and arrive unannounced. Yes, she would leave for South Africa by the next mailship. Had she headed Wernher off with her vague acceptance of his offer...?

Back in her apartment she hastily summoned the architect. During the past few months they had had many discussions on the house Penlynne had promised to build on her return to Johannesburg. Fortunately the young architect had sufficient sketches ready for her to take out for Penlynne's approval. The house was going to cost a fortune and the furnishings another. But if Pen was to become 'king' of Johannesburg, and all the talk said he would, then it was her duty to be at his side and together they would watch every detail of a house suited to his new status.

George Borcherd had hesitated at buying material and hiring

craftsmen to go out to South Africa without Mr Penlynne's authorisation. Dorothy had quelled his hesitation with an imperious gesture.

'You have my authority.'

'Very well, Mrs Penlynne.' As she watched him leave she felt both elated and apprehensive. She was reassured about her decision to push Borcherd when she boarded *The Moor* two weeks later and found Lord and Lady Gordon Lennox, son of the Duke of Richmond, going out to see South Africa for themselves and in search of investment opportunities. She was able to warn them that Johannesburg was a rough place and was delighted when they accepted her invitation to stay at Bloukoppen – 'our temporary abode.'

In Cape Town she was seized by a great affection for the country of her birth. Her eyes filled with tears when she heard the accents of Malays and the people of mixed race. She felt so close to Penlynne that it took all her resolution not to wire him and spoil the surprise. At the same time she felt a sinking apprehension about his reaction. They had been separated now for almost two years.

The train was held up by washaways in the northern Cape where the swirling red flood of the Orange River tore at the crumbling banks for two days before it began to subside enough to trust the bridge. How familiar it all was: the green willows trailing their fronds in the muddy water. She had picnicked with her father in places like these on idle summer days when the river was tranquil. Now she realised that the earliest she could hope to arrive in Johannesburg would be the evening of the ball. She resisted the temptation to telegraph Penlynne to meet her.

Gaslight flared over the platform at Park Station. When she left there had been no train. Johannesburg was incredibly changed. No cabs were available. The Hollander station master was apologetic. They had all been taken up for Mr Penlynne's ball ... the whole town was there. She stood hesitantly outside the station. The roads were still unmetalled, the streets only partially lit. It would be foolish to attempt to walk to Bloukoppen. She returned to the station master's office.

'I am Mrs Penlynne,' she said firmly. The man stood up.

'You must get me a cab at once.' Gratifying though it was to see the alacrity with which he moved to obey she had a feeling of increasing ... yes, it was as strong as fear. Waiting, she watched through a window the flare of lights at the Wanderers' Club. The far off sound of waltz music rose and fell on the hot night air. There was a sudden din of passing Africans, drums thumping and dogs barking. It was still unbearably crude.

Penlynne waited at the foot of the wide staircase. Kitty was still dressing. He had indulged her whim not to ask questions about her costume, not without some trepidation. She was impulsive enough to wear something entirely inappropriate to the occasion. He had invited hundreds to the ball at the Wanderers'. Everyone in mining and business and government, as well as distinguished visitors from overseas on hunting trips or looking for investment opportunities, would be there. The President had declined but would be represented by his Minister of Finance. The newspapers had filled columns for days in advance. The Wanderers' Club had been transformed into 'a faery bower of evergreens and potted plants'. It would be, he read, the greatest social occasion of the decade. Mrs Penlynne would not, it was regretted, be present, being overseas on account of her health. Miss Kitty Loftus, the noted actress 'of whom we have seen so little of late on the boards', would be the hostess.

The *Standard and Diggers News* noted that invitations had been declined by some clergymen. Penlynne did not care a damn. He glanced at his costume and in spite of its splendour he felt a trifle foolish. It had been chosen for him in London by Dorothy. She had spent a pretty penny on it. The jewellery in the turban was authentic and the scimitar an actual piece. She had even sent out enough make-up with instructions on how to use it to darken his skin, but in the end he had settled for remaining a white sultan.

At first he had been afraid that Dorothy would insist on his delaying the date of the celebration to allow her to be present. She seemed so interested in the whole affair that he suspected she might have heard rumours of the goings on in the house on the ridge. So far she had not hinted at this in her letters. She might wonder about the press reports mentioning Kitty as his hostess, but he would be ready with a plausible explanation if she did.

In her last letter she had written simply, 'Since I cannot be with you please have a splendid photograph taken. I know you will be a sultan indeed! I shall read all about it in the *Illustrated London News* and *The Sphere.*' The letter had ended with a plaintive, 'feeling rotten and missing you dreadfully. The papers here are calling you the saviour of Johannesburg and the Transvaal ... I am so proud of you.'

Penlynne did not think it immodest to agree with the opinion of the press. But to call a man a hero was to know only the most superficial details of the truth, the visible outcome. Few knew what hell he had gone through in the past six months. How touch and go it had been. He had felt the strain of keeping up a bold front when the entire MacForrest operation had looked like disaster. If it had failed, he would have been the biggest holder of useless, barren farmland in the Transvaal. Instead, only today he had stood on the edge of the red clay excavations for a twelve-storey building on the corner of Simmonds and Market streets. It was to be the finest commercial structure in Africa. From its boardroom he would be able to look out on the visible symbols of his optimism – the incredible march of mine dumps and headgear east and west of the first strike by Rawlinson at Langlaagte. True, they were not all his by any means and there were years of hard struggle ahead. He knew well enough that to wrest its wealth from the obdurate rock was going to take millions in cash, plus the skills of the best and most highly paid men he could bring over. He knew that he had the energy to cope with the demands. Johannesburg itself with its exhilarating climate and astonishing fruitfulness gave him each morning the stimulation he needed.

He was standing in his costume on the long Ushack carpet, admiring the richness and variety of its design, when he became aware of a rustle of female clothing. He glanced up the staircase and gasped. He was looking at the Gainsborough portrait of Sarah Siddons come to life. Marvellous creature! How had she done it? Sent to London for the material without his knowledge?

She swept down the staircase, her red-gold hair piled up to carry the huge, feathered hat. The billowing satin skirt rustled as she moved. He saw the fullness of her breasts beneath the wealth of lace. For a moment she stood there, immobile against the richness of panelled wood.

'Do I please you, sir?' Speaking with the careful accents the great tragedienne might have used. Then in a lapse into the comic London voice she sometimes affected. 'Don't knock me fevvers orf.'

'My God, Kitty,' he cried, 'you're marvellous. You'll set the whole town talking.'

'I suspect I do that already, kind sir,' she said, holding out her gloved hand to him. 'Is it windy outside?'

'A little. Hold your hat until we get into the carriage. I'll take you right to the door.' Looking at her he was surprised to see a minute film of perspiration under the careful make-up. Was it the warm night or did she feel a slight unease about the occasion, more grand than any she had ventured on before? He pressed her hand. 'You're magnificent. They'll all love you.'

'Not everyone,' she said.

'To hell with those who don't.'

'Just as well it's this month,' she panted, taking his hand into the carriage. 'In another week I couldn't have got into the costume.' They'd call the child Penlynne's bastard. Well, it could be educated at home. Kitty would have to agree to that. No use worrying about it now.

When she knew she was pregnant Kitty had been frightened to tell him. She had gone alone to Stewart MacDonald in his town rooms. 'Are you sure, doctor? There's no doubt at all?'

Stewart stripped off the rubber glove, his back to her at the basin. 'There's no doubt, Kitty.'

She looked away and he could see what idea had been in her mind. There were tears in her eyes as she said, 'Mr Penlynne's very good to me. He gives me everything. I'm afraid that he'll be angry or put out, him being so important an' all.'

'He doesn't know?'

'Not yet.'

'I think you'll find he won't be angry. He has a responsibility to you.'

She brightened at that. 'Will you come to my house when the time comes, doctor?'

'Surely.'

A few days later he received a handsome gilt-edged invitation to a costume ball. On the back in Kitty's untidy hand he read, 'Please come and bring your wife. I so want to meet her. She must be a very special girl.'

The ballroom was like a hothouse. Claude de la Roche leaned against a pillar on the verandah. He drew on his cigar, watching the swirl of dancers. It was really an extravagant affair; must be costing Penlynne thousands. It amused him to see the Dutch officials and their perspiring *vrous* looking so ill at ease in this atmosphere of foreign levity. Supper had been served without a blessing being asked! It intrigued him that Penlynne had felt obliged to invite him. His status in the town had changed dramatically since he let it be known that he had the sales rights of the French explosives consortium, Fabrique Nationale. The first shipload of dynamite had been unloaded at Lourenço Marques. It would be on the Rand shortly and in competition with the Nobel Trust franchise. He could greatly undercut that monopoly. Penlynne's mines alone were going to be worth millions a year now that the pyrites problem was solved and with the new hope of deep level mining ... all that shaftsinking and tunnelling.

De la Roche knew that his new social acceptability rested on his ability to undercut Nobel Trust. And of course he would for as long as it suited him. He had made money in liquor and had pull with the liquor licensing board about the granting of canteen licences. He had made shrewd buys in real estate and when in France he had purchased the title of an obscure baron, long deceased and his line extinct. In Johannesburg he rubbed shoulders with sharp-witted men from every country in Europe ... and held his own. No one here cared how a man got his start. Being penniless was the only thing held against a man in Johannesburg.

Penlynne had gone out of his way to be civil. 'Not in costume, Baron?' he asked as he danced by.

'Please excuse the omission.'

Penlynne paused. 'I hear the French explosives are in Lourenço Marques. I'd enjoy a chat with you about that.'

'Certainly, at any time.'

'Oh, have you met Miss Loftus?' Penlynne turned to make the introduction but she had melted away in the throng of dancers.

'You're a lucky man,' De la Roche said admiringly. She should have no hard feelings. Hadn't he brought her out here from a second-rate theatre company in London? A chorus girl.

'I don't believe in luck, Baron. I believe in making opportunity work for me. In business and pleasure.'

'Shall we say tomorrow then?'

De la Roche walked outside. He was impressed by Penlynne at close quarters. This was not a man to be taken lightly, he thought.

Stewart MacDonald was not enthusiastic about the 'Penlynne extravaganza' as he called it and he had no intention of wearing costume. The idea of changing one's personality with one's clothes did not attract him. He would not have accepted at all if he had not seen the expression on Mary's face when the card arrived. To her it was as if they had been especially chosen for some honour. She was radiant with excitement. He had not been allowed to see her costume and when she called him into the bedroom a few minutes before they were to leave he could hardly believe what he saw. A rosy-cheeked Scots fisher lass, the kind he'd seen so often crying herring in the streets of Glasgow. It brought tears to his eyes, a surge of nostalgia and love.

'Will ye buy my caller herring?' she dimpled at him.

What could he do but embrace her and kiss the bright face between the starched wings of the white cap. 'Och, Mary ... my Mary.'

Alexander MacForrest was to pick them up with a cab but when the appointed time came and went and no MacForrest Mary was in a fever of dismay. 'What are we to do, Stewart?'

'I'll fetch a cab, or a ricksha.'

'We canna turn up in a ricksha. Are you sure he knew to bring the cab here? If you've got it wrong, Stewart!' She stamped her foot, caught between tears and laughter at the absurdity of turning up in a ricksha with a whooping Zulu between the shafts.

Indeed, Stewart would not have been surprised if either he or MacForrest had got it wrong. The arrangement had been made in haste, both men preoccupied, Stewart with a dozen men down with enteric, newcomers who had been drinking the fouled underground water, and MacForrest with a chemical paper to write. They had become friends after discovering that they had studied at the same university. The man was lonely and soon became a frequent visitor. He had a dry wit and a nice light tenor voice and was fond of the old Scottish airs Mary stumbled over at the piano. He had confided that Penlynne was a hard taskmaster ... but fair. It was to Mary that he had burst in with the first news of success. The process was vindicated. He was beside himself with delight.

'What will you do now?' she asked him as she placed a hot griddle cake before him with her own apricot jam.

'Do?' he said, rapturously licking the spoon. 'I'll be away hame. I've a mind to buy the auld Buchanan estate on the River Dee and be a laird. I'm gaun to be a rich man, Mary MacDonald.' And soberly, 'It's a fact, lass.'

Later he showed them both figures that seemed to them to be in the realms of fantasy. 'This time next year, my dears, I'll be asking you to be my guests on my steam yacht. No, seriously, look at the figures. A thousand tons of ore will give you two thousand pounds of treated residues, with an eighty percent recovery – it's better than twelve hundred ounces.'

'You mean ... gold?' said Stewart incredulously.

'What else, laddie! It's the process! But what we're talking about here is six thousand ounces of gold from Rawlinson's Star alone. Call it twenty-five thousand pounds. A month! Aye, a month! And ten percent's coming my way.'

He was pencilling the tablecloth till Mary put paper in front of him. 'I could pick up the Buchanan estate for twenty thousand or thereabout. Aye, salmon and a deer park and the moors stocked with grouse and pheasant. I used to walk the moor when I was a bairn and get my backside warmed by the gamekeeper.'

'Och, you're havering,' Mary laughed.

'It's a solemn truth. If you've any money put by, Stewart, now's the time to snap up shares. Buy now.'

'Buy what?' said Stewart in bewilderment.

'Anything. Any damn thing at all. Sae long as it's gold!'

Apart from the fact that he had nothing to spare, at the time it had seemed to him lunatic counsel with Johannesburg still in the depths of depression, mines hardly operating, goods stacked in the market place and shops that had flourished a year ago boarded up. Whole districts stood empty. The only thing that still flourished was sickness.

Well, MacForrest had been right. He was leaving for home within a few days and to judge from the way he had been fêted and celebrated in town he could well have no remembrance whatever of his promise to pick them up for the ball. Every newspaper sang his praises. The man who had saved the Rand.

When half an hour had ticked away on her mother's wag-at-the-wa' clock, its pendulum sounding ever more ominous in the silence, Stewart set off on his bicycle to look for a ricksha. As he cycled over the dark rutted road he was thinking what an extraordinary thing it was that one man's ingenuity could save an entire community. They were saying in town that he'd changed the course of gold mining ... and even more ... of history in the sub-continent. Was it any wonder he'd forgotten to fetch them a cab!

A mile short of Ferreira's Town his bike punctured and he was obliged to get down, cursing the new pneumatic tyres, the roads and MacForrest. Och, my puir lass, he thought. I've really got to do something for her sake. And her so uncomplaining. Maybe it was time to take a room in town and put up his brass plate.

Dorothy Penlynne was not prepared for the luxuriousness of Bloukoppen. When she had last lived in Johannesburg there had been nothing to match this opulence, clumsily Germanic though it seemed to her taste with its dark panelling and heavy pieces. The maidservant had stared at her and spoken vaguely about her master's movements.

'It's alright,' she assured the German girl, 'I am Mrs Penlynne. I'll wait for my husband. You may go.'

Alone she wandered into the dining room, noting that the table seated twenty. Many of the leatherbound books she saw in the library were French and German. She went silently upstairs, her feet making no sound on the Turkey runner. Her heart was beating fast. She was anticipating she knew not what but already she sensed that Penlynne did not live here alone. The house, for all its sombreness, suggested a lighter presence. She opened door after door off the main gallery, all unoccupied bedrooms. Toilet things in the bathroom confirmed her fears. In a silver-backed brush she found a few strands of hair the colour of the Venus in the Botticelli canvas.

Penlynne's room was characteristically sparse and neat. She smelled his pomade and saw his dressing room, the rows of shining shoes. A door opened off it and she felt herself in the presence of this other woman, her taste evidently rich and frivolous. She saw the huge bed with its embroidered canopy. A fresh bowl of roses competed with the heavy odour of cosmetics. On a

243

gilded escritoire she saw a silver-framed photograph of Penlynne, the dark, intelligent face smiling confidently. She put it down with trembling hands and closed the door, her anger mounting.

She went downstairs to the library and rang the bell. No one came. She poured a glass of sherry and sat down to await the return of her husband and the red-headed woman. She dozed in the chair, then fell into an exhausted sleep. She woke when a maid pulled back the curtains. '*Grüss Gott!*' the girl exclaimed.

It was daylight outside. Penlynne and the woman had not returned. Almost at that moment she heard the grating of carriage wheels on the drive, loud voices and laughter. Evidently Penlynne had brought his guests back to the house for breakfast. She remained where she was, seated, listening, trying to isolate and identify the voice of the red-headed woman from the rest. Momentarily she was seized with panic; then with a great effort she rose and opened the library door to confront them.

In the harsh light of morning they looked absurd in fancy dress, particularly Penlynne, as if his folly had drained him of some vital quality. The red-haired woman was leaning on his arm, looking, Dorothy thought, like a tawdry imitation of a great lady. One of the party caught sight of her. The laughter subsided. Penlynne looked stunned. The woman took his arm, as if to draw him quickly upstairs. She had a startling beauty, slightly coarse. Dorothy felt glad of that. It would have been harder to bear had the woman been one of the London set she had so recently left behind.

'Please go upstairs, Kitty,' she heard Penlynne say. Then, turning to his guests, he said with renewed authority, 'I'm afraid the party's over.'

The dozen or so strangers moved to the door and Kitty, staring defiantly at her, went slowly up the stairs. At the turn she stopped and looked back as if to appeal to him. Then she went on up.

To Dorothy everything seemed to be happening in a vacuum, in a strange annihilation of reality. She must not faint, she told herself. He was coming towards her. He seemed immense in the turban, regality itself with his dark beard and glittering eyes, the scimitar trailing somewhat absurdly at the hem of his robes. Othello, she thought. Then he was taking her hands.

'Why on earth didn't you tell me you were coming?'
'I thought to surprise you.'
'Indeed you did ... but why?'
'I thought you'd be pleased to see me.'
'Well, what can I say? I'm sorry it had to happen this way.' He shrugged. 'No use beating about the bush. As you see I've not been living the life of a celibate.'
'I see that.'
'For God's sake, Dorothy, what did you expect? You've been away a long time and even before you left...'
'I'd rather not discuss that.'
'Very well. Later perhaps.' He pulled at the bellrope. 'I'm ordering breakfast. I'm ravenous. I expect you are too. What time did you arrive?'
'Too late for the party.'
'We can sort this all out,' he said quietly, his eyes steady on hers. She realized with shock that his eyes no longer held the expression of vulnerability she remembered. This man was a stranger.

She was dismayed by his sang-froid and the ease with which he appeared to have overcome the shock of the moment. Perhaps it's for the servants, she thought, as he ordered his man to 'set for two on the terrace and take a tray up to Miss Kitty.'

'I'm not hungry, Pen,' she said.
'Please yourself.' But his expression had softened, although he remained seated some distance from her.
'I'm sorry, Dorothy. Dash it all, you should have let me know.'
'So you could get rid of the evidence.'
'You'd have heard pretty smartly. No, that's not what I meant. Anyway, we'll move your things into the guest room.'
'You don't expect me to live here, surely?'
'It's a big place.'
'Nothing on earth would induce me to live here.'
'Of course not. I'm rather confused myself. Where will you go?'
'To an hotel, I suppose.'
'No, no, that's impossible.'
Her composure suddenly crumpled and she began to fumble in

her handbag. He viewed her fumbling with distaste and impatience.

'Really, Dotty, you should have cabled.' There was a discreet knock at the door. 'Come in,' he called curtly.

'Breakfast is served, sir.' The servant spoke as if nothing unusual had occurred. Penlynne waved him out.

'Will you join me?'

'No.'

He gave her an uncertain smile and went out onto the terrace. A moment later he returned. 'I really had no intention to hurt you, Dorothy. In a way I expected you to know.'

'I had no idea ... none.'

'I expect we'll come to some arrangement.'

'Then you have no intention of giving her up?'

'I would prefer you to turn a blind eye. I shall book you in at Heath's. It's really quite good though not up to standards you've enjoyed in Europe. Then we can talk things over properly. Or would you prefer to spend a time in Durban?'

He was speaking as if it was all quite simple, just another arrangement. And presently he would bathe and shave and go to the office and get on with important matters. He was showing a degree of insensitivity which left her numb. What was she to do? Return to Europe? Join her mother in Kimberley for a while?

'Come, Dotty,' he said, taking her arm and leading her onto the terrace. 'You must be exhausted. Won't you lie down upstairs until I've made arrangements?'

'I'd prefer to leave right away,' she said.

'I understand.' For the first time there was a note of conciliation in his voice.

'I wonder if you do,' she replied.

Chapter 22

Four months had gone by since the night of Penlynne's ball and it was still being talked about. Stewart MacDonald was reminded of it when he opened a letter from Alexander MacForrest. It was postmarked Monte Carlo. The chemist had a worse hand than a doctor's prescription. He was there to buy a summer villa, having achieved his ambition of buying the Buchanan estate '... but not a fit place for winter after Africa.' He hoped Stewart had taken his advice and bought in 'when shares now standing at pounds were a few shillings a job lot ... and then no takers!' He enclosed a Kodak print of himself against a pillar covered with bougainvillea. 'Purple – magnificent!' He asked kindly after Mary but never a word of the evening of the ball when he'd forgotten to turn up.

MacForrest penned a lengthy postscript: 'Nothing will bring me back to that abyss of dust, flies and niggers. Do you see anything of Penlynne? He was all gratitude for a while but now I seem to note a grudging tone when his cheques arrive. It's as well that I've got him tied to a contract. If there's one thing I do miss about that bleak and awful town it's the good stink of cyanide! Yours aye, affectionately.'

Stewart had seen nothing of Penlynne but everyone in town knew that his wife had returned unexpectedly. It was from Kitty that he had a personal account of the scandal. She had come to him in a state of bewilderment, misery and indignation. When he opened the door of his consulting room she looked like a hurt child. He did not forget that she was an actress but the face beneath the towering hat looked as guileless as one more sinned against than sinning.

'Come in,' he said. 'I didn't expect you today but since you're here we'll have a look, shall we?'

As she removed her hatpin some strands of the amazing red-gold hair tumbled loosely about her shoulders. Really, she was enchanting, prettily gloved, her boots beneath the long skirts which she carefully adjusted of the best. She was redolent of expensive cosmetics but wearing no jewels – which rather surprised him. When she drew off her gloves he saw her nails were bitten to the quick and when she began to speak the whole facade of brazening it out started to collapse.

'I don't know which way to turn,' she wept. There was a flush on her cheek and as he leaned forward to take her pulse he smelled alcohol. Covering her face with her hands she began to tell him about that morning .... She had waited upstairs for Penlynne to come up. Two hours went by. At last he came. Instead of cradling her in his arms and assuring her of his tenderness and protection he spoke of Dorothy and how dismayed he was that she had turned up like that. 'Bit of a shock for her, you know.'

'But it's her fault,' she had shouted at him.

'Keep your voice down, Kitty. I don't want to rouse the household.' His indifference to her distress only provoked her to shout louder.

'Stupid bitch! Leaves you for years and then turns up to spoil everything.'

'Be quiet at once.' He went out in a cold anger, leaving her crumpled and weeping into her pillow. She did not leave her room all day. She heard him giving orders to the servants and their muffled whispers on the landing. At one stage there was a knock on her door. A tray had been brought up.

'Take it away!' she screamed. Nothing would induce her to eat while he continued to treat her so cruelly. He had installed a telephone so he could call her from his office. It never rang. It was late afternoon when she heard his footsteps on the stair, his hand on the door. She turned her head away as he came towards the bed.

'Feeling better?' he asked, turning her face towards him.

'Yes,' she whispered.

'They're bringing us up a tray.'

'What's going to happen?'

The trolley was wheeled in and they ate in silence. At last he told her what he had in mind. 'She'll stay at the hotel. She's planning to build a house.'

'You mean she's staying?'

'Everything will go on as it was before. This is your house and I'm still looking after you.'

'But it can't be the same,' she wailed.

'It will be the same,' he said firmly. 'Nothing has changed.'

It all came out in a tearful jumble as Stewart examined her. When she was calmer he bent over her, his gloved hand checking the position of the foetus.

'Nothing amiss,' he said cheerfully.

'What's to become of me?' she said.

'Kitty,' he said, 'as your doctor and an old friend – no more drinking. You must think of the child.'

'He says he's happy about the baby but I dunno if he's telling the truth. He's often with her and her posh friends from London.'

He took up his pen. 'Iron tablets,' he scribbled. 'Rather necessary for new mothers. No strenuous exertion, short walk each day, plenty of rest and not too many late nights. And Kitty, no intercourse from now on.'

'You must be joking,' she said. 'He hasn't been near me for ages ... that way.'

Dorothy Penlynne seated herself on a rock. From the low koppie she looked north to the blue smudge of the Magaliesberg range some twenty miles away. This was the site she had chosen for her house. Between it and the mountains a yellow prairie of winter grassland undulated into the distance. Round her skirts a chill south wind bullied the coarse plants among the rocks. Aloes in brilliant flower decked the slopes with their burning coals. She watched a hunting falcon beat up and down the ridge. This was the place. She would build on this rocky slope which was so remote from the unplanned disorder of Johannesburg only a mile away. Up here the air was clear of the red dust of the valley. The house she planned would far outdo Bloukoppen where Penlynne had installed the Loftus woman. It would be equal to anything on the Bois de Boulogne. She would entertain the cream of foreign visitors. Even royalty will not feel out of place in my house, she told herself defiantly.

Up here on the rise, the chill wind buffeting and blowing her hair against her cheeks, Dorothy brushed tears impatiently aside. Nothing could hurt her now, not even Pen. He had advised her not to walk alone on the koppie. She had pretended she had no idea what he was getting at. She would do as she pleased, go where she pleased, with him or alone, at any time. She was not afraid. She would build a great house. She would bring antiques from Europe, paintings and gilded mirrors, Persian rugs and tapestries and Venetian marble and bronzes.

Miners had already begun to blast out the carriage drive that would lead up to the front door. She could hear the dull, rhythmic thudding of the drills on stone, the boss boy's steady chant and the response of the drillers. Up here she would keep out any contact with that Africa. Society would beg and grovel to be admitted to her dinners. Whether Pen liked it or not she was the wife of the most important man in Johannesburg. And she meant to fulfil her role as his equal, impervious to opinion.

As for the actress! When Pen told her that the woman was expecting his child she had received the news calmly, as though he were talking about some casual mutual acquaintance, of no particular interest to either of them. When she pictured Kitty it was as a bold, voluptuous woman, never as the mother of Pen's child. She could not grasp the reality of that. It all seemed far into the future. If indeed it were possible at all.

She had moved into the hotel that first morning and she saw that her ability to do so had impressed him. She had a choice but she went back into the same building where the aftermath of her agony had been played out.

She rose from her seat, smoothing out her skirt about her legs. The hem was filled with hooked grass seeds which penetrated the fabric and her stockings. It was a reminder of harsh things. The monotonous chant of the blacks came up to her with the steady thud of hammers. She knew that Pen had come to realise that she was made of sterner stuff these days than the pitiful creature he had sent away to his father's home in London. Then she had felt broken and defenceless. Now she felt strong in her resolve to make this gossiping camp forget that there had ever been a Mrs Penlynne other than the chatelaine of the great house on the ridge.

She had written to Penlynne: 'I realise of course that in our strange situation, with the ocean between us, you could probably not have done otherwise than take a woman into your house. It was foolish of me to suppose that your work would keep you busy all the time. And even more foolish to think that we could make a fresh start when I felt well enough to take up our married life once more. Nevertheless I have no plans to leave you. It seems to me that when the house is ready we shall present, to outward appearances at least, a fine exterior. You shall see that I am not afraid of gossip. It appeals to me to be in a position of wealth and prestige, and I admire you for achieving this position for us.

'Until the house is ready I shall continue to live here. George Borcherd has moved in. He is a very decent young man and a lively companion. You will be surprised at the number of friends I have been able to make in high places during my stay in London. Friends who will be an asset to you in many ways. Already I have letters to answer from parties interested in coming to look around Johannesburg. I am sure that you will be very busy entertaining a stream of important visitors.

'The house, as I plan it, will cost a great deal, but it will be a fortune well spent. I have given Borcherd the order to go ahead in every respect. Your suggestion that I should live in Bloukoppen when the Loftus woman goes to Cape Town for her confinement is really tactless. It is an ugly house. So clumsy and heavily Teutonic. To me, all the place lacks is a German band to play sausage-and-beer music on Sundays.'

She read the letter through a couple of times, tempted to soften a phrase here and there, but on reflection decided to leave well alone. She was in no sense ready to meet him on conciliatory terms. Perhaps such an offer would one day come from him. She was still not sure whether she wished it to happen or not.

For several days after writing she felt nervous about his reaction. Would he accept her terms or would he conceivably ask for a separation? She hoped it would not come to that. If it did, how would her new-found strength react? It was possible the affair would come to an end quite abruptly. These liaisons seldom lasted. Her tentative plan was to bide her time. Separation was just conceivable. Divorce, never.

In the next few weeks she drove daily to the site in her dog cart to watch the house going up. She revelled in the activity, the sound of trowels ringing and the masons' chisels shaping stone. She could read the plans as well as Borcherd by now. Her chief pleasure was the feeling that her initiative had set all this in motion. Penlynne had been to the site several times, although he had said nothing to her. She knew how much her contacts in England meant to him. She had made a journey of light years away from that other age when she had been a barefoot child running between the bleached tents of the Orange River Diggings. Now she was Mrs Dorothy Penlynne ... and might yet be Lady Penlynne. She would relinquish none of that future, a future in which she would hold the reins that controlled his life.

The scaffolding was second-storey high by the time she noticed that a view of Bloukoppen could be seen from the upstairs bedrooms. She ordered George Borcherd to alter the plans. He seemed put out and a few days later told her that Mr Penlynne had refused to authorise the additional costs.

'You had no right to go to Mr Penlynne behind my back,' she stormed at the astonished architect.

'But Mrs Penlynne,' he began, his untidy hair blowing into his eyes. 'It will be a very considerable sum ... and delays.'

She was fond of him but the flash of sunlight from the windows down there had been too much. 'How dare you, George? Your orders for this house are from me.'

He began to stammer, never having seen her in such a rage before. 'Perhaps you would prefer it if I withdrew from the work, Mrs Penlynne, though I should be sorry. I have enjoyed our collaboration and admire your judgement very much.'

At once Dorothy Penlynne put out a conciliatory hand.

'No, no, George, of course not. I want you to continue; besides I am going to need you to draw plans for the city art gallery I'm thinking about. I want it to be the finest in the southern hemisphere.'

'I'd be honoured to work with you, Mrs Penlynne. I've always dreamed of doing a project like that.'

'Make the alterations, won't you,' she said.

'Very well, Mrs Penlynne.'

She went back to the hotel, thinking with rage and distaste of Penlynne's recent announcement to her that he had given Bloukoppen to Kitty Loftus as a gift. She knew that this was the basis of her outburst but it rankled. 'And who, may I ask,' she flared at Penlynne, 'is to pay for the upkeep of that establishment?'

'I have made her a shareholder in African Gold Recovery. It's the least I could do for her and the child.'

'So you don't intend to give her up?'

'I wish you could take a more mature view of this,' he said.

'You're indifferent to gossip.'

'This isn't London. It's a small town. Everybody knows everybody's business. If they can talk about Lord Randolph Churchill as a syphilitic they can say what they please about me. I'm living my life, Dorothy.' He stood swinging the bauble on his watchchain and she tensed herself for his next thrust. It came smilingly.

'I thought that to be the chatelaine of Far Horizons would be quite an achievement for the daughter of a minor official at De Beers.'

'My father was a decent man,' she said. 'No doubt there will be a sharp distinction between the guests you entertain at Far Horizons and those calling at Bloukoppen.'

'Perhaps you stayed away a mite too long, Dorothy,' he replied coldly. 'The snobbery of London society has never applied here ... though no doubt it's coming.'

That the turrets of Bloukoppen would remain in sight to gall her dismayed Dorothy. It was almost as if Penlynne wished to remind her that her influence as a hostess would still be dependent on his generosity. 'Another ten thousand I refuse to spend, Dorothy. Already people are calling this place Penlynne's Folly.'

'What may I ask are they calling your infatuation with this actress? If that is the right word to describe her talents.'

'My infatuation is my own affair. Call it folly if it pleases you.'

Later in the afternoon she received a note from him.

'Dear Dorothy, I have decided to give in on this matter of the alteration. Please go ahead just as you wish. Pen.'

Dorothy never knew the exact reason for his change of heart. She hoped that it was an indication of contrition and she read the note many times hoping it might convey his regret. Actually, at this moment he had too much on his mind to waste time wrangling with her over what, to him, was really a triviality. One day he would have to re-think his attitude towards her, and it would probably be with regret for his present position, but in the meantime he had much on his mind. Josiah Rawlinson was seeing state officials and Kruger, urging them to declare the MacForrest process a government monopoly. Penlynne did not underestimate their power to do so. They had turned everything they could into state revenue for their ramshackle republic. Dynamite, timber, liquor. Iniquitous taxes on every item of mining machinery railed in. Wringing the neck of the golden goose, he called it.

Penlynne was not keen to find himself in politics but if it was the only way to prevent Kruger crushing them and ruining the mining industry, not to speak of his own rise to power, then the time might come. Appeals to the old tyrant's reason usually proved hopeless. Suppose the *uitlander* community were to demand the vote, rouse a popular clamour and force Kruger from power? There were thousands of hotheads on the Reef ready to be followers of a resolute man. He had always declined invitations to speak at patriotic dinners and smoking concerts. Now he saw that they could be a useful forum, promoting the idea that under one flag, the flag of England, and the sovereignty of Her Majesty Queen Victoria, newcomers would be able to enjoy the freedom they needed to develop a great country. A British country.

Josiah Rawlinson sat in the shade of the wisteria arbour watching his grandson. The tottering child seemed to him to step out with the right kind of Rawlinson vigour and purpose.

'Spencer,' he coaxed. 'Look here!' He held up a sovereign. 'Katherine ... watch this.' The boy grasped the piece of gold and put it to his gums.

'That's it, lad,' Rawlinson laughed. 'Test it. Don't just take my word for it.'

'Do you want him to choke on it, father?' Katherine protested but she had to laugh when Walter Fairbrother Spencer Gardiner used his own judgement and cast the gold coin among the sweet-williams and grasped at his grandfather's trousers. It was hard for him to remember Katherine as the strong-willed girl in Kimberley, whooping her horse alongside the men, riding down ostrich in the veld, her hair tucked up under a boy's cap.

Her father noticed fine lines around her eyes. The Rand's thin air and harsh light soon left its mark on women. Her mother's portrait, taken in a tin shanty in Kimberley, was unlined ... she was always twenty to him.

These days he often came to Katherine's house on the Parktown ridge, especially when Gardiner was away. And that was often enough. He would call the house by telephone before driving over. He had no desire to see his son-in-law after the way the man had joined forces with Penlynne. It grieved him but that was the way it was. Sometimes he tried to draw her out but she was not responsive. Watching her now he could not quite put his finger on her air of ... was it melancholy? Did Gardiner ill-treat her? Did she feel already that she had missed out on something? Certainly she lacked for nothing that money could buy. The establishment kept a butler, a French chef, an English coachman and his laundress wife, a children's nurse from Manchester and English housemaids. The Scotch gardener was as cantankerous as any of his tribe. Walter had done well for himself in switching his allegiance and if he proved the deep levels he'd be a millionaire.

That his daughter was married to a man who might one day in the not distant future rival her father, and even outstrip him, was hard to take. He wished she would confide in him. She talked about clothing she was having sent out from England and all the little details of Spencer's progress but she never discussed her husband.

He groaned inwardly. Gardiner and Penlynne and this chemist fellow MacForrest with their so-called Cyanide Process had every mine owner along the Reef paying through the nose for their system. It was a great triumph for Penlynne that the Gold Recovery Syndicate had already recovered over a half a million ounces of gold from tailings, worthless rock till now.

Rawlinson never saw the grey swirl of the cyanide plant at his own Star without feeling his collar grow tight and his heart pound. Even in his new offices the stink of cyanide on the wind reached him, never failing to remind him that Penlynne had refused to let him in on the syndicate and had blocked his efforts in London too when he tried to buy there. Even here in Katherine's garden he could smell a faint bitter odour. No wonder the gardener grumbled that the acid-laden wind scorched his blooms and tainted his vegetables.

He could never forget that day at the refinery when he had watched the public test pouring. The burning stream of gold had almost scorched his eyeballs. By God! MacForrest had done it after all. He'd recovered ninety-six percent pure gold. It meant that every heap of broken rock discarded as useless on the sixty miles of the Reef had recoverable gold.

It gnawed him that it would not be the name of Rawlinson that would be remembered as the saviour of the Rand. And he was the true pioneer of them all. They had scoffed when he bought up farmlands. Rawlinson's cabbage patches! Well, millions had come out of them and millions more were still to come. He had a report on his desk now. It calculated that by the turn of the century, in a mere five years, the reefs would yield up twenty million sterling a year, of which some three million would be his and his shareholders' here and in Europe.

At the last board meeting the figure of two hundred thousand paid out to Penlynne had been a matter of concern. Alfred Kellerman, his manager at the Witbank Colliery, voiced what they all felt: 'How did we get into this situation?'

The suggestion of error on his part enraged Rawlinson.

'Rather the question is ... how do we get out of it?' He glared around the table at the men he would be relying on to run his companies when he retired to England as Muriel was nagging him to do. They were all experts in their own fields but none of them had the stuff of greatness. There wasn't a Penlynne or a Gardiner among them and maybe it was his own fault that he had chosen men who seldom challenged his decisions.

'However, gentlemen,' he said, bringing himself under control, 'I believe I have the measure of the situation. We should now urge the Government to take over the cyanide treatment monopoly, as being in the interests of the state security...' He paused, watching their reactions as they stirred, meeting each other's eyes. 'Penlynne's monopoly on this thing is a danger. In a year or two he'll have more power than the state. It's outrageous. One man and a chemist having the sole rights to a trick with chemicals ... that's all it is, gentlemen. One of our own assayers could have come up with it.'

He relished the murmur of assent. 'Of course, if Penlynne lets us buy in that's another story.' They saw him glare through the blue haze of cigar smoke with the bloodshot eyes of an old boar. 'So far he's refused all reasonable approaches.'

'Suppose we simply refused payment,' Kellerman suggested.

'On what grounds?'

'Challenge the patent.'

It had sounded good to him and the board decided to consider ways and means. Rawlinson thought a really first class lawyer, a

Boer, if possible, could carry Kruger's judges with him if they could find the smallest technical reason for rejecting the patent. Especially if he was convinced that here was an *uitlander* plot to rob the republic of royalties.

'What's worrying you, daddy?' Katherine's voice brought him sharply out of his thoughts. She placed a cup of tea on the garden table beside him and motioned the nanny to take the child. She kissed her father's forehead, something she had not done for some time. Her cheek brushed against the grit of beard beneath the dark, sun-reddened skin. She had been urging him for months now to take up residence in the Park Lane house and leave his anxieties to his managers and the Board. The high choleric flush of his cheeks worried her. His reactions were becoming slower than they used to be.

'You should retire now, daddy. You know you should.'

'I have to get everything settled here first, darling. This cyanide business. It's ruination to us. I don't expect Walter's spoken to you about it but between them he and Penlynne are bleeding us white.'

'I'll speak to Walter, father. Would that help?'

'No, no, my girl. It's not for you. This is men's business. I just hope that they'll see reason before they ruin us all.'

Katherine bent to snip the head of a fading rose, scattering petals on the flagstones. Bright sunshine glanced off the silver tray. He sensed that she was burdened by some inner conflict ... perhaps of loyalties. She looked up suddenly as if she had made a decision.

'I think it's unfair that they should treat you so, father.'

'It's business,' he said with a mildness he did not feel. She was about to say something significant. He waited, hardly breathing, as she resolved her conflict.

'We had a visitor last week. He told Walter that there was a chemist in Australia, a Dr Hahn, who had been using cyanide for ten years. In one of the outback mines. What does that mean? Walter put him down pretty quickly.'

Rawlinson was too old a hand to show his elation. She had handed him the key. He nodded ponderously, mustering the calm that had been his strength in the old days. He looked up at her with those blue eyes which had lulled many with their penetrating blueness and unexpected twinkle. He wondered how far she was conscious of having betrayed her husband. Was this a way of hitting back at him for his infidelities? Surely she knew of them?

'I might look into it, Katherine,' he said drowsily. 'Don't bother Walter with my problems; he's got his own. This deep level madness .... But there, girl, it's not for you. You'll always have your father...' He closed his eyes and pretended to nod. He heard her tiptoeing away.

He chuckled. He had the chink in Penlynne's armour for sure. The process was no patent at all. The maid came for the tea tray and he sat on, watching the shadows lengthen. He could feel his old strength returning. His strategy was not yet clear but it would come.

Chapter 23

Mary was rolling pastry when she saw Stewart return from the meeting of the Health Committee. He looked more grave than she had ever seen him. 'What is it?' she said as he threw the reins of the trap to the stable hand.

'Come inside,' he urged, shutting the door. She was in her third month of pregnancy and one of the few women he had ever seen who actually bloomed. 'Mary, the committee's in a panic. The smallpox is getting out of hand. There were twenty more cases in this last week, three of them fatal. There's no way we can hold this thing. Serum from Europe's been held up and what stocks the Government had turned out to be sterile.'

He began to wash his hands at the sink as if afraid to touch her in case he contaminated her. Without turning he said, 'I want you to take the next train to Durban. I'll send for you when this is over.'

'I'm not leaving,' she said.

'I have your ticket; the train goes tomorrow evening.'

'It'll hae to go without me then.'

'You won't be the only woman going. It's been decided as a sensible precaution.'

'How do you think I'd feel, leaving you?'

'What about the child?'

'You're my husband. What about you?'

'I have to be here.'

'There are other doctors. Why you? I'll go, Stewart, but only if it's wi' you ... no other way.'

He saw he could not persuade her otherwise. It moved him deeply but he did not show his feelings until she came from behind and pressed her thickening body against him.

'Did you really think I'd ever leave ye, Stewart?'

The first sign of the disease had appeared over two months ago. Stewart had been returning to his rooms in Marshalltown when a messenger from Height's Hotel brought an urgent request to come at once. In the hall he was met by the manager, a Swiss, the pallor of his trade accentuated by fear. There was an air of disorganisation with guests coming downstairs carrying their own baggage. Bells were ringing and no one answering.

'The staff ... they've all run away!' cried Zimmerlei. 'Upstairs! The Englishman ... it's the pox.'

Stewart went upstairs to find a man in his late thirties. He was already beyond speech. 'He came in from the lowveld,' Zimmerlei said from the door, a cloth over his mouth and nose. 'Been on a hunting trip. Took to his bed two days ago. I thought he was on the drink.'

Stewart threw back the covers. The neck and naked chest showed unmistakable signs of smallpox, still in the early stages. The red pepper papules on the man's face, neck and arms were without the characteristic umbilication that came later but the man was in a high fever and delirious. The haste of guests and staff to leave was warranted. So was the despair of Zimmerlei, whose fashionable hotel would have to be quarantined and fly the yellow flag.

Stewart had come across what was called '*kaffirpokken*' in mine workers but this case had developed with a virulence that looked to be quickly fatal.

It was at a meeting of the Health Committee that Stewart met Leonard Penlynne again. He had hardly been aware of him on *The American* except as a presence, at the captain's table and sitting at the green baize in the card room, extraordinarily noticeable and yet not flamboyant. He had wondered then what his business was and had been told he was 'in mining'. They had not spoken to each other at the ball. Penlynne was not a member of the committee in the first weeks of the scare. His presence at the table now meant that the mining industry was concerned.

'I remember you, doctor, from *The American*,' Penlynne smiled and shook hands. Stewart was impressed by his air of pleasant authority. Almost at once he was the dominant figure in the room where members of the committee had been unable to agree for weeks.

'If this gets out of hand – and what is there to prevent it? – it will spread like wildfire through the mine compounds. Blacks will desert in thousands. We'll be left without labour and I need not tell you what effect that will have at a time when confidence has just revived. Serum is available in the Cape. What are we doing about supplies? Is there enough for mass inoculation?'

By the time Stewart felt he had to get Mary out of the town the outbreak was out of control. The serum from Europe arrived but it had not stood up to the voyage out and the heat. Calf vaccine produced in Grahamstown had been mixed with glycerine and was too viscous to penetrate the scarification of the skin. Neither was more than ten percent effective. The tents on Hospital Hill had increased to the extent that guards had to be hired to prevent the escape of patients and the suspected victims quarantined with them.

Wherever his work took him in town Stewart saw the yellow flag flying over houses and mine compounds where contacts and patients could no longer be restrained and had fled, carrying the disease from one end of the Reef to the other. Drunken guards deserted. Every morning the death waggon went past his room flying the yellow flag. As it trundled through the streets and past the market square people scattered and one could hear shouts going up ahead of its coming. 'Look out! Here comes the death cart!'

Stewart refused to allow Mary to go into town but he knew that she went to the market just the same. 'I've seen the cowpox at hame, on the farm,' she assured him.

'You haven't seen this,' he said grimly.

His disgust of the disease and his horror of her being disfigured were constantly with him. He did not know that while she went about her house she was repeating like an incantation: 'Oh dear Jesus, let it not happen to him.'

The doctors on the Smallpox Committee could not agree. It was round this table that Stewart came face to face once more with the ship's doctor from *The American*. He sensed the man's antagonism at once. Fordyce looked to Stewart to have further deteriorated in drink and he was astounded to meet him here with his hot pebble eyes and scanty, perspiring locks. The man had given it out to the Health Committee that he had had considerable experience in the control of smallpox in India and the Sudan.

It seemed the sanatorium in the Karoo had been a financial failure. The sick of Europe had not responded to his advertising and he was now seeking an appointment. The committee, at their wits end, scourged by the press, were willing to listen to Fordyce's claims for the old-fashioned arm-to-arm vaccination. The pustules of a victim were scratched and pressed against a scratch on a person to be treated. 'Humanised lymph, gentlemen. I've used it in scores, hundreds of cases. This new calf lymph is no better than water.'

Stewart objected. 'You can't be serious, doctor. You must know that there is the chance of syphilis, tuberculosis and many other diseases being transmitted by this dangerous ... discredited method. That it is, in fact, illegal in England.'

'Are you presuming to correct a man of my experience, doctor?'

'I am.'

'How long have you been qualified, doctor?'

Stewart flushed. 'I qualified in an era' – he used the word with emphasis – 'when the method you recommend had been discarded. I must urge the committee to find a way to procure a more effective calf vaccine. Producing it here may be the answer.'

Fordyce gave him a pitying look. 'You are perhaps not aware, doctor, that calf vaccine can be so virulent as to infect your subject with a fatal dose. Yes, gentlemen, fatal! Or be totally ineffective.'

'Gentlemen ... gentlemen!' Leonard Penlynne called for order as the doctors around the table took sides on the issue. 'I must remind you that this committee will be a laughing stock or worse if we cannot agree on methods of control. It is no use arguing that it is for Government. Government had issued us ineffective serum, refused to finance a lazaretto. It is for us to decide, and gentlemen, we may not leave this table without a decision. The press is outside.'

The meeting broke up about midnight. Mary met Stewart on the doorstep. 'That fool Fordyce,' he groaned.

'Dinna take on so, Stewart.'

'It's you,' he said. 'I'm terrified for you.'

'We're in it together, Stewart.'

'There's got to be an answer.'

'It's in the Lord's hands, Stewart.'

'The devil's more like.' Holding her face between his hands, trying not to see it pustulated and suppurating, that face he loved to look at when she was about her domestic work or turned towards him on the pillow. No, she must be got out of this. Only yesterday a delirious black who had staggered away from the compound hospital had come raving and shouting to the door. Tonight's paper had editorialised: 'No doubt there are those in Pretoria who would like nothing better than to see the *uitlander* community decimated and the labour force scattered back to their kraals.'

When Penlynne appeared at Stewart's rooms a few days later he was impressed by the man's sincerity. 'If I put up the money for this experiment you spoke of, to produce calf vaccine here, will you take it on?'

'I've no experience in this field ... none.'

Penlynne was opening a letter and passing it over.

'It's from a Swiss, a man named Theiler. He's a veterinarian working for Nellmapius at Irene. He claims that with five calves he can produce five hundred tubes of serum in three weeks. What have we to lose by trying?'

'What about the committee?'

'To hell with the committee. I'm ready to go over their heads. If you concur.'

Stewart recognised the moment. Everything that was instinctive and impulsive in his nature urged his acceptance. But to fail... To feel the lash of his peers. He knew that many of his colleagues had simply given up using the imported lymph. That a Swiss vet could produce an effective vaccine seemed a wild chance. The red face of Fordyce rose before him. He knew the surgeon would do everything in his power to discredit him if Theiler turned out to be a chancer. The cry would be: arm-to-arm inoculation could have turned the tide. Blame MacDonald.

Penlynne was picking up his gloves and hat, an extraordinarily immaculate man for one of such clumsy frame and heavy head. The clothes that once fitted him so badly now seemed to be part of him. Rosebud in buttonhole, as if he had stepped out of a box, as Mary would have put it – 'neat as a squirrel.' What were his motives? Surely not altruistic? But did it matter?

'I'll go over to see Theiler tomorrow, Mr Penlynne.'

'Good man. You shan't lose by it.'

Stewart found Arnold Theiler in a stable on the Irene estate of

Hugo Nellmapius. He was in his twenties, as huge as a blacksmith, heavily bearded and as physically clumsy as a farmhand in his farrier's apron. He was cursing two blacks holding down a horse and drenched in sweat. Stewart saw that his left wrist supported a wooden hand in a black glove. He was dextrous with both.

'Stand out of my light,' he shouted in German and then, seeing Stewart, he straightened up and ordered the blacks to take away the horse. 'I have a remedy for the *perdesiekte*, the horse sickness.' His face shone with the glow of an enthusiast. 'I shall have Government contract ... much money.'

Stewart had come straight from Nellmapius. What Theiler had just said confirmed the Hungarian's belief that Theiler was a good vet, 'but stubborn, very stubborn. He came here without papers. His story was that they had been lost by the steamship company. I gave him a job as a labourer. You'll see he wears a glove. A clumsy, impatient man. He lost his hand in a chaff cutter. He plays with serums.'

'He claims to have produced lymph from calves.'

'He also claims to have a cure for the *perdesiekte*. I do not say he is a crank .... He has skill but the lymph he produced here with my beasts gave no better results than the imported.'

Theiler walked Stewart to his room. It was little better than a lean-to but the man had set it up as a laboratory. 'I now have microscope and books from Switzerland. I know now I can produce good lymph.'

'Your diplomas and certificates .... The committee will ask for these before they can appoint you.'

'These I have not got,' he said with the greatest affability.

'You mean, you have no qualifications?'

'I am qualified, Zurich qualified. My papers are held by the office of the Commandant-General more than one year now.' He grinned hugely and brandished the wooden hand. 'Tomorrow I get them. Tell Johannesburg Theiler is coming!'

Leonard Penlynne's announcement that he had set the Swiss up in an experimental laboratory in a stable in Market Street caused an uproar. 'I am doing this on my own initiative,' Penlynne cried. 'The committee can accept it or reject it. Call it unofficial if you will. But if you accept, Dr MacDonald will be our link with the work.'

'And the cost?' Faces were bleak and hostile.

'Theiler asks fifty pounds for the three weeks. And the supply of calves, at thirty-five shillings each.'

'And who may we ask is the lymph to be tried on?'

'There will be no lack of volunteers,' said Stewart.

'Perhaps yourself, doctor,' sneered Fordyce.

'Perhaps.'

'Then let me warn you just once more, doctor ... and gentlemen, calf lymph can be fatal. Thank God it will not be my responsibility.'

'Gentlemen,' Penlynne pounded for order, 'need I remind you that people are going down daily. I wish a man like Theiler had been in Kimberley where I saw smallpox do its work ... unchecked. And need I remind you that not all that long ago the disease all but wiped out Cape Town.'

Nothing he said carried any weight.

As Stewart walked with Penlynne to his club afterwards he blurted, 'At least they didn't knuckle under to that brute Fordyce...'

'I shall make sure that gentleman has no entry into any of my mines,' said Penlynne. In a private room of his club they sat down in deep leather chairs beneath trophies of big game which snarled and stared with glassy eyes between the gas brackets.

'If you should ever wish to join my company, MacDonald,' he was saying, his luminous, dark eyes on Stewart, 'do not hesitate. I will not ask you how you find conditions under Rawlinson. Enough said!'

Stewart went home with Penlynne's mandate to oversee the project. He told Mary that he had found him a very impressive man.

'I hear funny stories about him,' she said. 'And that woman up at the house on the hill.'

'He's certainly not lacking in courage,' said Stewart.

'Don't you see,' she cried. 'It's no' him that's got the courage ... it's you.'

Arnold Theiler's stable in Market Street was quickly famous. People took the tuppeny tram ride from the market square just to stand outside its doors. Children peered through the cracks and scattered in terror when the Swiss came out. The blood of the calves he slaughtered ran out under the doors and when blacks were seen burying the remains horror stories went the rounds. Stewart went often to the stable where the Swiss worked with furious energy. It was already winter and freezing but he bunked down in the stable with his calves, taking their temperatures hourly. The place was half-laboratory and half-stable, with a table for the post mortems. Thousands of test tubes were readied for serum. The man worked with a meticulous care that impressed Stewart. He was certainly no ordinary vet.

Stewart found him there one morning, his breath smoking in the frosty air. 'You come in good time,' he said. 'My first calf has take!' He showed the pustule on the shaven neck. Theiler was right. His graphs showed rising temperature.

'Tomorrow I draw five hundred doses from this little lady. Tell them, the Health Committee, Theiler is ready.'

The committee was hastily convened that evening. Penlynne took the chair with what Stewart thought to be commendable lack of triumph. 'Well, gentlemen, we have five hundred doses. The press is clamouring for its issue. I propose we delay no further.'

'No doubt Mr Theiler has tried out his vaccine ... but not on himself,' said Fordyce with a grim smile.

'The method is proven in Europe. I urge you to proceed.'

'Perhaps Mr Penlynne will volunteer a guinea pig from his plentiful supply.'

'Are you insinuating, sir,' said Penlynne hotly, 'that I misuse my Kaffir labour?'

'It is your experiment, Mr Penlynne, not ours.'

'Very well. I think Dr MacDonald and I will manage what is necessary.'

Stewart had expected to see Fordyce's face fall. Instead his complexion turned almost apoplectic with triumph. He got up and opened the door. 'By your leave, gentlemen.'

He ushered in a woman in black. The men rose and she was seated, nervously twisting her hands. She was in her forties, a Swiss, wife of the consul in Pretoria. She told her story in reasonable English. Theiler had used his earliest experimental lymph on her son. The boy was dead.

'It was too strong for his blood, sirs,' she said. 'Herr Theiler regretted it. I do not blame him; he wished only to help.'

When she had gone Fordyce turned to Penlynne. 'You knew

this of course,' he accused. 'But in your haste to be the saviour of the town you overlooked it. Gentlemen, it is as I warned.'

Penlynne had gone white to the lips. He looked at Stewart.

'Did Theiler tell you of this?'

'No, sir.'

Penlynne rose. 'The experiment is concluded, gentlemen. You have my resignation from the Health Committee. And my apologies, Dr Fordyce.' He went out without another look at Stewart.

Stewart roused up a sleeping ricksha boy and ordered him down Market Street at his best speed. '*Tshetsha ... tshetsha!*' The flying boy needed no urging as his feet barely skimmed the surface. Stewart saw the fluttering rags on his back, aware, but hardly seeing them. He was choking with anger against the Swiss. How could the man have concealed such a thing, led him on with his enthusiasm ... 'Tomorrow we inoculate three more calves. Soon we have plenty, plenty!' Stewart paid the boy and pounded at the stable door. There was light under the edge and he heard the chink of glass, then the sudden bellowing of a calf.

'Theiler, open up!'

The Swiss appeared with his mouth full. 'I enjoy my supper. Please join me. I hope you eat Wiener schnitzel. I eat schnitzel every day.' He stopped joking when he saw Stewart's expression.

'Come in, come in. Something is wrong?'

There was a dead calf on the floor, its blood running in the gutter. 'For post mortem,' said Theiler. The stable, lit by two hurricane lamps, looked to Stewart like something between a witch's kitchen and a slaughterhouse. For moments he was too aware of what would have happened if he had gone, as his first impulse had been earlier that evening, back to his home with a phial of serum and used it on Mary. He held it up in shaking fingers. 'Why did you not tell me about the boy Rettler?'

'He died, ja.' Theiler said it matter-of-factly, as if it was nothing to be regretted unless, perhaps, it was to discredit him now.

'Your lymph killed him. That's what his mother says.'

'Ach, Vrou Rettler, poor woman.' He was mopping up gravy with bread and wiping crumbs from around his beard. 'It was too late for lymph. The poor boy was already past saving. But she wept ... and her husband. They begged me and I gave them. Ja, it was strong, but it was too late.'

'The committee has rejected your work. Mr Penlynne has resigned.'

'Ja,' said Theiler, wagging his great head. 'I have rejected been before, many times. Never mind. We have goot veal!' Mouth full, he walked to his racks of test tubes and held up one of the newest batch of lymph.

'I have goot lymph this time ... ja, I know.'

He rolled up his sleeve and Stewart saw three angry pustules already at the stage of suppuration. They stood grinning at each other. It was all Stewart could do not to grab the man in his arms and dance him round the stable. He hired a cab and drove back to Langlaagte as if the devil was at his back, standing up on the board and shouting at the horse. Somewhere along the track his hat whirled off his head. He hardly noticed. He had the precious phial that would make his darling safe.

He leaped down from the vehicle and she came in her dressing gown onto the stoep. 'Take it off ... there, sit down, bare your arm.' She let the gown fall to her waist. He dabbed on the fluid and scratched the flesh, her eyes on his face. 'Oh, my Mary,' he said. Slowly he sank to his knees and as his lips touched the swelling that was their child he tasted his own tears on the warm, rounded smoothness and felt her hand in his hair.

'Och, my man,' she said softly, 'did it mean sae much?'

Chapter 24

It was August and vile weather. The veld was burnt out. The dryness of winter had shrivelled everything and the south winds were gritty with dust. There was nowhere in town where one could escape the irritation and discomfort. Tempers were short. There were fights in hotel bars. From the windows of Rawlinson's office the market square was more often than not under a cloud. The white dust from the cyanide dumps blew round every corner. Shops carried the notice: Closed on account of the dust.

Rawlinson was in good spirits. It had taken weeks to make contact with Dr Rudolf Hahn but Hahn's letter had arrived while he was going over the latest figures of payments to African Gold Recovery. Between them, he and other mine owners had paid out to Penlynne nearly half a million sterling in royalties. But here in Hahn's words was what he'd been hoping for.

'... I have used cyanide and also cyanide of potassium as recommended by the Americans Rae and Simpson as long ago as 1886. I was then called out to South Africa when the gold fields in the Cape, at Knysna, had problems. Rae's process treated gold with an electric or galvanic current in conjunction with suitable chemicals, including cyanide of potassium. By the joint action of electricity and chemicals, the gold was brought into a state of solution. Unfortunately the Cape strikes were not sufficient to justify further mining and the process was lost sight of. I would be pleased to give expert advice and accept your offer of passage out, also facilities to conduct experiments *in situ* to compare the MacForrest process with that patented by Rae and Simpson. As to your information that the MacForrest process was patented this year in terms of the Patent Act (1887) of the Republic of South Africa I must point out that the application was granted ten years later than that to the American patentees...'

Rawlinson felt a tremendous surge of elation and energy. What he wanted now was a lawyer well-versed in Roman-Dutch law. The case would be held in the Supreme Court in Pretoria. His man would have to be Dutch, not English. Christiaan Smit was the obvious choice. The opportunity had come for the lad to repay his debt. Christiaan had married during his convalescence from wounds received in the Magato affair. Some girl he had known since childhood.

Pretoria was hot and steamy as Rawlinson hitched his horses in the broad market *plein*. It was crowded with waggons and armed men on horseback. It stirred him to see warlike preparations. The Pretoria commando was going out against Magato again. The Venda troublemaker was to be crushed once and for all.

He crossed the square towards the scaffolding on the face of the new Palace of Justice, a building as handsome as any in Europe, built against a background of thorn trees and a scattering of small houses, most of them thatched. As he stepped into the coolness of marble and had a look inside the empty chamber where the arms of the Republic hung above the bench he thought: so this is how Kruger spends my money. It was said that Kruger's judges were ill-paid. Maybe it was time to distribute a few sweeteners. Outside there was a volley of shots, cheering and a clatter of hooves. When the square had emptied he went across to Christiaan's rooms and stood for a moment to admire the brass plate.

'Oom Josiah!' As he took the young man's hand he was struck now, as before, by an unusual quality in the energetic figure, the broad forehead and the penetrating blue eyes that were curiously motionless.

'Well, Christiaan, now I'm the one in need of help.'

'My talents will always be at your service, Oom Josh.'

'I could have brought out the best lawyer in Europe ... but I've chosen you.'

'I'm honoured.' His young man's face with its beginnings of blonde beard was stern and unsmiling now. Rawlinson felt convinced he had done right. It was a young mind he needed to fight Penlynne. Shrewd, fresh and uncontaminated by too much contact with cynical men. In the meantime, strong letters to the press on the evils of monopoly. The mining community must be told that it was being bled white. Wages could never rise so long as mine owners were held to ransom by the cyanide syndicate. A public agitation against Penlynne and Gardiner must be at white heat when the case opened. He had not been mayor of Kimberley and the youngest M P in the Cape Assembly for nothing. He knew the pressure of opinion even on judicial judgements.

'Will Oom please be seated.' Christiaan moved a book and a bundle of wild grasses from the leather chair.

'What's that you're reading?'

'Xenophon ... his campaign in Persia.'

'Is there a war in those parts?'

'This one's in 400 B.C.'

'And you're reading it now?' It was a respectful question.

'This man was one of history's greatest strategists. He beat the Persian Empire's best armies with a handful of ragged Greeks.'

'And what's that to you, boy?'

The young Boer walked to the window. He looked down on the red square and across to the post office building standing among bluegum saplings. Without turning his head he said: 'They say in Europe we're going to have to fight England.'

Rawlinson made no reply but the shock of the statement went through him. Christiaan's acceptance of the idea was what hit him hardest. If the Boers won such a war, and they had thrashed the British troops before this, just as they had put an end to Dingaan's impis ... if they won again it would put paid to any ideas he had of being first governor of a British occupied Transvaal. He began to realise that it was this very thing that, even above the cyanide crisis, had been delaying him in this country.

'Oom did not come over to discuss the ancient Greeks,' he heard Christiaan say.

Rawlinson stayed over in Pretoria for two days. He was delighted with the way Christiaan grasped the essentials. 'First look into the patent application. Examine the specifications. See if there have been any earlier applications and look for careless wording.' That was how he briefed him. Next day Christiaan had a copy of the application.

'It was made last year, Oom. It's very technical. It seems to cover substantially three points: namely, the use of dilute solutions of cyanide, the use of zinc as a precipitant and the employment of caustic alkalies for neutralizing acid ores.'

'How can anyone patent that? Any fool can dilute cyanide.'

Rawlinson snorted his contempt. 'Can you patent a chemical action? That's nature, ain't it?'

Christiaan flicked through the document, already marked with slips of paper for comment. 'MacForrest's patent consists of not using more than eight parts of cyanogen to a thousand parts of water. Suppose we could demonstrate that it could be done, as efficiently, by using ... say ten parts?'

'Wait till Dr Hahn arrives,' chuckled Rawlinson. 'I'll give him every facility to try.'

They lunched on greasy mutton, sweet potatoes and pumpkin heavily spiced in the Boer manner, followed by *vetkoek* as sweet as wild honey and bitter coffee. It put Rawlinson in a fine humour as a change from the tough roast trek ox and leathery Yorkshire pudding at the Rand Club. He was glad to see that Christiaan did not touch liquor; neither did he smoke. He ate sparingly, his mind active on the case.

'I believe our tactics must be to challenge the patent on three grounds. Firstly, that MacForrest was not the true inventor. Secondly, that the invention –'

'So-called invention.'

'Precisely! ...was not of a patentable nature. And finally, that the specifications are insufficient to have qualified for a patent.' His stern young face relaxed in a smile.

'I'll beat them for you, Oom Josiah, never doubt it. Call it a debt repaid.'

Where the new road up to Far Horizons turned round the koppie there was a place where Leonard Penlynne enjoyed to stop the carriage and point out the view. On one side they could see the town and its headgears and dumps. On the other they could stand beneath the branches of a protea tree and see a landscape that was still untouched Africa. Wild, empty and beautiful, in a way that bore no resemblance to Europe. They could feel the gusts of hot wind on their faces and sometimes hear the bark of baboon. 'Yes, we still get the odd leopard,' Penlynne would smile.

The trick was to drive round the next bend. There stood Far Horizons, its wrought iron gates swinging open to the salute of a black warrior in an old army tunic as the carriage swept on up the drive to the mansion. It was so unexpected, so magnificently sited. A mixture of chateau and English Gothic, of turrets and tall windows, doors that opened onto wide stone terraces with Italian statuary of classic figures and ponds where fat carp slithered among waterlilies beneath the bronze figure of a heron.

Penlynne revelled in the effect on visitors. He could not resist the showmanship. It was still so novel. 'There it is, Alexander!'

'Aye, it's a fine place,' MacForrest admitted, his face burning under the thatch of uncontrollable ginger hair. 'Of course, you must excuse me if I say it's nae a patch on Kirkbride, my place on the Dee ... and I got it for a song.' He added with a wink, 'This'll have cost a packet, cost Gold Recovery a packet, eh? Well, I dinna grudge it to you, Penlynne.'

Penlynne smiled civilly but he was riled by the impudent allusion that Far Horizons and indeed everything he had was due to the man at his side now here in connection with the case. And very reluctant to leave the pleasures of his new life.

'Come along in,' Penlynne said. 'My wife's expecting you.'

Dorothy came down the stairway to meet her guest, a figure of such elegance and distinction in grey silk that Penlynne was hard put not to applaud. To the manner born, he thought, in her surroundings of rich hangings and fine carpeting with the glint of silver and polished wood and the dark glow of paintings by Dutch and Flemish masters, among them the exuberant fruit and flower arrangements of the 17th century of which Dorothy was particularly proud.

'You must be exhausted,' Dorothy said. 'First a rest, then we'll show you round.' She was graciousness itself where a day before she had been furious at Penlynne's suggestion that MacForrest be put up at Far Horizons.

'Must the man stay here, reeking with chemicals? You know I'm expecting friends from London by the next mailboat.'

'He must have the best of everything. I want you to understand that, Dorothy. Your best hospitality.'

'How long is he to stay?'

'Till the case is over.'

'How insupportable! He won't fit in with our other guests.'

'Have you any idea how important that man is to us? For God's sake, Dotty, use your head. You wouldn't be in this house now if it weren't for him. I hate to dwell on it but he saved all our skins. Johannesburg should raise a monument to him. I grant you he's no gentleman but treat him as if he were visiting royalty ... you simply must!'

She took his rebuke with outward dignity. 'And you? What can I expect of you during the visit?'

'The usual. You know very well the terms of our arrangement. They were your own conditions. I am not to live under your roof as long as ... nothing's changed, my dear.'

'You'll be here tomorrow night for dinner, I take it.'

'Of course ... of course.'

They were dining Judge Fourie of the Supreme Court, Stephen Yeatsman, editor of the *Oracle*, and various mine officials. Gardiner and Katherine would be there and Penlynne had himself asked Etienne Esselen, a very able Boer lawyer he had in mind to brief to fight the case for African Gold Recovery.

The immediate anxiety was to examine the patent. It had to be watertight. Walking with MacForrest on the terrace in the cool of the evening, Penlynne was shocked to hear the chemist admit, with disarming candour, that he knew others had used cyanide before him.

'Aye, William Skey, on the Thames Gold Fields in New Zealand. He used it to keep the mercury clean.'

'When was that?' said Penlynne, trying to keep a tone of anxiety out of his voice.

'Ten years back.'

'Did he use it to extract gold?'

'Certainly not,' MacForrest chuckled. 'He passed over that application with his eyes shut.'

'Alexander, you do realise that you will have to make full details of your experiment available to the court?'

'Mr Penlynne,' said MacForrest, as red as a turkeycock, 'I made nearly two hundred experiments with many different chemicals before settling on cyanide and I insist that my use of it is unique. And the patent valid.'

'We are going to be challenged by experts, Dr Hahn for one. Rawlinson's sparing no expense in bringing in authorities.'

'Let them all come!'

He was sanguine to the point of euphoria. Fortunately the hearing was set down for some weeks ahead, long enough to allow Hahn to set up his tests at the Star and MacForrest to prepare his defence. In the meantime Penlynne had other things to think about. This man De la Roche with his stranglehold on the dynamite trade. At the last moment of their negotiations he had joined forces with Nobel Trust and together they had the mining industry in a vice.

His only escape was in the hours he managed to spend with Kitty at Bloukoppen. Hours which had dwindled considerably of late and at a time when he knew that her need for him was greatest. She was difficult and querulous and demanding and he was more than ordinarily tense. He was now realising the irony of his situation, that the child he had wanted with Dorothy had been denied him while the child he had not wanted was inescapable.

There were times when he thought ... what on earth am I doing here with this woman? I should be up there at Far Horizons. One evening he blurted out that he wanted the child to be born in Cape Town.

'I want you near me when it's born,' she pleaded. 'Are you now suddenly afraid of scandal?'

'It's not the scandal.'

'What is it then? Is this your way of getting rid of me? Now you're so busy with your important people up there?'

'It's not that, Kit. I'd like you to get away from it all. What about my finding a pleasant house for you by the sea? I'll get down from time to time. The child can be educated in England.'

'You're trying to get rid of me,' she wailed, sitting up in her nakedness, her white belly swollen with the child, like some Etruscan fertility symbol, he thought. And quite ravishingly beautiful with the fullness of her breasts and the glow of health in her cheeks.

'Nonsense,' he said in his most persuasive way, twisting his fingers in the red coils of hair below her navel. She flung his hand away. 'I only want the best for you, Kit. You know that.'

'I'm nothing to you.' She leapt from the bed and stood at the door, shaking with fury, her hair tumbling everywhere. 'Get out! Go back to your wife up there and your guests that you think of more than me. I'm not leaving here. It's my house and my child's going to be born here.'

'Calm yourself, Kitty, we'll work it out.'

'We will not work it out. I've already done that. You go to your fine friends. I'm used to being alone here while you're over at Far Horizons.'

'But Kitty...'

'Let me finish. Perhaps you wonder sometimes how I'm passing the time while you're up there. Well ... I'm not always alone as you suppose. I've got friends, too, friends who like coming here. Friends who are not ashamed of me.'

'Kitty, please. Calm down.'

She had assumed an expression he had never seen before, a look of pitying scorn. 'You'd be surprised how jolly some of my parties are – even without your company.'

'What are you getting at?' His rage was building to meet hers.

'Don't delude yourself that you're the only "king" in Johannesburg.'

In that moment he almost struck her.

'No one ... no one talks to me like that,' he said coldly.

She threw on a gown and walked out of the room, the heels of her slippers with the silver pompoms tap-tapping the wooden floor. Doors slammed. Then silence. He looked at his watch and began to dress. He felt a sudden deep depression coming on. There was a very good chance that African Gold Recovery would lose the case. How was it that he seemed to have lost control of everything so quickly? One thing he could see, and with total clarity – if he lost the case Kitty would be a luxury he could no longer afford. He did not think this without regret, even remorse. What he saw around him was of his own making. Her slavish adoration and childish affection were what he had craved and needed to overcome the years of total failure – and in particular, with Dorothy.

As he let himself out of the front door and took up the reins of the trap he glanced back at the window on the second floor where she so often sat to await his coming. How often had he let himself in with his latchkey, his heart hammering with anticipation, to meet her flying along the passage and into his arms. He had believed himself the only one. Now he found himself besieged with images of men he had never met and men he knew ... especially Walter Gardiner.

He flogged the pony to a trot. If there was a price to be paid in these things he was not yet ready to admit it. He was Leonard Penlynne and he paid the price he chose. Not a penny more. No one ... nothing, was going to undermine his drive to succeed.

By the time he had reached the top of the drive at Far Horizons his mind was clear again. He gave the reins of the blowing, lathered pony to a groom. 'Give her a good rub down and a whiskey mash. I drove her rather hard.' He must never let himself become a prey to his feelings. Emotionalism was one of the prices of imagination and sensitivity. Control. Control was everything. Iron control.

Chapter 25

Sitting in the saddle half a mile from the drilling rig, Walter Gardiner was not listening to the steady thump-thump of the machinery. In the silent heat of midday he could hear the drip-drip of blood from the carcass of the springbok slung from the saddle-horn, its wound a mass of loud-buzzing flies. The blood pattered and splashed ... and then ceased. The horseman he was watching approach had become recognisable. From the size of the figure and the tall white helmet he knew it for his father-in-law.

'Well, Gardiner,' said the old man, reining in, 'not many buck left around here. Ten years ago they were in their thousands.'

They spoke game for a few moments, Gardiner waiting for the inevitable.

'I was over at the house last night. Katherine's too much on her own. When I gave her to you I took you for a solid fellow, sown his wild oats. She didn't look happy to me, Gardiner.' His hot eyes were challenging.

Gardiner had been expecting this outburst for a long time. He had other problems than old Rawlinson's anger about his treatment of Katherine. The coming cyanide case he had left to Penlynne. His concern was to prove the deep levels. If he were wrong it wouldn't much matter whether the process belonged to African Gold Recovery or the devil. He had been drilling here in the south hills of Johannesburg for eight months now. The cores coming up were negative. Negative. Negative. Already the diamond-headed drill was cutting lava at a depth of two thousand feet and there was no sign of gold-bearing conglomerate. He longed for the sight of the white quartzite pebbles, a sign that he had struck the Main Reef.

People took him for a man of stone because he had learned to control his feelings. Control had brought with it an ability to hear the other man out and disarm him with silence. He had long ago learned that anger was a luxury for fools. It gave Gardiner an advantage knowing that he could hold his temper with the man, hear him out. At least Rawlinson had had the self-control not to seek a confrontation at the Rand Club or some other public place.

He was restless in the saddle. The old man had been at it for ten minutes. 'I'm taking this meat in to the boys at the rig,' he said.

'You're never at home, Gardiner. Alright, a man has his work, even if this drilling is fool's work. And you'll have to admit I'm right one of these days. There's nothing down there ... stone and more stone. I've been looking at your drill cores. Shale, dolomite and lava. I've proved that all the gold on the reef's in a riverbed, maybe a thousand feet wide, tilted on its side. After that ... nothing. What the hell makes you think you're going to find it again out here ... two miles from the Main Reef!'

'You were talking about Katherine,' Gardiner reminded him but Rawlinson was plainly as agitated about the one matter as the other. Both affected him as a man who could not bear criticism or to fail on any level.

'I know my daughter's young and, mark you, she's not complaining to me. It's not her style. She's got too much spunk for that. But I can't stand to see her alone in that house I gave her. At that great table, eating alone – except for the servants and that young Englishman. This lord fellow.' His anger had evidently found a fresh focus at the mention of Charles Warewood.

'He's quite harmless ... and company. It's an enormous house and there are other guests there as well, coming and going. Katherine's by no means alone.'

'He asked for her hand. Did you know that?'

'Certainly.'

'He's still sweet on her by the look of it.'

'Give him time; he'll get over it.'

Charles Warewood had returned to Johannesburg still suffering from intermittent bouts of malaria, his face yellowed and drawn. He looked years older. Gardiner had had no objection to the man's accepting Katherine's offer to be their guest until he was fully recovered. He spoke little enough. It was only indirectly that Gardiner learned of the abortive coup. The expedition had been called back in haste when Rhodes' intention had been leaked. Of course Rhodes had denied hostile intention –

and Rhodes being Rhodes there had been no public censorship.

'In any case,' Gardiner went on, 'there's the staff and her maid. The child has an English nanny. I'm at home as often as I can be.' The horses were fidgeting and the rifle was turning into a rod of burning metal, scorching his forearm. Away on the dry hills to the south he could see the game herds moving in a shimmer of heat towards the Klip River.

'Home,' said the old man. 'You're more often at that woman's place. What do you want with that old whore?'

'If you're talking about Mrs Talbot...'

'Oh, it's *Mrs* Talbot now she's got her own hotel!'

'Stick to your own affairs, father-in-law.'

'Katherine's happiness is my affair.'

'Katherine and the boy are my concern.'

'He's my grandchild.'

Rawlinson wheeled his mount and picked his way down the stony slope. At the drill rig he reined in for a moment. In the saddle, removing his white helmet to mop his brow, he had the look of an angry monarch. Gardiner did not deny his stature or his power but he guessed that the truth of his visit was less his concern for Katherine than his fear that the deep levels would strike it rich. If that happened, all this south land now Penlynne's and Gardiner's would have eluded him. Gardiner guessed that if he ever struck the gold-bearing conglomerates ... and by God, it looked unlikely now ... Rawlinson would turn the full battery of his hatred on him. No doubt about it.

He'd be up to some devilry with the Kruger Government. Quite likely urge it to proclaim the whole new field as government monopoly. One thing he did admire about his father-in-law was his independence. He was a native-born South African. Could have been a Texan. Same kind of background, same kind of spirit. He'd given it to Katherine. Spencer was a hell of a fine kid, something he'd never expected to happen in his life.

Why was it then that Katherine had failed to satisfy him? It went far deeper than sexual inadequacy – and he'd be the first to admit that his tastes were unsuited to a girl of her kind. With a man nearer her age it might have been better for her. There was a gulf that no amount of eagerness to please on her part and no amount of understanding on his could bridge. It was simply her immaturity. He could talk to her of his problems only in the way a father might discuss them with his daughter and get a concerned look and a hug. What he needed was the ear of a woman who had lived and suffered and knew men.

It angered him to hear Jenny Talbot talked about as a whore. As far as he was concerned she was a woman. She had kicked about the world of men as he had. And been kicked herself. Maybe this was part of the reason he could talk to her. They would lie together naked on top of the bed for a long time, the wooden fan churning the hot air and the smoke of their cigarettes. She made no demands. She asked for nothing and he gave her nothing, aware that gifts would be hurtful and connected with previous gainful encounters. It was an association he could not have explained but when he left her it was with a deeper sense of satisfaction and content than he had ever known. He felt young and confident. Physically she was nothing to look at any more. In her early forties, he judged. Close to his own age. Her face was not exactly hard, more disillusioned than bitter, and she had a turn of expression that always saw the ironical ... yet was oddly, pleasingly uncynical. The way she'd earned her money in the past did not concern him. With his background it was hardly for him to censure her. Respectability was what she was aiming at, he guessed, and maybe this was the one town in the world where she could have a past and have it forgotten.

He did not have a conscience about her, except when he was home with Katherine, but he accepted this bad feeling as the price he had to pay for the good feeling, though he knew that gifts to Katherine were no substitute for what the girl was searching for. He made much of the child, of course, but when he found Katherine's eyes pleading with him he would turn away with some light remark.

More important to him at this time was his relationship with Penlynne. Penlynne's background as a manager of diamond mines in Kimberley in no way qualified him to take a chance on the deep levels. Burdened with the coming cyanide case – and the Rawlinson press predicted he would lose it – the man was understandably anxious about the progress of the drilling.

'What have you got to go on, Walter?' had been his initial question. 'There's no geological precedent for your proposal.'

'It's the way the reef outcrops. Where Rawlinson and the others are working it's like ... call it the rim of a saucer. The rest of the saucer is still underground, miles away. It's a question of angle. Here it's on the surface. There it's two thousand feet deep.'

'I'm willing to gamble on it, Walter.'

Gardiner's first test drilling was made some six hundred yards from the outcrop along which a score of mines had developed – Stanhope, Geldenhuis Estate, Langlaagte, Wemmer, George Goch, Jubilee, Crown Reef, Little Wonder, and of course Rawlinson's Star. They had all sunk vertical shafts to follow the surface gold, 'the first row deeps' they called them. Some went down three hundred feet or more. The current thinking was that this was about the end of it.

When Gardiner put down the first diamond drill at the Village Main Reef he was referred to as 'that daft Yankee'. When he struck the reef at 517 feet and it was two feet thick, his critics paused and waited for the assay report. All this had happened when he was still with Rawlinson.

The old man had scorned the assay report. 'You're talking about four pennyweights! You propose to sink a shaft to recover values like that! Do you take me for a fool?'

That was when he first went to Penlynne. He was convinced that his hunch was correct. If it was possible to strike the reef on the first row deeps, and again on the second, it would be possible to hit it again on a third, say a mile away.

'Look, Penlynne,' he urged, 'the descending angle is proven. We have to take a chance and try again at say, two thousand feet.'

'How long will it take?'

'Call it a year ... a year at worst.'

'Alright,' said Penlynne. 'If you're right we'll have more offers of capital than we ever dreamed of. If you're wrong I'm going to finish up with ten miles of useless, barren hills and be vilified as the biggest fool in South Africa. I've been called a fool before. I've been called a lot worse.'

Gardiner rode down to the test rig, cut loose the buck and had a look over the morning's cores. Peter Harris, his Australian driller, shook his head. 'We made only six feet this morning. Stripped the drill. We're still in lava. Five hundred and sixty feet of it so far.'

Gardiner looked at the drill cores laid out on the ground in strips hardly thicker than his thumb. Two thousand three hundred feet so far. He knew their story all too well. Carbonaceous shale ... dolomite ... sediments ... quartzite ... lava. They told a fascinating tale to his geologist. Joe Williams always said: 'It took millions of years to lay it down, Mr Gardiner. What an opportunity we've got to read the record.'

'I haven't got all that time, Joe.'

Williams looked stricken when there were times that it seemed Penlynne would call off the probe. Sitting around the campfire at night, meat sizzling and the fat flaring, he used to paint the picture for them, his face glowing.

'A hundred million years ago. Maybe longer. No life, Mr Gardiner, not even plant life. Just a great sea and what we're after – the conglomerate pebbles with the gold – was brought by waves, tides and currents and deposited in a great arc. It could be a hundred miles long. Yes, boys, from here to the Free State.'

That always got a laugh. 'So what's it doing down there?' Peter Harris would wink around, hurl his empty bottle into the darkness to shatter on the rocks.

'It was all buried in lava, Pete.'

'You're too dead right, mate.' Then Harris would pick up his lamp and go over to the rig to watch the drill growling and coring.

Gardiner often slept out with them. There was a fortune in it for him if he was right. Ridicule if he was wrong. Let the drill core barrel come up empty of the pay streak at the two thousand five hundred feet mark, the lowest depth Penlynne would go to, and he'd have backed the wrong horse. It would have been better to stick with Rawlinson.

In this kind of mood it was no use to go home to the house on the ridge and entertain guests. Pointless to spend hours in the billiard room and no consolation to listen to Katherine's chatter about Spencer's progress and the alarms of his infant sicknesses. He had to go where he could forget. Jenny Talbot could wipe it all out for him.

He always went up the back way to her personal rooms, a sitting room with a modest bedroom, and generally he turned up very late, often when the town was deathly quiet, the gaming rooms empty at last and the bars closed. He'd take a hot bath and she'd be sitting at the end of it with a drink, her gown half open.

She'd put on no fancy gear for him and as often as not her hair hung loose.

She never said to him, 'Where were you last week? I looked for you.' More like it would be, 'Have you eaten?' While he luxuriated in hot water and relaxed with the liquor she would go down to the kitchen and come up with a grill of game chops and liver, kidneys and eggs and a jug of coffee. Sometimes they made love. It didn't always seem necessary to him, though as she lolled there in an easy chair, her gown open, legs swinging and her face in a wreath of smoke he would sometimes change his mind about talking. Other times they'd play poker for high stakes. Neither had any intention of paying.

Only very gradually did her own story come out. And then he was never sure if it was the truth, if there ever had been a Major Talbot. Yet there was just that trace of ... you could call it class. He was never sure, for example, if she had gone to the lowveld gold fields in the eighties as a barmaid, and the rest, or as the wife of the British ex-officer in search of fortune. 'He never struck it. Only enough to keep going. And he died of fever.'

'So you went to work?'

'If you're ever down there you could see his grave. It was at Joe's Luck. A lot of boys died there up those jungle creeks, panning gold. And a lot made fortunes.' He knew exactly what she was talking about. The half-crazy struggle to follow the streams roaring and cascading from a jumble of forested mountains. The small clearings with the smoke of cooking fires and men's clothing spread on bushes. The sound of singing, water falling, dynamiting of boulders. The sudden appearance of a startled buck and the crack of a rifle. The first-comers got out nuggets that weighed by the pound. Then gradually, inevitably, there was money in it only for the big men with capital to follow the lode into the heart of the mountains.

While it lasted it was a great life with a kind of lusty cameraderie a man never quite shook out of his system. Like the army ... except that this offered reward as well as death. The women followed the men. All kinds of women, but those who made it into the remoter parts where there was nothing more than a corrugated iron grog shop ... well, they were pretty worn out with being lovers and mothers to old men and boys, some of them real miners, most of them chancers and hopers. Boys from every country you could name.

It amazed Gardiner to hear her speak warmly of those men. Transport riders, hard cases, hunters with contracts to shoot for mining companies. Bums, no-goods, army deserters. Maybe it was because they were like herself. Doing the only thing they were able.

'You never married again?' Extraordinary how he could find a sympathy for this woman which he could not give to Katherine.

'The boy's at school.' She offered it as a mere statement of fact and not, as he saw it, as a justification of what she had done.

'Where, for God's sake? Here, in Jo'burg?'

'St Saviour's College. Grahamstown.' If he stiffened at her side it was only long enough to register that this was where Katherine proposed to send Spencer. A church school with masters from English colleges.

'How old is the kid?'

'Eleven.' She got up and, slipping into a gown, opened a drawer in the bureau and returned with a bundle of letters in a boy's erratic hand. 'He's very religious. Writes about becoming a priest. That'd make up for his mother.'

'Don't be a damn fool,' he said.

'I'm going to lose him anyway. He's going to hate me just now.'

It was then that Jenny Talbot admitted the boy was the illigitimate son of an English gentleman wastrel kicked out by his family after being disgraced by his regiment. The old story. Losing at cards and embezzling mess funds. 'They gave Rupert a thousand quid and told him never to come back.'

'Do they know about the boy?'

'Would I ever tell them? No, but I gave him his father's name.' The portrait of the boy, taken in Grahamstown by a studio photographer, showed a tall, fine-boned youngster with a round cap perched on a mass of curls. Typical British schoolboy of the upper class, looking dreamily into the distance.

'The image of Rupert.'

'What will you do ... Jenny?' It was the first time he had ever called her anything but 'Red' and she showed her pleasure.

'Sell up here. I've been offered a fair price.'

'Who wants it?'

285

'The Baron ... De la Roche.'

'That bastard! Look out for him.'

'I'm not so simple,' she laughed. One thing she told him about De la Roche he'd never heard before. He was English-born. As a Catholic orphan of eight years old he had been sent to Belgium to be raised in a church orphanage, hence his mastery of French and his accented English.

'Did you know he's the one who brought out Kitty Loftus – her that's up at Bloukoppen? It's true. She came out with an English lot. Most of them married now.'

'Does *he* know about that? Penlynne?'

'I expect he'd have a fit. He was never one for the girls.'

Gardiner wondered how much Penlynne knew about the origins of the startling beauty he kept in the big house on the Berea hill. It was a side of Penlynne he found hard to equate with the man's ambition to be respected and a social leader.

'He found her in a show. An actress. But before that she was one of the girls.'

Gardiner was wondering how Penlynne would react if he knew De la Roche's part in her coming to the Rand. He suspected that he found the man's grasp of the dynamite business too important to have any desire to investigate his beginnings. Penlynne had a great gift of blindness when it suited him. But when a man was past use he could drop him like something red hot. That was worth keeping in mind.

'What about old Rawlinson?' he asked.

'I used to send girls out to him once a week. Out there to the old house at Langlaagte. He's mean. Never gave a penny more than he had to...'

This woman was the repository of many secrets, he began to realize. She was carrying them like a trunkful of dirty old rubbish she could never get rid of. One day the virtuous of the town would turn on her and on the committee you'd find Rawlinson, and probably De la Roche as well, cheek by jowl with rabbis and parsons.

By that time who knew where he would be? His ambitions did not run to power for its own sake. Freedom to make money was all he really wanted. His main task as an engineer at this time was the sinking of the first deep level shaft to meet the main reef on the second row deeps. He had drawn plans for the first steel headgear which would carry a cage of forty men down a thousand feet. Every girder was coming from Europe; even the cement. The government monopoly on cement given to bribers had produced concrete that crumbled into powder. Every day on the job there was a snarl-up of some kind. Skilled men were at a premium and walked off the job all the time. He needed welders, carpenters, boilermakers, turners and fitters. Every kind of chancer turned up.

More than once he had seen workmen crowded around a small dark haired Welshman with one sleeve tucked into his pocket. The word 'brothers' was being shouted and when he walked among them he found himself confronted by this angry little man.

'Brothers unite! Join hands against the tyranny of the owners. The Penlynnes, the Rawlinsons. Raise the glorious banner of the free worker. Free to choose his hours, free to choose his work and free to call no man master.'

'Get the hell off my job,' Gardiner warned him. 'And you guys, we got a shaft to sink.'

It was the new cry of the eight hour day the agitator was ranting about. Gardiner knew the type and how to deal with them on his own ground. 'I find you here again and you're inside for trespass. Got it?' He heard the men growl. In the States he would have been in among them with his fists, picked out the loudest mouth and felled him. But these runty little British ... they had a temper he could not measure.

He had hesitated to take the matter to Penlynne and the Association of Mine Owners. It reflected on his control of the job. But the problem was there. Mine managers all over were aware of a disruptive influence. Owen Davyd. Lost his arm on Rawlinson Star. A union man. Bitter as hell. What had the men to complain about? There wasn't a tradesman in the Transvaal who wasn't making a pound a shift. And each and every one had his nigger to carry his tools and do the heavy work. The white tradesman sat on his ass and smoked. The black did the job for two bob a day. Smart too. Some of them knew the job as well as their masters. Until now the game had been to close one eye to it but now the men were getting uppity, snarling and downing tools. There looked to be a showdown coming.

'If it comes, gentlemen,' Penlynne had told his board, 'it will be our opportunity. The men who walk off this job will not walk back on. The skilled Kaffirs will take over, except for foremen and key men who'll stand with management. We will not, gentlemen, find ourselves at the beck and call of union leaders. We will not permit the poison of socialism to cripple us and infect good men, loyal men who know when they're well off and grateful for it.'

You saw them on a Saturday afternoon and a Sunday at the races and on the sportsfields. Mechanics and carpenters on tennis courts! They had never been better off in their lives. As Penlynne put it: 'There's a chance for every man here to be a capitalist in his own right. It's up to him.'

'What about this man Davyd?' he was asked.

'If Mr Davyd is all we have to worry about ... the problem will not last long.'

More and more blacks were coming down from the mountains. Tough Basutos who had beaten the Boers time and again and were now under British protection. He had no doubt that Penlynne was right when he called them the workforce of tomorrow. And they'd do it for a fraction of the money. Some of them went back maimed to their stone kraals up there in the crags, the clouds and the winter snows, but they accepted the risks. As they lashed broken rock into the skip they were like parts of a glistening black machine. He'd often seen a machine boy, waiting to drill for the next round of shots, grab the shovel from a worker not pulling his weight. The heckling, shouting and jeering was done in high spirits. They were proud of their manhood and when they lashed the rock they did it with a rhythm that was thrilling to watch. None of your trade union whining here.

The white worker had no idea what was at stake or how much he owed to men like Penlynne. When he returned to his house Gardiner felt no pang for them. They had the right to quit if it didn't suit them. So had he. Right now he was living like a prince but it might not last forever. Everything hung on the test drilling. When he rode over the rocky track to Peter Harris's borehole and saw the drill rods getting longer and the cores still coming up barren ... when he saw his analyst shake his head over the latest assay he felt grim. He was already on the limit Penlynne had set. How much deeper would they have to go? The sneers of Rawlinson were intolerable.

But if he was right ... why, the shaft he would sink here and the gold it would recover would be the first from that primordial shoreline. Along its buried verge the headgears would march across the Transvaal veld like the oil rigs in Kansas.

Chapter 26

The knock at the door was not that of an hotel servant. Penlynne rose from his chair in the private suite he had taken in the Republic Hotel for the duration of the case. Rawlinson loomed in the doorway. The sight of his bulk filling the aperture was totally unexpected although Penlynne had been aware that Rawlinson had rooms on the same floor. The man had a reputation for being totally insensitive. He smiled genially at Penlynne.

'May I come in?' Penlynne stood aside. 'Pen, I've been thinking about all this business. You and I made the Rand. I was the architect of the first phase. I panned the reef. I showed the first payable gold. You've had the vision of the second phase. You mastered the pyrites problem and gave the Reef its new lease on life.'

Rawlinson was most to be wary of at his most expansive, when he could descend to sentiment and draw on anecdotes of the fraternal past to demonstrate his good intentions.

'Come to the point, Josh.'

'The point is,' said Rawlinson, seating himself, 'it's a great pity that we're working against one another. A double pity in my case as my son-in-law went over to your side. I believe you're expecting him?'

'Later this evening.'

'That's why I've come to see you now. Family disagreements being what they are, I wanted to speak to you alone.'

'What is your point?'

'Well, in my view, it's still not too late for us to get together. I won't live forever. When I'm gone you can run the whole shooting match. You haven't a dog's chance of winning the case, you know. MacForrest's patent will be declared null. African Gold Recovery will be eliminated.'

'We'll see,' said Penlynne, but he had felt the thrust. The sight of the great crag of a man lolling there, mopping his head in the moist heat of the Pretoria evening, momentarily unnerved him. In Kimberley, as Rawlinson's manager, the man had bullied and abused him, underpaid him, held him to the terms of the contract he had signed in ignorance in England. All those years at a paltry wage while Rawlinson got rich. Then, when he was able to buy a few claims, the bottom fell out of the diamond market.

It was one of Penlynne's deepest fears – a return to the poverty of his early twenties. At this moment Rawlinson seemed to assume the proportions of the man who had stood on high ground, shouting down into the pit where Penlynne laboured. Could it be true that Rawlinson had the judges in his pocket? An ugly thought but by no means improbable. If the judges upheld MacForrest's patent it would be years before it could be challenged again, if ever. But if Rawlinson won the case the cyanide process would be open for use by anyone.

Rawlinson's eyes were all but disappearing as his head sank on his chest, moulding the mass of reddened flesh. He seemed extraordinarily passive, almost asleep. He opened his eyes suddenly and they were as bright as diamond chips.

'Call it off, Pen.'

'*You're* challenging the patent.'

'I mean call off the grudge. Let's shake and agree that the cake's big enough for the three of us, yourself, Gardiner and me. I'm here to offer you the best deal you're likely to get this side of paradise. For a share in African Gold Recovery I'll drop the case.'

'What kind of share?'

'Fifty-one per cent.'

The sheer audacity of the offer was almost laughable. Penlynne poured himself a brandy. He offered the decanter to Rawlinson who refused, but Penlynne saw that the hand which held a match to his cigar trembled. He wondered what the legal experts under this roof would think if they knew of this meeting – his own team going over the final details in their room, MacForrest making a late check on a 60-page paper detailing his experiments.

'Really, Josh, that's outrageous.'

Abruptly Rawlinson sat upright, his eyes blood-red. With his great curving mustache and his bared teeth he looked like a wild boar. 'What kind of fool are you, man! If you lose the case, everybody loses. Any Tom, Dick and Harry can use the process.

It's free to all. Make a deal with me. I'll call off the case and we split.'

'And if I win?' asked Penlynne and he sat down because he could feel his knees trembling.

'You can't win. You haven't a snowball's hope in hell.'

There was a knock at the door. Both men were startled.

'Who is it?'

'Coffee, sir. You ordered just now.'

As Rawlinson watched Penlynne walking towards the door he felt the strain of the encounter. He was not as young as he used to be. His heart hammered. He knew that his face was flushed. Sweat poured off his body, soaking his shirt.

Penlynne opened the door. The passage was empty except for the man with the tray. Penlynne took it. He realised that standing here holding the coffee tray, in his nightshirt, he was facing the most critical decision of his life, a decision which would affect not only his own holdings but the very future of the Republic. He had one of those sudden, terrifying insights that come like a warning and are never repeated.

He looked at Rawlinson. He could see that the smile of conciliation was already hardening into one of triumph. The man was sure of his power, of finally getting what he'd asked for two years ago. And all it would cost him would be the fares out for his expert witnesses and the experiment Dr Hahn had set up at the Star reduction works.

Rawlinson's eyes bored into him and his hand was outstretched to shake on it.

'No deal,' Penlynne heard himself saying into a kind of roaring vacuum that seemed to isolate him from all reality.

'You'll fight it then?' Rawlinson's voice ground out the words as he rose to his feet. For a moment he towered over Penlynne, his face a study in baffled rage. He raised the ebony cane with its ivory and gold inlay ... restrained himself as if by a great effort.

'By the living God, Penlynne, you'll live to rue this day.'

'I believe not,' said Penlynne. The man was gone but his presence lingered behind him. Immense. The man was a giant. He had left his imprint on the very air Penlynne breathed.

By the end of the first day Penlynne was all too aware that Rawlinson's young advocate, Christiaan Smit, was a man of unusual ability. He could turn from addressing the bench in Dutch to question a witness in English or German, apparently with equal facility. 'Where does he come from, that fellow?' he asked Esselen at the morning remission.

'A protégé of the plaintiff,' said Esselen with a curtness that indicated his own concern at having to best such an opponent.

'We haven't heard the last of him, that's certain.' To Penlynne he was like a fresh blade springing out of a field of stubble. There was an alertness, an eagerness and, in the poise of the head, a confidence that made the excellent Esselen seem ponderous.

MacForrest looked thin-lipped when Esselen told him that Smit, speaking in Dutch, had made a telling analysis of the patent laws of America, England and the Republic.

'In those countries,' Smit argued, 'it is possible to patent an invention if it is merely imported from abroad. The word "inventor" does not have to mean that he was the originator of the article. Over there Mr MacForrest would be regarded as the first and true publisher. In other words, his first use of the article would constitute his claim to originality. Until recently in our own state there was an enactment that tended to show that our law-makers agreed with this ... and indeed they did, until the case of Andrews vs The Rawlinson Star Gold Mining Company. The plaintiff Andrews won the case against Rawlinson Star.'

At that moment Penlynne had looked at Gardiner. They both saw what was coming. What had been a humiliating defeat for Rawlinson at the time the old buccaneer was now using to his advantage. One had to admire his nerve.

Smit's voice rose as he made his point. 'In that case the court decided that in the Republic the words "first and true inventor" must be taken in their natural sense. An importer is not an inventor. The true inventor is the person who made the discovery himself and did so before anyone else in any part of the world. In the case of Patent 47, the MacForrest Claim, this cannot be said to be true.'

MacForrest went very pale on hearing this, the pallor of anger. Penlynne had to restrain him from crossing the lobby to accost Rawlinson.

After the recess Advocate Smit examined the chief witnesses. MacForrest snorted audibly when the American professor Raymond Harris quoted previous instances of the use of cyanide.

'Indeed, sir,' Harris pursued, 'patents have been issued in the States. No doubt,' he said tendentiously, 'the defendant was not aware of this, experimenting as he was in his misty Scottish laboratory.'

Penlynne felt MacForrest quiver with suppressed rage. 'Keep calm,' he whispered, gripping his arm. 'You'll have your say.'

'I'll grind his bones,' MacForrest said. When Dr Hahn entered the box he focused his eyes on the German as if he would pierce him to the soul. Hahn was bearded and dressed in formal black, high collar and cravat. He rapped his gold pince-nez to emphasise his points. He brought into the stand so formidable a sheaf of notes that even Esselen winced. He chose to speak in German and gave his evidence with precision; very emphatically.

He had made experiments at the Rawlinson Star, yes.

He had compared the processes of the American Simpson and MacForrest, yes.

'And your conclusion, doctor?' urged Smit.

Dr Hahn pawed his papers and adjusted his pince-nez. Suddenly he made his answer in English, as if he were hurling it at the head of MacForrest. 'Both processes are satisfactory. In the case of Simpson it is superior, yielding a finer quality of gold. The MacForrest process tends to leave a residue of copper.'

He began to quote from his graphs. Smit interrupted.

'In commercial terms, doctor ... if you will.'

'According to my tests with the MacForrest process, one hundred tons of tailings have yielded £81.21.11d. The Simpson process had yielded £94.2.9d.'

Esselen gave a pitying smile but Gardiner and Penlynne strained forward in their seats.

'In other words,' pursued Christiaan Smit in English, 'not only did Simpson's claim and patent anticipate MacForrest's, but under trial it is found to be superior. On this basis alone the court would be justified in declaring the defendant's patent void.'

The court was adjourned at this point to allow for examination of expert papers, all of them testimonies sworn by chemists and metallurgists in America, England and Germany, all of them supporting Rawlinson's case. The big man and his team passed Penlynne and Gardiner on the steps. Rawlinson's walk had the confident majesty of one who has just added another conquest to his empire. They passed out into the sunshine, a flutter of black gowns around the monarchial figure. Suddenly he broke away and came over to them.

'It's still not too late to pull out, Penlynne. Think it over before the court sits again. A sixty percent interest will satisfy me. I'll be in Johannesburg for the next day or so. You know where to find me.'

Penlynne and Gardiner had elected to stay over in Pretoria and go over their case with the utmost care. The hot air of the day had hardly abated but the coolness of evening was taking its place when Penlynne and Gardiner, in shirt-sleeves, waited for Esselen to join them. Great moths flitted in at the open windows and rustled against the lamps. They had two days to go through it all again. MacForrest was being uncooperative; even surly.

'We've got to demonstrate MacForrest's exact claim,' Penlynne said. 'Show how he arrived at his results, what makes his process unique.'

'Does he know himself?' said Gardiner. 'I've begun to have doubts that a chemical process is patentable. The man insists that his patent is not the use of cyanide, but the use of a *dilution* of cyanide. This is what he calls "selective action".'

'Then he's got to be explicit about this "selective action".' Penlynne was tensely walking up and down. 'As I understand it, cyanide dissolves gold while leaving base metals untouched ... that's selection!'

'I think the man's going to crack,' said Gardiner.

'He's got to pull himself together. Understand he's fighting for his interests, same as we are. He's in some cloud of outraged scientific honour with his precious theory under attack. Harris and Hahn have been formidably impressive witnesses. MacForrest's simply got to match them. So far his attitude to their evidence has been truculent and defensive. I've told him he's got two days to recover his composure. If the case is lost he's ruined. I told him so quite bluntly this afternoon.'

'What about our loss?' said Gardiner.

'Incalculable.'

'You think we should have taken the old man's first offer?'

'Say no more about that.'

'He'd likely negotiate for a much smaller share.'

'Forget it. I'll never knuckle under that man.' He changed his tone. 'Walter ... I wasn't born yesterday.'

Esselen arrived some time later. The Hollander with his owlish eyes, his air of sobriety and probity, had come straight from MacForrest. He looked both bemused and agitated.

'Sit down, Esselen, I'll get you a drink.'

'How am I going to argue "selective action", Mr Penlynne? We'll be torn to pieces.'

'It's all we've got,' said Gardiner.

'You'll do it brilliantly,' Penlynne assured him.

'Unfortunately,' went on the Hollander, 'nowhere in MacForrest's claim of invention is there mention of a dilute solution having a specific power of selection.'

'We know that,' said Penlynne. 'It was an afterthought. Just the same we must argue it as confidently as if it had been stated in the patent claim.'

'Smit will argue that Simpson knew of it ... years ago.'

'Yes, but did he patent it?'

'No.'

'Did he even mention it in such a phrase?'

'No, it's MacForrest's. The weaker the solution, the more action on gold.'

'Has he figures to demonstrate it?'

'Plenty. Oh yes.'

'Then "selective action" has to be our weapon.'

'It's all we've got,' said Gardiner dryly.

'Not so,' said Esselen. 'The fact is a patent can only be cancelled, and this is the nub of it, if there has been a previous publication in this country. If nothing appeared here in a scientific journal, imported or printed locally, then an inventor could duplicate an invention without knowing it. We're in the strong position that in our law "first inventor" means first to make use of ... and that surely was MacForrest!'

'Of course,' said Penlynne. 'There are no scientific journals published here. Patents are flouted every day and rarely challenged.'

'The benefits of backwardness,' said Gardiner, tongue in cheek.

'There is still MacForrest's testimony and the impression he makes on the court,' said Esselen. 'It is all important. In a case like this which will turn on the interpretation of a few words, call it legal hairsplitting, Rawlinson could easily get the verdict.'

'Especially if he has been at the judges,' said Gardiner.

'Even to one of them,' agreed Penlynne. 'A single assent will be enough to turn the judgement. One of the three holds the balance.'

'Would it be too late to make it clear to one of them that an upholding of the patent by the court would be amply rewarded?' said Gardiner. Then, seeing the look of dismay on Esselen's face, he hastened to add, 'Forgive me my sense of humour, Esselen.'

'The bench is incorruptible,' said Esselen stiffly.

'Sorry I upset him about that,' said Gardiner when Esselen had gone.

Penlynne did not commit himself. He had not heard from Judge Fourie since the dinner party at Far Horizons when he had calculatedly invited the judge. Perhaps he had not been broad enough in his hint that a substantial piece of company-owned land, excellent for a plantation of mining timber, could be picked up for a nominal sum. But he said nothing of this to Gardiner. He had always kept his inner counsel closed. That was the real secret of power.

On the morning the case resumed MacForrest appeared at breakfast looking bright and alert. He appeared to have recovered his rational attitude and scientific detachment. He ate heartily. So did Walter Gardiner who all his life had enjoyed a good breakfast, crisis or no. Penlynne was not disposed to eat. He was tense and irritable. Esselen took only black coffee.

'There's nothing like the parritch,' declared the Scot cheerfully as he spooned away at oatmeal porridge.

'I intend putting you on the stand right away,' said Esselen.

'Oh aye,' humphed MacForrest. 'My evidence will be conclusive. Never fear.'

'One must never underestimate the enemy, Mr MacForrest.'

'"Selective action", that's the basis of it,' beamed the chemist as Walter and Penlynne watched him attacking lamb chops and kudu liver with relish, sweat in the crinkles round his eyes, a dribble of egg on his beard. When he wiped it, Penlynne felt as much a shock as if it had been blood to see the yellow stain on the napkin.

'It worries me,' pursued the lawyer, 'that the words "selective action" are not used in the specification. And there is no precise description of its application.'

'Man alive, the verra process of chemicals in action is its own demonstration, its own description. The weaker the solution, the greater the action. I demonstrated this. No one has before or since.'

The court rose on the entrance of three judges in the scarlet gowns of Roman-Dutch courts. The next hour will tell, thought Penlynne as he searched the face of Mr Justice Fourie. There was nothing in the dark sunburned features under the grey wig to show that he had reacted in any way to the offer of the previous night when Penlynne, meeting him in the corridor of the hotel, had given him a cordial invitation to inspect the land he had mentioned at the dinner party.

'My wife and I would take it as an honour if you spent a weekend with us when this business is disposed of.' The judge had nodded civilly. No more. This morning his expression was severe. Christiaan Smit was seen to whisper something to Rawlinson. Esselen fiddled with his papers. Penlynne raised a finger to acknowledge the presence of Stephen Yeatsman, editor of *The Oracle*. Extraordinary how blank the faces seemed. Everyone drained of his persona, the sounds of court officials unnaturally loud, a small gallery coughing and shuffling discreetly.

Esselen began to lead MacForrest. 'Will you tell the court what is meant by "selective action"?' MacForrest's explanation seemed unnecessarily complicated and incoherent to Penlynne. And far too long.

Then Smit rose. 'Do I understand correctly that a weak solution would be eight percent in a thousand parts of water?'

'You do, sir.'

'Expert evidence has been given in this court that Simpson succeeded with a two percent solution. Would you consider this an infringement of your patent?'

It sounded so innocuous but Penlynne caught himself straining for MacForrest to take his time.

'I would sue,' said MacForrest vigorously. Penlynne groaned inwardly. Now the man's temper was up he would probably rush at every gate with his head down. He tried to signal him, to no avail.

'Mr MacForrest, what do you say to a weakened solution being used in Australia some ten years ago?'

'Pure trial and error, a fluke. My patent was granted on the first scientific observation of the principle.'

'Are you calling a scientific principle ... patentable?'

The chemist hesitated only a second but Smit knew how to take his advantage. 'For example, Mr MacForrest ... suppose Professor Röntgen had applied for a patent for his discovery, the action of the rays named after him. Do you suppose any court would have granted him the right, the sole right, to radiant energy? Why, sir, by your logic he could have been granted a patent to the sun!'

'Will you kindly answer the question, Mr MacForrest,' said Mr Justice Jorissen with just a trace of judicial appreciation of the point.

'I've nae answers to foolishness, sir.'

Christiaan Smit indicated that he had finished with the witness. Esselen rose as MacForrest came to his side and sat down heavily, very pale now and under stress, obviously aware that the next few minutes could be critical. Esselen showed no sign of dismay. Indeed, he rose with a confidence that was impressive.

'Let us say that it is granted that the process of dilution was something that any workman could have stumbled on, as my learned friend has argued.' At these words everyone in court became reanimated. Penlynne was aghast and MacForrest had to be dissuaded from rising to protest. There was as much dismay in Penlynne's side as there was a cautious triumph in the Rawlinson camp. Why was the man conceding? Why was he throwing away the argument for selective action?

'I ask the court now to examine the plea of the plaintiff Rawlinson. It will be noted that nowhere in the plea does it give details of a previous use of a dilute solution by parties other than MacForrest. I draw the court's attention now to Patent Law, Article 37. I quote: "When a person disputes the validity of a patent on the ground that it is not new he must state the time and place of the alleged previous use." This the plaintiff has failed to do. On this ground I ask the court to dismiss the case.' He was as matter of fact as if he had known he was leading to this all the time and had not, in fact, made his decision as he rose to speak.

Rawlinson and Smit buzzed furiously together. MacForrest gave a sob of relief. It was astonishing that both sides had missed this point until now. Smit was rising. 'I ask the court leave to amend the plea.'

The grey wigs on the bench seemed to be grouped in a red and grey cabal, their wigs separated, the implacable faces turned towards them. 'Application to amend the plea is refused. If the plaintiff wishes to follow this point it will have to be done in another action. At the present stage of this case it is too late.'

Rawlinson's rumble of displeasure was audible. Smit's face was stiff. MacForrest went so white that Penlynne pushed his head between his legs. Slowly the chemist recovered.

'Have we done it then? Have we won? Surely that's it?'

'Well done, Willem,' said Penlynne loudly as Rawlinson and Smit went past. Rawlinson turned.

'The judgement is still to come.' With a confident nod he went out, holding the young man's arm.

'How long will that be?' Penlynne asked Esselen.

'With this amount of material ... two months.'

'And our chances now...?'

Esselen shrugged. 'As good as they were when we began. Or as bad.'

Chapter 27

Isadore Isaacs had no cultural interests but he knew he had chosen well to take Rachel to see the Yiddish Players presenting *Shulamith, the Converted Priest*, a piece highly praised by the Yiddish newssheet. Strange girl. Nothing he had done or said could persuade her to go on living in the house he had rented on the Berea. He had made every comfort available to her. He had respected her religious prejudices. Their ways of life were irreconcilable and only her sense of duty to him had made her stay as long as she had. Tonight was their last evening under the same roof.

From the day she arrived in Johannesburg Rachel had felt ill at ease. Her life in Cape Town had been placid and in surroundings mellowed by centuries. Almost without being aware of it she had absorbed something of the culture of Europe. To a girl of her sensitivity there was a feeling there among old walled gardens, courtyards and tree-lined walks that the world was a sanctuary in green leaf. Johannesburg was a rude awakening. She had known from the first moment she saw the mine headgear and the mountains of broken rock that her life was about to change. In her first few days in the city it had shocked her to see penniless Jews as wretched and ragged as any in the old country.

'There are soup kitchens, Rachel. Nobody goes hungry,' Isadore had said. 'Remember, ten years ago there was nothing here.'

She had grown up in an atmosphere of educated people. She had not been excluded from the currents of liberal thought, the strivings for better things for everyone. Jewish households, small and large, took in immigrants from all over Europe until they were ready to move on up-country. There was no feeling that one was better than another. Musician or artisan. To most, Cape Town was a garden of paradise.

It was when she was serving in the Working Men's Club that

she heard for the first time of the yearning to rebuild the Holy Land. She had become an idealist without being aware of it. Her compassion had been deeply stirred by these ragged hopefuls. Isadore's letters begging her to make a home for him had seemed an answer. She would do it. She owed it to him.

From the very beginning his rebuffing of Abe Cahan had dismayed her. She had served him many times in the club. He was doing carpentry work to make his fare up-country. A strong, gentle man. She had not felt strange telling him of her life in the East End of London. On the journey up he had travelled Third but somehow he had always contrived to be standing at every halt to hand her down. What would he say if he knew that her brother was *yahudim* ... ready to disown his Jewishness? Abe, a man who read his *siddur* daily.

As the lights went up at the end of Act One Isadore had a sensation of being watched. Rachel felt him stiffen as he looked across the red plush, the smoke agitated by scores of fluttering fans. 'What is it?' she said. He broke his gaze and asked to be excused for a moment. At the same moment she saw a striking Jewess leave the side of a man in an opposite box.

Isadore pushed through the crowd animating the foyer. Rosetta Judelsohn was standing by a pillar almost as if by prearrangement. Immediately she brushed past him as if she had never seen him. Once again he had an extraordinary presentiment of being warned. He turned and saw that she had stopped at the door of the cloakroom. She looked directly at him across the foyer ... then went inside. For a long time now he had felt that Judelsohn was moving towards something. His overtures had not been renewed but there were rumblings in the trade.

In the bar he ordered a drink. Two men in evening dress entered behind and crowded him, one on either side. He had the impression that they were out of breath and had just come in from the street. He recognised the brothers Judelsohn.

'We seem to have missed the first act,' said Simon, speaking across Isadore to his brother.

'The best is to come, I believe,' smiled Idel.

'Yes, the second act is good drama,' said Simon, his eyes glittering. They were both almost feverish. And yet as cold as ice.

'I prefer comedy,' said Idel. 'What about you, Mr Isaacs?'

'I mind my own business.'

'That's wise, Mr Isaacs.'

'Keep out of my way,' said Isadore in a low voice.

'In a crowd like this,' smiled Simon.

'A man could be dead on his feet,' said his brother.

'He'd only fall down when the bell rang,' said Simon.

At that moment the bell rang and the throng at the bar began to dwindle. 'Enjoy the second act,' said Idel. 'It livens up.'

'You don't need to tell Mr Isaacs,' chided Simon. 'He knows what's to come.'

Isadore found his hands trembling as he paid for a box of bon-bons for Rachel. The bell was ringing loudly in the foyer. Later he realised that this was the reason why he had not heard the bells ring as the fire pump went past. In any case there was a fire almost every night in one camp or another. A paraffin stove knocked over in a shanty. A shelter of boxwood blazing up. There was so little water that most fires burned out unless there was rain and an abandoned digging nearby flooded with water.

He gave his sister the bon-bons but he could not enjoy her pleasure in the play. Abruptly he rose and drew her after him.

'What is it?' she pleaded.

'We must go,' he muttered. He reached the street with a presentiment that it was already too late. He saw the glare in the sky and began to run. Others were running from all directions. Figures huddled in doorways and in alleys between buildings were suddenly illuminated. Bars spilled men into the streets. Cabbies were turning frightened horses away from the glare and the stink of smoke.

The nearer Isadore got the brighter the illumination. As he ran, his chest tight against his starched shirt, wrenching at his collar, he could read the names of shopkeepers. His own tailor. A general store. A draper's. Windows opened above the shops and people in nightclothing looked out. He seemed to see everything with a kind of preternatural calm, already knowing what he would find. The very brightness of the blaze warned that it was no ordinary fire.

When he turned the last corner into Pritchard Street watchers' faces were lurid. Streams of blazing spirits were running in the street. Barrels of alcohol were exploding, shooting sheets of fire that joined with burning pools, linked and ran in an eerie blue. Already the iron sheeting of the roof was buckling upwards. The rafters were falling inwards towards the inferno.

He stood helpless, watching showers of sparks blowing into the darkness towards the shanties on the verge of the market square where hundreds of waggons were drawn up, their tents white in the glare, teams of oxen stirring restlessly, bellowing. He looked on, appalled. Unrecognised. The hoses were too short. The brick facade was bulging ominously. Heat drove them back. He stepped into a doorway across the street.

Something in his memory responded. He was standing helplessly in a doorway; the very doorway where De la Roche had found him lying on his first night in Johannesburg. It seemed impossible. They had wiped him out in a single night. As he watched the facade came down with a roar and a mighty thud. He dug his nails into his palms as the heat seared his face. None of them – not Judelsohn, not Pastolsky, not Schlossberg, none of them, not from the East Rand to the far West – none of the syndicates was going to intimidate him.

Start again? Of course he'd start again.

Because of the fire it was a week before Rachel moved out of his house. 'I'm going to work, Issy.'

'There's no need ... where then, in God's name?'

'The Immigrants' Shelter.'

'But Rachel. You've had your sufferings. It's over!'

Passionately she burst out. 'You of all people should be able to understand.'

'What will people think of me?'

'It is something I have to do.'

'Where will you stay?'

'Mrs Landau's. The boarding house.'

He was appalled. It was a collection of rooms of plastered mud with a patchwork of rusty iron and reeds for a roof. Jews of all kinds lived there, mainly artisans and job seekers. It was one of dozens of its kind, some of them owned by businessmen, others built on rented ground. Quagmires in summer, freezing in winter, filled with raucous drunks and miserable women brought from one kind of poverty in Europe to another in a hostile land. Children and infants everywhere.

'You're not going there!' he cried.

'Please don't try to stop me.'

'Oh, I see,' he said coldly. 'It's the Litvak. The shoemaker. You've been seeing him.'

'Mr Cahan's a carpenter,' she said calmly.

He rose up and made to seize her by the wrists and restrain her. Then he relented. 'All right then. Go.' He scattered some gold and silver on the table. 'At least do me that favour. Mrs Landau won't keep you for nothing.'

'Some day I want you to meet Mr Cahan,' she said.

They embraced, tears in their eyes, and he saw her into a ricksha. He turned back to the house. The money still lay on the table. All but half a sovereign. He shook his head with a kind of reluctant admiration. It had not occurred to him until that moment that there was any kind of guts other than his own.

Chapter 28

'It's been a hell of a time,' said Walter Gardiner, stretching his legs in the 1st Class compartment as the locomotive panted up the long gradient towards the halt at Irene.

'Six months and a week,' said Penlynne. 'It was the mass of expert evidence, I expect. However, it will be concluded by midday.'

'You're pretty cool about it, Penlynne. We could both be wiped out this morning.'

'So I'm informed by the press.'

At Irene Halt other passengers got down to drink coffee and marvel at the Nellmapius estate with its plantations of trees, its acres of steam-ploughed cultivation, dairy farms and nurseries. In ten years the Hungarian Jew had made of the barren landscape a progressive farm on the lines of the best in Europe. For some minutes Gardiner and Penlynne looked over the fields in admiration. Naked blacks in loincloths worked at a steady pace under the supervision of German farm experts. Compared to the ragged, unkept fields of the Boers with their haphazard agriculture, their contempt and suspicion of ideas that had not been approved by their grandfathers, Irene was a wonder.

'Trust a Jew!' said Gardiner tongue-in-cheek to Penlynne.

'I've never found the Jewish half a hardship,' responded Penlynne. 'It's the Gentile I have trouble with.'

'Going to stretch your legs, Pen?'

'I'll keep out of sight. They'll have reporters waiting.'

'They'll know soon enough, I guess.'

Penlynne stopped short and made a swift note with a gold propelling pencil.

'I saw Tomlinson of *The Times* at Park Halt.'

'*The* Times?' said Penlynne whimsically. His figures seemed to please him.

'*The* Times ... New York!'

They were aware that the world press would be represented in the Palace of Justice today. For weeks there had been low key speculation in the financial press of Europe about the possible effects of an African Gold Recovery defeat. Neither man showed signs of undue strain, though at this moment Penlynne's cheeks had a high daub of colour and his eyes were bright.

'What's the betting on us, Pen?'

'I hear Rawlinson was offering ten to one against today.'

'And MacForrest? Where's he got to?'

'I sent him off to the farm for a few days. He's better out of the way.' He went on with his figures. When African Gold Recovery was floated in London and Paris the share issue had been snapped up on the strength of the prospectus. Today £5 shares stood at ten times their par value. The MacForrest process had set off a boom on the Bourse and on the London Exchange. As it became increasingly frenzied it affected the shares of hundreds of mining finance companies and brought a spate of company promotions. Europe's enthusiasm was such that any company that had even remote mining connections traded in an excitement that had lost all sense of proportion.

It was hard to recall that before the process had been perfected Johannesburg had been bankrupt, with out of work men queuing at soup kitchens. Penlynne and Alfred Beit had bought left and right at give-away prices until today their holdings included mines as far east and west as Benoni and Roodepoort.

Penlynne's confidence in winning the case had consistently been made public in the *Oracle* and his optimism cabled to Europe. All his shares stood at peak prices. He was a millionaire. Looking back, it all seemed to have been effortless. How could he ever have conceived himself a failure?

'How about contingencies?' said Gardiner suddenly. 'Have you thought of that?'

If they lost today he was still a mining engineer. What of Penlynne? African Gold Recovery was financing everything he owned, including the deep level adventure. He had to hand it to the man for nerve.

'You look after deep level mining, Walter. I'll handle finance.'

'I do have a mild interest in AGR,' said Gardiner with mock humility. He took a nip from a silver flask and proferred it. 'I understand Mr Justice Fourie has decided to retire from the bench

307

and take an interest in a bluegum plantation.'

'So I believe,' said Penlynne drily.

'I'm wagering that AGR stock will be up twenty percent tomorrow.'

Penlynne smiled secretively and laid back his head, closing his eyes till the train jolted to a standstill in Pretoria station. Esselen met them with an open carriage. He smiled vaguely as they drove through the town in its midsummer greenery of subtropical shrubs and roses. What gave the capital its special charm for Penlynne were the running furrows of water where of an evening expatriate Hollanders fished for eels at their front doors. Esselen got many a wave and a shout of encouragement. Was it the man's personal charm or the popularity of his cause?

'Judgement will be given in Dutch,' Esselen reminded them.

'It's Greek to me,' shrugged Gardiner.

'I can manage,' said Penlynne.

'Afterwards we'll get a good translation,' Esselen assured them.

'Will it really matter?' said Gardiner. 'A simple yes or no will suit me. I'll be in the hotel bar.'

'I'm touched by your confidence,' said Penlynne.

There were three judges on the bench: Justices Kotze, Fourie and Jorissen, the Chief Justice of the Republic. Mr Justice Kotze gave judgement first. He had the judicial face *par excellence*. Rat trap mouth and fleshy jowls and a delivery as cold as cod three days dead.

Much of what he said went over Penlynne's head but he caught phrases that were hopeful. 'MacForrest can be said to have carried forward Simpson's patent in a somewhat improved manner.' Then the deflating: 'The substitution of equivalents to achieve the same result is not such an invention as will sustain a patent.'

When he heard that and saw Esselen's face stiffen Penlynne left the court. When he resumed his seat twenty minutes later Esselen handed him a note. 'Judgement for the plaintiff with costs against us.' Penlynne wiped his hands with a silk handkerchief and nodded. He had seen what was coming from Rawlinson's air of buoyancy. It's our man now, he thought. As Mr Justice Fourie began Penlynne began to shake with suppressed mirth. Esselen inclined his head towards his client.

Penlynne had just realised that the fact that Fourie had gone through with the land deal meant no advantage after all. He'd have been a fool not to. Now he'd quite likely give judgement to Rawlinson just to demonstrate his incorruptibility. He wiped tears from his eyes as the livid, leathery face under the grey curls droned on. Very soon Penlynne heard the words he dreaded.

'... the first and true inventor can have no other meaning than that the person so described did so before anyone else in the world.'

Let every man find his own remedy for defeat, Penlynne thought. I have mine.

Fourie continued for twenty minutes, painstakingly discussing the experiments described by the foreign experts. 'The chemist Skey is, in my view, the man with the best claim to be called discoverer. It is, however, one thing to discover, another to make practical use of. We have therefore to enquire if there was anything new, anything original in MacForrest's invention. It is also fair to ask: was Simpson's work actually an anticipation?'

Penlynne felt his legs trembling. He could hardly face the bench as Fourie turned the final page of his judgement.

'It has been ably argued by Mr Smit that Simpson's solution is also dilute ... and actually the same as MacForrest's.' He paused a long time, as if savouring what was to come. 'However, the plea to withdraw patent rights from the defendant cannot stand up for the reason that the pleadings were faulty. Therefore my judgement...'

In the rush of emotions Penlynne did not actually hear the final words dismissing Rawlinson's plea. As the flood of sensation slowly ebbed he looked up and saw the newspaperman Stephen Yeatsman give a reassuring nod. One all!

Mr Justice Jorissen was senior judge of the Supreme Court of the Transvaal. He had a reputation for cutting to the very heart of a case with elaborate sarcasm and heart-stopping pauses. He would appear to lose the thread of his delivery only to follow with some crushing demolition of an advocate's shrewdest argument.

He looked over his half-lenses and it seemed to Penlynne that the red-robed figure had more than mortal power as he glanced down at the court and began in a rapid, nasal Dutch. Gabbling it off, Penlynne thought, like a hunched old vulture tearing at a

309

carcass. He could almost feel the blows, the most innocuous words stripping him to the bone. He could feel Esselen's hiss of indrawn breath. This was it then ... here it comes.

'... this so called "selective action" is only a consequence, an accident. It is no part of the invention proper, in any shape or form. Mr Esselen for the defendant has surely confused the result of the invention with the invention itself! But assuming that we have to deal with a real discovery, is it now, in accordance with our law, a new invention in the realm of industrial use?' He paused to sip water.

'Not every discovery by which our knowledge is increased is patentable...'

Surely it was coming now? But no. He went on for three-quarters of an hour. At one stage Penlynne nodded off in the unventilated courtroom but he sat up sharply when he heard the name MacForrest.

'... unfortunately an unwilling and wary witness...'

Just before the finale Gardiner took his seat next to Penlynne. He was red-faced and euphoric. 'How're we doing?' he nudged.

'Shut up,' said Penlynne, tensely trying to catch the final words.

'... the use of cyanide is no invention of MacForrest and if the defendants think they have discovered it, it is their misfortune to have discovered something already known. Others after Columbus have discovered America.'

'What did he say about America?' said Gardiner.

'He said,' said Penlynne drily, 'that we've lost the case.'

'We'll appeal, of course,' said Esselen firmly but it was obvious that he was shocked by the outcome. People were clustering around Rawlinson and Smit. No one came near the losers.

'There'll be no appeal,' said Penlynne calmly. 'Don't look so down, man. You did your best and thank you for putting up a good fight."

Gardiner looked on, sobered. If he was astonished at the way Penlynne had taken the verdict he showed it only by a meditative chewing on the corner of his mouth. Presently they found themselves alone in the empty courtroom. Penlynne took out his notebook and looked at some figures.

'I think we got out AGR at a good average price.'

'You mean...' Gardiner was groping to understand.

'I've had it in train for the past two months. I got shot of the last block an hour ago.'

'You're a cool hand! Suppose we'd won?'

'There never was a chance. I saw that after the first week. Still, the law being what it is, it was worth the fight.'

'My God, I believe you enjoyed it.'

'I think I did.'

An orderly who looked in at the court a moment later was astonished to see the two men roaring with laughter and clutching at each other.

It was not until they were on the train back to Johannesburg that Gardiner thought of MacForrest. 'He's wiped out then, I take it.'

'I expect he'll go back to his laboratory and invent something, perhaps even something original.'

'How did he get into this at all?'

'He was investigating a gold solution for sensitizing photographic plates.'

'I guess he's over-reached himself with that property he bought in Scotland.'

'The man's an eccentric.'

'How will you break it to him?'

'I'll go down to the farm tomorrow.'

Gardiner said no more. He took a swallow from his flask. It had just occurred to him that his own interests, linked as they were with the fortunes of this man with the first traces of grey in the dark beard that obscured his mouth and the glittering dark eyes ought to be looked at carefully. For the first time in his dealings with Penlynne he felt a twinge of apprehension. It was mingled with his admiration for the man's astuteness.

White Gate Orchards was one of Penlynne's peripheral investments and very near to his heart. Now that the railway line linked Johannesburg with the sea and the new fast mailships were doing the trip to England in nine days there seemed the possibility of a vast market in fruit. He often went down to the farm in the Witpoortjie Valley, some fifteen miles from town. The soil was good, the land sheltered from the bitter winter winds. The young citrus trees were growing well. He enjoyed the orderliness, the feeling of growth, the drowsy heat and the sight of clear water piped from the kloof rushing in the irrigation furrows.

There was a brick house for the manager, a block of rooms for the labourers and a guest house under thatch. Long before he reached the lands he could smell the heavy fragrance of orange blossom. The nearer he came the stronger it became. It made him quite heady.

The German manager was not in his house. Everywhere there was a hot, heavy silence. He hitched the spider and walked over to the guest house. The scent of orange blossom was almost overpowering. He knocked. 'MacForrest! Alex! Are you there?'

He pushed open the door. Dazzled by the brilliance outside he was momentarily blinded. Then his sight focused on a pair of bare feet dangling at waist height. Bare shins, bare thighs and the shock of a gingery nakedness. MacForrest's trousers had slipped to the floor, leaving him only his vest for decency as he hung there, his head of hair flaming grotesquely above the black, unrecognisable features.

Chapter 29

Kitty stood at the top of the stairway at Bloukoppen. She looked splendidly theatrical. Her *peignoir* had fallen open and her hair was loose. She had just thrown a silver-backed hairbrush downstairs at Penlynne. Behind her the Welsh woman wet-nursing the child stood gaping. Penlynne thought he had never seen Kitty look so fine, not even in his first glimpse of her at The Globe theatre.

From being the comparatively simple girl he had fallen in love with she had developed a taste for every kind of luxury. The heavy Germanic furnishings of Karl Marloth's choice had been replaced by the style of a French *demi-mondaine*. Heaven knew where she had found the taste. Copied from magazines or her own ideas, it was undeniably sumptuous, and if there were lapses into vulgarity he had treated them with amusement. For instance, the lacquered figure of a Moor standing at the foot of the stairs with a silver tray for visiting cards. To his knowledge there had never yet been a visiting card on the tray.

There were white marble figures of undraped Grecian women holding aloft electric lamps of bronze. These he rather liked. In every public room there were fine carpets and in the huge dining room with its coloured glass windows there was a Gobelin tapestry showing Diana the Huntress. Upstairs next to her bedroom was a small salon where she received friends. The odour of cigar smoke often hung about this intimate room and he had more than once challenged her about it.

The hangings of her bed were pale amber-coloured silk, embroidered with gold thread and all over the house china, bronzes and costly embroidered fabrics jostled for attention. Curiously, there were none of the ornate gilded mirrors he might have expected. A solitary maid was no longer enough. She had demanded a full staff and in the coach house there were four horses and two carriages.

'It's your money,' he said indulgently for they were all in a river of gold thanks to African Gold Recovery's total grip on the cyanide process. In his infatuation for Kitty he had never regretted giving her a substantial block of his own share allocation.

The child's nursery had been decorated in sky-blue and silver, the cot covered in lace and ribbons like the cocoon of a princeling. It was absurd in its extravagance but he had not interfered. A man had to indulge the whims of his mistress.

The day he came to tell her he had lost the case he was grave-faced.

'I'm sorry you lost, Penny ... but what does it have to do with us?' she asked appealingly, drawing him down on the couch beside her and about to prattle on about the servants. 'The coachman is insolent, Pen. I want you to tell him to go.'

'He'll have to go in any case, my dear.' She looked at him blankly. 'You have no more income.'

'You mean ... you're poor again.' Her face paled and seemed to have fallen in. There was a sudden reversion to the expression she must have had in the days of her childhood in London. Her face, always so calculatedly bright, so ready to please, was suddenly pathetically waif-like, at variance with the extravagant *peignoir*, the embroidered slippers, the billowing hair. Slowly her colour returned. The shock of what he had said had given her a wild, distraught beauty, her eyes like a pair of enormous green stones, staring so wildly he saw himself reflected in her dilated pupils.

'Are you putting me and my child on the street?' she said in disbelief, very calmly and articulating with difficulty, as if the words were stuck somewhere between realisation and expression. 'Are you planning to throw me out ... me and a child the image of its father?'

'Calm down, Kitty, please. I can't throw you out ... even if I wanted to. What a girl for drama you are. The house belongs to you.'

'What's the trouble then? No, don't tell me. I don't want to know.'

She put her hands over her ears like a child. Gently he pulled them away. 'The company's bust, Kitten. You must understand. You'll have to put this place on the market. You'll get a good price the way things are, I'm sure. My misfortune has been good for other people. I'll educate the boy. I promised you that in any case.'

'And me? What about me?'

'We'll have to think about that.'

She looked at him as if she could not believe what she was hearing. 'But you're still a rich man, aren't you?' She said it with such childish appeal that he had to turn his back on her to recover his composure. Really, it was much more painful than he had imagined. The newspapers here and in Europe had made a meal of the case. Stock markets in London, Berlin and Paris had been in a panic when it was known that someone had been unloading African Gold Recovery shares before the judgement in the case was made public. No one had accused him openly and his own paper, *The Oracle*, had given the impression that he had suffered as much as anyone and blamed Rawlinson for having engineered the crash. The total effect has been a loss of confidence in the Kaffir market. The familiar cry had gone up: 'Johannesburg is a dangerous investment.'

At the peak of the panic there had been a telephone call from Rawlinson, the bull voice oddly thinned and diluted by the instrument. 'I'll see you wiped out if it's the last thing I do on this earth, Penlynne.'

'Oh come,' said Penlynne. 'You brought the case and I believe you won it. Why be uncharitable?' He winked at Gardiner.

'Decent men won't speak to you after this.'

Penlynne felt a terrific surge of pleasure. 'I did what I could in the circumstances. I believe you'd have done the same.'

He heard the instrument click.

'He'll have a stroke one of these days,' said Gardiner with quiet relish.

It was true that Penlynne could have continued to support Kitty at Bloukoppen, perhaps in a less extravagant style, but the birth of the child had been a profound shock to him.

'This backstairs child' – it was in these words Dorothy had let him know that the whole of Johannesburg was talking about it. She pushed in front of him a periodical with a reputation for barbed commentary. 'Have you seen *The Critic*?'

'I don't read that muck.'

'This may interest you.'

'It is understood,' *The Critic* noted, 'that there will be a slackening in the scale of entertaining at Bloukoppen in the next few weeks. Sounds less harmonious than music will be heard. Miss Kitty Loftus has been unavailable for comment but we understand the refreshment at Bloukoppen will be less spirituous and more mammalian than heretofore.'

'Of course it may not be your child,' Dorothy said in a curiously detached manner, as if considering the possibilities of an alternate father among their friends. He had to admire her skill. The way she reduced his mistress to something beneath her dignity.

'I accept responsibility,' he said, trying to match her coolness. 'The child ... the boy ... will be educated in England. He'll be no embarrassment to you, I promise.'

She gave him one of those disturbing, penetrating looks. 'You can't really believe that, surely? This boy will be your heir. Have you thought of that?'

'I must admit it has never occurred to me.'

'You surely don't imagine that this woman will not see to it; bring him up in the expectation of an inheritance from his father?'

'It is a possibility.'

He saw the brightness of her eyes and the swelling of her bosom, her struggle to retain self-control. He wanted to reach out his hands and give her assurance. But how could he? To wound her and comfort her in the same gesture would be abominable.

'Really, I find you strangely unimaginative in this matter.' Her eyes were glittering, her voice hard and angry now.

He made a conciliatory movement of his hand.

'You will send her away, of course.'

'Of course.'

If she accepted it as a victory she did not show it. She simply nodded and left the room. He was impressed. She really was a superb woman. She had not deserved this. It did not occur to him that he might be fully reconciled with her. He had never wholly left the house but it would have been grossly insensitive to do more than appease her wounded feelings. He would go to Bloukoppen at once and be done with it.

A few days earlier he had brought Kitty a silver and mother-of-pearl teething ring for the child and a Punchinello of ivory with silver cap bells to distract him in his cot. She had received it with delight, lying on the chaise longue dandling the infant, a dribble of milk at his mouth and his blue eyes still smoky.

'Oh, I knew you'd been thinking about him, Pen. I've been having such fun with names. Leonard for one, of course, and then I thought he could have my mother's name, in the meantime.'

A name for the child brought him the realisation that he would never allow the boy to be called Leonard; or Penlynne for that matter. That was when he understood how deeply committed he was in this house, this affair he had entered into so ardently and without thought of the consequences.

Now as he stood here telling her everything was over, that all this had to go, he saw that she was suddenly calm. Like a child at the end of a tantrum. 'I'll get rid of the servants,' she said carefully, 'and I daresay I don't need two carriages, though the landau was nice for the races. I'll economise. The servants steal dreadfully and waste a lot of food.'

She turned her smile on him with a winsome confidence that six months ago would have clutched at his heart.

'You'll see, Pen. I'll be so careful now. I can manage very well. You'll be proud of your Kitten.'

'It won't do, Kitty. You'll have to move to somewhere much more modest. There's no more income.'

'And what about you? You and your precious Dorothy?'

'That's different.'

'Different, is it?'

'It is.'

'You and your snobbery, your stiff dinner parties, your stuck-up friends ... and her ... her and that black man. Oh yes, I heard all about it. A decent man wouldn't touch her after that.'

He raised his hand to strike her. She caught at his wrists, clawing his hands, her nails raking like hot coals, drawing blood.

'Take that back,' he heard himself shout. 'I demand you take that back, you little guttersnipe. I know what goes on up here when I'm not around.'

'Why shouldn't I have a friend and you up there at Far Horizons most nights ... treating me as if I was dirt.'

'De la Roche, I suppose, renewing old acquaintance. I expect you'll do very well, Kitty, with me out of the way.'

He meant none of it but abuse poured out in an uncontrollable stream of anger and shame. The child had been an embarrass-

317

ment to him since the moment he first saw him in her arms and recognised something of himself suckling at the full breasts. Kitty had held up the small red-faced creature with its tufts of dark hair, its angry old-man expression, its puppy eyes. Kitty had never looked so pretty. There was a look of searching hopefulness, a need for reassurance he was unable to give. He had bought her a pearl pendant. He could smell the milky woman odour of her body as he bent over to fasten it and when she raised her face to be kissed her eyes were full of tears. She grasped his hand and held it to her cheek.

Well, it was over. They had both said their worst. He broke away from her and heard her follow. 'You bloody swine,' she screamed. 'You rotten Jew bastard. Get out! Get out of my house.' The silver-backed brush fell at his feet. 'Take it. Take everything!'

The front door slammed. She sat down on the top step. She looked like a child who had just had a tantrum and was debating with herself whether to start screaming or go to the nursery and break something. How long she sat there she had no idea. Scared servants came to the foot of the stairs and receded. No one dared to pick up the silver-backed hairbrush lying at the front door. In the nursery she could hear the child squalling.

She would never see Penlynne again, she knew that. It seemed impossible but it had happened. From all this ... to nothing. Was that what it meant? Was it true that he would never come through that door again and run up the stairs, shouting, 'Kits ... Kits! Look at this!' Or, 'Look what I've brought you!' Suddenly ... emptiness, all in the past and only this nightmare now, this numbing unreality of the present. She sat dry-eyed and saw the light of the late afternoon sun come through the stained glass window as it brightened and glowed towards sundown. Soon it would be dark. The hall clock ticked with preternatural loudness.

Josiah Rawlinson came more frequently to Katherine's house. He was obsessed now to be gone to England. He spoke of it as 'home' though it had never been his birthplace. He wanted his knighthood, to hear men call him Sir Josh. He wanted to be clear of the Transvaal before there was a war. 'It's only a matter of time, Kathy. They'll bring the whole place to rack and ruin. I want you and the child with me in London.'

His winning of the cyanide case seemed to have made little difference. She could not understand what was pulling him down. 'It's nothing, nothing,' he would tell her when she knelt beside his chair or put Spencer into his lap. She was distressed, torn between her love for him and a sense of loyalty to Gardiner – diminished but still there.

One day she decided to speak to Muriel Rawlinson about it. The Scotswoman was in her sewing room. She had never been able to shed the habit of making her own clothes and the truth was she was as skilful as any dressmaker in the town, particularly in the making of hats. She was deft with buckram and canvas, her velvet roses and her swift needle.

'What's worrying him? Do you no' ken, girl! It's that man of yours. Your father's afeared of him, out there with that drilling. I dinna understand it m'sel' but he thinks it'll be the ruin of him. Penlynne and your husband – they'll have it all yet, he thinks. I've tried to tell him he's a millionaire over and over and they canna hurt him. He's like a child. It isna his, ye see.'

With a quick snap of her teeth she severed a thread. 'There! Is that no' bonny!'

Katherine took her knowledge to Gardiner, coming to him with a severity that took him by surprise. 'If you find what you're looking for out there in the south, what then? Why does it worry my father so much? Tell me, please, Walter.'

'Because he's a bad loser. That's why I left him. He can't stand for anyone else to have a piece of the pie. He comes out there often enough to tell me I'm wasting my time and other people's money. He disputes the theory ... there are no deep levels!'

'Are there?'

'If there aren't, the next stop will be Brazil. It'll be all over here. There will be no great Wit Waters Rand gold field.'

He did not tell her that he was already drilling two hundred feet below Penlynne's limit and that in his heart he was almost ready to admit defeat. She saw that he was bone-weary and haggard. She wanted to reach out and comfort him.

'I'll go with you, Walter. Anywhere you say.'

'Don't be too hasty with offers, baby. It's tails I lose, heads your father wins.'

'You're my husband.'

'You're a good kid,' he said. The lean face twitched and he went quickly out of the room. She followed him to the gun room where he had taken down one of the weapons he so carefully oiled and cleaned. He was squinting down the barrel of the weapon he had used that night when he went after the leopard. His feet were on the trophy. She smelled gun oil and sensed the black despair of the man. He was further away from her than ever, untouchably distant. She could not know that he had given himself another hundred feet. Ten days drilling at this rate.

He came suddenly towards her, his face enigmatic. 'Forgive me, Kathy,' he said. 'You deserved better from me.' She went quickly into his arms. Holding him she was aware that she was holding only the shell of a man. Whichever way the drilling went he was already dead to her.

On the eighteenth month, almost to the hour, Peter Harris's drill bit came up with a core of conglomerate pebbles. It had probed a layer twenty-four inches deep, penetrating it at 2,001 feet. When the tiny button of gold had cooled in the kiln and been weighed it assayed at twelve pennyweights per ton.

'Gold has been proved at half a mile below the surface,' wrote an exuberant Penlynne to Wernher in London. 'Never has a tiny sample of the earth's inner crust been so fraught with greater significance. The core measured only one seven-sixteenth of an inch. Is it not amazing! It has opened up limitless possibilities.' He added a postscript: 'I have not seen Walter Gardiner for two days. But I think I know where I shall find him.'

Gardiner had gone directly home. He had a sudden, overwhelming desire to be with his young wife and son. He found Katherine in the wisteria arbour reading a book. She looked up at his footfall, plainly confused by his appearance at this hour.

'I did it, Kathy,' he grinned, lifting her and whirling her about. 'Now pack. I've got a yen to see young Spencer paddle in the ocean at Durban.'

If Dorothy Penlynne felt a sense of wellbeing with the return home of her husband she did not go out of her way to show it. The wounds of his behaviour went too deep for that and she was not yet ready to make more than conciliatory gestures. The emotional energy she had expended on the affair and the building and furnishing of the house had been recharged. The truth was she was ready to embark on another great project. The art gallery was premature. She accepted that. What now? The intellectual and cultural diversions of Europe which could have occupied her restless mind were conspicuously absent here. She raged to plunge into something more challenging than flower arranging and tennis parties, soirées and charades and the never ending 'at homes'.

She noted with amusement that George Borcherd followed her about like a little dog. 'Oh, do go and design something, George,' she would say. 'For heaven's sake don't look so forlorn.'

She had not encouraged him 'that way' but it was obvious that he was in love with her. She did toy with the idea of revenging herself on Penlynne and it was deeply gratifying to find herself physically attractive to an agreeable and talented young man, albeit ten years her junior. An affair might have assuaged her restlessness but it would certainly have brought less desirable complications.

One afternoon the footman brought in the card of Lady Violet Hurlingham. The moment the woman came into the drawing room Dorothy had a sense of being in the presence of the real thing. Lady Violet made no gushing references to the furnishings and paintings. It was as if she never saw them. She had a hard hand and the dry powder round her eyes as she lifted her veil aged her face. The eyes were fine, almost violet and much alive. Her clothing had been good but was shabby. The voice had the note of demand Dorothy admired and associated with privilege.

'To what do I owe the pleasure, Lady Violet?'

'I have come, Mrs Penlynne, to ask you to be patroness and president of The Albion League of British South African Women.'

'What is that, pray?'

'We are dedicated' – Dorothy noted the stress on the plurality of it and had her doubts – 'to the ideal of creating a British homeland here in Africa. Of bringing to this country the best and noblest of English blood ... and of working people raised in the traditions of our motherland.'

'We?' queried Dorothy. 'Who, if I may ask, are "we"?'

For answer she was handed a pamphlet decorated with Union

Jacks and a sketch of a woman with outflung hand, supporting a sturdy babe, a group of adoring soldiers and artisans brandishing tools and weapons clustered at her feet.

'Our objective, Mrs Penlynne, is to support our men in the coming struggle to plant an exalted civilisation in this barbarous land. Will you accept?'

Lady Violet snapped up the lace-thin bread and butter fingers served with china tea and it occurred to Dorothy that the woman was actually in need. But she had asked for no money. She would speak to her husband, she said, thinking as she did so that it was somewhat less than dignified to find herself admitting the need to do so.

She was astonished to find that Penlynne was immediately enthusiastic. He sat down at the escritoire of Dutch marquetry, rosewood inlaid with silver and ivory, and wrote a cheque for a hundred pounds.

'Surely she does not need this? There is, after all, a committee.'

'Tell her to take a room in town. Arrange a meeting in the Odd Fellow's Hall. I will speak.'

'We,' she mused. 'I don't believe there is anyone but herself.'

'It has to come,' he said vigorously. He looked at her with a challenging manner, not sexually, but as a man measuring the worth of another. 'You have all the qualitites needed, Dorothy. Energy, enthusiasm ... fortitude. I am seeing beyond the moment. Great oaks from little acorns grow.' His face softened as he sat down and took her hand. 'You really are a remarkable woman, my dear. I believe that together we could achieve much.'

He sprang up and went to the window in his energetic way. 'Dammit, Dottie,' he cried, turning from the panorama of mountains, 'why am I talking like this? What I should be doing ... what I mean, and I mean it sincerely, is to ask your forgiveness for my callous and shallow behaviour. You have borne it with great dignity ... and forbearance and I believe that in this town it has been noted with admiration.'

As she listened she felt something crumble within her. It had not been easy for him and it was not easy for her to accept his apology with a rush of generous enthusiasm. But to deny him now .... No, that would be to perpetuate the whole cycle of bitterness, resentment and anger. It was to be unfair to herself, if nothing else.

'Thank you,' she said, trying not to break down entirely.

One of the features of Far Horizons was the vast bath of white marble carved in the shape of a swan with wings partly raised. Its gold beak gushed hot and cold water. It was sunk in the centre of a lofty room tiled to the ceiling in the Moorish manner and embowered with a conservatory of exotic plants which reached their pale greenness towards a skylight, deeply blue.

Penlynne entered the bathroom one evening before dinner without knocking. Dorothy was floating in the clear water in a faint aura of scented steam. Her body looked beguilingly pink and the whole room with its silver jugs and basins, crystal and gold appointments, had the atmosphere of a seraglio. A mood of voluptuous ease. He felt a sudden resumption of his desire for her.

'I beg your pardon,' he stammered, averting his gaze for fear of embarrassing her.

'I thought it was my maid,' she smiled. 'Do pass me the towel.' She rose from the water, arms outstretched, her flesh rosy and glistening. Then, turning her back, 'Ring for Helen, will you please.'

At table that night she was unusually flirtatious with young George Borcherd. Penlynne had sometimes wondered about her relationship with her architect, the possibility of an intimacy which had gone further than an aesthetic companionship. Certainly the young man's attachment to her seemed deeper than mere gratitude for patronage. He danced attendance and was invariably seated on her left hand. They shared small private jokes. Watching them now he felt a stab of jealousy and marvelled at the experience.

Since their reconciliation he had on more than one occasion tried the handle of her bedroom door. It was always locked against him. Well, he would try again tonight.

In the morning Penlynne opened the french doors and stepped out into the sunlight, drawing deep breaths as he looked across dewy lawns towards the shimmer of the Magaliesberg. He wore only his dressing gown and his feet were bare on the paving. It was a splendid new day, but so was every day in this most invigorating of towns. Up here the air of the plateau was as sharp and clear as crystal. It was all immensely satisfying. Not merely wealth but the feeling that he had emerged at the top of the pack, a man sought after on all sides. And yet, there was so much further he could go!

He broke off a long-stemmed rose and nosed its fragrance. The potential of the Transvaal was immense. It wanted only progressive government. He did not want to go into politics but he intended to make damned certain that the right politics prevailed. When Dorothy's son is born, he thought, not doubting it for a moment, it must be under the sovereignty of England.

He was about to ring for his man to take the rose upstairs to Dorothy. Then he thought, no, I shall take it up to her myself.

Chapter 30

The moment he approached his former employer Stewart MacDonald knew that Rawlinson was done for. The loud snoring from the figure on the bed was unmistakable, the puffing out of the cheeks on expiration and the florid colouring of the massive face, grey hair straggling on the pillow. It was like looking on an india rubber effigy which had been pricked and had collapsed. Stewart lifted an arm. It fell back in a limp and helpless way. The great diamond on the thumb seemed to emphasise the uncharacteristic feebleness of the large hand and its horny nails. The right cheek was paralysed. He passed his hand over one staring eye. There was no movement but he believed Rawlinson had responded.

'Can you hear me, Mr Rawlinson?'

'Aye, he can hear, doctor,' said Muriel Rawlinson, on her knees at the bedside. 'He could say a few words a while back. Then he gave a kind of shiver and he begun this snoring. He was trying to ask for Katherine. She's at the coast wi' her husband. Durban ... they've been wired for. The train'll be in in the morn. I think he understands.'

She held the limp hand to her cheek. 'It's awfu' ... awfu' to see him like this. A mon like him. It's the stroke, is it no'?'

She did not ask directly if he would recover but he sensed that this was what she needed to know. He took her from the bed, walking her across an immense spread of green carpeting and sheepskin rugs. She held his hand and searched his face.

'The truth, please, doctor.'

'Hemiplegia,' he began. 'It could be from a clot from the heart or an embolism of the cerebral artery. He may make a recovery, a gradual recovery with some use of his limbs and speech. The next few hours will tell.'

'I'll do anything ye say.' He ordered hot bottles for the feet and ice for his head. She helped him turn the hulk onto its side while he performed an enema to reduce temporarily the blood supply to the brain.

'The indignity of it,' she said. 'A mon like him, helpless as a bairn.'

They raised his head and shoulders and settled down to wait, the woman on one side of the bed, Stewart on the other. The heavy, darkened curtains were drawn and the gas lit. 'Katherine is a' he cares for,' she said without resentment. She was gradually lapsing into the speech of her girlhood, the girl who was standing next to the uniformed soldier in the wedding photograph he had seen in the sewing room.

He wondered what she was thinking, this so-late wife of a man who was never going to be better than a hulk in a wheelchair. Rawlinson was not a heavy drinker but there was much in his life to suggest a reason for arterial deterioration in his late fifties. Stewart had seen it often enough in his sudden rages at the Star, the apoplectic flush, the gasping for breath.

'When did this come on?' he asked the woman.

'Well, I first noticed the difference ... oh, it was lang sine. He come home one night and he sat down in his chair. Well, Muriel, he says, they've done it. That son-in-law of mine. Then he sat for sae long a time I thought, he's fallen asleep. I'll see to his supper. He's worn himsel' oot wi' this deep levels business.'

When she returned with a tray he was talking as if she had never left the room. 'I just prayed at the assay, let it come up with four pennyweights. If there's any justice, I said, and I know there isn't, let it be worthless...'

'Then he said, Why did you put out the light just now. I said, what are you saying ... it's no' yet dark.'

'Did he have any trouble walking after that? Or with his arm?'

'Aye, he used to put his spoon into his hand wi' the other one. I thought, oh, it's just that he's getting cranky. And then he stopped doing it.'

So that was the first stroke. A mild one.

'And today?'

'He came in the front door and he stood in the hall and shouted. 'Lady Rawlinson ... are ye at home to Sir Josh!' I heard him running up the stair, roaring my name. I cam' oot of my sewing room and there he was, laying his length on the carpet.'

'What did he mean? Was it a joke?'

'It's Lady Rawlinson I am a' right,' she said with a grimace. 'And that's Sir Josh on the bed ... for a' the good it'll do him now. He got news of it today and it's kilt him. I begged and pleaded for months. But no, he was going to win the case first. Then it was the deep levels. He hasna been himsel' for months. A puir, worried creature. Nothing but enemies all round him. But he'd do for them all yet!'

Rawlinson lay unconscious. The snoring deepened but became gradually irregular. Stewart opened his bag. He took out lancet and tourniquet, opened a vein and bled him of about a pint, the red blood spurting into the basin she held for him.

'You won't faint?' he said. She merely grunted.

The snoring diminished and Stewart saw recognition come into his eye. The man attempted to move his considerable bulk, without effect. A sound of harshly articulated clicks came from his throat, the sound blurred by the helpless tongue. It was meaningless to Stewart but the woman's response to it satisfied him.

'Kathy ... she'll be here directly. Just lie quiet.'

He could pass into a coma as the night drew on. And if he did it was likely he would never come out of it. The pulse was reedy and irregular, his breathing increasingly harsh and spasmodic. The abdomen laboured. Yet whenever Stewart shone light into the man's face he saw the flicker of awareness. If his heart held out he would make it to the morning. And if that, there was the faint possibility. The man was holding on...

In his diminished world Josiah Rawlinson was aware of everything except his inability to move. He was urging them to bring Kathy to his bedside. Why did no one obey him? He had urgent things to say to her. Why did she never come? Ah, it was his anger with her husband. She was punishing him for that. Why did they look into his face as if he could not hear them, as if he weren't here. Could they not hear his orders? Who was this woman? Ah yes, his housekeeper, Mrs Ferguson, a good creature, if unlovely. Always ready with a man's comforts. The young man with the beard? Where did he know him from? Ah yes, the Star. In the dimness of the room, in the deep red shadows of lamplight and stifling curtaining, he saw a young woman enter. He stretched out his hand to her but she did not see his gesture. Kathy, my darling child, it's your father calling. No, it was not the child. Sheila! he cried. Someone was praying in the room. For Sheila, surely ... not for him.

Stewart, suddenly aware of a change, bent forward to check respiration. He saw water well up in the staring eye. It gathered there, brimming over and spilling. Through the fluid the pupil stared, magnified as through a lens. It was as if a great tear had flowed uncontrollably from the deeps of the man.

Muriel Rawlinson slept and Stewart sat on at the bedside. He had sat at the side of many a man who had died in the Rawlinson Star and it had never failed to move him that the event that all men dreaded came so calmly and ultimately with so much dignity. It was no different at this bedside than it was at another. In the end there was only the man. This man had been a giant. Let them say what they would about him; there were few who could recognize the hour and seize the opportunity as he had. But now he was no different from any of the human kind.

Presently Stewart heard the sound he had not noticed all night, although it had never ceased. The heartbeat of the man had faltered and stopped but this sound he was hearing, as if for the first time, was the pounding surf of the rock crushers. Roaring like the tide surging in. He rose and pulled apart the curtains. Long rays of light were streaming between the mine dumps, reaching out and piercing into the room. The great diamond on Rawlinson's thumb blazed up. The clay face was touched by a kind of golden illusion of grandeur. It gave the effigy of Sir Josiah Rawlinson, Bart. a serenity he had never experienced in life.

As the young doctor crunched his way down the gravel drive he saw the gates part and an open carriage come swiftly through. He raised his hat. Katherine Gardiner, her husband and son swept on up to the front door.